Copyright © **2021** by **Raneem Hasan**

CW00664271

Typewriter Pub, an imprint of Blvnp Incorporated
A Nevada Corporation
1887 Whitney Mesa DR #2002
Henderson, NV 89014
www.typewriterpub.com/info@typewriterpub.com

ISBN:_978-1-64434-157-5

DISCLAIMER
This book is a work of fiction. The characters, incidents, and dialogue are
drawn from the author's imagination and are not to be construed as real.
While references might be made to actual historical events or existing
locations, the names, characters, places, and incidents are either products
of the author's imagination or are used fictitiously, and any resemblance to
actual persons living or dead, business establishments, events or locales is
entirely coincidental.

LOVING TRAGEDY

RANEEM HASAN

type
writer
pub

I would like to dedicate this book to my twin sister, Rua Hasan. Thank you for always believing in me.

PROLOGUE

Ariel was astonished by the beautiful surroundings as she opened her eyes. She was at a place she have never seen before, a place people could only see in their dreams. Ariel took in her surroundings, wondering on how she even got there in the first place.

Her eyes became teary as she saw the beautiful waterfall that was right front of her. The water flowed in perfect harmony. She smiled softly as she absorbed the beautiful nature that was in front of her.

Trees and flowers surrounded her as she stood in the middle of this beautiful wonderland.

Where is she? How did she get here?

Was it possible that she slept walked? She is one weird girl after all. Sleep walking wasn't new for her, she did it several times before. It might have sounded like a weird explanation, however, she couldn't think of any other answer on how she got to a place like this.

Ariel was pulled out of her thoughts when she heard soft steps coming from behind her. She jolted to the direction the noise was coming from. She squinted her eyes as she saw a body emerging from the trees. Ariel's eyes widened and a large smile took over her lips as she saw him.

Troy.

Troy came walking up to her. A smile made its way to his lips as Ariel stood at her position, before slowly taking a few steps towards him.

"Troy," she said, smiling from ear to ear as he stood in front of her. It's a loveable smile reflecting her's and warming her heart. "What are you doing here?" she asked, looking at her surroundings before staring at his beautiful dark eyes. "How did we get here?"

Troy let out a soft chuckle that made her insides turn. He shook his head as he grabbed her hands with his warms ones. Ariel glanced at their joined hands in shock. She once again looked up at him, noticing that his face was rather close than before.

"Troy?" Her voice got stuck in her throat. She felt her cheeks heat up as she noticed how close they were to each other. This was something unusual. Surely, she was extremely happy. However, it was weird because Troy would rarely do stuff like these.

She has always wished to be this close to him. She has always wanted to hug him and to express her hidden feelings. However, she was nothing but a scaredy cat. She was living in this world of hers, too scared to even tell Troy on how she truly felt. She didn't want to lose their remarkable friendship.

It was too valuable to put it at risk.

"Shh," Troy hushed, shaking his head. "Don't say a word. Let me talk."

Ariel only nodded, gulping as she got more nervous.

Ariel's eyes followed Troy's hand as it raised and softly landed on her soft brown hair. He started stroking it lightly. She shut her eyes as a soft breath escaped her lips.

"My little mermaid," he whispered, making her open her eyes. That nickname always made her stomach turn. Sure, it was one weird name that he always called her, but it was a special nickname for her. It's a nickname only Troy would use.

He started calling her that ever since she was a child. She can clearly remember the first time he called her that. It was exactly after they both watched the Disney film "The Little Mermaid". Troy liked the fact that they both shared the same name, so from that day on he would call her his little mermaid.

However, it wasn't the nickname she liked, it was the fact he would say "his" little mermaid.

"You are so beautiful," he whispered as he continued to stroke her hair. She smiled up at him as her cheeks heated up even more. His words never failed to turn her face as red as a tomato. "I've been meaning to ask you this question," Troy said, making Ariel nod her head.

"Go ahead, ask."

"Ariel," he whispered under his breath, which Ariel acknowledged. "Will you be my girlfriend?"

Ariel's eyes widened, and soon brimmed with tears as she registered his words in her mind.

This is not happening, it can't be. After all these years she hid her feelings towards him, he finally asked that one question she longed to hear from him. She placed her hands over her mouth, trying to cover her shocked yet happy expression.

She closed her eyes for a brief moment, preventing those emotional tears from falling down her cheek. She then opened her eyes and screamed her answer.

"Yes! Yes, I'll be your girlfriend!"

Troy eventually dissipated.

Ariel's eyes widened as she took in her surroundings. Her face turned into an expression of horror as she witnessed all the stares she got from her classmates and her teacher. Laughter emerged in the classroom while some shook their heads at her. Ariel felt her cheeks heat up as the realization hit her.

She was daydreaming again, but this time, she talked out loud for the whole class to hear.

3

This is an uncontrollable habit that she couldn't get herself to stop. She sulked in her chair as the laughter finally died down. Her teacher shook his head.

"Ariel, is there anything you'd like to share with the class?" the teacher wondered, causing some to snicker. Ariel shook her head, and the teacher acknowledged.

"Alright then, since all distractions are put aside, let's get back to class."

The class resumed. Ariel shook her head in embarrassment. She was thankful that the teacher didn't persist about what she said was daydreaming about. She heard someone next to her whispering her name. She turned to her right to see a smirking Clare looking right at her.

"What?" Ariel whispered. Clare shook her head at her.

"Daydreaming again, huh?" she teased. Ariel huffed and shrugged her shoulders. "Why don't you just tell the guy you like him?"

Ariel glared at her for suggesting the most stupid thing ever.

"Really? So our friendship could get lost in the wind? Yeah, never happening," Ariel argued. Clare shook her head and let out a sigh.

"Fine, you keep daydreaming and hiding your feelings, never knowing whether he has the same feelings for you or none," Clare warned. She then put her attention back to the class they were in.

Ariel frowned but then shook her head. This was better than nothing. She could never confess, or else she'd lose everything she already has.

She'd lose Troy.

She walked out of her class as the bell rung. The hallway was filled with talks about the dance which was taking place tonight for the freshmen of this school. Ariel and Clare decided to go together. They were not in the need of a man to take them. It was

Ariel's first year of high school so she wanted to make the best of it.

Deep down, she wished that Troy would ask her out to the dance, but he didn't. It was disappointing.

She was pulled out of her thoughts when an arm wrapped around her shoulder. She looked up to see a familiar smile which never failed to make her heart beat fast.

"Hey, little mermaid. How was class?" Troy asked, making Ariel remember the scandal she caused. Her cheeks flushed but she shook her head, pushing those embarrassing memories at the back of her head.

"It was fine. How about yours?" she asked. He just shrugged his shoulders before smiling.

"You're coming to the dance tonight, right?" Troy asked.

Ariel nodded as a response. "Yes. Why?" Ariel wondered.

Troy smiled from ear to ear before stopping in front of Ariel's next classroom, giving her a soft peck on her cheeks which caught her by surprise. Her eyes widened as Troy took a step backwards.

"You'll see," he answered. He turned around and continued to walk towards his class, leaving Ariel standing there bewildered.

*　　　*　　　*

Ariel and Clare walked through the gym doors where the dance was taking place. Music blasted through the air as many freshmen danced on the center.

The high school arranged this dance to welcome the freshmen, as they did annually at the beginning of the school year.

Ariel looked at her surroundings. She was looking for a specific person but frowned when she couldn't find him. Clare excused herself and wandered off, leaving Ariel alone with a bunch of people she hardly knew. Ariel sighed and walked to the corner of the room, waiting for Troy to make an appearance.

Finally, when she caught glimpse of him, he came walking up to her. He engulfed her in a tight hug which made her catch her breath. There was no doubt, friends or not, they had a strong connection that no one else could feel but them. He soon pulled away and smiled down at her.

"You look beautiful," he whispered, which made Ariel smile.

"Thank you, Troy."

"Did you come here alone?" Troy asked.

Ariel shook her head. "No, I came here with Clare," she replied.

He nodded his head and cleared his throat, which made Ariel raise a brow at him. "Is there something wrong?" she wondered. Troy shook his head but looked at her with a sheepish smile.

"No, I've just been meaning to ask you a question," Troy said.

Ariel looked at him closely. "What is it?" she asked.

Troy cleared his throat and grabbed onto her hands, which took her by surprise. Troy was acting strange at the moment. He never acted so nervous around her like how he was right now.

"Ariel, I know I'm too late, but, will you be my girlfriend?"

Ariel had to pinch herself to know that she was not daydreaming once again.

*   *   *

The month went by fast. Everything was like a blur. It was by far the happiest time of Ariel's life. Many things happened these past few days. It was too difficult for her to register the fact that she was finally Troy's girlfriend.

Never in her life she thought that a day would come when she'd label herself as Troy's girlfriend. It was unusual, but she was extremely happy. Ariel has been madly in love with Troy ever since she was a child. They were so close to each other.

They knew each other as their parents were close friends. They always had a strong connection, however, she feared that Troy wouldn't hold the same feelings as she did. She always thought that he only saw her as a little sister. She was terrified to confess and throw all these years of friendship in the garbage.

However, last month he confessed to her and they're now a thing. It was too good to be true.

A goofy smile appeared on her lips as she walked down the stairs. She was getting ready to go to Troy's house as she did every single weekend. She had many things to tell Troy and discuss with him.

As she walked towards the living room, she found her parents whispering to each other. However, they immediately stopped when they saw her.

Ariel smiled at them. "Good morning," she said.

"Good morning, honey," her mom replied. "Are you going somewhere?"

Ariel nodded her head and smiled. "Yes, I'm heading over to Troy's place. We need to discuss about some stuff and I have a math quiz this week so I figured he'd help me," Ariel answered. Her parents frowned and glanced at each other before looking back at her with a sad expression.

"Honey, come sit down. We need to talk," her dad said in a careful tone.

Ariel furrowed her brows. Her heart sinked as she thought of many ugly scenarios. She didn't like the tone of her parents. She knew something was wrong.

Ariel took a few steps forwards before speaking. "Mom, Dad. What's wrong?"

Her mom patted the seat that was next to her. "Please, Ariel. Sit down."

Ariel sat down quietly next to her parents. They glanced at each other again, then turned to their daughter with a look that frightened her. Aa lump was starting to form inside her throat.

"What's wrong?" she repeated.

Her mom sighed before finally speaking. What Ariel heard next made her world crumble to the ground right in front of her eyes.

"Honey, Troy isn't here anymore," her mom whispered sadly. "He's gone."

CHAPTER ONE

"Ariel!" my mom yelled from down the stairs, making me rush with whatever I was doing. "Hurry. You're going to be late for your first day of school!"

I sighed and immediately grabbed my bag, placing it over my shoulder. I ran down the stairs, coming face to face with my parents. I gave them a lazy smile as my mom only rolled her eyes. I walked up to them then gave them both a kiss on the cheek.

"Good morning," I said in a soft voice. I then sat at the dinning table and started with my breakfast.

"Good morning, sweetheart," my dad greeted, flipping through the pages of the newspaper as he sipped his coffee. "Do you need me to drive you to school before I go to work?" he asked.

I smiled at him and shook my head. "No thanks, Dad. Clare is going to come and pick me up. She'll be here in a couple of minutes," I replied. I got up as I held my plate and walked to the sink, setting it down as I munched on the last bite.

My dad nodded his head and that's when I heard a loud honk. I knew that it was Clare. "She's here," I said, walking to the door before looking back at my parents. "I'll see you both after school."

"Take care, honey," my mom said. I smiled at her. With one last wave, I walked out the door and towards Clare's car. She smiled at me once I sat in the passenger seat. She started the car.

"Hey," Clare greeted. I smiled at her and got comfortable in my seat.

"Hey to you," I greeted back. "How's life?"

She glared at me as soon as I asked that question. I knew she hated that question but I couldn't help but ask her that every time I saw her.

"Life's great, as always," she muttered under her breath. "And now we start our senior year in high school. Even better," Clare continued, her voice laced with sarcasm, making me chuckle at her.

"Yeah," I sighed. "We're seniors now. Time flies by so fast. It feels like we were just freshmen yesterday."

Clare glanced at me before focusing her eyes back on the road. A frown covered her features as I sulked in my seat. "Yeah," she whispered. "Can you believe it has been three years since that day?" Clare asked in a sad tone. I glanced at her before sighing, looking outside the window.

"Yeah. It has," I muttered. "Three years."

"Do you ever think about him? Wonder how he is? What's he doing?" Clare asked, looking at me with concern for a brief second before turning her attention back on the road.

I let out a troubled sigh before rubbing my face with both my hands and shrugging my shoulders. I'm used to Clare bringing up this subject every once in a while, although it still bothered me. "I do, all the time," I replied. "I wonder how he is, what's he doing and how his life is after the surgery." Clare's frown deepened as I continued to speak. "I wonder whether he still remembers me or not."

Clare shook her head. "Ariel, I don't think a person could ever forget the person they loved," she told me.

I shook my head in return. "No, I actually think that he forgot about me," I said. "My parents told me that after the difficult surgery he took to remove the brain tumor, he lost his memory."

"But maybe he still remembers you," Clare suggested.

I scoffed. "If he still remembers me then don't you think he'd be back by now?" I lamented. "Clare, it's been three years, and he isn't back. He clearly forgot about me. He moved on with his life."

Clare gave me a sad look before speaking, "And maybe it's time for you to finally move on."

I looked at her. My frown deepened even more. "I'm trying. I really am. But—"

"But you're still madly in love with him? I know. I'm your best friend, after all." She caught me. I offered her a sad smile. "But this isn't healthy, Ariel. Try to move on. You're gorgeous for goodness sake. Many wish to have you. Heck, Ozan is madly in love with you. Yet, you don't even notice."

I frowned and shook my head. "Don't say that Clare. Ozan is our family's friend. Both our dads are buddies. I could basically call him my cousin."

"But he's not your cousin. And he's heads over heels for you! He's gorgeous too! What do you want more than that?"

"Clare, please. I don't like to talk about these stuff." I sighed, shaking my head. "I'm trying to forget, but it's just difficult."

Clare nodded her head, giving me a sad look. "I understand. I just want the best for you," she said.

"I know. Thank you," I said, smiling at her. "You're right. Maybe it's finally time to actually forget. Just like he did," I said to myself. Clare gave me a confused look as we parked outside the school.

"What did you say?" she asked. I shook my head.

"Nothing. Come on, let's go," I told her. We got out the car and walked towards the school doors. We were greeted with

11

many familiar faces As soon as we walked into the school campus,. Clare and I walked to the school office to get our schedules. I was relieved to see that Clare and I shared many classes.

As we were walking to our first class, a familiar face showed up in front of me. He engulfed me in a hug. I smiled as Ozan tightened his arms around me, making me laugh.

"Hey," I whispered as we pulled away from each other.

He smiled at me. "Hey, Ariel. I missed you."

"I missed you, too. How are you?" I asked as we continued to walk to our class, ignoring the look that Clare offered me.

"I'm good," he replied. "It's been a while since we've seen each other. How come you didn't stop by at my place over the summer?"

"I was pretty busy and didn't really have time. Besides, you went to Turkey for like a month?" I told him. Ozan smiled and nodded his head. "How was it there?" I asked.

"It was really nice. I got to see many family members. It's been years since I've last seen them," he answered. I smiled up at him.

"That's great. All I did this summer was sleep," I chuckled.

Ozan raised a brow at me. "Pretty busy, huh?" We all laughed while I just nodded my head.

"Tell me about it," Clare chuckled.

Luckily the three of us had the same first class so we both walked towards the classroom. I remained silent as Ozan continued to tell us about the stuff he did in Turkey and how he enjoyed his stay. Ozan came from a Turkish background. However, he lived here in New York for all his life.

My dad and his dad work together. That's how we got introduced to each other. We've been friends for more than two years now. I've caught onto the stuff that Clare says. However, I always try to brush it off. I just can't see him that way.

I shook those thoughts out of my head as soon as we made it to our first class. We sat down and that's when the teacher walked

12

in. She made a motion with her hands which made everyone else behave.

And that's how my senior year began.

*   *   *

The school bell finally rang. Many students in my class sighed in happiness. I got up from my seat as what the rest of the class did. It was the first day and I already dreaded my classes. I walked out the room and towards the cafeteria, where Clare, Ozan and I decided to meet for lunch.

As soon as we gathered, we went to grab some food. Ozan and Clare kept complaining about their classes while I was in my little world.

I kept replaying the conversation I had with Clare this morning. I was honestly tired of waiting. I have always convinced myself that even though Troy has lost his memory due to that surgery, he'd still remember me and come back.

He never did.

I guess after that surgery, his family started off new. Troy's dad and mine were very close friends, but after they moved away, we all lost touch with them. I can still vividly remember the day when my mom tried to explain to me that Troy was sick. They moved away to provide him with the best medication. I was devastated by the fact that the person I was in love with was gone and sick.

Later on, I found the devastating news that Troy has lost his memory due to the surgery. Since that day, something inside me told me that he'd never come back, that everything has changed. However, I always tried to convince myself that I was wrong.

I wasn't.

What made it worse was the fact that I never got to say goodbye to him. I never got to tell him how much I love him. Now it doesn't matter anymore, because he doesn't remember me.

13

He's gone now, and it's finally time to move on.

I was pulled out of my thoughts when Ozan wrapped his arm around my shoulder, making me look up at him. "Easy there. You were almost going to bump into the pole," he chuckled. I smiled at him and shook my head. I walked towards a table with the tray of food in my hands.

"Sorry, I was daydreaming."

Ozan raised a brow at me. "Daydreaming of what?" he asked. I shrugged my shoulders.

"Nothing particular," I muttered as we all sat down. Ozan nodded his head, looking at Clare who only shrugged her shoulders at him. We began eating while talking about our classes and how annoying our teachers were. Ozan kept cracking lame jokes which made Clare snort out of laughter. She made the whole cafeteria look at her.

I chuckled at her and shook my head. "Can you control your laughter?" I teased. She glared at me and threw a fry at me, which only made Ozan and I laugh.

"I hate you all," she muttered under her breath, which only made Ozan and I laugh harder. We got up when the bell rang, then made our way to our classes. Unfortunately for this class, I did not have Ozan nor Clare as a classmate. I entered the class with a sigh. The teacher was not present yet.

I sat down on a chair as more students entered the class. After a couple of minutes, the teacher walked in, prompting everyone to sit down as she began with the introductions and rules, like what all the other classes have done.

After half an hour of the teacher just basically talking about the school year in general and what we'll be doing this whole year, I got bored and raised my hand, catching the teacher's attention.

"Yes?" she asked.

"May I go to the bathroom?" I asked her. She gave me a pointed look and placed her hand on her hip.

14

"You just had lunch break. Why didn't you go then?" The teacher asked. I sighed.

"It's urgent," I lied. She rolled her eyes but excused me anyway. I got up and walked out the door and towards the bathroom. The hallways were perfectly empty as I walked through them. This is what I usually did when I got too bored. I'd walk around the school campus then return to my class.

The air around me was silent. I continued to walk around the campus when something disturbed the perfect silence. Something loud. I winced when loud bangs echoed in the hallway. It took me a second to realize what that sound was, and when I did, my blood turned cold.

Gun shots continued to be heard from within the school campus. I could not figure out where exactly it was coming from. I looked around but I couldn't see anyone. I stood at my spot, too afraid to move. My heart beat was accelerating. It felt like at that moment, my legs couldn't function anymore. That's when I heard screams coming my way. I looked up front, and I saw him. A man slowly walking towards me in all black, holding a gun with his hand.

I ran. I didn't care that he saw me running away. I just dashed towards the nearest hiding place, and that was the bathroom. I immediately entered it and locked the doors. I continued to hear gun shots and screams as I hid in a stall and locked the door as well.

All of a sudden, the principal came on the speakers, telling us that we are going on a lockdown drill as there is an armed man on campus. Everyone was ordered to remain silent and to lock the classroom doors.

That's when I knew I was in deep trouble.

I held back the frightened tears that threatened to escape as I heard him banging on the bathroom door. This was not the time to cry. I gulped and immediately pulled my phone out from my back pocket and dialed 911. I still hoped they were already on their way.

The operator answered and I immediately told them the situation I was in. I started to cry as the man continued to bang on the door and as I heard gunshots, but what made me lose it was when I heard him yelling, "He's going to get you! You're going to die! You can't hide forever!"

I sucked in a breath but tried to ignore the man's words.

"Are you okay?" the operator asked from the other end.

"Please, come quick," I whispered. "I'm scared."

"They're on their way, just stay with me," she told me. I tried to hold my cries as the lunatic only continued trying to bust down the door. I thanked the Lord that our school doors were made of metal.

The man continued to scream that he was going to get me and that he's still coming for me even if he gets jailed. I stood in the bathroom stall for what felt like hours as the operator only asked me numerous questions, which I didn't respond to.

It felt like at that moment, I lost my voice. All of a sudden, the screaming stopped. That's when I heard yelling of other men. I'm guessing that the police have finally arrived. I let out a relieved breath and opened my stall door, before the bathroom door got busted down by a police officer.

I saw the gunman in handcuffs, staring right at me. It was like his eyes could see right through my soul. It frightened me. Other police officers came to my aid. They started to pull him away but his eyes remained on me. He suddenly blurted.

"He's coming for you. You can't run. He'll get you!" They pulled him away before he could say anything else.

I stood there baffled. My head is still registering everything that just happened. I looked at my surroundings. I noticed many police officers guarding the area. Some were asking me many questions but I just stood silent. I was just too shocked.

"He" is coming for me? What was he saying?

A police officer started to ask if I knew the man but I only shook my head. Everything else was a blur. After what felt like a long time, my parents arrived at the school campus, and so did many other worried parents.

My mom took me in a tight hug as she bawled her eyes out. I cried as well. My dad was yelling and the cops tried to deal with him. One cop told him what the man said to me and that's when my dad went silent.

The whole school is in a sensitive moment right now, and it was only the first day.

After what felt like an hour, we were all excused early for today. The principal assured everyone that the man was caught and will go behind bars. I got in the car with my parents as my mom continued to ask if I was okay. My dad only remained silent, looking like he was thinking of something. I only nodded my head.

I was scared, even though he was caught. What the gunman said kept playing in my head. He could be a lunatic for all I know, but I still wondered about what he meant. When we arrived home, the air around us was tensed.

"I'm going to go rest for a bit," I told my parents. My mom gave me a sad look and nodded her head.

"Go ahead, honey. You need it."

I walked upstairs and laid on my bed. I closed my eyes and drifted off.

I woke up later in the evening and recalled everything that happened. I sighed and ran a hand over my face. I checked my phone to see numerous calls from Clare and Ozan. I told myself I'd reply to them later as I got up and walked down the stairs and into the living room. I frowned when I saw my mom and dad sitting on the couch, talking about something serious.

They turned their attention towards me as I made them aware of my presence. My parents had a sad expression on there faces which made me frown.

"Mom, Dad . . . What's wrong?" I asked as I walked up to them. I sat next to them as they stood silent for awhile.

"Honey, your dad and I were talking and we've decided on something. And it's for your safety," she whispered, grabbing onto my hand. My frown deepened. "."

"Decided on what?" I questioned. I gulped. I'm so afraid of what I might hear. My parents looked at each other for a second before looking at me. My dad started to talk, something that I've never thought to hear from him.

"We've decided that you're moving out of here. We're sending you away."

CHAPTER TWO

"You're what?" I exclaimed, registering their words in my head. "You're sending me away?" I asked. I can't accept the fact that my parents would say something like that. They would never do that. I knew them. They were so protective over me that they wouldn't let me go anywhere that was out of their sight.

Why would they want to send me away?

"Yes, Ariel. You're going to get out of here as soon as possible," my mom replied, grabbing onto my hand and giving it a squeeze.

"It's for your safety," my dad continued.

"What's wrong with my safety? Why the hell do I have to leave my home that I've lived in for my whole life?" I raised my voice. I couldn't believe it. Did this have something to do with today's shooting? Is this why they're doing this?

They're probably just paranoid. However, I never expected for my parents to say such things.

"Ariel," my dad said, looking at me firmly. As soon as I saw that expression, I shut my mouth and let him speak. "You know that I would do anything to keep you safe. You know that, right?"

I nodded my head and he continued.

"I fear that what happened today wasn't a coincidence and that someone's trying to put your life in danger," my dad told me.

His soft voice held something in them that I barely heard from my strong dad.

Fear.

"But what if it was just a coincidence?" I asked. My dad shook his head.

"Honey, I can't take the risk. I have many enemies and their target might be you," he said firmly, sending shivers down my spine as I heard those words. "I've always feared that someone might use you to hurt me. After today, I'm sure that's a possibility. So I won't let you stay here and have me worried."

"Enemies? What do you mean?" I questioned worriedly.

"Ariel. I'm a businessman. I have many people out there who are trying to hurt me in and out of the business. Whether if it's someone who's trying to get to me or not, I'm not risking it," my dad explained.

It took me some time to register his words in my head. It was difficult to process. It was difficult to realize that I'll be leaving the place I call home, and going to a place who knows where. This is the place I was born in. How could I leave? Just thinking about it was breaking my heart.

"Oh, Ariel," my mom said softly, wiping a tear that trickled down my face. "Don't cry. We'll make sure you're sent somewhere that will make you feel at home. I promise you, you won't stay there for long."

I just nodded my head as I tried to hold back the tears. However, I didn't do a good job, because as soon as I saw my mom's eyes swell with tears, more tears started flowing down my cheek. My mom pulled me in for a tight bear hug as I cried onto her shoulder. Moments later, I felt strong arms wrapped around us and that's when I knew my dad was also taking place in this family moment.

I needed this. It wasn't like everyday you hear that you'll be moving out of the place you call home.

"It's okay, honey. Everything will pass," my mom assured, playing with my hair in a comforting manner as my dad rubbed my back. "You won't even realize that you're gone. We'll make sure to hand you over to the most trustworthy people we know."

After a moment, my cries died down and I pulled away. I wiped my face and stared at my parents. Their faces held pain and sorrow, which caused my frown to deepen. I realized that they were doing this for me. They weren't doing this for their own well-being. But for mine.

I ran both hands over my face, and with a sigh, I whispered, "Fine, I'll go wherever you want me to go." My mom to smile and grab my hand.

"Thank you, honey. Trust us, this is all for you," my dad whispered as I nodded my head in understanding. "I promise that as soon as I realize there is no threat, you're coming back," he added. I nodded my head again and sighed.

"But where will I be going?" I asked. "And when will I be going?"

My parents looked at each other for a moment before looking at me. "You'll be staying with a family that I trust," my dad said, glancing at my mom before turning his attention back at me. "And you'll be leaving tomorrow evening."

"Tomorrow? Isn't that too soon?" I questioned, feeling my stomach turn at the realization.

My frown deepened but my dad shook his head.

"No, the sooner the better," he claimed.

I didn't even have time to process what was happening. *What about my friends? Will I have time to say goodbye to them?*

"Will I even have time to say goodbye to my friends?" I asked to myself. My dad smiled at me as I gave him a confused look.

"Did I mention that Ozan is coming with you?" he asked. My eyes widened as I processed what he just said.

"What?" I asked. "Ozan is coming with me? Why?"

"Yes. I spoke with his father about what I was going to do and he insisted to send Ozan with you," he explained. "His father and I are great friends, so I trust that boy. I accepted because I didn't want to send you away alone, and I know if something happened, Ozan would help and do his best to protect you. Besides, you won't feel alone if you're with him."

I slowly nodded my head, understanding what he meant.

Was Ozan willingly going to give up his life and come with me? That was something difficult to believe. I shook those thoughts out of my head and told myself that I have to see Clare and Ozan before I left tomorrow.

"Come on, let's go up to your room and start with packing up your bags," my mom said. I looked at her then shook my head.

"No, it's okay. I'll do it myself," I told her.

"You sure?" she asked. I nodded my head and got up, giving them a smile as they gave me concerned looks.

"Yes. I'll start now because tomorrow I want to meet up with Clare," I claimed, taking a few steps backwards. They nodded their heads and with one last smile, I walked up stairs. I entered my room and looked at it with sadness, realizing I'll be gone from here by tomorrow. But with one last sigh, I started with packing my stuff.

The next morning came. I'm completely ready. I had my bags all set up by the entrance door and I was dressed up. Clare decided to skip school today so we could meet up one last time with Ozan. Ozan and I aren't attending that school anymore so it wasn't a problem.

I felt my stomach turn at the thought of leaving my best friend. Clare and I are like sisters. We've been glued to the hip for years. Troy and I were the closest people before he walked out of my life, but as soon as he left, Clare and I formed a very strong bond.

With a sigh, I walked down the stairs. I was alone in the house as my parents went out. Mom went outside to get some stuff for me from the grocery store and my dad attended to something urgent. However, Dad promised me that he'd be back in an hour and wouldn't take long.

My parents weren't too comfortable when I told them that I wanted to go meet up with Ozan and Clare, but I assured them that we would be in a public place, so nothing could possibly happen.

After a couple of seconds, I heard a honk. Clare was outside. I rushed and immediately entered her car. I could see the sadness in her eyes.

"Awe, don't look at me like that," I told her while hitting her arm which made her laugh. "Leave the tears for when I'm in the airport. You're coming to drop me off, right?" I asked.

She scoffed. "Of course I am. Now buckle up." I smiled and buckled up as Clare started the car. We decided that we were going to eat breakfast in a diner. I could sense the sadness from Clare for the whole ride but I tried to brush it off and make her smile.

I knew she was incredibly sad, and so was I.

"I wish I could come with you, like what Ozan is doing," Clare said softly. I immediately shook my head.

"Don't say that. You have a life here," I whispered. "Besides, we won't be gone for long," I assured her and myself. Clare nodded her head as I gave her a comforting smile.

"Hopefully."

As soon as she parked her car, we got out and walked into the diner that we usually ate breakfast at. Ozan was already at a table and when he saw us, he got up and waved at us. We greeted each other and sat down. We immediately ordered food.

I glanced at Ozan and he smiled at me. I frowned, and he followed.

"What's wrong?" Ozan asked.

I sighed. "Ozan, are you sure you want to come with me? You know it won't be easy and you'll be throwing your life away," I told him. He smiled and nodded his head.

"I'm sure, Ariel. I'm not leaving you alone at a time like this. Besides, I want to come with you," Ozan assured me. I smiled at him and grabbed his hand.

"Thank you," I said.

"Oh, come on," Clare said loudly, not letting Ozan speak. "You guys are like a new dating couple. Gross." I immediately took my hand away and glared at her as Ozan laughed. Clare smirked at me.

"But you'll miss us," Ozan claimed, smiling at her. Clare smiled back but shrugged her shoulders. It made me smile as well.

"Yeah. Unfortunately, I will."

*   *   *

Clare dropped me home. I only had a few hours left before my flight took off. She decided to wait outside as I got ready, so she could come with me to the airport with my parents. Ozan and I decided that we would meet in the airport as he had a couple of stuff to do. I walked in the house to find my mom and dad sitting in the living room. They smiled as they saw me and got up.

"Have you been waiting for long?" I asked. My dad shook his head.

"We just arrived," he said. "Are you ready?" I nodded my head.

"I brought some stuff for you. I thought you'd need it," my mom said, raising a bag that was in her hand. I smiled at her but shook my head.

"Mom," I whispered. "You didn't have to." She just shook her head and smiled.

"You go upstairs and see if you didn't forget anything while I place these inside your bag," my mom said as she opened my bag

24

to place the stuff she bought for me. I nodded my head and walked upstairs, opening up my bedroom door.

I screamed.

My eyes widened as I looked around my room. Tears threatened to escape as I processed what happened. Immediately, my parents ran upstairs as they heard my voice.

"What happened? What's wrong—" My mom laid her eyes on my now messed up room. My once nice and organized room was all upside down. It was a disaster. Papers were scattered across the floor. Books that once laid on my bookshelf were now in pieces. My shelves and drawers were broken. It was like a hurricane passed by.

I looked at my parents. My dad stiffened. He shook his head and pushed me backwards.

It didn't take a second for all of us to guess that someone broke in while we were gone and damaged my room.

The question was, who?

My dad immediately closed my bedroom door as my mom placed a hand on my shoulder. I looked at them worriedly. I was not sure what to do.

"What happened? Who did this?" I asked my parents.

"Let's head to the airport," my dad commanded, ignoring my questions.

"What about my room?" I asked, frowning.

"I'll take care of it. Now I'm definitely sure about sending you off," he answered. We walked down the stairs as my mom tried to comfort me and telling me that everything was going to be okay. My dad said that he'll speak with the police but first he had to see me get on my flight for assurance.

I kept replaying what I just witnessed a while ago, which brought shivers right down my spine. Was this linked to what happened yesterday? Was someone actually trying to hurt me? My frown deepened. I held back the fear. I didn't want to look weak.

I felt sick in my stomach.

25

Without a minute to spare, we took out my bags and walked out my house and into Clare's car. She smiled at me but as soon as she saw the expressions that were on our faces, she frowned.

I explained to her what happened. She started yelling and immediately started her car and drove to the airport. It feels like I'm running for my life. The whole ride was filled with tension as I thought of what happened back there. As for my dad, he was on the phone arranging security and to have the the security cameras checked.

I was honestly scared. Before, I didn't really see a good reason on why I should leave. Now after what happened, I kind of want to.

I was never a brave and strong girl. I was one of those girls who would breakdown and cry. Back then when Troy was in my life, I was a little stronger. He was my rock and would always help me when I needed him, but after he left, I just got weaker.

He took a piece of me when he left.

I shook those thoughts out my head. Now wasn't the time to think about him.

I ran a hand through my hair and sighed, glancing at my parents through the mirror. "Where exactly will I be going?" I asked them.

My dad looked at me. "You'll be going to California."

"California?" I questioned. He nodded his head.

"Someone will meet you outside the airport and take you to your destination," he explained, making me nod my head.

"So, who will I be staying with?" I asked. My parents glanced at each other before looking at me.

"You'll see when you get there." That's all my dad said, which made me frown. I looked at Clare who just shrugged her shoulder. I had a bad feeling about this. I tried to shrug off that feeling and calm myself down.

Hopefully, everything will be okay.

We met up with Ozan as soon as we made it to the airport. We had little time before our flight took off so we were in a hurry. After a while, Ozan and I were ready to board our flight. I glanced at my parents and Clare. I frowned. I do not know when will be the next time I would see them.

I felt my eyes swell. My parents took me in for a hug. I hugged them as tight as I could, inhaling their scent one last time.

"I'll miss you guys,"—I exclaimed, tears falling down my cheek—"so much."

"Trust me. I'll miss you way more," my mom said, pulling away and wiping the tears off my cheek in a comforting manner. She gave me one last kiss before I looked at my dad. He kissed me on my forehead before looking down at me.

"Take care of yourself, okay?" he said softly, his voice holding pain in it. I nodded my head then looked at Clare who had tears rolling down her cheeks. Ozan and I hugged her before pulling away.

"Be careful, you guys," she said. We nodded and smiled at her.

"You too, Clare. We'll make sure to update you on everything," Ozan told her.

She nodded her head.

"Take good care of Ariel, Ozan," my dad told Ozan. Ozan nodded his head and reassured him that he would do just that.

"Please, be careful," I told my parents, but my dad said not to worry. To make me feel better, he claimed that he was already arranging security.

We started to head to our flight. I looked back to see my parents waving at me. I waved back at them with a sad smile on my lips.

"Have a safe flight!" my mom yelled.

Smiling at them one last smile, we walked away and borded our flight, leaving my parents to watch me.

*　　　*　　　*

Our five-hour journey to California was soon going to end. We had a couple of minutes till the plane was going to land. I was tensed during the whole flight, which Ozan sensed. He asked what was wrong. I then basically told him what happened with my room and that I was just really worried. I was nervous for what was going to come.

Ozan tried to assure me that no matter what would happen, he would stick by my side. I was thankful for that.

"Are you ready?" Ozan asked as the plane landed. I nodded my head, and with a breath, we got up and took our bags. We soon walked out the plane and not too long, we were walking out the airport.

"My dad said someone is going to pick us up," I told him, looking around, not too sure who we were looking for.

"Ah, I think I found that someone," Ozan said, smiling as he pointed at someone. I followed the direction to where he was pointing and saw a man standing next to a car, holding a paper which had our names on it. I smiled at Ozan and nodded my head.

"Great," I told him. "Come on, let's go."

We walked up to the man. He introduced himself as an acquaintance of the family we are staying at. He will be driving us to our destination. We entered the car and welcomed us in a polite manner. He then started to drive off.

The driver then started telling us how he knew my father from years ago. He assured that he was a very nice and has no ill-intent, and that we shouldn't worry because the family he works for is a very lovely family.

His words calmed me down and my nervousness started to ease up.

Ozan kept making small conversation with the driver while I just sat there quietly and stared out the window. Not long after, we arrived to a very big house and the gates opened, allowing us to enter. I started flabbergasted at the scenery that was in front of me.

This place was beautiful. Surely these people were rich.

Ozan had the same expression on his face as he looked around. The car soon came to a stop. We exited the vehicle. The man told us to leave our bags and that someone else would come and take them.

Ozan and I walked up to the front door and nervously, I rung the doorbell. "Here goes nothing," Ozan said, smiling down at me. I looked up at him, thankful that he was with me at a time like this.

I heard the door open. I looked at the person who opened the door. As soon as I laid eyes on the person, my heart stopped. My eyes widened as I stared at the person who was looking at us with a raised brow.

My breath was stuck in my throat and Ozan gave me a confused look, but I wasn't able to utter a single word. I was too busy registering everything in my head.

This person in front of me was the person I never thought I'd ever see again in my life.

Right in front of me, Troy stood there, looking at me like he has never seen me in his entire life.

CHAPTER THREE

I stood there, my heart sinking as I watched Troy look at us in confusion. I wasn't able to utter anything. My breath was stuck in my throat, creating a huge lump that I couldn't swallow. It was like my heart accelerated ten times than its usual pace.

Ozan looked at me with confusion as I stared wide-eyed at Troy. I felt my body stiffen and my mind going blank.

I couldn't help it. I wasn't prepared for this, not now, not ever. It's been three long years since I've last seen him. It's been so long since I've been this close to him. All the feelings I've tried to hide for three long years slapped right back at me in the face.

My heart was pumping with many emotions: fear, sadness, and confusion.

I snapped out of my trance when Troy cleared his throat, raising a brow, specifically at me.

"Yes?" he said in a very deep voice that I haven't heard in so long. "Is there something you need?"

His voice has definitely changed. It surely sent shivers down my spine. As I stood there speechless, wondering if we were somehow at the wrong destination, a woman that I recognized came into sight. Our attention turned to her.

"Oh, dear," she gasped and smiled. She turned her head to the opposite direction. "Damon, they arrived!" she called before turning her attention back to us. "Welcome, welcome! Don't just stand there. Come in." She looked at Troy who soon stepped aside and opened the door wide, indicating for us to come in.

Ozan without another second, stepped into the large house with a smile on his face. I however, hesitantly walked in. I felt Troy's eyes on me, making me glance to his direction to see him inspecting me. He was looking at me with this weird expression, like he was trying to understand something.

Our eyes met and his face went blank. I immediately turned my attention to Rose, Troy's mother. I haven't seen her in years, but she still looked like her usual self. She was smiling at me from ear to ear. Seconds later, Damon came into sight, Troy's father.

I gulped as I saw them all together. They were my favorite people on earth, other than my own parents, of course. Troy's parents always treated me like their own child. However, ever since they left, I've tried to erase them all from my memory.

Unfortunately, that never seemed to work.

"Ariel." Damon gave me a smile. "Welcome. Make yourself comfortable, sweetheart. I hope you both had a safe flight."

I only nodded my head, not knowing what to say after three long years. How come my parents didn't tell me that we were going to stay here? Why haven't they given me a heads up? I felt betrayed in some way. They should've told me that I was going to stay with Troy and his family.

How on earth will I be able to stay with them?

"We had a nice flight, sir," Ozan answered, smiling. Damon shook his head and indicated for us all to sit down on the couches.

"Don't call me sir. Just call us Rose and Damon. Right, Ariel?" Damon argued, looking at me. Troy's parents would always make me call them by their name without using honorifics.

"Yes, dear. Rose and Damon is enough," Rose said, smiling to all of us.

I cleared my throat and nodded my head. Troy looked at us in confusion before turning his attention to his parents, raising a

31

brow. "So, I'm guessing you guys know each other?" he wondered. They looked at him, before frowning. Rose nodded her head and looked at me with sad eyes, before turning her attention to her son.

"Honey, these are the people that I've told you about. The ones who will be staying with us for a while," Rose explained to her son. Troy slowly nodded his head in understanding. The way she talked to him made a big lump get stuck in my throat. Like he didn't know me at all.

"Oh, I see," he murmured, placing his hands in his front pockets, staring at me like he could see right through my soul.

"Son, this is Ariel,"—Damon pointed at me—"and this is Ozan. And this is my son, Troy," Damon finished, looking at Ozan specifically.

"It's nice to meet you guys. I hope we won't be a disturbance," Ozan told them.

Damon immediately shook his head. "You don't know how happy I was when your father called," he claimed, looking at me. "I immediately accepted when he asked for some help. We were great friends in the past, we still are. However, due to some circumstances, we drifted off."

By the time he finished his sentence, there was a frown on his face. I immediately knew what he meant and looked down to my feet, unable to control my feelings. I looked up at Troy with a sad expression as he stood at the corner of the room. Our eyes met again and I immediately looked away.

Rose looked between us with sad eyes before she cleared her throat. "Um, honey." She turned to Troy. "Can you go call Julia to come down here? I'm sure she'll be delighted to see who came."

My eyes widened as she talked about Julia, Troy's little sister. She's younger than me by four years, but we were both incredibly close friends until they all left. Troy nodded his head and silently walked upstairs. As soon as he was out of sight, Rose looked at me and stepped closer.

"Oh, Ariel," she whispered. "I know you're confused and scared. Many things have happened over these last three years."

I looked up at her through blurry vision. "What happened? I mean, I know what happened but, how could he forget me?" I asked. I did not care if Ozan was looking at me in confusion.

Rose held onto my hand and rubbed it in a comforting manner. "Why did you guys leave without even saying goodbye? Why wasn't I able to see him for the last time as the person I know?" I questioned, getting more and more upset. Rose and Damon both held guilt in their eyes as I spoke.

"Honey. When we realized that he was sick, we didn't think of anything else except for his health. His state got so bad that we immediately came here for medication. He didn't want to see you because he didn't want you to see him in that state," Rose started to explain. "We weren't planning on staying here. We thought that shortly after the surgery we'd return. However, after he lost his memory we decided to stay here. We wanted to start off new."

I looked down with sad eyes, unable to comprehend what she was saying. I understood that they wanted to do the best they could for their son, however, that doesn't change the fact that I went through hell these three years without him.

I don't think anyone knows how madly in love I was with him. To this day, I was still recovering from that love.

"We tried everything to make him regain his memory. He was a total mess back then. He didn't even remember us, his parents," Damon said, sitting next to me, trying to comfort me. "At one moment, we decided we'd return back to New York because maybe then he'd remember, but Troy refused. It took him time to finally get used to us. To this day, he doesn't remember anything that happened before three years. He's a completely different person now."

"Nothing?" I wondered, very disappointed.

Rose shook her head. "Nothing. Trust us, we told him about you, about every close person to him. But nothing has ever changed."

A tear fell down my cheek and Rose immediately wiped it away. Ozan was staring at me with a confused expression, but he remained silent the whole time. That, I was thankful for.

I was too heartbroken over the fact that he went through so much pain, and that he has forgotten me. What will I do now? How could I live with him and act as if nothing ever happened between us?

It was surely impossible to hide these feelings.

"Don't be sad, Ariel. Think of this as another chance. A new page," she said. I only shrugged my shoulders. Before I could say anything else, I heard someone yelling out my name.

"Ariel?"

I snapped my head up to see Julia standing at the door, looking at me with a shocked yet happy expression. She came running towards me, pulling me into a crushing hug. A small smile made its way onto my lips and I immediately hugged her back.

"Hi, Julia," I greeted. "I missed you."

She pulled away from me and looked at me with blurry eyes. "Oh my God, Ariel. I've missed you more," she whispered. We hugged each other again before pulling away. "Wow, you've gotten prettier from the last time I've seen you." I smiled at her.

"You also look great. You've grown so much," I claimed, noticing Troy walk back in the room.

"Come, let me show you to your room. It's right next to mine," she gushed out in happiness, making my smile grow.

She then glanced at Ozan and smiled at him.

"Hello, I'm Julia," she greeted him, shaking his hand.

"I'm Ozan," he replied back.

"Ozan? Wow, an unusual name," she exclaimed, making him smile.

"Yes, it's a foreign name."

34

She then nodded. "Then come on, I'll show you both to your rooms," she claimed happily.

We both nodded in agreement. "Make yourselves comfortable. If you need anything then don't hesitate to ask," Damon told us. "I bet you're tired so have some rest then we'll gather for dinner."

"Thank you, Damon," I told him, smiling. We walked off with Julia. Troy stood in the corner, his arms crossed over his chest as he looked at me intensely. I tried to ignore his stare as I passed him. Ozan was stiff and looked between me and him carefully.

Julia soon showed us to our rooms. She told me to make myself comfortable before she left. As soon as I entered the room, Ozan came walking in. I looked at him in confusion.

"Mind telling me what that was back there?" Ozan questioned, making me frown. I sat down and he followed. "Did something happen that I do not know?"

"Ozan," I whispered. "Basically, Troy is my ex."

"What? Really? He's your ex?" Ozan exclaimed. I let out a breath, allowing him to process my words. "You're telling me your ex-boyfriend forgot about you?"

I nodded. "We were very close friends. We soon started dating before he left. I found out that he left for a surgery and later lost his memories," I explained, frowning at the memories of the past which has hurt me severely. "I loved him a lot. He meant so much to me."

"Oh," he whispered, looking down at his hands. We sat there in silence for a few moments, then he said, "So, do you still have feelings for him?"

That caught me off guard. I didn't know what to say. I was afraid of my answer. Three years is a long time, but I knew I couldn't forget it completely. I decided to just shrugging my shoulders. I guess he understood what I meant. He nodded his head before standing up.

"I know it will be difficult at first, but you'll get used to it. Besides, we won't be staying here for long," Ozan told me, smiling at me. It made me feel much better. I smiled back at him and nodded my head.

"Yeah," I murmered in a soft tone.

He placed a hand on my shoulder. "I'll be going back to my room to start unpacking. You do that same," he ordered, making me chuckle.

"Yes, sir." I said. He left, leaving me sitting in the room. I stared at the blank white wall as I thought on how I'll be able to survive living under one roof with Troy.

I've locked myself in the room for hours, too afraid to go out and bump into him.

How would I react if I did? What would I say? Should I act as if I didn't know him and go on with my life? That was surely impossible. I'm a horrible actress. I can't just hide my feelings. I've never been that type of person to do so.

I shook my head and decided it was time to go out. I'll be staying here for awhile, I can't hide in here forever. I have to get used to it, whether I like it or not.

I got up from the bed. I unlocked the door then opened it. I inhaled deeply before stepping out. It was almost time for dinner so I decided to go downstairs and see if Rose needed any sort of help. I have to interact with them.

Out of nowhere, Troy got in front of me, catching me off guard. My eyes widened. I was speechless. He was so close to me that I didn't know what to do. It's been years since I've been this close to him.

Troy looked as handsome as ever. He changed but not to the point where I wouldn't recognize him. His dark brown eyes studied me, before his lips turned upwards into a smirk, making me confused.

"Ah. Ariel, right?" he asked. I slowly nodded my head and cleared my throat while stepping backwards.

"Yes," I answered hesitantly.

"Just like the little mermaid," he claimed, catching me off guard. "Ariel . . ." he said softly. My eyes widened as I feel my heart rate accelerated. It's been years since I've last heard someone say something like that. Only Troy would call me the little mermaid.

"So, I'm guessing if you know my family, then you know me?" he asked. I nodded again, not uttering a single word. "How?"

What should I say? I wasn't prepared for this. I felt my heart fall to my stomach. However, I summoned all the strength I had left to speak.

"Um, well . . ." I started. I looked at the floor, not knowing what words to say. "We were—"

"Wait," he said. His smirk grew and so did my confusion. "Don't tell me you're the girl my parents told me about? The girl who 'loved' me?" he chuckled. I didn't find that funny at all. Instead, I averted my gaze away from him and looked down to the floor, not knowing what to say.

He went silent. I looked up at him. He was staring at me with a confused expression, then before his face went blank.

"Wait. You are that girl?" he asked. I swallowed. Hesitantly, I nodded. I shouldn't hide the fact that we were close in the past.

"Yes," I said with a little bit of courage. "We were best friends. We then soon dated."

His dark orbs remained emotionless as I spoke. He didn't show any sense of confusion nor happiness.

We remained silent for a moment when out of nowhere, Troy chuckled, placing his hands in his front pockets. I furrowed my brows as he only shook his head, making me gulp.

"How pathetic of me," he said with a smirk on his lips. His words were like a slap to my face. My heart sank as I heard those words. "Really pathetic." His smirk dropped and his expression turned into a glare, which disappointed me to a whole new level.

"I've dated someone like you? I'm kind of glad that I don't remember," he said in a deep tone. "How stupid of me." With a shake of his head, he walked away, leaving me standing there in shock.

I felt my eyes brimming with tears as I replayed his harsh words. His words were like cold water splashing onto me. It hurt, really hurt. It was like a stab to my chest, especially since it came from someone I really loved. I felt a heartbroken tear slowly fall down my cheek as I stood there in the empty hallway.

How stupid of me. What did I think? That he'd come running into my arms as soon as I told him? I felt pain deep inside my chest.

One, because of his words.

Two, because I realized that my Troy wasn't the same Troy at all.

He changed.

CHAPTER FOUR

After staying in my room for what felt like hours, I finally mustered all the confidence I had left and exited my room. I didn't want to however. If I had the chance, I would have just locked the door, went under the sheets, and not do anything else. After my encounter with Troy, all I wanted to do was to dig a deep hole and never come out of it.

I felt shattered and heartbroken by his words. I know it has been three long years since I last saw him. It should not affect me, but it hit me hard. Whether he was far away or not, my feelings towards him have never completely drifted away.

I tried, however. I tried a lot to forget him and to stop thinking about whether he's fine or not. I tried to completely take him out of my mind, but my heart wasn't able to. He carved himself inside my heart from day one, and that is why I wasn't able to let go of him.

However, I came to learn that even the people you love most could change. Even the people you think that would stick by your side till the end could do so. Unfortunately, I was a let down. I don't blame him, though. What he went through must have been difficult and terrifying.

I just wished that there was some way to bring the old Troy back.

Yes, what he said hurt me, severely. However, I have to try to get along with him for now. We're living under one roof after all.

I was too afraid to see him again. What should I say? How should I act with him? I pushed all these thoughts aside and slowly walked down the stairs. I shouldn't just stay in my room. That would be too rude. Dinner was about to start so I decided I'd see if I could help with anything.

As I made it to the living room, I saw Rose setting the table. She glanced my way and smiled at me, gesturing me to come in.

"Hello, dear. Did you rest well?" she asked.

I nodded my head and gave her a soft smile. "Yes. I did," I answered. "Is there anything I could possibly help you with?"

Rose nodded her head. "Yes, that would be very nice of you. Why don't you get the rest of the stuff from the kitchen while I call everyone to come down for dinner?" she answered. I only nodded in agreement and made my way to the kitchen, while Rose walked up the stairs.

As I entered the kitchen, I saw that there were many things I had to put on the dining table such as plates, cups and the rest of the food. I brought them one by one so I wouldn't drop anything and cause an embarrassment to myself. Of all times I could be clumsy . . .

I walked back to the kitchen to grab the plates when I heard someone behind me. I immediately turned around to see Troy standing right behind me. My grip on the plates tightened as I stared into Troy's dark eyes in surprise. He was looking at me with a blank expression, making me take a few steps back.

Silently, he walked to my side and filled in a glass of water. He drank it as I stood there. After a couple of seconds of just standing there in silence, I took a few steps backwards. Troy placed the cup back on the counter as his eyes stayed glued to mine.

I found the situation very uncomfortable. I looked down to the floor but then decided on saying something. I didn't want us to be enemies. In fact, I wanted us to be close. Yes, that doesn't change what he's told me but still, I couldn't bare to be like this with him.

I cleared my throat. "Um, Troy?"

He raised a brow, his expression still blank. He didn't speak so I was guessing that his silence was a way to say go on.

"I don't want us to be like this," I whispered softly, looking to the floor but raising my head when I heard him snicker.

"What?" he questioned. "Do you want us to be a loving couple and be how we were like in the past?"

I gulped. My eyes widened and I immediately shook my head. "No. That's not what I meant," I tried to clarify. He raised a brow then slowly started walking up to me, making me take a few steps backwards. However, I wasn't able to take any more steps when my back collided with the wall.

Troy, however, didn't stop with the slow steps. He was soon standing right in front of me. Both of our eyes connected as his breath fanned my face. I swallowed and felt my cheeks heat up at how close we were.

I missed being this close to him for so long.

"Oh, really?" he whispered, grabbing onto my chin. "Then what did you mean exactly?"

I sucked in a breath. I can't handle this. His eyes were staring at me like he was able to see right through my soul. My eyes glanced at his lips but immediately looked back at his eyes so I wouldn't do something I'd regret.

I couldn't help it. No matter what he said to me, no matter what he did, I still loved him.

"Uhh . . ." I whispered, biting onto my lips. "I-I meant in . . ." I stopped to catch my breath. My heart was probably beating ten times faster than it usually did. Troy was still staring at me with a serious expression as his fingers still gripped my chin.

"I meant in being civilized and getting along," I whispered so softly that I wasn't sure that he heard. He raised a brow and

41

brought his face closer to mine, making my breath get stuck in my throat.

"Really? Is that all you want?" he asked, his breath fanning my lips. It took me a moment to register his words. Hesitantly, I nodded my head, not uttering a single word. At a moment like this, I didn't trust my voice.

"You sure?" he asked in an intimidating voice. I sucked in a breath and bit my lip, thinking of his words. I almost started to speak and say something that I'd regret when someone called for me from the living room.

"Ariel? What are you doing in there?" Rose yelled. "Get the plates so we can start." I immediately looked down to the plates in my hand then looked up at Troy.

He was still staring at me blankly. I stepped aside and rushed out the kitchen. I did not say anything to Troy. I inhaled and walked back to the living room, hoping that my face wasn't red. I set the plates on the table as Rose and Julia were talking about something.

After a moment, Damon and Ozan came in while Troy made his appearance. I immediately looked away from him as I felt his eyes on me. I smiled up at Ozan and sat next to him. Julia sat to my other side while Troy sat directly in front of me, making me feel uncomfortable.

We started dinner.

"I hope you two feel comfortable in our house. If you don't, then don't hesitate to say so. We'll surely do something about it to fix it," Damon told us. We smiled at him.

"No, don't worry. We're very comfortable," Ozan replied while I nodded my head. "Thank you."

"Don't worry, Dad," Julia said with her mouth full. "I'll make sure they're very comfortable. Rely on me." Ozan and I laughed at her while Rose glared.

"Julia, have some manners," she scolded. "Don't talk with your mouth full." Julia immediately shut her mouth, which earned a

42

chuckle from Ozan. I glanced at Troy to see him shaking his head at his sister, making her blush.

"Idiot," he muttered but all of us heard him. Julia glared at him while I sat there, staring at Troy with sad eyes as a memory came flooding in my head. I looked down at my plate.

If only I could relieve those days.

*   *   *

"Troy!" I yelled, waving my hands in the air as I jumped eagerly, getting Troy's attention from the distance. "Come on! I'm hungry, for goodness sake."

Even from far away , I could still make out a smile on Troy's face. It made me smile from ear to ear. I continued to jump as Troy speed walked towards me. When we got closer, I ran up to him and jumped on him, making him stumble a couple of steps backwards.

I giggled as Troy groaned. "Easy there, my little mermaid. Why are you in such a hurry?" I looked up at him as he was smiling down at me.

"I'm hungry, Troy!" I whined. "Let's go eat. Come on. Any more time and I'll die from starvation." Troy laughed at my dramatic behavior. I furrowed my brows and glared at him.

"What?"

"Ariel, when was the last time you've eaten?" he asked, deepening my frown. He was smiling from ear to ear, something I loved to see on his face. It always made my insides melt.

"Um . . . an hour ago?" I hesitantly answered. "But still," I shook my head and grabbing onto his hand. "Let's go eat something. I'm starving." He shook his head but chuckled, making me glare at him again.

"You're such a drama queen," he teased.

"Oh, yeah? Well, I can do better, jerkface!" I spat out like a child. He raised his brow but wrapped an arm around my waist, pulling me towards his chest.

"Seriously?" he mused out. A smile crawled onto my lips and I nodded my head. He laughed out then took something out from his pocket.

I glanced at it and smiled when I saw it was a chocolate bar.

"Here," he said, handing me the chocolate bar. "Take this for now to tame your deadly starvation before we find something to eat." My smile grew and I immediately opened it, stuffing it in my mouth.

I moaned as I munched on the delicious chocolate bar, while Troy only watched me in amusement. I stepped closer to him as I continued to eat it.

"Thank you," I said with a full mouth. "I love you so, so, so, so, so much," I cooed while hugging him. He laughed and then shook his head.

"Don't speak with your mouth full," he chuckled. I shrugged my shoulders then took another bite.

"You still love me," I claimed, making him sigh.

"That, I do."

My smile grew as I took my last bite, making him chuckle once again.

"Idiot."

CHAPTER FIVE

I stared at the blank ceiling for what felt like hours. It was just one of those night when I'd just stare blankly into space and not fall asleep. I'd think about my life and what's going on with it. It was one of those nights when no matter how much I try to shut my eyes and fall to the dark, I couldn't.

I stayed like this for awhile. I went to bed early, but I have yet to fall asleep. I'm not sure why I couldn't. I guess it was because my mind was too worked up about the situation I was in. More likely, because I have school tomorrow. It's been about two days since we've arrived in California, and tomorrow is the day when Ozan and I start senior year for the second time this year.

I was quite nervous, but Ozan will be with me so I shouldn't really be. Troy is also in the same school I'm going to attend and honestly, I don't know how to feel about that.

I guess deep down in me I was happy that I'd be in the same school Troy was in like the good old days.

I sighed and ran a hand through my hair. I forced my eyes shut and told myself to push these thoughts aside and sleep, for tomorrow I'll wake up early and regret this. However, for the hundredth time tonight, my body wasn't cooperating with my mind.

I blame it on Troy. Ever since I came here, I haven't been able to take him off of my mind. What made things worse was the fact that we're living under one roof. I'd see him whenever I step out of my room. However, he'd either ignore me or give me a blank expression, to which my heart would always break to.

I couldn't help it. If I wasn't able to forget him at the time he was far away from me, how do I expect myself to forget him when he's so close to me? It was impossible, no matter what he says or does.

Sighing, I sat up and glanced at the clock, seeing it was almost midnight. I frowned and ran a hand through my messy, tangled hair. If I don't sleep anytime soon, then I'll surely burst. I hated waking up very tired. I shook my head and got out of my bed. Maybe a glass of milk will help.

I just pray that I wouldn't bump into Troy.

Slowly and quietly, I opened my bedroom door and looked out. The hallway was empty and dark. I sighed and gently closed my door. I started making my way down the stairs. The house was dark so I trailed my hand on the wall to make sure I wouldn't be my clumsy self and fall. I don't want the whole house to wake up.

I prayed that nobody was awake. I know I wasn't doing anything wrong, but it felt weird sneaking around a house which wasn't yours.

I entered the kitchen to see a back facing me. I immediately aborted my mission and turned around. However, before I could take a step forward, a voice stopped me.

"Ariel?"

I looked back and sighed in relief when I only saw Ozan.

Thank God. I feared that it could be Troy.

"Ozan," I said, stepping into the kitchen as he raised a brow at me. "What are you doing here at a time like this?" I wondered. Ozan gave me a sheepish look and smiled.

"Oh, damn it . . ." he cursed, making me frown. "You caught me red handed. I was about to steal all the food and make a run for it," Ozan claimed. It only made me frown more. Ozan began laughing at my expression. I hushed him so no one could hear. He stopped but shook his head.

46

"I'm checking if they have any medicine for headaches," Ozan said. "I've had this massive headache for hours and it's not going away."

My eyes widened and I immediately walked up to him, placing the back of my hand on his forehead. "Really? Are you feeling sick?" I asked worriedly. Ozan's eyes widened, a small smile coming onto his lips. He grabbed my hand and slowly took it off his forehead.

"I'm okay," he assured. I then realized that we were too close to each other in a very dim kitchen. It didn't make me feel comfortable. I cleared my throat.

"Oh. Okay," I whispered. "That's good. I just came down here to get myself a glass of milk because I couldn't sleep."

Ozan nodded his head. I took a step backwards, but he did not let go of my hand. I cleared my throat again as he remained silent, looking down at me with an unusual glint in his eyes.

"Go look for any pain killer while I get myself a glass of milk," I said. Ozan nodded his head, but before he could say anything, the dim kitchen's lights turned on, making me immediately squint my eyes.

I looked behind me and my eyes widened when I saw Troy standing there, giving us a look that sent chills down my spine. His eyes held a hint of surprise in it before it lowered down to my hand. I followed his gaze and then realized that Ozan was still holding onto my hand.

My mouth fell open. Without a second thought, I pulled my hand away from Ozan, who looked upset from Troy's arrival. Troy's expression immediately went blank.

"Troy?" I called out. He didn't say anything. He just opened the fridge and took out a water bottle. He slammed the fridge close, not uttering a single word to us.

"We weren't able to sleep that's why we're down here," Ozan told to him. Troy remained silent. After a while, he suddenly snickered.

47

"Next time, why don't you stay in one of your rooms when you can't sleep?" Troy finally blurted before walking off. My eyes widened at what he said and I immediately looked at Ozan, and Ozan didn't look so happy.

"Oh God," I said. "What if he thought wrong and misunderstood?"

Ozan shrugged his shoulders. "So what if he does? I don't care. It doesn't matter," he muttered, opening a cabinet as he started looking through it. I frowned and took a step back.

"Well, I do care," I whispered. I immediately turned around and rushed out of the kitchen. Ozan asked where I was going but I ignored him. I didn't want him to get the wrong idea. There was nothing going on between Ozan and I.

I caught up with Troy who was walking up the stairs.

"Troy," I called. Thankfully, he heard me and stopped on his tracks. He turned towards me.

"What?" he asked, looking at me as if talking to me was the last thing he wanted to do. I frowned at his attitude but took a step closer to him.

"Umm . . ." I muttered, getting a bit nervous.

"Come on. Speak. I have better things to do other than talking with you." he ordered. My eyes widened at his words. I looked at the floor for a second before looking back at him.

"What you saw back there wasn't—"

I don't care." He cut me off, making me frown.

"What?" I whispered.

Troy took a step closer to me and brought his face closer to mine, making me hold my breath.

"I said I don't care. You can do whatever you want and I won't give a single damn," he claimed before turning around and continuing up the stairs, leaving me in the dark. I stood there, shocked. I was flabbergasted from what happened. I closed my eyes as I felt the tears threaten to fall again.

I didn't want to be weak, but I couldn't help it. When he says words like that to me, it just breaks my heart.

I shook my head as a tear escaped through my shut eyes. I was stupid again. I slowly walked back up to my room, not wanting milk anymore.

My appetite was ruined, and so was my mood. I went straight to bed.

I groaned in misery as my alarm clock went off, forcing me to sit up. I frowned desperately as I looked at the clock that hung on the wall.

It was so damn early. All I wanted to do was cry, and the thought of school made me want to cry harder. After what happened last night, I didn't sleep at all. I just laid in my bed, under my sheets as I shed tears. I felt weak. Yes, I'm not a strong girl, however, I've never really cried for little things.

These days, I've become something else, and it was all because of him. My heart became weak when it came to him, and I couldn't tell my heart to do otherwise.

I forced myself out of my bed and inside the bathroom to get ready. After, I exited my room and walked down the stairs. I inhaled before walking in the living room to see Rose and Julia sitting down, talking.

"Good morning," I said. They both looked at me and offered me a welcoming smile.

"Good morning, sweetheart. Did you sleep well?" Rose wondered.

I smiled at her. "Yes, I did," I lied. I glanced at Julia who was ready as well. Julia was in middle school so I only attended the same school with Ozan and Troy. I just wished that Julia was a couple years older so I wouldn't have to worry about making friends in my new school.

"Breakfast is ready. You go eat so you and Troy can head off to school," Rose said, smiling at me. I frowned as she brought up his name. It reminded me of what happened last night.

49

"Me and Troy?" I asked. She only nodded her head before Julia frowned.

"Uh, Mom," Julia interrupted. "Troy left a while ago." Rose scowled from what Julia had just said.

"Are you serious?" she asked, looking pissed. I frowned as I watched Julia nod her head.

"Yes," she replied, giving me a sad look. Rose shook her head and then sighed.

"I told that boy to stay so he could take you with him," she whispered. "I'm so sorry, Ariel. I'll be sure to talk with him so he wouldn't repeat it another time."

I immediately shook my head.

"No, it's okay. I'll go with Ozan," I told her, trying to smile as I hid the pain I felt.

Rose frowned again. "Honey. Ozan isn't going to school today," she said. I frowned and gave her a confused look.

"What do you mean?" I asked.

"Ozan is quite sick so he'll be staying home for today."

"Oh,"—I nodded my head and sighed—"it's okay. I'll just use the GPS on my phone and walk there."

"Oh, dear. If only Damon was here. Then I would've let him drive you to school but unfortunately, he's at work," Rose said. I smiled at her but shook my head.

"It's okay, really. I'm just going to go check up on Ozan then head off to school," I insisted, backing up.

"What about breakfast?" Julia asked, frowning.

"I'm not that hungry," I said softly. "Thank you, though." Rose smiled at me. I turned around and walked towards Ozan's room. I entered his room and hear him coughing. He immediately opened his eyes and looked at me. I frowned at his sight.

"Ariel?" he croaked.

"Are you really sick?" I asked. He rolled his eyes at my question.

50

"No. I'm pretending so I won't attend my first day of school," he said which made me frown even more.

"You just had to get sick on the first day of school?" I huffed in a joking manner. He rolled his eyes again but smiled this time.

"It's not like I asked to be sick." He coughed. I sighed then nodded, smiling at him.

"Well, get some rest and get well. You're coming to school with me tomorrow, whether you like it or not," I told him, making him smile.

"Yes, ma'am."

I chuckled. "I'm going to get going."

"Be careful," he called out as I walked out his room. Eventually, I walked through the main doors and took out my phone, following the directions the map told me. I walked for awhile, not knowing where I was exactly.

I shook my head as I noticed that I was getting late.

If only Troy hadn't left, then I might have been in school by now. I continued to follow the directions when I started to get worried. Supposedly, the school is only a couple minutes away from the house, yet I've been walking for ten minutes now.

I'm almost panicking. I looked at my surroundings then back at the map. I was surely lost. Damn me for using something I'm not good at. I was seriously getting afraid.

Many scenarios popped into my head which frightened me even more. *What if I was kidnapped then killed by some stranger? What if I was actually in some kind of danger and someone gets me then kills me?*

I kept thinking of the "what ifs" when a car pulled up next to me. I got more nervous. I sucked in a breath and prepared to make a run for it, when the window slowly went down. My curiosity kicked. I looked to see who was the person inside the car.

My eyes widened when I saw Troy sitting in the driver's seat. He gave me a blank look, before looking forward as I stared at him. He stood silent for a moment before speaking.

51

"Get in."

CHAPTER SIX

Huh?" I said stupidly as I stared at Troy. He faced me and gave me a glare. I guess he did not want to repeat what he said.

"I said get in," he demanded. I looked at him for a couple more seconds before finally opening the door and getting in. Troy, without a second thought drove off and I secured my seatbelt on. Troy didn't utter a word while I just remained silent.

I glanced at him. He's concentrating on the road. I sighed.

"Why did you leave without me?" I asked softly. Troy glanced at me for a split second before putting his attention back on the road.

"Because I didn't want to wait," he responded with a blank expression. I furrowed my brows at his tone and adjusted myself in the seat.

"Well, that was kind of rude," I told him, mostly myself as I frowned. "I could have gotten lost. Or worst, kidnapped."

He raised a brow and glanced at me, before shaking his head. He remained silent, however. I inhaled.

"Well, why did you come back then?" I asked, raising a brow. He cleared his throat and shrugged his shoulders, not even sparing me a single glance.

"My mom called. So I turned back so I wouldn't have to hear any more complaining," he muttered in a blank tone. I frowned and looked down at my lap.

"Oh, it wasn't because you felt guilty?" I wondered, looking up at him through sad eyes. His head immediately snapped over to mine and his grip on the steering wheel tightened. The expression that was plastered onto his face was a hard one. One that brought shivers down my back.

All of a sudden the car stopped. If it wasn't for the seatbelt I was wearing, then my body would have surely jolted out of the seat. I looked at Troy as he glared at me, which made me frown severely. I sucked in a breath as he brought his face closer to mine, my eyes widening as his face got closer to mine.

"I told you, Ariel," he gritted out. The way he said my name made me freeze. "I don't f*cking care. Now get out of my car." My eyes widened at his harsh words and I blinked to prevent the tears from falling. I was flabbergasted, not able to utter a single word.

I looked out the window to see we were right outside a school. I opened the door and got out, giving him one last sad look before I slammed the door shut and walked away. I shook my head at myself. I didn't know why I kept trying with him.

Stupid Ariel.

I ran both hands through my brown hair as I tried to cover up my sadness. I just couldn't help it. For a second, I thought he actually cared. I thought that he came back for me, but he didn't. It was only because Rose called him.

I shook my head once again before I walked in the school campus. I didn't know where to go and where to get my schedule. I had no clue. That also didn't help with my nervousness. The last time I went to school, something horrifying happened. It didn't take a genius to figure out I was not so excited.

I quietly walked in the school as no one spared me a single glance. I tried finding the main office but I was completely lost. I didn't know where to go. I was debating whether I should ask for someone's help but before I could do so, a girl came walking next to me, offering me a smile.

54

"Hi," she greeted, making me stop in my place as I looked up at her. "Are you new here?" she asked. I nodded my head.

"Yes, I am," I answered. "Today's my first day."

"It's nice to meet you. I'm Randa," she said, giving a welcoming smile at me. I smiled at her as she reached out her hand. We shook hands.

"I'm Ariel," I said. "It's nice to meet you, too."

"So, Ariel. Did you get your schedule?" she asked me. I shook my head, frowning.

"I was actually looking for the main office but kind of got lost," I whispered, a little embarrassed. She chuckled then started walking again.

"Then follow me," she offered. "The office is this way." I followed right behind her as we made our way through the crowd of people walking down the hallway. I thanked the Lord that He sent me someone to help me. I didn't know what I would have done if I got myself in some embarrassing situation at the first day of school.

Randa seemed like a nice girl and I was thankful for that. She was pretty as well. She was tall and had nice black hair. I noticed we shared the same eyes though. We both had blue ocean eyes which kind of took me off guard when I first saw her. I couldn't help but feel a little relieved at the fact that maybe I've made a friend.

"So, you're new here?" Randa asked, glancing at me curiously. I nodded my head.

"Yes, I actually am," I responded, smiling at her.

"You're not really from this town, are you?" she asked, raising a brow.

"I from New York," I answered.

"Really? Cool," she exclaimed. "My boyfriend used to live." I nodded my head but before we could say anything else, we stopped in front of the main office.

"We made it," Randa said. I nodded my head and opened the door, before walking to the women that sat in the front desk. She looked up at me and offered me a welcoming smile.

"I'm Ariel, the new student," I greeted. "I would like to get my schedule."

"Ahh . . . Ariel," she murmured, looking over some papers. She then took out a paper, handing it to me with a smile. "Here is your schedule. Have a nice first day. If you face any problems, don't hesitate to report it to us."

I took the paper from her and smiled, nodding my head.

"Thank you." I turned around and walked out the main office and to where Randa was standing, waiting for me.

"You got your schedule?" she asked, stepping towards me. I nodded my head and showed it to her. Her eyes scanned over it for a second then smiled. "Great. We have first, second, fifth and seventh period together." I smiled and nodded my head at that.

"That's nice," I claimed. She clapped her hands before stepping forward.

"Then come on, let's get to class before we're late," Randa said, grabbing onto my hand. I nodded my head and that's when we made our way to our first class. I couldn't help but feel relieved that I wasn't alone for my first day of school.

I just hope that nothing goes wrong today.

I wasn't used to going to school without seeing Clare or Ozan. We were always together and we mostly had all our classes together. Ever since Troy left, Clare, Ozan and I became so close. I felt a piece missing inside me now that Clare was not with me.

I made a mental note to call her once I got home. I called her only once ever since I came here and updated her on everything. I told her that I basically live in the same house with Troy and she went nuts. She could hardly understand what was going on, and to be honest, neither did I.

I told her that Troy changed so much and he wasn't the same person I new before. He wasn't my old Troy.

56

However, even after everything he did, deep down I hoped that there was still something in him that would remember me. Something that would remember the love he felt for me and what we had. However, it was too difficult to keep holding on.

That doesn't change how I felt about him. The feelings I've held for years are so difficult to erase. It's difficult to empty them out of my heart.

It's surely impossible for me. I've never loved someone like I loved him.

I drastically shook my head as memories from this morning flooded into my head. I frowned and couldn't help but feel my heart fall to my feet. It hurts me so much when I hear harsh words like those coming out of his lips. Those were lips that once talked nicely to me and once told me that he loved me.

I might be stupid because I still care for him and I keep trying to communicate with him, but I do stupid things for the people I love, even if they don't deserve it.

"Ariel? Hello?" Randa exclaimed, waving her hand in front of my face, pulling me out of my thoughts. I looked up at her to see her raising a brow at me. "I've called your name three times. Where was your mind at?" She asked. I sighed then gave her a small smile.

"I'm sorry," I whispered, running a hand through my hair. "I have this bad habit of drifting off into space." She nodded her head.

"I can see that," Randa chuckled. "Come on, second period finished. Go to your third period and we'll meet up in lunch. Okay?" I nodded my head, getting up from my seat as we both walked out of the classroom.

"See you in lunch," I told her, waving at her. She waved back at me before we walked away, making my way to my third class.

After greeting myself to teachers a couple of times and enduring torturous classes, it was finally lunch time. I sighed in relief as the teacher excused us from the classroom. I couldn't help feeling that today was a long day and I still got a couple of more classes before it was time to leave.

So far, I haven't had Troy in any of my classes. I would see him walking around the school campus every now and then, to which he'd completely ignore me. I sighed and walked out of the classroom as many kids rushed down the hall. I walked alone to the lunch area, following where mostly everyone was walking to.

I didn't know how I was going to find Randa through the huge crowd of students.

I was actually quite thankful that Randa invited me to sit with her friends and her in lunch. Now, I didn't really have to worry about finding friends. She seemed like a sweet girl and I could tell that we'll get along really well.

I walked down the hallway, looking for Randa but the crowd blocked my sight. Eventually, I saw her in the distance and waved my hand at her. She offered me a smile and came walking towards me.

We greeted each other before we started walking towards the cafeteria.

"So, how were your other classes?" Randa asked.

"They were fine," I answered, shrugging my shoulder. Randa nodded her head, smiling at me.

"You'll get used to them. Don't worry," she assured me. I smiled at her and nodded.

"I know. Thanks."

We entered the cafeteria and Randa started to look around, looking for someone.

"I wonder where he is?" She muttered, furrowing her brows as she scanned the large room filled with students.

"Who?" I questioned, looking at her.

"My boyfriend," she answered. I only nodded my head and scanned over the room as well. I do not knowing who exactly I was looking for though. All of a sudden, Randa smiled from ear to ear. I'm guessing that she found the person she was looking for.

"There he is," she claimed, walking towards the person. I slowly followed behind her as she speed walked towards someone before hugging him. I couldn't exactly see who the person was because of the many people that were covering my view.

As soon as I walked closer, I completely stopped dead in my tracks. My eyes widened and my breath got stuck in my throat, creating a huge lump that I couldn't seem to swallow. My heart sank as I saw Troy wrap his arms around Randa's waist, before kissing each other.

Right then and there, I wished that the floor would open up and eat me, so I could never see the sight I was looking at ever again.

CHAPTER SEVEN

You know that moment when time just stops? When you feel like everything is in slow motion and you're not able to escape it, no matter how much you blink?

That's exactly how I'm feeling at this moment. I saw in the distance something that was familiar. It was something that I used to do. Only this time, it's with someone else. I was witnessing something that felt so painful, tearing my heart slowly as I gasped for air.

At that moment I regretted everything. I regretted coming here and leaving New York. I regretted that I never got over him. This was all because of my stupid, weak heart.

Staring at them hurts. My vision blurred and tears threatened to fall down my cheeks. I can't handle it. Watching Troy hold someone else was like a stab to my heart.

I closed my eyes for a second. With a breath, I opened my eyes and told myself it wasn't the time to be weak. I'm stronger than this. I can go through this. I shouldn't break down.

Randa and Troy broke apart as Randa started to speak. Troy's eyes followed to me. His eyes immediately hardened as Randa looked over to me with a friendly smile, waving for me to come to her.

With slow steps, I hesitantly walked over to them with shaky breaths. As soon as I was close to them, Randa's eyes changed from happiness to a look of concern. She placed her hand on my shoulder and frowned slightly.

"Ariel? Are you okay?" she asked. "You don't look so good. Do you feel sick? If you do, then we can take you to the nurses office." I immediately shook my head.

"No," I argued. "I'm okay." She nodded her head then smiled, looking at Troy.

"Ariel. This is my boyfriend," she said, pointing at Troy who only stared at me blankly. Her words made my heart sink. I swallowed and inhaled, not knowing what to say. "His name is Troy."

"We know each other," Troy interrupted, my eyes widening as Randa had a curious look onto her face.

"Really?" she asked. "How?"

Troy's eyes remained on me for a moment before he slowly averted his gaze to Randa.

"She's the girl I told you about. The one that is staying at my house with a friend," Troy replied.

Randa nodded.

"Oh, I see."

I nodded my head as Troy stared back at me. I looked away and placed my eyes onto the floor.

"Well, that's okay. I hope you're comfortable at his place," Randa said, smiling at me. I looked up at her and nodded.

"I am. Rose and Damon are very nice to me," I claimed. Randa nodded again before telling us to go sit on a table as the rest of their friends arrived. Troy didn't utter a word as Randa and a few more people I've never seen before gathered and sat at a table.

Randa introduced me to the rest of the group as they all welcomed me. I smiled at them and sat down in front of Troy and Randa. Troy stared at me intimidatingly before I looked away.

A girl named Haya kept asking me numerous questions. Another boy who introduced himself as Ethan also tried to start a conversation with me. I would only reply with short answers to each of them. My mind wasn't cooperating correctly. It was only focused on Randa and Troy. I couldn't help but feel like puking.

How am I going to continue to play along like this didn't affect me?

Could I actually be Randa's friend?

I just hoped that maybe if Ozan is with me tomorrow, things might turn out better.

The rest of the day went downhill. I found out that I have Troy for the sixth and seventh period. Randa was also in my seventh period class, which was not fun especially that they're together. Troy as usual would only stare at me. I've endured those two classes to what seemed like eternity.

Troy didn't really show much affection towards Randa. He'd just stay quiet as Randa did all the talking, hugging and holding hands. However, it still broke my heart that he called another girl his. It broke my heart even more to see another girl calling him her boyfriend.

I would avert my eyes from them as much as possible, so I wouldn't break my heart further than it already was. I decided that I shouldn't show Randa how I felt. Randa is a sweet girl. I should endure it. I was not a relationship wrecker, no matter how much he meant to me.

It's not like anything will ever happen to Troy and I from now on. It was surely impossible. I had to hide what I felt, and maybe just try to move on.

After what I witnessed today, I came to realize that I didn't want to endure this heart break nor put myself in this misery. Troy didn't care, so I shouldn't try to bring back something that maybe wasn't meant to be brought back.

After today, I just wanted to leave California more than ever.

My thoughts were interrupted by the final bell. Everyone got up from their seats and rushed out the door. I slowly stood up as Randa came up to me, smiling.

"Are you going home?" she asked. I nodded my head.

"Yeah. I am."

Troy came walking towards us before I continued to speak. "I'll be walking home, so I better go." Randa furrowed her brows before looking at Troy.

"Walking? Why won't Troy just drive you there? You both live in the same house, after all," she asked. I shook my head but before I could speak, Troy butted in.

"I'm driving you home. Orders from my mother," he said blankly, shrugging his shoulders before looking away. I sighed before nodding my head, not wanting to upset Rose.

Just endure it, Ariel.

"Let's go," Troy ordered before walking off. I nodded and Randa smiled down at me.

"You'll get used that. He's kind of rough," she told me. I only nodded my head.

"I know," I said as we started walking behind him.

"He lost his memories three years ago," she said. "That's why he's like that." I nodded my head once again. I didn't bother adding a comment. After a while, I looked back at her and decided to speak.

"Do you know anything from his past?" I asked. I want to know if she knew anything. She shook her head.

"Troy never talks about it. He can't remember anything before three years," she claimed. "I've known him ever since he came here but we just recently started dating, like a month ago. He's always quiet and doesn't open up much. Even with me."

I looked down the floor and nodded, not knowing what to say.

Who knew that a person like the old Troy could completely turn out to be so different. Some people really do change.

I soon got in Troy's car and said goodbye to Randa. Troy immediately started the car and drove off and this time, I remained silent, not uttering a single word. Troy stayed silent as well as he concentrated on the road. I looked out the window the whole ride, feeling empty inside.

We soon stopped at a red light, and I glanced at Troy to see him looking at me. He immediately averted his eyes away and I inhaled deeeply breath. I decided not to question and for once to keep my stupid mouth shut.

Maybe if I do, then nothing hurtful will come out of his mouth.

We eventually arrived at the house. I exited the car immediately and entered the house.

I was thankful that I didn't run into Rose so I could just get to my room. As soon as I made it to my room, I slammed the door shut and slowly sunk to the floor. I let everything go. Everything I was holding back for the whole day, I let it all go at that spot and moment.

Tears fell down my cheeks as I replayed what I witnessed today. It was exactly as what I remembered from our past. It hurt me so much. I cried as I remembered the love that Troy and I shared. The love that kept me going these three years.

Now it's gone.

I eventually stopped crying and wiped the tears off my cheek. I still sat there, staring off into space. I inhaled deeply then ran both hands over my face. I felt much better after I got it all out.

It was true. When you cried, you feel much better than holding it in. I knew it was going to be very difficult, but I have to be strong. Hopefully, I won't stay here for long so I shouldn't do this to myself. I shouldn't constantly feel like the world was closing on me.

A knock at the door pulled me out of my thoughts. I immediately wiped my face when I heard Ozan's voice.

"Ariel? Are you in there? Can I come in?" Ozan called out.

I immediately got up from the floor. I cleared my throat and ran my hands over my face. "Come in."

A smiling Ozan came in, closing the door behind him. His smile immediately dropped when he saw that my eyes and nose were pink from all the crying. "Ariel? Are you okay?" he asked, stepping closer to me. "Were you crying?"

I didn't say anything but walked up to him, pulling him into a hug. I'm so thankful that I have him with me. He immediately wrapped his arms around me as I placed my head against his chest. I blinked to prevent the tears from falling all over again. Ozan's worried voice ringed in my ears.

"Ariel? What happened?" He asked.

"Please, don't leave me alone," I whispered, my voice cracking at the end as a tear fell. "Don't ever leave me alone again. I only have you at this moment."

Ozan's arms tightened around me. He then started rubbing my back in a soothing manner.

"I don't know what happened," he whispered, pulling away as he looked into my eyes. "But know that I've got your back. You're not alone."

I nodded my head as he gently wiped a tear off my cheek. We hugged again and remained like that for a while. My head against his chest as he rubbed my back, comforting me. Thankfully, he didn't ask what happened nor did he push for me to talk. That, I was thankful for.

We just stayed like that for awhile, and I was thankful that he stood by my side, not letting me go at a moment that I felt weak.

After awhile, Ozan left my room. I slept for two hours. When I woke up, I was very hungry. I mustered all my strength and exited my room. I hesitantly and slowly walked down the stairs into the kitchen.

Thankfully, I haven't bumped into Troy. I didn't even want to see him. Just seeing him hurt me so bad, and I didn't like that at all.

As I entered the kitchen I noticed Rose standing by the counter. She walked towards me and smiled. I smiled back at her as I stepped closer.

"Ariel," she called. "How was your first day of school?" She tilted her head at me. I cleared my throat.

"It was nice," I lied, giving her a small smile.

"That's great," she exclaimed, patting my back. "Are you hungry? Dinner is almost ready." Rose started to take out some plates.

"Yes, I am," I replied.

"Okay, then could you possibly help me get the table ready?" she asked, offering me a sweet smile.

"Of course," I answered, smiling back at her. Rose handed me the plates and spoons, then took out the food from the oven.

"Place these on the dinner table," she said. I was about to walk out of the kitchen but I remembered something.

"Rose."

She looked back at me and raised a brow. "Yes, honey?"

"Why didn't you tell me Troy had a girlfriend?" I wondered, looking at the floor for a second then looked back at her. Her eyes immediately averted my gaze. She emptied her hands then walked over to me.

"I'm sorry, sweetheart," she whispered, putting her hand on my shoulder. "I didn't tell you because it's not important."

"What do you mean?" I questioned, looking at her with a confused expression plastered onto my face.

"I mean that I know it won't last. Ever since we've came here Troy would date a girl then soon break up. He's going through a faze, I guess. His relationships never last long. I honestly don't think he cares that much about her. He never brought her here nor does he talk about her that's why I didn't tell you. So don't be that upset," Rose explained.

I nodded my head, smiling wistfully at her. "It's none of my business honestly on who he dates. I just wished I could have

66

known earlier to have prepared myself," I whispered to her. "He could do whatever he wants."

"I'm still rooting for you, though. I know that with time, maybe you could bring back our old Troy. Troy loved you so much. And I don't think a love like that could ever be forgotten," she said, smiling back at me

I shrugged my shoulders then took a step back. I do not know what to say or think. "I'll go set the table," I said. Rose only nodded her head. I turned around but abruptly pulled back when I rembered one more thing.

"Oh, Rose. One more thing," I said. She looked at me again.

"Yes, sweetheart?"

"You didn't have to call Troy to pick me up and drive me home. I prefer to walk next time," I said, giving a soft smile at her.

She tilted her head at me. "What do you mean?" she asked.

"I mean, it's not necessary to make Troy my personal driver. I'll walk next time," I explained.

She looked at me for a second then shook her head. "But Ariel, I never called him to pick you up or to drive you home," she said. "I thought you walked?"

My eyes widened. It took me a moment to register everything in my head. I slowly nodded as Rose looked at me with confusion.

"It's nothing. Forget it," I said. I turned around and walked out of the kitchen before she could ask something else. I darted to the dining room and started to set up the table. I ran a hand over my face.

I felt confused. One question kept circling my head.
Why did Troy lie to me about that?

CHAPTER EIGHT

The end of school looked like a scene straight out of a school shooting. All the students got up from their seats and made a rush outside. It was as if everyone was being held hostage with a gun pointed at their heads.

I got up from my seat and grabbed my bag. I calmly walked out the classroom and then searched for Troy across the halls. After making it in front of the school campus, I smiled as I saw Troy waiting in front of his car. His hands were in his pockets as he gazed around the area.

I waved at him and then our eyes locked. He smiled warmly at me, a smile that I loved so much. I sped toward him until he eventually took me in his arms. I wrapped mine around his large figure. I placed my head against his chest and finally got to inhale his scent and relaxed.

"Hey, my little mermaid," he said, pulling away and looking at me. "How was school today?" he asked. I shrugged my shoulder as I let out a long, exhausted breath out of my lips.

"It's honestly so boring without you," I muttered, placing my head against his chest one more time. "How was your football practice today?" I asked him this time, looking up at him. He leaned in to kiss my forehead, making me smile.

"It was fine. We still need some more practice," he replied, slipping his hand on mine. "Come on, let go get something to eat. I bet you're hungry."

I immediately smiled and nodded my head eagerly, getting hungrier as we brought up the subject. Without a second thought, I opened the car door and hopped in. Troy soon started the car and drove off towards the city as I hummed along to the music that was playing in the car.

Troy was just concentrating on the road, not even glancing my way. That's how Troy was when he drives. He was a very safe driver and was very serious when it came to driving. He just recently started driving as he passed the legal age of driving. I, however, still needed a year. Troy is a year older but he entered school a little late.

I let him drive in silence as I continued to hum. Soon, I started to sing. I noticed that he started smirking. I narrowed my eyes at him as he continued to keep his eyes on the road, his lips slowly cracking into a smile.

I stopped my singing as I tilted my head in confusion.

"Why are you smiling?" I asked, crossing my arms. He started to chuckle and shaking his head.

"What's so funny, Troy?" I asked.

For the first time since we've gotten into the car, he glanced at me for a second then smiled that reached his eyes.

"Ariel, even though I call you the little mermaid, I don't actually mean you're her," he said, his eyes twinkling with amusement. My eyebrows furrowed and I slapped him on his arm.

"Are you saying I don't have a good voice?" I questioned, looking daggers at him.

"That's exactly what I'm trying to say," he chuckled. I dramatically gasped and sulked in my seat as I glared at him. He made a quick glance at me to see my expression.

"For your information, my voice is way better than yours!" I said. I stuck out my tongue at him. He raised a brow at me while chuckling at my dramatic behavior. I rolled my eyes.

"Yes, I admit. You do have a better voice than me," he said, letting one hand go from the steering wheel as he grabbed onto my hand, giving it a comforting squeeze.

"Yeah, yeah. I know," I muttered while smiling at him. He laughed at my behavior. We eventually stopped at a diner and got out the car. At this point, I was starving. I'm always hungry after school. Troy, however, was used to it by now.

We walked into the diner hand in hand and settled down at a table. A young waitress came walking towards us with the menus. She smiled widely at Troy as she stood in front of us,.

"Hello, I'll be your waitress today," she said, handing Troy a menu. Troy only nodded his head as I narrowed my eyes at her. The way she looked at Troy made me feel uneasy. I cleared my throat to get her attention.

She then handed me the menu with a blank expression. Troy obviously didn't seem to be aware of her actions so he didn't utter a single word. She then looked back at Troy, completely ignoring me.

"I'll be back to get your orders. If you need anything, don't hesitate to ask." She walked off.

Troy opened the menu and started to scan through it. I just looked at him with a frown on my face. He surely noticed what I did, because he raised his brow at me.

"Is there something wrong?" he asked, placing the menu on the table. "Did you not like the food that they offer here?" I narrowed my eyes at him, shaking my head.

"No," I muttered annoyingly. He raised a brow for the second time at me.

"Then what's wrong?" he asked. "Why do you look upset?"

"Did you seriously not notice?" I questioned, my frown deepening. He looked at me confusingly.

"Notice what?" Troy asked. I am getting annoyed by the minute. I sighed while running a hand through my hair.

70

"The way that waitress acted towards you?" I told him. He looked at me weirdly as a smile crawled onto his lips.

"How did she act towards me?" he asked, raising a brow. I huffed and shook my head. "What?" Troy pushed.

"She was clearly into you," I finally admitted, frowning as I told him.

He chuckled, shaking his head. "No she wasn't. She just gave us the menus," Troy argued. I narrowed my eyes at him and I couldn't help but feel extremely annoyed.

"You just weren't paying attention. I saw how she was looking at you," I muttered, crossing my arms against my chest as I looked away from him. Troy soon grabbed my hand and squeezed it, making me look at him.

"It doesn't matter how she was looking at me. What matters is how I look at you," he said.

I started to ease up a bit after he said that. He then kissed my hand which cracked a smile onto my lips.

"And I look at you with so much love, and you know it," he soothed.

I chuckled. He always knew what to say to make me feel better. That's what I really loved about him. He'd always try to make me happy even if I was extremely annoyed.

"Yeah, yeah, I know," I muttered.

He smiled at me. We talked for a bit while we waited for our orders to be taken. Eventually, the same waitress came walking towards us, making me feel uneasy. She stood in front of us, and as I expected, she did not once glance at me but stared right at Troy, like she could see right into his soul.

"Is your order ready?" she inquired. Troy nodded his head and grabbed onto my hand.

"I would like the number two that's on the menu," he told her, glancing at me with a smile. "What about you, honey?" Troy asked, making the waitress look at me with a frown.

71

I gave her my most innocent smile. "I'll have the same," I answered.

She nodded her head and wrote our orders down. After, she faced Troy once again. "Your food will be here shortly," she said. I then saw the waitress winking at Troy before walking away.

My jaw dropped at her audacity. I held the urge to jump at her. I could imagine myself tearing her to shreds. Troy looked a little surprised but shrugged his shoulders.

"Tell me you noticed that," I said with a frown painted on my face. He nodded his head but squeezed my hand in a comforting manner.

"I did," he muttered. "But just ignore it."

"Ignore it? How can I ignore it? She doesn't even care that I'm here." I raised my voice at him and looked away. I pulled my hand away from him and crossed it across my chest.

"Oh, Ariel," he muttered. "Don't do this."

"I'm not doing anything," I muttered grumpily.

"Yes, you are. It's not my fault she's looking at me," he said, making my frown deepen. "I was clearly making it obvious that you're my girlfriend."

I huffed, shaking my head as I looked at him. "Obviously, you weren't making it obvious 'cause she didn't even acknowledge my presence and only stared at you like I wasn't even here," I muttered in a very annoyed tone. He smiled, but remained silent. I raised a brow at him.

He suddenly got up from his seat. I looked at him with my eyebrows wrinkled. Troy then cleared his throat.

"Troy, what are you doing?" I asked him. He glanced at me, smiling from ear to ear.

"Acknowledging you," he answered, looking around the diner. "Everyone!" he yelled. The rest of the diner glanced at him. My eyes widened and I immediately grabbed onto his hand.

"Troy," I hissed. "What are you doing? Sit down."

He glanced at me with a smile, then turned his attention to the many people who were now looking at him.

"This is my girlfriend,"—he yelled, pointing at me— "and I love her so, so, so, much." I felt my cheeks heat up as everyone looked at us with large smiles. I tugged on his hand as I tried to hide my blushed cheeks behind my hair.

"Troy, that's enough," I hissed. "Sit down." Troy started laughing as customers looked at us in awe. He eventually sat down. I placed my hands over my flushed cheeks.

"There, now everybody knows that you're my girlfriend," he claimed, smiling widely. I smiled warmly at him, grabbing onto his hand as I chuckled.

"You're crazy," I exclaimed. He laughed but nodded his head. He then raised my hand towards his lips as he planted a soft kiss on it.

"I am. But you still love me," Troy claimed. I gave him a warm smile as I nodded my head.

"I do."

*   *   *

Memories from our past flushed into my head as we sat on the dining table. I couldn't help but remember the times when Troy and I were just an amazing couple. We cared and loved each other so much, even if it didn't really last for long.

I averted my gaze away from my plate and onto Troy, to see him staring at me. It was like he was trying to understand something. His eyes seemed hard as he looked into my soul. He slowly looked away and I followed. Ozan and Julia were bickering about something as Rose and Damon talked to themselves.

I just remained quiet, not knowing what to say or do. Eventually, I got up from my seat and smiled at Rose. "Thank you for the delicious meal, Rose," I thanked her then grabbed my plate.

"I'll be going back to my room. If you need any sort of help then don't hesitate to call for me."

Rose gave me a warm smile. "You're welcome, honey. And don't worry, Julia will help me clean the table." I turned around and placed the plate in the sink.

As soon as I entered my room, the phone from my pocket vibrated. I took it out to see my mom calling me. Ever since I arrived here, I've only talked to my parents a couple times. I didn't try to hide that I was very upset with them, but eventually, I kind of gotten over it. My dad explained to me that he had nowhere else to send me off to. If I would've known earlier, I might have decided not coming.

I answered the call. "Hello?"

"Ariel, honey," my mom said from the other end. "How are you?"

"I'm good. How about you?" I asked her.

"We're good. We miss you so much," she said softly. I sat down on my bed and sighed.

"Me too, mom. I miss you both so much," I said. "Is there anything new?" My mom exhaled from the other end.

"At the moment, no. We have security all around the house but nothing new has happened," she explained. "But there is one thing that were looking into."

I furrowed my brows. "What is it?" I asked, getting a little worried.

"We've tried to see the security footage of the day when someone entered your room but all the footage from the street camera outside our house was deleted. There's nothing from that day," she said, sending shivers down my spine.

I gulped and breathed out.

"What does that mean?" I asked her, my heart falling to my feet. How could there be no footage? Who deleted them?

She stood silent for a moment.

74

"I don't know, honey," she sighed. "But all we know is that you'll be staying in California for awhile."

CHAPTER NINE

I groaned then raised a brow as I faced Ozan. I ran both hands over my face. I'm definetely not happy with his behavior at this moment. He offered me a foolish smile.

Ozan chuckled and raised both hands in front of his face.

"Hey, what's that grumpy face for?" he asked, smiling from ear to ear as I rolled my eyes at him. "If you stay like that any longer then that expression will glue to your face."

I slapped his arm which only made him giggle. I sighed and waited until he was done with all the laughing. When he calmed down, I looked at him with a raised brow at him for the second time.

"Are you done?" I asked, tilting my head as I looked at him. Ozan's smile was still plastered onto his face and I could clearly tell the he was trying so hard not to burst out in laughter due to my seriousness.

"Oh, come on, Ariel," Ozan said, moving his chair closer to me as he smiled from ear to ear, showing his teeth in the process. "Don't be like that."

"Don't be like what?"

"A party pooper," Ozan answered with his arms crossed. I scowled and slapped him again on his arm. "Ow!" he winced, pouting at me like a child. "That hurt. What was that for?"

"That's for being immature. I'm a party pooper? Remind me to never study with you ever again." I replied, crossing my arms.

Ozan frowned and soon pouted his lip.

"What's wrong with studying with me?" he asked, raising a brow. "I'm an awesome study partner," he defended.

Are you serious? I rolled my eyes at him. A sly grin slowly made its way onto his lips which eventually turned into a laugh.

"Okay, okay. Don't look at me like that," he said in between giggles. "I might not be the best, but hey, I'm awesome and I make studying quite fun," Ozan exclaimed, smirking at me.

I shook my head and rolled my eyes for what felt like the hundredth time today. "You make studying fun?" I asked, raising a brow. "You're not even studying to even make it fun. Heck, I've been trying to get this section of the notes in my head but all you've been doing is distract me." I narrowed my brows at him as his smirk fell. He sighed.

"Okay, fine. I can get quite distracted. I just can't seem to concentrate," he finally admitted. I've been telling him that for past few hours!

I made an oath to myself to never study with Ozan ever again, and I mean ever.

It has only been a week since our first day of school has started here in California, but a couple of our teachers have already lined up quizzes for the following week. So today, a Saturday, Ozan and I have decided to study all day instead of going outside or something.

It's not like we could do anything else if we wanted to. We were new here so we had no idea where to go or who to go with. It's not like Troy wouldn't mind taking us somewhere. However, as soon as we started, I immediately regretted it. Ozan was the worst person to study with. He won't help you. He'll just distract you and make things even more difficult than it already is.

We've been sitting in my room for what felt like hours, trying to get the information in our head but Ozan gets distracted with the smallest stuff. I'd be in the middle of explaining something when Ozan would bring up something from the past and he'd be

77

like, "Do you remember this . . . ?" and "remember when we did this . . . ?"

It didn't help either when he'd just stare off into space and start yawning.

"If this goes on then nothing will be entering our heads, Ozan," I exclaimed, looking at him. He shrugged his shoulders as a small smile made its way onto his lips.

"It's not my fault, honestly," he mused. I leaned against my chair and offered him a confused look.

"What do you mean it's not your fault? Am I the one who's distracting you?" I asked, sarcasm laced in my voice. I could see the smile growing on his face. Ozan moved his chair closer to mine and leaned towards me. I instictively backed up my head.

"Yes, a matter of fact, you are," Ozan said.

"What do you mean? You're the one distracting me," I pressed, gulping as his head moved closer to mine.

Ozan slowly shook his head, his eyes slowly moving down to my lips then back to my eyes. His eyes had an unusual glint in them, something I wouldn't see much. I sucked in a breath at our closeness, something which definitely left me uncomfortable.

"No, Ariel. You're the one distracting me," he said. "I can't seem to concentrate when I'm around you."

My breath immediately got stuck in my throat. Ozan's lips inched to mine. I immediately moved away and got off my chair in discomfort. Ozan immediately looked at me with a surprised expression. We remained silent for a moment. What should I do?

"Uh . . ." I muttered. "I'm going downstairs to grab a cup of water," I stupidly said. I rushed out of my room without even waiting for a response.

I immediately stopped in my track when I realized what just happened. Ozan almost kissed me.

I was in shock. I always knew in the back of my head that Ozan felt something for me but I always tried to brush it off and push it in the back of my head. Ozan was a very close person to me, but, thinking of him in another way didn't really work out for me.

I immediately shook my head and ran both hands through my face. I tool a long, deep breath. I didn't know what to think. Why did I just run out like that? Now it will definitely be awkward when I see him. I sighed. I continued my way down the stairs and towards the kitchen.

Maybe a glass of cold water will help me cool down.

I was about to enter the kitchen when I heard voices. I stoppped dead in my tracks as I listened in. I heard Troy's angry voice arguing with Rose, who seemed annoyed with her son. I could also hear Julia's voice. They all seemed like they were arguing about something.

I decided not to interrupt their private conversation and took a couple of steps back.

"How long will she stay?" Troy bellowed, his mother shushing him.

"Troy, honey, please, calm down before anyone hears you," she whispered. I frowned.

"You're not answering me," he said. "How long will she be staying here? How long will I have to keep seeing her? It's pissing me off." My eyes widened. I immediately knew he was referring to me. Rose hushed him again.

"Troy. Why is it bothering you so much? You're being extremely rude. She's a guest and she'll be staying here for as long as she wants to," Rose beamed. "You know why she's here. We already told you. Her parents fear that her life is at threat. We are very good family friends, that's why they sent her here. She'll stay here for as long as she needs to and you need to stop complaining. Don't forget that she used to be your best friend."

"Here's the thing, Mom," Troy started. "I forgot her. I forgot everything. There is nothing for me to remember. I will neither remember her nor will I remember anything."

"You're not even trying," Julia spat back this time. "Maybe she could bring back your memories if you just give her a chance."

"I won't give her a chance because she means nothing to me," he claimed harshly. They went silent. I stood there, heart to my feet as I registered what he has just said. My vision blurred. His words stabbed my fragile heart. I can't help it feeling. It hurt so much to hear that I meant nothing to him. Nothing.

My breath was stuck in my throat. I couldn't seem to swallow.

I heard Julia sigh in frustration. "That's it, I'm not talking to you about this subject anymore. We tried everything Troy, but you're not trying at all. You're the one who's blocking your own memories, and if you don't change that then you'll never remember anything." She walked out of the kitchen, but immediately gasped when she saw me.

"Ariel? Did you hear everything?" Julia stammered. Rose later on followed Julia's shock. They now know that I was standing there. I was looking hurt as ever.

"Oh, Ariel." Rose walked up to me. Before she could say anything else, Troy walked right past me, not even sparing me a single glance. Julia glared at him, while Rose looked at me with guilt.

Meanwhile, I looked down on the floor, trying to prevent any tears from escaping my eyes.

"Ariel, honey," Rose murmured, placing her hand on my shoulder. "Don't be upset about what he said. He just needs time to get used to you."

I shook my head and took a step backwards. Rose kept trying to comfort me, but all I did was turn around and walked towards my room, not knowing what to feel. I entered my room, thankful that Ozan wasn't in here anymore.

I slowly sat on my bed and stared off into space, replaying his hurtful words into my head. A tear slowly fell down my cheek as I thought of what he said.

I meant nothing to him.
Nothing at all.

My head snapped up when I heard my bedroom door open. Julia hesitantly walked into my room then closed the door behind her. She looked at me with a sad expression.

"Ariel," she said. I looked at the floor. I heard her walk up to me to sit on my bed. "I'm sorry for what happened back there."

I shook my head, my eyes still set on the floor. "There's no need to apologize. He was just being honest," I said softly.

Julia sighed, making me look up at her through sad eyes.

"My brother changed that day after the surgery," she exclaimed. "He changed and ever since then, he became a new person. Yes, he's mean and harsh, but I believe the old Troy is still there deep down inside him. I just think that someone needs to push him, to be his motivation."

"And I can never be that motivation," I told her. "He hates me." Julia immediately shook her head.

"No, he doesn't," she argued. "He's just confused. Ever since you came here, you've been affecting him. I know it. He's confused and scared. He just needs time to get used to it and maybe then, he'll finally open up to remembering. Troy has never ever tried to remember. He's too scared to."

I looked at her with sad eyes. I don't know what to say.

"Just please, Ariel. Don't give up on him. You're our only hope. Maybe you can bring back our Troy."

I can't utter a single word. I knew I could never bring back the old Troy, because the old Troy is gone.

CHAPTER TEN

I spaced off in my last class as I wait for the final bell to unleash me from this hell hole. I was relieved that it was finally Friday. I wasn't able to concentrate with whatever the teacher was saying because my head was going haywire. I'm having a headache with all these emotions and thoughts running in and out of my head.

I ran a hand over my face as I eyed the clock. Any minute now and I would be out of here. I always dreaded the final class, not because of the teacher nor the subject, but because I shared it with Randa and Troy. I also shared the class before this one with Troy, which makes me extremely uncomfortable as he sits rather close to me.

I share most of my classes with Ozan, including this one, which I was thankful for. At least I didn't have to worry about making friends with anyone because I have Ozan with me. However, I've been kind of avoiding Ozan this whole week. Ozan kind of went on like nothing happened after the other day, but for me, I was a little uncomfortable. It wasn't something serious though since I still talk to Ozan normally.

The person who I've been completely avoiding was Troy. I've been ignoring him like the plague. What happened that day really hurt me, and I don't want to go through that again.

I bet the whole house noticed our behavior. We avoided eye contact and even being in each other's presence. Maybe, this was for the better. Maybe by doing this, I won't get hurt.

Yet, I was still hurt. Just seeing him hurts me. Seeing him with another girl hurts me even more. I dreaded this class, because Randa was glued to Troy's side and never seemed to let him go. They sat next to each other so she would always show affection like holding his hand, playing with his hair and hugging him.

I always tried to avoid looking at that. I even stopped sitting with Troy and Randa at their table at lunch. It was a torture sitting with them so I just started sitting on my own, and obviously Ozan would sit with me too, so I don't feel so alone.

I was very thankful for Ozan. Yes, he did stuff which made me uncomfortable but he means so much to me. I'm grateful for having him by my side. I don't know what I would do if I didn't have him.

The final bell pulled me out of my thoughts. Everyone got up and rushed out the classroom. I immediately followed while grabbing my bag. I then waited for Ozan to get out. Usually, Ozan and I would just walk home by ourselves. We didn't bother asking Troy for a ride. He didn't even ask us if we wanted a ride home to start with.

Ozan walked out of the classroom and smiled at me. I returned that smile then walked up to him.

"Come on, let go home already so I could just sleep," I told him while running a hand through my hair. Ozan chuckled. We started walking.

"I swear, I was about to fall asleep back there. Thank goodness today's Friday. I can finally sleep." Ozan grunted. I nodded my head in agreement as we walked off the school campus.

"Tell me about it," I murmured.

On our way home, we talked about anything. The walk home took only ten minutes. As we arrived, I saw Troy's car parked outside. It's obvious that he'd arrived earlier that us.

"Hello, kids. How was school?" Rose greeted. I smiled at her as she tooka couple of steps towards us.

"Tiring," Ozan and I answered at the same time, which made her roll her eyes.

"I'll be heading up to my room. I need to rest," I said, smiling at her one last time before walking up to my room. Troy came walking towards me, but I immediately looked away.

I glanced at him as we got closer to each other. I found him staring at me, so I averted my gaze immediately and walked past him straight into my room.

That gaze that he always gave me made a shiver run down my spine. Even though he wouldn't talk to me or anything, he'd always just stare. It was like he was trying to understand me or trying to read my mind.

I shook my head. Without a second thought, I hopped onto my bed, ignoring the fact that I was in my casual clothes.

I was exhausted. All I wanted to do was sleep. I closed my eyes and yawned. I was so close to drifting off when someone opened my bedroom door. Great.

I opened my eyes to see Julia by my door. She offered me an apologetic smile before stepping in.

"Yes, Julia?" I said, running a hand through my tired face. "Is there something you need?"

"No. Actually, Mom is calling for you," she said. I sat up. "She says to get downstairs because she needs you."

"Okay, Julia. I'll be down there," I said as I got up from my bed. Julia offered me one last smile then walked out of my room. I ran a hand through my hair and fixed my appearance.

I guess I won't be getting sleep after all.

I guessed Rose needed some help with the dinner or something. It would be rude of me to sleep and let her do all the work. I made my way down the stairs and into the living room to see Rose and Troy talking to each other.

I walked up to them hesitantly. They both turned to look at me. Rose smiled as she laid her eyes on me.

"Ah, Ariel. Come here," she said.

"Rose. Is there something you need?" I wondered, glancing at Troy for a split second. She nodded her head as Troy just stood there in silence.

"Yes. A matter of fact, I do," she answered. "We have guest coming over for dinner tonight, Damon's employee and his family. So, I need some stuff before I start working on the dinner. That's why you and Troy will be buying me these from the grocery store," Rose explained, handing me a grocery list.

I furrowed my brows and so did Troy. We glanced at each other then looked back at Rose.

"You want Troy and I to go grocery shopping?" I asked. She perfectly knew that I was trying to avoid him, and now she wants me to go grocery shopping with him?

"Yes. Now get along so I could start with dinner," she replied.

"Why do I have to go with her?" Troy questioned, raising a brow. "Why can't she go with Julia?" I frowned but nodded my head.

"Yeah," I murmured. "Why do I have to go with him? Anyone else but him." Troy looked at me and his frown deepened.

"What do you mean by that?" he asked, not looking too happy. "What's wrong with going with me?"

I raised a brow at him and scoffed. "What's wrong with you? You're a jerk, that's what's wrong. And I don't want to go with a jerk," I told him.

"A jerk?" asked.

"Yes, you're a jerk," I admitted. "Let Ozan or Julia come with me. I'm not going with him." Rose looked at us with wide eyes as Troy glared at me.

85

"I'm not wasting my time to go grocery shopping with her," Troy said to his mom. "I'm a jerk, after all," he scoffed out. I frowned at him and Rose shook her head.

"No," she said. "You both are going together. End of discussion." My eyes widened as I offered her a confused look.

"But why?" I asked.

"Because you two need to learn to communicate with each other," she answered. "You both are living under one roof after all, and constantly ignoring each other isn't going to work in my house."

Troy opened his mouth to argue but Rose glared at him.

"No arguments. Now get going and get me the things that's on the list," she instructed. She eyed me this time. Looks like she isn't going to back down from this.

I sighed and Troy groaned. We both walked out of the house silently.

"Let's get this over with," he muttered. "The faster we finish the faster I finish with you."

I looked up at him with a frown on my face. I just remained silent as we drove off. I kept my gaze outside the window.

Well, there goes my sleep.

Troy drove in silence. I could feel the tension in the air. After five minutes in the car, we parked in front of a supermarket. I hopped out of the car. Troy and I walked silently into the store side by side. As we entered, Troy looked at me.

"What's the first on the list?" Troy raised a brow. I then scanned the list.

"Vegetables. We need to get vegetables," I answered, looking up at him. We walked to the vegetable section.

I still found it so weird that Troy and I were here in a grocery store, buying food together. I never would have thought that I'd be buying groceries with Troy.

We picked out some vegetables in silence. Troy placed some rather small potatoes in the plastic bag.

86

"What are you looking at?" he asked with a raised brow. I shook my head and took the potatoes out of the bag and replaced them with larger ones. Troy frowned at me.

"Why did you do that? Those potatoes were perfectly fine," Troy asked, taking the ones I placed in the bag out and replacing them with the ones he placed in. I looked at him, shaking my head.

"These are too small," I said, bringing it up to his face so he could see. "We need bigger potatoes." I took them out for the second time and replaced them with the bigger ones.

"There's no difference," he argued.

"There is," I argued back.

"No, there isn't."

"There is."

"There isn't."

I shook my head. "It doesn't matter. Let's just continue." Troy nodded, glancing at the bag of potatoes one last time.

"Sweet pepper," I muttered, pointing at them from across the room. We walked up to them and Troy grabbed another bag, opening it as I picked red ones, placing them in the bag.

Troy frowned at the bag. "What?" I asked.

"I don't like the red ones," Troy muttered, taking them out from the bag and replacing them with green ones. "These are better."

I gave him a look that said 'are you serious'. "No, they aren't," I argued, placing a red one in the bag. "These are better. I like them more." Troy shook his head and placed another green one.

"No, these are."

I placed another red one in the bag as I shook my head in disagreement. "Uh, uh. These are."

"No, these are."

All our bickering made a few people look at us. I can't believe we're doing this.

"Okay, that's enough. We're acting like children," I said. "We'll take both colors. How does that sound?" A small smirk made its way to Troy's face then he chuckled. It definitely caught me off guard.

"We could've done that from the start," he claimed, my heart beating as I stared at his grin. "You make buying vegetables more difficult than it seems. Remind me to never go grocery shopping with you ever again."

I scoffed. "No, you're just stubborn. You like things to go your way," I told him, placing the bag of sweet peppers in the cart. Troy crossed his arms, raising a brow.

"I'm stubborn?" he said as we walked down the section. I looked over at him, nodding my head.

"Yes, you are," I answered. "And you're also a jerk." I muttered the last part.

"Why do you keep calling me a jerk? I didn't do anything," he argued. I scoffed at him as I continued to place some stuff into the cart.

"You didn't do anything? You've been a jerk to me ever since I came here," I said.

"No, I haven't."

I placed what was in my hands in the cart and turned to give him a serious look. "You have. All I wanted was to have you back in my life but you've completely changed. You're an asshole and all you've done ever since I've came here was be a jerk."

Troy looked quite surprised with my words. His expression turned into an serious one. He took a couple of steps towards me as he brought his face closer to mine. "That's just how I am. I am an asshole and the old Troy can never be back," he claimed, his eyes hard with no emotions. "Never."

I stared at him, feeling heartbroken by his words. I looked down on the floor. "Why?" My voice was so soft that it took Troy off guard. "Why aren't you even trying?" I asked.

Troy took a couple steps backwards. We remained silent for a moment while staring at each other. Troy looked like he didn't know what to say. Many emotions glinted in his eyes all at once as he stood there.

Troy opened his mouth to say something when all of a sudden . . .

"Everyone, get down to the floor!" a man yelled from the entrance of the supermarket. Seconds later, the man started to shoot in the air. People started screaming as the gunshots echoed. "Give me your money or I'll shoot you!" the man continued. "I'll shoot. Give me all your money!" he continued. Everyone started screaming.

A couple more gunshots made me scream as I feel my heart beating rapidly. It was like history was repeating itself. Troy was alert and grabbed my hand. He pulled me to the opposite direction from where the shots were coming from.

I wasn't concentrating on where Troy was taking me. I was concentrating on the cries I heard as gunshots continued to erupt in the air. People ran past us in fear. Everyone was running around the place. It was so chaotic. I felt like I was reliving what happened in New York.

Troy continued to pull me deep inside the supermarket. We abruptly stopped in front of a door. Without a second thought, Troy opened the door to what seemed like a small storage room and pulled me inside. He quickly locked the door. He pulled me to his chest as I gasped for air. We continued to hear yelling, crying and gunshots.

"Oh my God. Oh God," I softly gasped as the sounds drowned my ear.

The room was dim, but I could still make out some things in the room, including a worried Troy. Troy wrapped his arms around me.

"Shhh, everything will be okay. Just remain quiet." I nodded my head as I placed my hand on my mouth. Troy rubbed my back in a soothing manner.

We weren't sure of what we were going to do. The screaming did not stop. It only heightened my anxiety. Troy remained silent, trying to calm me down.

"Oh God. Oh my God," I kept murmuring under my breath as tears started to fall down my cheeks.

"It's okay," he whispered. "Don't cry."

I shook my head. "I can't. I'm scared. It's like I'm reliving what happened in New York," I whispered. I feel my heart beating rapidly.

Troy grabbed my face between his hands. "Don't be scared," he consoled. "Nothing's going to happen to you. I promise."

I continued to shake my head.

"Calm down and take a deep breath. I promise you'll be okay," Troy whispered into my ear, slowly pulling away and looking into my eyes.

I took a deep breath and gulped. "You promise?"

Troy nodded. "I promise."

CHAPTER ELEVEN

The air around us was tensed as I stayed wrapped in Troy's arms. It felt like hours have already passed. We didn't dare to move or make a sound. We stayed in the dim small room.

Moments later, everything went silent. There were no more screaming and gunshots. Everything was quiet. The only thing I could hear was our heavy breathing. Other than that, nothing.

We didn't know what was going on.

I looked up at Troy in confusion. He shook his head at me. Troy placed his point finger across his lips then slowly placed his ear on the door.

Troy listened for a while. I watched him in silence. I was starting to get anxious in this closed off room. I wanted to get out of here badly.

Troy's eyes widened. He took a couple of steps towards me then released a relieved breath.

"What is it?" I asked.

"The cops are here. I think they got him. I'll go out to check. You stay here until I tell you to come out," Troy answered.

I felt relieved but was hesitant about what Troy said.

"Are you sure you're okay with going out there alone?" I gave him a concerned look. Troy nodded his head as he made his way towards the locked door.

"I'll be fine. As I said, the cops are here," Troy replied. He unlocked the door and opened it slowly. I squinted my eyes and Troy walked out the small room, closing the door behind him.

I anxiously stood by myself in the room. A troubled sigh escaped my lips as I waited for Troy to be back. I placed my ears on the door to try to make out something but I couldn't hear a single thing. It was too difficult to hear something as this room was at the back of the supermarket, and guessing, everyone was at the front of the market.

I waited for a couple more minutes. I'm getting nervous. I was ready to walk out but the door opened itself with Troy on the other side. I released a long, relieved sigh.

"The cops got him. They took him out of here and they're interrogating some people," Troy said.

"Is anyone hurt badly?" I asked, biting my lip.

Troy snickered but shook his head. "That bastard was only using a fake gun that only released sounds to scare everyone. No one was injured," he answered.

"Oh," I muttered under my breath. "Thank God no one is hurt."

Troy nodded his head and placed his hand on my shoulder, taking me by surprise. "Come on. The cops want to interrogate us shortly so we could go home. I bet my mother is worried," Troy muttered. I took a couple of steps towards him, running a hand through my hair.

"What about the groceries?" I asked him, looking around the chaotic place that people caused as everything went chaotic.

Troy raised a brow at me and gave me a blank expression. I looked at him confusingly.

"What?" I muttered.

"Ariel. Is that all you're worried about right now?" he asked.

I slowly shook my head. "No."

He nodded. We started walking towards the entrance of the market.

"We'll make someone else get the groceries from somewhere else," Troy said, facing me. "Let's just head home." I sucked in a breath as I saw the cops by the entrance. The last time I witnessed a scene like this was during the first day of school back in New York.

Troy must have noticed me because he offered me a concerned look. One officer came walking towards us. To comfort me, he placed his hand on my back. I nodded my head at him. I'm so thankful that he was being understanding. The officer asked us a couple of questions which Troy answered. I stood there in silence thinking about the hand that was rubbing my back. It made me shudder. I felt my heart racing. Troy for once, showed me emotions other than anger and hatred. Today I witnessed a different side of him, a side I knew was brried deep down within him.

After a while, the officer excused us to leave. We walked towards the car while releasing a long sigh. We silently hopped in and drove off. I kept quiet, replaying what happened today in my head. I noticed from the corner of my eyes that Troy kept glancing at me.

"You know how you said you were reliving your past? Were you talking about that incident that happened in your school? The one my parents told us about?" he asked out of nowhere.

"Yeah. Three weeks ago, we had a shooting incident in our school back in New York," I explained softly. "The man was threatening me. I don't know whether he was just crazy in the head or really had the intentions to hurt me, but after a day, someone broke into my room and trashed it. That's when my parents feared that I was under a threat," I explained to Troy.

"That's why they sent you here. I didn't think it would be that serious," he said. I nodded my head at him. "

"Yeah. That's why," I whispered. Troy glanced at me another time before looking back at the road.

"Do you think you're under a threat?" he asked.

"I don't know, honestly. All I know is that I'll be staying here until my parents are assured that my safety isn't threatened," I replied. He nodded his head in understanding and didn't saying anything else. I bit my lip, debating whether I should ask him the question that was circling my head.

"Troy," I called, making him glance at me. "Does my presence really bother you?" I muttered. I wasn't sure if he heard me. However, his blank expression told me that he did. All of a sudden, I noticed that he parked in front of the house. He remained silent.

Troy brought his face closer to mine. "Yes. You bother me so much. I hate it," he answered.

What took me by surprise was the fact that his expression completely changed in one second. He was perfectly fine a while ago but now he went back to being an asshole. I opened my mouth to speak but before I could do so, he got out of the car, walking towards the house.

I immediately ran towards him, grabbing onto his arm. He looked at me with a hard expression plastered onto his face.

"Why?" I murmured under my breath, looking up at him. "Why does it bother you so much? What did I ever do to you?" I asked him. He released his arm from my grip and completely ignored me.

I immediately stood in front of him. "Answer me, Troy. Why do you hate me so much?" I pleaded.

He looked at me, remaining silent for a moment. "Ariel. Get out of my way," he muttered, but I shook my head.

"Not until you answer my question." I stood my ground. Troy snickered.

"I'm not forced to answer you," he exclaimed roughly . He walked past me towards the house. I stood there as I watched him disappear from my sight. I glanced sadly at the ground and ran a hand over my hair.

94

Of course nothing changed. Why the hell did I think that he'd change the way he looked at me just because he showed a different side today? Why did I hope that I'd receive a different treatment from him?

Stupid Ariel. When will you ever learn?

I slowly walked into the house and saw Troy explaining everything to a worried Rose. She then rushed towards me and placed her hands on my shoulder as Troy stared at me blankly.

"Oh, honey. Are you okay? Are you hurt?" she asked worriedly. I nodded my head and offered her a small reassuring smile.

"I'm okay, Rose. I'm honestly just tired," I said, glancing at Troy. "I'm going to my room to rest." Rose nodded her head, offering me a sad smile.

"Okay, Ariel. You get some rest. I'll deal with the dinner because we're having guests over soon. You don't have to come down here if you don't feel like it." Rose patted my back.

"Okay, thank you." I walked towards my room. I jumped onto my bed and finally welcomed the darkness with open arms.

I woke up when I heard my bedroom door open. I rubbed my eyes as I sat up. I smiled softly when I saw Ozan walked in. He pulled me in for a hug which caught me by surprise.

"Ozan?" I said groggily. He pulled away and sighed in relief.

"I just heard what happened," he claimed. "Thank God you're okay." I offered him a small smile, nodding my head.

"I'm okay," I assured him. "I was just scared." He frowned.

"If only I was with you," he muttered, shaking his head. "That's why I'm here in the first place, to look out for you. And the time when you needed me the most, I wasn't there." I immediately shook my head at him in disagreement.

"No, don't say that," I argued. "I'm perfectly fine. It's not your fault. Besides, Troy was with me." His expression turned sour. He remained silent for a while before slowly nodding his head.

95

"Yeah, Troy..." He muttered. I remained silent, looking at him in concern as he shook his head. "I'm just glad you're okay. The guest who are coming will arrive soon. You don't need to come down stairs. Just rest."

I shook my head and smiled softly at Ozan. "I'm fine. I have rested enough. I'll be down in a couple minutes," I told him as I got off my bed. Ozan followed suit.

"Okay. Then I'll be waiting for you downstairs," he claimed. I nodded. With one last smile, Ozan walked out of my room. After one long breath, I walked to my closet and pulled out something to wear. After ten minutes, I was completely ready. I could hear the doorbell ringing. They have finally arrived.

I wasn't planning on going downstairs, but after resting, I felt completely better. I was also quite curious to see who these people were.

I could hear the chatter already. When I entered the living room, I saw Rose and Damon welcoming a man, a woman and a teenage boy that looked around my age. Rose smiled as she saw me and waved at me to come over. I walked at them and offered them a welcoming smile as they looked at me.

"Hello," I greeted, standing next to Rose.

"Layla, Luis." Rose gestured at her guests. "This is Ariel, my friend's daughter. She's staying with us for a while," Rose introduced me to them. They smiled at me and shook my hand.

"It's nice to meet you," I said.

"It's nice to meet you, too," the lady greeted back. "This is my son, Rex. I think you two attend the same school." She pointed at her son who offered me a smile. I nodded at him and greeted him as well.

"Really? This is my first time seeing you," I told him. He nodded his head at me.

"You'll be seeing me more often. I recently transferred," he explained. I nodded my head at him in understanding. Soon, Ozan and Julia came and greeted them as well, and then Troy. After they were done with the greetings, Rose showed them the way to the dining table so we could start with dinner.

The whole time I was looking at Troy who just ignored my presence, making my stomach fall at the realization. We eventually sat down as they all started with their food, chatting while doing so. I sat next to Ozan while Rex sat in front of me, talking every now and then.

Luis and Damon were talking about work while Rose and Layla chatted about something else. Rex looked at me as I ate.

"So, you're new here to California?" he asked. I nodded my head at him.

"Yes," I answered. "I was in New York before I came here."

"That's nice," he smiled. "I've lived all my life here in California but we just recently moved around here."

"Really?" I asked.

"Yes. Have you explored California yet?" Rex asked. I shook my head.

"No. Honestly, I didn't really have time to do so," I said, frowning.

"Then I'll be your tour guide," he claimed, making me raise a brow at him.

"Tour guide?" I muttered.

"Yeah. I'll show you around California. If that's okay with you," Rex said, taking a bite from his food. I slowly nodded my head, understanding what he meant.

"You'd do that?" I asked. He nodded.

"Yeah. So you could get to know the place well."

I smiled at him. "That would be nice." We continued to chat as we ate our food. I kept seeing from the corner of my eyes that Troy was staring at us in silence. He didn't even eat his food. He only sat there.

I tried to ignore him and continue with my food as Rex kept chatting with me. Ozan remained silent as well as he listened

97

to our conversation. After a while, we all finished our food and Julia and I helped Rose clean up the table. After a while, the guests finally excused themselves.

Damon opened the door for them as they bid them goodbye. "Thank you for the delicious food, Mrs. Rose," —he then turned to me—"and I won't forget that promise I made to you," he winked before finally walking away with his parents. Rose closed the door.

"I'll be heading up to my room. If you need anything, call me," I told Rose. She nodded her head and offered me a soft smile.

"Thank you, sweetheart."

I smiled at her and walked up to my room after saying goodnight to Julia, Damon and Ozan. As I entered my room, I immediately changed into my pajamas and laid in my bed.

I didn't really feel sleepy as I have already slept today, but I was emotionally tired. After ten minutes of just laying on my bed, a knock on my door made me frown. I got up, wondering who would knock at my door as I clearly stated I wanted to rest.

I walked towards the door and opened it. I was surprised when I found Troy. He looked at me as I gave him a confused expression, not expecting for him to be knocking at my door.

"Troy?" I called, opening the door wider. "Is there something you need?"

Troy let out a sigh and ran a hand through his hair. "No," he answered, causing for me to frown. "I just wanted to make sure you were okay after today."

I sucked in a breath as those words left his mouth. I stared at him surprisingly, not ever expecting for him to be knocking at my door to see if I was okay.

"I-I . . . I'm okay." My voice came out softly. He nodded his head and inserted his hands to his front pockets.

"That's good," he muttered under his breath. "Get some rest, you need it." I slowly nodded my head and that's when Troy turned around and started to walk away.

"Troy," I called out. He stopped and looked back at me, making me step out of my room and step towards him. "I didn't get to thank you for what you did today. So . . . thank you. I don't know what I would have done if you weren't with me."

Troy only nodded his head as I offered him a small, sad smile. And with one more glance, he walked away and down the hall, away from my sight. I sighed and entered my room, closing the door behind me as I softly smiled to myself.

I couldn't help thinking that even though this Troy was a complete jerk, deep down inside him hid something else. A side which truly and actually cared.

CHAPTER TWELVE

I strolled down the stairs, holding onto my bag as I hummed a song that has been stuck in my head for ages. I took my time as I walked towards the kitchen to grab something to eat before I headed off to school with Ozan. I glanced at my watch. I still had more than thirty minutes till my first class started.

I walked into the kitchen and smiled up at Julia and Rose, who were eating their breakfast on the kitchen counter. I kissed them both on the cheek.

"Good morning," I greeted, placing my bag onto the counter as I grabbed a piece of bread. They both smiled at me, greeting me back.

"Morning to you, too," Rose said. "You look rather happy today. Did you dream about something good?" Rose asked, smiling at me with one raised brow. I chuckled out and placed my bread in the toaster, waiting for it to be ready.

"No. Not really. I am relaxed though." She was sort of right. I was in a good mood today. There wasn't a reason behind it but I guess maybe it was because I slept like a baby last night.

"Oh. Well, that's very nice," Rose said in a happy tone, taking a bite out of her breakfast. "You still have time before class starts, so sit down and eat." I nodded my head and took out the toast from the toaster, spreading cream cheese onto it.

I filled myself a glass of juice before sitting down, taking a bite out of my toast. We chatted for a bit as we continued to eat.

Julia was telling me how her exams has started and how she has to start studying.

It's been a month since I have started attending the school I went to and haven't really studied that hard since I've started.

I bet that the teachers were going to start giving out exams, that's why I made a mental note telling myself I should start studying.

Surely, not with Ozan.

I was pulled out of my thoughts when Troy came walking into the kitchen. We all looked at him as he strolled in with a natural expression on his features.

"Morning," he muttered, looking at Julia and his mom.

"Good morning, honey," Rose smiled at him. Troy's eyes eventually landed at me. He greeted me with a nod. I offered him a small smile in return then I went back to eating my toast. Troy opened the fridge and grabbed a bottle of juice to fill himself a cup. I glanced at him numerous times as I continued to finish my toast.

Troy and I were rather neutral for the past two weeks. He didn't really act as if he hated me anymore. We talked here and there but not for long. He was actually tolerating me now. Why? I still don't know. I was rather happy of this change of attitude. It wasn't big, but it was enough for me to hold on. I was willing to take anything.

Troy drank the juice then placed the cup in the sink. I caught him looking back at me. I glanced at my watch. I should get going before I'm late.

"Where's Ozan? We're going to be late," I said out loud. He would usually be the first one to be down here. Julia smiled but shook her head as she got up.

"Poor guy, laying in bed as he spills his guts out," Julia chuckled slightly as she grabbed onto her bag.

"What do you mean?" I asked.

"He's sick. I think he caught a stomach bug. He's been puking the whole night." Rose explained. I frowned as I looked at them.

"How?" I asked. He was perfectly fine just yesterday. How did he get sick all of a sudden?

"I think he's pregnant." Julia snickered. Rose glared at her.

"Julia. Don't joke like that. The poor kid is tired," she scolded, which only made Julia laugh. Rose turned her attention back at me and continued to explain. "I think he ate too much from yesterday's meal, that's why he's like that."

"Well, I'll get going before I'm late. Bye." Julia waved as she walked towards the door. Rose smiled at her. With a sigh, I grabbed my bag and looked back at Rose.

"Well, I should get going too, before I'm late," I told Rose, glancing at Troy for a second. Rose nodded her head and with one last smile, I walked out the house. I was eventually walking down the streets towards my school all alone.

I really hate walking alone without Ozan. Ozan kept me company but now since he wasn't here, my mood went downhill. He just had to be sick.

As I was walking towards the school, a familiar car stopped right next to me. Behind the wheel was Troy who slid down the window.

"Get in," he muttered. I raised a brow at him.

"Huh?" I murmured.

"Come on Ariel before we're late," he said, urging me to get in. I stood there for a moment before getting into the passenger seat. He drove as I sat there in silence, confused on what happened back there.

"I'm not letting you walk alone," Troy said out of the blue.

"Excuse me?" I questioned. Troy sighed, glancing at me.

"I'm not comfortable in letting you walk alone without Ozan," Troy muttered. I wasn't sure I heard correctly. I slowly nodded my head, smiling at him softly.

102

"Thank you, I appreciate it," I told him. He put his attention back on the road. He nodded his head and continued driving. A while later, his phone rang. He glanced at his phone and so did I.

I frowned as I saw 'Randa' on the screen. He huffed before answering it.

"Can't talk right now. I'm driving," Troy said then ended the call right away. My eyes widened at his attitude towards her. He placed the phone down before raising a brow at me.

"What?" he asked.

"What was that?" I asked him. He shrugged his shoulders.

"I'm driving," he muttered. I slowly nodded my head but looked back at the phone again when I heard it ring. Randa was calling again. Troy sighed frustratingly before completely turning his phone off. I'm not really sure what was going on.

"Did something happen between the both of you?" I asked after a moment. Troy glanced at me then shook his head.

"No," he murmured. I raised a brow at him. "What?" he reacted.

"Why are you acting like that towards her?" I asked. He shrugged his shoulders.

"I'm always like that. She knows it." he muttered.

I looked away from him. "You could hurt her feelings," I said softly.

"She knew that this was going to happen once she got into it. It's not like it's going to last long," he said. I opened my mouth to speak but stopped when he parked the car in front of the school. "Come on, head to class before you're late."

I glanced at him. I decided not to interrogate further before he got angry. I got out the car but before I closed the door, I smiled at him.

"Thanks for the ride," I said. He nodded his head. I closed the door and walked towards my first class, starting a long and tiring day.

I breathed out in relief as the lunch bell finally rung. Everyone got up from their chairs and made their way towards the door. I got up as well and grabbed my bag.

"Don't forget about the test tomorrow," the teacher shouted while everyone prepared to leave the classroom. "And remember, study smart, not hard."

A frustrated sigh escaped my lips as I walked out the classroom. I'm thinking about how I was going to study today. I had to get serious. I surely didn't want to fail.

I walked towards the cafeteria, knowing that I'll be sitting alone today as Ozan wasn't here. Within five minutes, I finished ordering my food and made my way to an empty table. I looked around the cafeteria and frowned when I didn't see Troy.

I forced my mind to shut those thoughts out.

I was in the middle of eating when someone sat next to me and placed their food tray on the table all of a sudden. I looked at the person and smiled when I saw it was Rex. Ever since I've met Rex two weeks ago, we started talking every now and then. I started seeing him many times within the school but he never once came and sat down with me in lunch.

He smiled at me before speaking. "Hey, Ariel," he greeted.

"Hi."

"I see your friend isn't with you today," Rex stated. I nodded my head at him.

"Yeah, he didn't come today. He's quite sick," I explained to him.

"Oh . . . well, that's not good," he muttered but shrugged his shoulders. "I saw you sitting alone so that's why I'm here to keep you company."

I chuckled softly. "That's very nice of you, but why didn't you ever come and sit with us for lunch before?" I asked while taking a bite from my pizza. He shrugged his shoulders but smiled.

"I didn't feel welcome because that friend of yours would stare daggers right at me whenever I would try to approach you,"

Rex chuckled. I frowned at his words but shook my head in disagreement.

"Oh, don't say that. You are welcome to sit with us," I argued, continuing to eat as Rex sipped his juice.

He nodded. "Thanks. I'll keep that in mind," he stated. "And don't think that I forgot about that promise I made to you," he pointed out. I laughed out, nodding as I remembered.

"Right. The tour around California?" I clarified.

"Yes. I am a man of my words," he claimed, making me smile.

"Where exactly would you take me?" I wondered, raising a brow at him.

"Anywhere you like," he answered. "I'll show you around the place."

I nodded my head. We talked for a while as we ate. I soon frowned when I saw Troy and Randa walking into the cafeteria. Randa looked pissed but Troy looked like he didn't give a single care in the world. Troy sat down on the table in front of us. Randa was saying something but Troy only ignored.

Troy and I made eye contact. His eyes drifted on Rex. I glanced at Rex to see him looking at me suspiciously.

"What?" I murmured, taking a last bite from the pizza that was in my hand.

He stood silent for a moment, looking between Troy and I.

"Is there something wrong with the two of you?" he asked. I shook my head and grabbed a tissue to wipe my lips.

"No. Nothing's wrong," I muttered. I glanced at Troy who's eyes were still on us. I turned back to Rex as he nodded his head.

"Oh, okay. It's because he keeps glancing towards us," he pointed out. I shrugged my shoulders.

"He's like that," I only said. He nodded once again and then glanced to his watch before giving me an apologetic smile at me.

105

"Well, I have to head to class. It was nice sitting with you, Ariel," he said as he got up from his seat and grabbed onto his backpack. "I'll see you around." I offered a soft smile at him.

"Okay. See you around," I said. He smiled at me and brought his hand towards my face, catching me off guard. His thumb wiped something from my cheek, making me blush.

"Tomato sauce," he pointed out, showing me his finger as he chuckled lightly. I immediately grabbed a tissue and started to wipe the area he wiped. He let out a chuckle before winking at me, waving.

"Bye, Ariel. See you later." With one last smile, he walked away. I ran a hand over my face in embarrassment. I looked back in front of me to see Troy still staring right at me, making me frown. He immediately averted his gaze away and got up. He started walking away.

"Hey! Where are you going?" Randa called out which Troy completely ignored. She huffed and walked after him. I watched them disappear from my sight. I have no idea what that was all about.

It didn't take a genius to figure out that Troy's attitude towards Randa wasn't so pleasant. I wasn't sure if that made me a bad person but I was kind of relieved about that. You can't really blame me for that. I loved him, even till now. Still, I did feel quite bad for Randa even though I didn't know her well.

I shook my head and got up. I cleaned up the trash and walked towards my next class.

*　　　*　　　*

As soon as I got home, I placed my bag on my bed and took out my physics book and notebook. I don't have much time. If only I didn't walk home, I could have saved more minutes for studying.

106

"What happened to 'I'm not comfortable in letting you walk alone'?" I muttered to myself, mimicking Troy as I shook my head in disappointment. I pushed those thoughts aside and flipped through the pages of my book.

After a moment of staring at a bunch of words that didn't even make sense, I decided to open my notebook. "Remember, study smart, not hard," I told myself.

After a moment of reading the pages, I knew I was in deep trouble. "Sh*t. I'm going to fail . . . Dammit. Why is physics so difficult?" I asked myself as I ran a hand through my hair. I barely understood anything. Physics is my most dreaded subject. I never did good at this.

After what felt like an hour of just staring at a bunch of pages that didn't make sense, a knock to my door made me huff. "Come in," I groaned. I was surprised when I saw who walking in. "Troy? Is there something wrong?" Troy placed his hands in his pockets.

"No," he muttered. "Mom is calling for you to come down for dinner." I nodded but frowned when I glanced at the book in front of me.

"Tell her I won't be eating," I told him. He raised a brow.

"Why?" he asked. I huffed and pointed at the book in front of me.

"I have so many things to study for tomorrow's test. I can't seem to get anything in my head." I sighed as I ran a hand over my face in frustration. Troy took a step towards me and glanced at the book.

"Physics?" he murmured to himself.

I nodded. "Yes. A difficult subject." He chuckled. "What?" I frowned.

"It's not that difficult . . ." he told me, shrugging his shoulder.

"It's very difficult," I argued, looking up at him.

"Well, not for me. It's pretty easy." he claimed.

"Easy? You're serious?" I said. He nodded. I stared at him with wide eyes. I looked back at the book, wondering how the hell I was going to study and finish everything when something rang in my head. I immediately got up from my chair and stood in front of him.

"Troy," I said softly. He gave me a suspicious look.

"Yes?"

I immediately grabbed onto his two hands and held them tight, looking up at him with pleading eyes as he stared down at his hands, looking taken off guard.

"Can you please help me study?" I pleaded with my eyes. He looked at me for a moment.

"Excuse me? You want me to tutor you?"

I nodded my head. "Just this once," I said. He snickered which caused me to frown before he pulled his hands away from mine, shaking his head.

"No," he said bluntly, my frown deepening. "I'm not a tutor." He turned around and walked towards my door. My heart sank as he walked away, causing for me to sit down on my chair in disappointment. I scolded myself for asking a stupid question, not really thinking straight.

Very stupid, Ariel. Great going.

I stared at the book for a moment before glancing at Troy to see him still standing by my door, staring at me with a blank expression. His hard eyes softened for a moment as our eyes met and that's when he sighed out and ran a hand through his hair, shaking his head.

"Dammit," he cursed to himself. "Fine, I'll help you. Only this once," he muttered. A huge smile made its way onto my lips. I got up from my chair and pulled him into a tight hug.

"Thank you so, so, so, so. much," I gushed. I won't fail after all. Troy stiffened so I pulled away. I gave him an apologetic smile. "Sorry, got carried away." He stared at me intensely before sitting next to me.

"But you owe me," he muttered, opening the book to the first page.

"Deal."

He glanced at me and chuckled. I placed my chin on my hand as I watched Troy flip through the pages in admiration. I couldn't pull my eyes away from him..

I smiled to myself, so thankful that I have him here with me even though he was a huge jerk.

CHAPTER THIRTEEN

"This is the formula for this question," Troy stated, writing the formula down on a piece of paper. I stared at the formula, forcing the information into my thick head. "Now answer the question," Troy ordered. I slowly nodded and grabbed the pencil. I tried my best in answering the question in front of me. I felt Troy staring at me intensely as I struggled. After a few moments of doing nothing, I sighed in frustration and looked over at Troy.

"Don't look at me like that," I told him, making him raise a brow.

"Look at you like what?" He questioned.

"Like that," I exclaimed, pointing my finger at him. "You're pressuring me when you're standing right over my shoulders. I get nervous." A small chuckle escaped Troy's lips and he shook his head, a tint of amusement clear in his eyes. He nodded his head and scooted away from me, looking away.

"Fine. Is this better?" Troy asked.

"Yes. Great," I said, looking back at the paper and finally answering the question. Troy and I have been studying for the past hour and he taught me stuff that I didn't even know. We answered a few questions to make sure I actually understood it. At first I did horrible, but then I started to get the hang of it. I was definitely sure that if he didn't agree to help me, I would have failed tomorrow.

"Okay. I'm done," I said, looking over at Troy. Troy moved closer then glanced at the paper.

"Good," he murmured. "Now let me give you another question." He started writing on the paper as I huffed in frustration.

"Oh, come on. Don't you think that's enough questions? You're starting to sound like a real teacher." I pouted and crossed my arms. Troy looked at me and offered me a glare. I did my best to held the smile that threatened to appear.

"Well, I'm sorry for trying to help you not fail your test," he said, placing the pencil down. A light chuckle escaped my mouth. "Why are you laughing? What's so funny?" he asked. I shook my head and placed my chin on my palm, looking right at him.

"I find it funny that you get upset quite easily. I was only kidding. Go ahead, give me another question," I said. Troy narrowed his eyes at me. I tried my best not to crack another smile, which would surely annoy him.

"I don't get upset easily," Troy argued, shaking his head as he grabbed the pencil and continued to write down the question. I snickered loud enough for Troy to hear which made him frown at me.

"Sure you don't," I muttered, shrugging my shoulders. He let the pencil go once again and stared right at me.

"What do you mean?" he questioned.

I looked over at him. "You get upset or angry all the time for no reason. I've started to notice that," I admitted, shrugging my shoulders again.

"If I get angry or upset then it's not for no reason. There is always a reason behind it," he argued, his voice low.

"Then why were you angry at me today?" I pressed.

"I wasn't angry at you today."

"Really? Then why did you leave without me today? Just this morning you said you weren't comfortable in letting me walk alone," I said.

He stared at me for a moment. "I didn't leave without you because I was angry at you," he stated. I raised a brow at him.

"Then why did you leave without me?" I asked.

"Randa and I fought while I was leaving, so out of annoyance I left immediately. I forgot about driving you home." Troy explained.

Wow, he forgot about me. Even better. "Why did you guys fight?"

Troy shrugged his shoulder and grabbed the pencil again, continuing to write the question. "I honestly don't know," he muttered out.

I raised a brow at him. "What do you mean by that?" I asked. He glanced at me for a second.

"I mean, I don't know why she was angry. She kept complaining and I honestly didn't care. Then she got angry and started yelling at me." Troy looked as if he didn't give a single care about the subject. He soon gave me the paper.

"Answer this question," he ordered. I nodded and read the question. We went silent as I started to answer. I felt Troy's intense stare, making me look over at him. He smirked and raised his hands defensively up in the air. He then moved away from me. With that, I went back to answering.

"So, are you close with this Rex guy?" he asked.

"Excuse me?" I murmured, raising a brow at him.

"The guy that came over and ate dinner with his family," Troy muttered out. I nodded my head, shrugging my shoulders.

"I'm not that close with him, but he's a nice person. Why are you asking?" I said.

He shrugged. "No reason. I was just curious," Troy answered. I nodded but continued to stare at him. He shook his head and pointed at the paper that was in front of me. "Come on, finish this question. It's your last one." I smiled at him and nodded.

"Finally . . ." I muttered. I then gave it to him and he scanned the paper.

"Good. Looks like teaching you wasn't a waste," Troy muttered with a smirk.

I smiled at him. "So, I won't fail tomorrow?" I asked. He shook his head.

"I don't think so," he chuckled.

"Oh, thank God." We both chuckled a bit. I stared at him, making him raise a brow. "You know, you could be a great teacher one day," I stated. Troy shrugged his shoulders.

"Teaching you is very difficult. Never doing that again," he mused. I playfully slapped his arm in response.

"So, how will I owe you?" I asked with a raised brow.

He shrugged his shoulders. "I don't know. I'll think about it," he said. I nodded my head another time. I got up and started tidying up my school materials into my bag.

"Thank you, Troy. Seriously. If it wasn't for you, I wouldn't know what I would have done," I said, staring at him genuinely. He got up from his seat and placed his hands in his pockets.

"Don't thank me. You owe me, anyway." He smirked slightly, walking towards the door. I nodded my head and smiled.

"Of course, I do," I chuckled.

"Just revise before the test," he ordered. He opened my bedroom door and stepped out without saying another word, leaving me standing therer from my sight. I smiled softly to myself as I recalled everything that happened.

I couldn't help but feel extremely happy.

I ran a hand over my face, putting away the notebook that was on my desk and decided to check up on Ozan since I didn't see him today. I walked out of my room and down the hall towards Ozan's room. I knocked on his door and opened it as soon as I heard him yell out "come in."

I walked in the room and frowned as I saw Ozan laying on his bed. He looking horrible as ever. He smiled softly as he tried sitting up .

"No, don't sit up. Lay down," I ordered. He laid back down. My frown deepened as I stared at him. "You look horrible," I stated, making him chuckle lightly.

"Thank you for your honesty," Ozan muttered as I sat at the edge of his bed.

"What's wrong? How do you feel?" I asked him.

"I feel the same as how I look. I feel weak and I keep puking my insides out," he answered in a low tone.

"From what exactly?" I asked him. He shrugged his shoulder.

"I guess it's a stomach bug," he muttered. I nodded before smirking at him.

"What?" he muttered.

"You're sure you're not pregnant?" I mused. He chuckled.

"I'm a hundred percent sure," Ozan pointed out, making me laugh. "How was school today?" he asked.

"Horrible," I spoke out, shaking my head. "We have a physics exam tomorrow and Troy helped me study." Ozan glanced at me.

"Troy helped you? Doesn't seem like he's the type of person to help someone . . ." he murmured. I nodded my head.

"He isn't. Let's just say I owe him something," I agreed. Ozan nodded at my words before speaking.

"If I stay like this then I won't be coming tomorrow either." I nodded my head at him before getting up, taking a few steps towards the door.

"Yeah, I think you'd be better off staying at home. I'm going to go down stairs to grab something to eat since I haven't eaten anything. You rest, okay?" I told him. Ozan chuckled.

"Yes ma'am." I returned the smile and stood in front of the door.

"Bye," I said, waving at him as I opened the door.

"See you," he muttered, waving back at me.

I closed the door behind me and walked towards the kitchen. I could feel my stomach growling.

*   *   *

I answered the last question on the paper then reviewed my answers briefly. I feel satisfied. I glanced at the clock to see that we had a couple of minutes left before class ended. I smiled to myself. I'm glad the exam wasn't too difficult.

If it wasn't for Troy then I would have surely failed this test. Most of the things that Troy and I studied yesterday was here.

I looked up at the teacher as soon as I heard him speak. "Time's up, everyone. Pencils down," he ordered, collecting papers as the bell rung. "You may all leave." He took all of our papers and placed them on his desk. Everyone rushed out of the classroom to talk about the test as I grabbed my bag.

I walked out the classroom and smiled when I saw Troy leaning against the wall, his arms crossed against his chest. He looked over at me as soon as I started walking towards him. He adjusted himself as I stood in front of him, before speaking.

"So, how was the test?" he asked, placing his hands in his pockets.

"It was actually very good. I think I'll get a B or something like that," I answered, my smile growing as I stared into his eyes. Troy nodded.

"That's good," he murmured. I sucked in a breath as we stared in each other's eyes in silence for a short moment, before he spoke. "Looks like my work paid off." We chuckled a bit before a small smirk crawled onto his lips.

"What?" I wondered as Troy took one step closer to me.

"I figured how you'll return my favor," Troy stated. I slowly nod my head.

115

"How?" I asked. I moved in closer as people rushed past us to their classes, bumping into me. Troy stood silent for a moment, staring right at me as I raised a brow at him, waiting for him to speak.

"Go on a date with me."

I stood there flabbergasted. My head could not comprehend what he said as his unbelievable words reached me.

CHAPTER FOURTEEN

I was loss for words. My eyes were wide as I stared back at his in search for any amusement but instead, I saw nothing but seriousness.

I felt like my world has stopped. Everything and everyone around me seems to be in a slow motion as soon as those words left his mouth. I was in a state of shock because I completely lost hope that I'd ever hear those words escape his lips.

I stood in front of Troy as countless students rushed past us towards the cafeteria. I'm sure no one spared us a single glance as their main priority at this moment was food.

I tried to muster any type of sound but it was like my voice has disappeared. After a few moments of staring at each other in complete awkward silence, I gathered all the breath that was in me to speak.

"What?" I only managed to whisper that I wasn't even sure that Troy heard. His lips twitched upwards into a sly smirk.

"You heard me," he said in a rather casual tone as if he was just talking about the weather.

"You want me to go on a date with you?" I asked him in a louder voice this time, but not loud enough for anyone else to hear as they walked past us.

Troy nodded and opened his mouth, ready to say something when a voice called out to him.

"Troy!" Randa rushed towards us. She soon stood in front of me then wrapped her arm around his. She stared at us with a hint of confusion. "Hey, Ariel," she greeted me with a smile then looked back at Troy. "Come on. Let go eat. I'm starving."

Troy only nodded his head at her. I stood in front of them in complete silence as I watched Randa pull Troy away from me. Troy glanced towards me.

"We'll continue talking at home," he said. He then walked away with Randa, leaving me standing there in utter shock.

I forced myself to breath in before I suffocate myself. I ran a hand over my face as my mind replayed everything that just happened a moment ago.

I stood still. How could he ask something like that from me? How? How could he ask that from me before walking away hand in hand with his girlfriend? Why? Did he take me as a fool? Did he think I was someone desperate enough that I would stoop down to that level? All so he can cheat on his girlfriend? No matter how hard I loved him, I would never stoop down to that level.

I couldn't believe it. I was angry. Very angry.

I forced myself to regain my senses and walk towards the library. I couldn't face him at this moment. I needed to think over this and process what I was going to say to him once I returned home. I already knew my answer.

That was a no.

Time passed, and school was finally over. Before Troy could even order me to get into his car, I rushed out the school campus and walked home alone. I decided to not let him drive me home so I could take this chance to think and practice what I was going to say.

I'd be lying if I said I wasn't nervous. Hell, I was very nervous. I also felt very upset. Upset over the fact that he asked me that when he has a girlfriend. I was also very confused. Many random questions kept circling my head in chaos. What changed all of a sudden? I know he stopped acting as if he loathed me but we weren't on a lovey-dovey basis. We were just neutral, and that is what makes me wonder even more.

I took my time in walking back home. As soon as I walked through the main doors, I immediately rushed towards my room. I didn't want to face Troy immediately. I was too nervous.

I shut my bedroom door. I placed my bag on the floor and laid on my bed, staring up at the blank white ceiling. My head replayed what he said to me earlier today.

Go on a date with me.

I immediately shook my head and forced that sentence out of my head. I would be lying if I said my heart didn't react to those words. Hell, my heart jumped out of my ribcage as soon as those words left his mouth. It all came to an end when Randa appeared.

It was like a slap to my face, like cold water splashing onto me that snapped me back to reality. I couldn't run away from it.

My thoughts were interrupted as soon as I heard a knock to the door. I immediately jolted out of my bed and stood up, running a hand through my tangled hair.

"Who is it?" I called out.

"It's me," Troy said in a low tone. "We need to talk."

I sucked in a breath. I took a moment to answer. "Come in."

The door opened and Troy stepped into my room. I stared at him as he closed the door behind him. We maintained eye contact. He soon stood in front of me.

"Ariel—"

"It's a no," I cut him off. He looked at me intensely.

"A no?" he asked.

"Yeah. I won't go on a date with you," I stated, looking at him right in the eye. I frowned as I saw a tint of amusement present in his eyes.

"Ariel—"

"Ask for anything else but that. You have a girlfriend and that's disrespectful. So, no," I interrupted him once again. He looked down at me with a tense stare which made me nervous all of a sudden.

"But—"

"Now if you'll excuse me, I have things to do," I spoke softer this time. I immediately walked past him and towards my bedroom door. I opened it but before I could even step a foot outside, he grabbed me by the arm and pulled me back, closing the door in the process.

My eyes widened as he backed me up against the wall. He placed his hand on the wall, trapping me. I stared at him with surprise clearly present on my features as he looked down at me intensely. However, I could see a glint of amusement in his eyes.

"Now, will you let me speak this time and not cut me off?" Troy said, raising a brow as he casually looked at me.

I remained silent for a second but soon gestured to let him talk.

"I want you to go out with me for one night," he said. He was serious.

"But I already said—"

"As my fake girlfriend."

My eyes widened at his words and my mouth hung open, welcoming anything to fly in it. I stared into his eyes for any sign of amusement but I saw nothing. He looked completely serious.

"Excuse me?" I forced myself to speak. "As your fake girlfriend?"

Troy nodded. "Yes. Exactly what I said."

"Why?"

Troy took his hand off the wall and stepped backwards but he still maintained eye contact with me.

"I'm going to this party on Saturday night and I need you to come with me as my girlfriend," he said casually as if he wasn't asking me to do something so big.

"Why do you need me to come with you?" I asked.

120

"The sister of the person who's hosting the party will be there," he muttered.

"So?" I questioned, raising a brow.

Troy let out a sigh. "She's my ex and she's still trying to get back with me. I've been trying to avoid her but I can't bluntly reject her because of her brother. The time I broke up with her, her brother was very pissed but I was able to make up an excuse. I know she'll be all over me that's why I need to have you with me so she could back off." Troy shrugged his shoulders.

I shook my head.

"Why are you asking me to do this? Why don't you ask your real girlfriend? That's her job," I pressed.

"Randa will be out of town for the weekend, and even though if she wasn't, I still wouldn't have asked her to come with me because of her temper and jealousy. She will surely cause a problem and I don't want that. My ex's brother and I used to be good friends before they moved away a year ago, and I need to stay on good terms with him because his father works with my dad," Troy explained once again.

"But—"

"You owe me, Ariel. Only for one night," he pointed out. I looked down.

"But what if someone recognizes us and tells Randa that you were with me?" I asked, looking back at him.

Troy shook his head. "The party is faraway from here. Nobody from our school will be there," he assured me. "I just need you to act as my girlfriend for that period then that's it."

I sucked in a breath and bit my lip. I gave it a thought for a moment.

"Fine. I'll go with you. Only because I owe you. If it wasn't for that then I wouldn't have agreed to go as your fake girlfriend." I said.

Troy nodded his head and took another step backwards, placing his hands in his pockets.

121

"Good," he stated. "We'll discuss more on what to do on Saturday. Other than that, that's it."

I nodded but stood silent. He turned around and walked out of my room.

After a moment, I sighed and sat on my bed. Even though I accepted, I wasn't too happy about this. I couldn't help feeling quite disappointed. Disappointed over the fact that he didn't ask me out genuinely because he wanted to, even though I was going to decline in the first place.

Of course, he would never ask me out. This is present Troy we're talking about. Not Troy from three years ago.

I know that it will be difficult for me to endure, for me to play along as his girlfriend when all I wanted to be was his true girlfriend. It will be difficult to play along and not feel affected whatsoever.

It's only for a short period of time.

Only for one day.

CHAPTER FIFTEEN

I stared at myself in the mirror for what felt like the hundredth time, making sure I looked presentable and not overdressed. I eyed the simple red dress I wore, debating with myself whether I should change quickly.

I couldn't help but worry about what I was wearing. The dress I wore was the only dress I owned at this moment and I didn't have any other choice. I was too afraid that maybe I'd make a fool of myself.

I ran a hand through my long brown hair which fell off my shoulders casually. I didn't really put on any makeup on my face but at the last minute, I decided that I should at least put something on my lips. After a moment of fighting with my inner self whether I should just ditch and just stay home, I forced myself to step away from the mirror and walk out my bedroom door and down the hall.

Troy texted me a moment ago that he was waiting outside the house and in the car. I quietly walked towards the main doors in hopes that no one would see me. Rose and Damon knew I was going out but I didn't tell them I was going to a party with Troy. That would just be awkward. I was sure if I told Rose the truth, she'd automatically assume that Troy and I were finally reliving the past. Unfortunately, that wasn't going to happen. I came into the conclusion that the idea was so slim. It's maybe not even possible.

I didn't tell Ozan either as I didn't really see him much. All he did this past week was stay in his room as he seemed quite off. I

123

talked with him several times but he was quite distant. He looked tired yet he still came to school. I made a mental note to myself to talk with him later and see if he was okay.

I sighed in relief as soon as I walked out the doors and towards Troy's car which was not so far away. I silently opened the door and got in, smiling at Troy softly as he looked over at me.

"Hey," I greeted. His eyes scanned me for a brief second before he nodded at me in response. He started the car as I closed the door behind me.

"You ready?" he asked. I took a breath, running a hand through my hair nervously.

"Kind of," I muttered honestly as Troy took off and stared at the road in caution. He looked over at me and raised a brow.

"Are you nervous?" Troy questioned, looking back at the road. I nodded as I stared at him, biting my lip as I tried to calm my nervousness, which didn't seem to work.

"Yes, a little," I answered as he glanced towards me. "I haven't really gone to a party before." Troy's lips curved upwards as he raised a brow once again.

"What?" I questioned, raising a brow at him this time.

"You've never been to a party?" Troy asked as his eyes remained on the road.

I slowly shook my head. "No . . . I'm not the party type." He nodded his head and his smirk grew.

"I can tell," Troy murmured, glancing my way before putting his attention back on the road. I frowned and shifted in my seat, looking at him as I raised a brow.

"What about you? You seem quite like the party type," I stated as Troy chuckled.

"Not much, but you could say that I do go to one every now and then," he answered. I slowly averted my eyes away from him then looked back at him with a frown.

"You were never the party type," I said softly. He seemed confused as he looked at me. "I mean, we both were never the

124

party types. We'd prefer to stay home and watch a movie instead of partying." Troy looked back at the road, staying silent for a moment. I waited for him to break the tense silence.

"You speak as if you know me very well, better than I do." He glanced at me.

"It's because I do," I told him then looked away with a sigh. "I mean, I did. I knew you very well, more than you knew yourself." A snicker escaped Troy's lips, causing for my eyes to land back on him.

"Were we really that close?" Troy asked, not even looking my way as he let out those words. I remained silent for a moment.

"Yes. We were very close," I replied as we made eye contact for what felt like minutes to me. Troy's face fell as he averted his eyes back on the road, a look of frustration crossing his features. I stared at him for what felt like hours as he remained silent, as if he didn't know what to say.

"Well, now those days have ended," he muttered. He did not even spare me a single glance. I looked away from him. A long sigh escaped my lips.

"I know," I whispered to myself. "So, is the party we're heading to far away?" I asked, trying to change the subject so we won't end up fighting or him ending up in a grumpy mood.

Troy nodded his head. "Kind of," he answered. "It's out of town so it will take a while." I nodded my head.

"What will I need to do?" I asked.

"You'll need to act as my girlfriend. We'll hold hands and act as if we're a loving couple. Do anything to keep her away from me. I know she'll try to approach me like usual. Just stick to my side and make it seem that I'm not available," he said.

I slowly nodded my head, biting my lip as he said 'loving couple'. I knew so bad that this was going to be so difficult to do. I knew that in the end, I'll end up hurt.

However, I have to do it. Just for one night.

"I still don't get why you can't just tell her to stay away from you?" I asked, raising a brow at him. Troy shook his head.

"I can't. I told you before that her brother and I were good friends and his dad works with my dad. If I somehow hurt her then problems might happen between us, and that's the least thing I want in my life right now," Troy explained, glancing at me as he spoke.

"Okay, then why didn't you just stay home? Why did you decide to go to the party?" I raised my brow at him for the second time.

"Because he's been pushing me to come to his parties for ages. So I decided I'll go to one party so he could stop," Troy answered. I nodded my head in understanding as Troy glanced my way. "We won't stay for long. Just for twenty minutes then we're out of there."

I nodded silently, hoping that his words were right and that no problems would surface tonight.

After a long tense drive, we finally made it to our destination. I could already hear the blasting music. Troy parked in front of a large house which screamed "party". There were many people surrounding the house. I hesitantly got out of the car as Troy came to my side. He reached out his hand. I looked at it for a second before slowly putting my hand in his.

"Don't be nervous. I'll be by your side," Troy assured. I only nodded. We walked towards the front door.

I couldn't help but stare at our joined hands. I could feel my heart beating fast. This was something we used to do a long time ago. It's bringing back many memories. I never thought that I would one day hold onto Troy's hand like how I would in the past.

Unfortunately, it was not for the same reason.

I forced my eyes to look forward and not at our hands. I sucked in a breath as we entered the crowded area. I couldn't help but feel more nervous. I was never the type to enjoy a crowded area like this. It brought me anxiety.

126

Troy continued to pull me through the large room. People were scattered everywhere. Some were dancing, some fooling around and some just standing as they talked to others. My eyes continued to scan the room as we walked through people constantly bumping into us.

We eventually stopped and stood at a less crowded area. Troy scanned his eyes over the place. He then stopped on someone before leaning in at me.

"There he is. Come on." Troy pulled me through the crowd as he walked towards the opposite side of the area. We eventually stopped in front of a large group of guys who were drinking and laughing. The guy in the middle smiled as he walked towards us. I figured this tall, buff guy was the host of the party.

"Well, would you look at that," the guy said as he stood in front of Troy. "Troy finally came to a party, after so long." Troy and him shook hands as Troy smirked up at him.

"You could say I finally had the time," Troy said. The guy chuckled.

"If someone heard you they'd think you're constantly busy. How are you? It's been a while since you've last shown up," he said.

"Things are okay," Troy answered, glancing at me. The guy looked at me then raised a brow at Troy.

"Who's the lovely girl?" he asked. Troy cleared his throat.

"Devin, this is Ariel, my girlfriend," he introduced us, causing for me to gulp as soon as he said the word 'girlfriend'. "And Ariel, this is Devin, the guy I told you about."

I nodded my head as we shook hands, putting on a smile. "It's nice to meet you," I finally said. Devin smiled at me.

"It's nice to meet you, too." He then looked back at Troy. "You've gotten yourself a pretty one, aye?" He smirked at a stiffened Troy. After a moment, Troy pulled me closer and wrapped an arm around my waist which made my heart jump out of my ribcage.

"I do. A beautiful one, in fact." he said, looking at me. I stared up at his eyes in silence, his words making me feel things I haven't felt in ages. I was speechless. The words that formed in my throat was stuck.

For a moment I believed his words. It was as if he was speaking out what he honestly felt. His words felt so genuine, until he averted his eyes away from me, bringing me back to reality.

I looked down at the ground, reminding myself that this was all a lie. This wasn't real.

I didn't pay attention to what they were talking about. I was in my own little world, replaying his words in my head for the hundredth time. Eventually, Devin had to speak with other people so he left, leaving me alone with Troy. We just stood there, waiting for something to happen.

After a while, Troy brought his face closer to mine.

"There she is." I immediately scanned the room for someone I didn't even know. Troy wrapped his arms around my waist and pulled me towards his chest, causing for my eyes to widen. He looked down at my eyes, staring at them for a moment before speaking out.

"She's walking towards us," he said, clearing his throat as our faces were closer than normal. I nodded but didn't look around. I was too caught up in staring up at his eyes.

They captivated me.

"What are we going to do now?" I whispered softly.

"This." He then softly placed his lips onto mine.

At that moment, my heart raced like it never before. I couldn't help but wish that this night wouldn't ever end, whether this was fake or not.

CHAPTER SIXTEEN

I pulled my phone out from my pocket and sat down in my room. I dialed Troy's number. He didn't answer the call though. It's strange. I dialed his number once again and waited for a response. However, for the second time there was no answer.

I stared at my phone. Why wouldn't Troy answer my calls? I got up from my bed, grabbed onto my bag and walked out of my room. I decided I'll go to him instead. I was quite worried. He didn't come to school today and now he wasn't answering my calls. I'm about to walk out the front door.

"Ariel? Sweetie, where are you going?" my mom called out, raising a brow at me as she placed some plates on the dining table. "Aren't you hungry? I just prepared something for you to eat."

I smiled softly at my mom. "Thank you Mom, but I'm not hungry right now. I'm actually going to head over to Troy's place. He didn't come to school today so I want to see if he's okay. I'll eat once I'm back," I told her.

My mom nodded, smiling at me. "That's fine, honey. Just don't be late," she stated, grabbing onto the plates she placed on the table.

"Okay," I said. With one last smile, I walked out the house.

Troy's place wasn't too far away from here so after ten minutes I was standing in front of his house and knocking on his front door. Rose answered the door with a smile.

"Oh, Ariel. I was just about to call you," she said.

"Really? Why?" I asked.

"I was going to ask you whether Troy was with you or not. He hasn't come back from school yet and I was getting a little worried," she responded.

I stared at her for a moment, completely silent. Her smile dropped.

"He's with you, right?" she asked, taking a step forward as she looked our surroundings.

I paused for a moment. She raised a brow at me. However, before she could say another word, I nodded my head.

"Yes, he's at my place," I said. Her frown disappeared. "I just came here to grab some of his books so we could study together for tomorrow's test."

If he wasn't here, then where was he?

"But why did you come? Why didn't he come to get them himself?" she questioned.

I paused, trying to find a reasonable excuse. "Umm . . . My mom needed Troy for something, that's why I offered to come instead." Rose nodded once again before stepping back, smiling down at me.

"Okay, you can go grab the books that are in his room," she said. I rushed to his room and shut the door behind me as I took out my phone, throwing my bag onto the ground.

I immediately called Troy once again. I prayed to God that he'll answer this time but he didn't.

"Dammit, Troy. Where the hell are you?" I groaned to. I placed my phone back in my pocket before running my hand through my hair and grabbing onto my bag.

I was very worried at this moment. If Troy wasn't here? Then where was he?

I then remembered. There is one place he would go.

I immediately walked out of his room and towards the front doors.

"Did you find the books you needed?" Rose asked, raising a brow. I made a fake smile.

"Yes, I did," I lied, tapping onto my bag. "I'll be going. I don't want to be late on Troy."

Rose nodded. "Okay, honey. Just tell Troy not to be late," she called out as I walked out the front doors.

"Will do," I yelled as I closed the door behind me. Without another second to spare, I rushed to the destination I hoped Troy was in.

I tried to call him again but as usual, he failed to answer. I don't know why he wasn't answering my calls, but I have a feeling I know where he was. My guts were telling me.

I stopped in my tracks as I stared at the bridge in front of me which led to the park Troy and I would go to ever since we were small. I walked under the bridge, finding Troy spacing out on our usual spot.

I was relieved as soon as I saw him.

"Troy," I called.

"Ariel?" he murmured as I sat right next to him. "What are you doing here?" He cleared his throat.

"Troy, I should be asking you that. What are you doing here? Why haven't you gone to school? Why weren't you answering my calls?" I asked. Troy didn't respond. Instead, he stared at the water in front of us.

His action only made me offer him a worried look. "Troy . . ." I placed my hand on his shoulder. "What's wrong? You're worrying me." Troy looked back at me and grabbed onto both my hands. He rubbed his thumbs over my skin in a comforting motion.

"Don't worry," he said, shaking his head. "There's nothing wrong. I just didn't feel like going to school today. That's all."

"Then why weren't you answering my calls, Troy? Are you sure there's nothing wrong?" Troy pulled my hands towards his lips and kissed them.

"There's nothing wrong, I swear. I just wanted to be alone for a while," he assured, smiling softly. I looked at him for a moment, not sure whether to believe him or not.

"Okay. I was just a little worried," I said.

"There's nothing to be worried about," he claimed, tightening his hold on my hands. "Everything's fine." I brushed the weird feeling that was in my stomach.

Troy smiled at me and placed his hand on my cheek. "I love you," he whispered, looking at my eyes.

"I love you, too."

He placed his lips onto mine, making me forget all my worries.

As soon as our lips parted, I was hit back with reality. My eyes snapped open to see Troy staring at me intensely as I was speechless.

"Troy?"A girl's voice hit my ears. We look at a red headed girl, who was way prettier than me. She was the definition of beauty, which made me question why Troy was trying to avoid her. She looked at us confusingly, before shooting daggers right at me. She then brought her stare at Troy, stepping closer to us. "You've finally came."

Troy stiffened. He cleared his throat.

"Yes, I did. I also brought my girlfriend with me." He looked at me for a second. I'm about to frown. The girl's face went hard. "Ariel, this is Dana."

I plastered a fake smile. I stretched my hand towards her. "It's nice to meet you," I lied. She stared at my hand for a moment then shook it, squeezing my hand tightly. She nodded but gave me a glare that sent shivers down my spine.

I cleared my throat and went back to Troy's side as he wrapped his arm around my waist.

"I missed you so much. How come you've never called me? We haven't talked in a long time," she asked Troy, smiling softly at him.

"I've been quite busy," he answered lowly, causing for a frown to appear on her face.

"Well, we can always make up for the time we've lost," she told him, stepping closer to Troy which left me uncomfortable. I then took a step forward.

"I'm afraid he's still busy," I told her. "Right, love?" I questioned, looking up at him with a soft smile. He looked at me intensely before nodding his head.

"Yes. You're right. I'm extremely occupied with Ariel." Troy said. Dana's expression fell. She stared at us for a moment.

"Oh. Okay then." she murmured. Troy nodded his head at her before someone called her name over the loud music. "Someone needs me. I'll be back so we can continue our conversation," she said. With one last glare, she walked away.

"Well, that was easier than I thought," Troy muttered, looking at me. "You did good." He smirked at me.

I frowned, remembering what he did a moment ago. He raised a brow at me as his smirk fell.

"That wasn't necessary," I told him.

"What wasn't necessary?" he asked.

"Kissing me. Please, don't do that again. It only hurts me."

"I . . . I'm sorry," he stated. "I wasn't thinking straight." I nodded but took a step back.

"I'm going to go to the restroom for a moment," I told to him, wanting to be alone for a moment to clear my thoughts. He nodded but took a step closer to me.

"Don't be gone for long," he said softly. "I don't want you to be alone around here." I nodded then immediately walked around the house and up the stairs, searching for a restroom. I sucked in a breath as I recalled the kiss.

I wished he didn't do that. It only brought me pain. It hurt me to know he did that with different intentions.

I was cut off from my thinking when I made it to the top of the staircase, meeting eyes with the girl who was shooting daggers at me not too long ago. I stopped dead in my track. Her arms were crossed.

"Why you?" she asked.

"Excuse me?" I questioned as she took another step closer to me.

"Why did he pick you? What does he see in you?" she asked louder, making me take a step back.

"That's none of your business," I said before walking away. However, she didn't give me the chance to as she stood in my way, backing me up.

"It is my business," she hissed. "It's my businesses because he's my man." I looked at her with an unbelievable expression before shaking my head.

"He's not yours. He never was."

Her eyes burned with anger. "He is," she argued.

"He's not." No wonder he was trying to get away from this girl. She was completely psycho. "I'm his girlfriend. Not you." I was surely adding fuel to the fire, but I couldn't help it. I hated how she was putting a claim on Troy. It pissed me off.

"He won't stay with you for long. He'll surely come back to me. I love him more than anyone has ever loved him," she hissed, stepping very close to me. I back up at the edge of the staircase. I looked back at her, shaking my head.

"Not as much as I do," I whispered to her. I was about to walk away from her when she grabbed me by my arm, digging her sharp nails into my arm.

"Listen, b*tch—"

"Let go of me!" I pulled my arm away from her aggressively knocking myself backwards. I tried to grab onto something but I plummeted down the staircase. I closed my eyes tightly as I hit my head very hard.

Everything went blank.

CHAPTER SEVENTEEN

I immediately got up from my chair as soon as the school bell finally rung. I dashed towards the classroom door, bumping to several students in the process. I ignored whatever comment my teacher had to say as I made my way to the cafeteria.

The hallways were packed with students. I huffed and forced my way through the crowd. I finally reached the cafeteria and smiled as soon as I saw him sitting on our usual spot.

Troy.

I walked towards the small table in the corner, where Troy, Clare and I sat at. A sense of emotion hit me as I got closer to him. I haven't seen him all weekend, that's why I was so excited to see him. He's always away every time I visit his place. Quite disappointing.

I also tried meeting up with him because I just had the urge to see him all weekend but he had no time to do so. It didn't bother me that much. I understood if he was busy. I only missed him, that's all.

I frowned when he didn't look up. Troy was spacing off at the table. He seemed like he was in deep thought. He was too serious to even pay attention to his surroundings.

I cleared my throat. "Troy?" I said.

No response.

I stepped closer. "Troy," I said louder this time. I then sat next to him. His head immediately snapped up. He looked taken aback from presence before remembering where he was. "Troy. Are you okay?"

He nodded. "I'm okay. I'm sorry. I just spaced off," he answered with a soft smile.

My brows furrowed at him, feeling a little concerned. It's been a while now and I've started to pay attention to his weird behavior. Something was off about him. I just couldn't tell what was wrong. Yet, whenever I would confront him about it, he'd only say there's nothing wrong and everything's okay.

I wanted to believe him, but something in my gut told me that there was something not right. I just didn't know what.

"Are you sure, Troy? You've been acting a little weird. Is there something you're not telling me?" I asked, lowering my voice as I placed a hand on his shoulder.

Troy grabbed onto the hand that was on his shoulder and brought it to his lips, leaving a tender kiss on my skin. He looked back in my eyes, which only made me worry.

"There's nothing wrong, Ariel. I'm just a little tired. That's all. Haven't been getting any sleep lately," he answered. My frown deepened as I stared into his eyes. I could immediately tell he wasn't tell the truth.

I opened my mouth to say something but was immediately cut off by Troy. "Please, Ariel. Don't argue." He pleaded with his eyes. I remained silent for a while. "I promise you, everything's okay," he insisted, yet I couldn't help but feel he was assuring himself more than he was assuring me. I slowly nodded my head and grabbed onto his hand.

"Okay. I just don't like it that you're tired. Make sure you get some rest once you get home," I said softly. Troy smiled and immediately nodded his head, kissing my cheek.

"I will."

I didn't get the chance to say anything else as Clare , placing her tray full of food on the table. "Hey, guys," she greeted as she immediately chugged on the food.

I greeted back weakly. Many questions ran through my head. Troy and I sat silently together as Clare babbled on and on about something but I paid no attention to her. I was in my own little world, thinking about what could be bothering Troy. No matter what Troy had said or done, I couldn't help but feel that there was something wrong.

He was hiding something.

Then everything went black. My eyelids felt heavy as I tried to open them but immediately failed when I felt a sharp pain. It took me a while but my vision slowly restored. The pain that was constantly pounding in my head only increased as the lights hit my eyes. I groaned at the pain in my body.

Someone started calling my name. I turned to the direction of the sound but stopped instantly as my head continued to pound.

"Don't move," Troy whispered. Out of nowhere, he appeared in my sight, concern written all over his face. That was when I took in my surroundings.

I was in a hospital room.

My eyes widened and I immediately looked at Troy. My mouth opened as I remembered how I got to this state. I fell down the stairs.

"Are you in pain?" Troy asked as I stared at him in shock. I'm still trying to register how the hell this had happened. "Do you want me to call the doctor?" He took a step back.

"Did I almost die? Was I in a coma?" I asked out loud. Troy's eyes widened. He looked at me, listening to me talk.

My eyes widened. "Oh my God. How long have I been in a coma? Please, don't tell me I've been out for months. Oh, God. My parents must have been worried sick about me." I gasped. Troy's eyes only widened as I freak out. I went silent. Troy opened his mouth to talk, but I immediately cut him off. "Don't tell me you've been visiting me every day while I was sleeping?" I wondered. His concerned look was immediately replaced with an amused one. "Oh my God. You actually do care. Well, actually it is your fault to begin with—"

Troy suddenly laughed.

"What?" I asked. He chuckled then stepped closer to the bed.

"Something must have happened to your head when you hit it," he said, his eyes twinkling with amusement.

"What do you mean?" I asked him with my brows furrowed.

"Ariel. Look down at your clothes." He pointed at me. I looked down to see the dress I wore at the party.

I was still wearing it, but the only thing that was different was the white cast wrapped around my leg. I frowned.

"You weren't in a coma," he assured me. "You just blacked out from the impact. The only injury you have is a broken leg." He pointed down at my right leg. I can feel the pain from it.

"A broken leg?" I asked.

Troy nodded. "The doctor said there's nothing serious. You could leave today after some tests. But what happened? How did you fall like that?"

I let out a troubled breath. "That Dana was trying to quarrel with me for coming with you. She ganged up on me and then I fell backwards," I answered.

I saw a small guilty expression crawl onto his face. "I didn't think she'd go that far." As soon as he said that, a male doctor walked in the room.

"Ah, Ariel. You're awake," he said, smiling gently at me as he closed the door behind him. "Is your head still hurting?" He questioned.

I nodded. "A little," I answered.

"Don't worry. The pain will subside. There's nothing serious. You're quite lucky that the it was a short flight of stairs that you fell from. Things could have gone worse," he assured me. I only nodded as he continued to talk. "We first need to conduct

138

some tests to assure you're fine to leave. You just need to rest that leg of yours so it could heal. We'll also prescribe you medicine for your head. You might feel some headaches but there isn't anything serious."—he pointed down to my leg—"You'll also have to make an appointment for a month so we can check on your leg."

I nodded again. "Okay. Thank you, Doctor," I said. Troy stood next to me. We both listened to some other stuff he had to say. After, he stepped back and headed towards the door.

"Get well soon," he told me, giving me a friendly smile.

"Thanks again." With that, he walked out the door. My eyes turned to Troy, seeing him staring at me intensely. After a couple of seconds of silence, he cleared his throat.

"Ariel, I'm sorry," he said softly.

My eyes widened. "You're sorry?"

He nodded. "Yes. What happened to you was all my fault. You wouldn't be in this state if it wasn't for me." He pointed at my leg, guilt clearly present in his eyes.

I frowned, thinking about what he said. "Well . . . It's kind of your fault but at the same time, I shouldn't have left your side. This wouldn't have happened if I stayed by your side," I told him, smiling softly at him.

He remained silent for a moment, his eyes staring at me with so much intensity. "God dammit." He placed his head in both of his hands, huffing out in the process. He then looked back at me, nodding his head. "I'm just relieved nothing serious happened. Things could have gone badly."

I nodded. "Yeah, I could have went in a coma." A grin slowly appeared on Troy's face.

"Thank God that didn't happen," he chuckled, making my heart flutter.

"It sounds like you actually care about me," I said, smiling softly at him. He cleared his throat, looking away from me.

"Uh . . . Well . . ." he cleared his throat again. "My mother would have killed me if something happened to you . . ." he said.

139

My smile was still present on my face. Deep down, I believed that he wasn't telling the truth.

I did not say anything else. Troy frowned again. "I'm still sorry. I shouldn't have asked you to come with me. It wasn't worth it," he apologized slowly.

"It doesn't matter anymore. Forget about it. I'm fine," I assured him. He nodded his head slowly. "Anyways, does anyone at the house knows what happened?" I asked.

Troy shook his head. "No. If my mom knew then she would have been immediately by your side," he answered.

"Yeah, surely," I chuckled.

After a couple hours of doing some tests, I was finally able to leave. I was told that I had to get some extra rest at home to deal with the headaches. Rose called Troy on the phone a while ago. It was getting very late so Rose wondered why we still have yet to return home. Troy had to explain to her everything from the party to me breaking my leg. She obviously was very worried, but Troy assured her that I was okay.

"You ready?" Troy asked, walking back in the room as I sat down, grabbing onto the crutches the doctor gave me.

"Yes," I answered, standing up. I instantly stumbled back but Troy grabbed onto me before I could fall. He wrapped his arm around my waist, making me stable.

I looked up to his eyes as he stared at me in concern. "Are you okay?" he asked.

"Yes," I replied. Troy helped me with the crutches They weren't that difficult for me to use. This wasn't the first time I've used them. However, Troy's hand didn't leave my back as he helped me walk out the room. I glanced up at him and smiled as he only looked at me in concern.

We eventually walked out the hospital and towards Troy's car in silence. His still kept a hand on my back. I couldn't help but feel many emotions as I recalled the whole day.

No matter what happened or what he did, I was pleased that he was by my side.

CHAPTER EIGHTEEN

As soon as Troy seated me on the passenger seat, he started the car and drove away from the hospital. I placed the crutches at the back seats and then made myself comfortable in my seat. Troy's attention was on the dark road. I glance his way every now and then.

I noticed that there weren't many cars on the road, which made me wonder what time it actually was. Troy returned my gaze and raised a brow.

"What time is it?" I asked softly. Troy glanced at his wristwatch.

"Half an hour before midnight. Quite late," he muttered.

My eyes widened at his response. "Quite late?" I murmured. "It's very late. I don't think I've ever been out this late."

He chuckled. "What's so funny?" I raised a brow at him. Troy looked at me, holding back a smile.

"Pardon me, I completely forgot you were a goody two-shoes." He was grinning. I dramatically scoffed, rolling my eyes at him.

"I'm not a goody two-shoes," I argued, crossing my arms. "I'm just not a troublemaker." He slowly nodded his head, his eyes twinkling with amusement as he glanced my way.

"Sure, like today wasn't the first party you've ever been to," he chuckled, keeping his eyes on the road.

"I told you before. I'm not a party type," I grumbled. He let out another chuckle. Troy did not look convinced at all.

"You're still a goody two-shoes in my eyes," he mused. I narrowed my eyes at him. "And I like it that way," he continued, smiling at me. My annoyed face dropped as I heard his words. I stared at him for what felt like a minute as he turned his eyes away from me and concentrated on what was in front of him.

I eventually cleared my throat and shrugged my shoulders. "Yeah, yeah. Whatever . . ." I muttered, holding back my smile. Troy chuckled. "But I'm never going to a party with you, ever again," I said.

His face dropped, a look of guilt taking over his features. I immediately regret what I just said. "Don't worry, I won't let that happen again," he said, glancing at me. "I regret taking you so bad."

"Forget about it. It's not important anymore," I stated.

Troy opened his mouth to speak, but was cut off by a sound. I frowned as soon as I realized that it came from my stomach. My cheeks went red. Troy giggled as I sinked in my chair from embarrassment, wishing that I would just disappear.

"I'm guessing you're hungry?" he mused. I avoided eye contact.

"You can't blame me. I haven't eaten all day," I grumbled with my arms crossed. I heard another chuckle from him, which only made me feel more embarrassed.

"Then we'll stop somewhere to eat," Troy said.

My eyes slightly widened. "You don't have to," I argued.

Troy shook his head. "I'm hungry too. Besides, it's the least I could do after tonight," he said softly. The next thing I knew, Troy was driving through a McDonalds drive-thru. A smile soon formed on my lips as Troy started to order the food. As soon as he was done, he looked at me and a sly grin took over his lips.

"I'm starving," he mumbled as he drove to the window. I giggled. "I think this is the best part of tonight."

"Yeah, obviously."

The lady standing by the window gave us the bag. Troy paid for it then drove away. I opened the bag, my stomach growling as soon as the smell hit my nostrils. Troy eventually pulled up in a parking lot of a local store. He turned the engine off and then unbuckled his seatbelt. I did the same. We were the only people in sight. The place was deserted at this time.

I ate one fry as I took out my burger. I then handed the bag to Troy.

"Dig in," I spoke with my mouth full. Troy smirked. Troy took out his burger.

I have never imagined that Troy and I would be sitting here in an abandoned parking lot eating McDonald's junk food with a broken leg. For a moment, I completely forgot that I even had one.

"What a weird night," I muttered, eating a fry as I glanced at Troy.

"Yeah,"—he took another bite from his burger—"I don't think I've ever been on a date this dramatic, but it wasn't that bad. At least we're eating some McDonald's." We chuckled.

"I think that's the best part of today. Now I don't owe you anything. We're tied. I don't think I'll ever ask you for a favor again," I said.

Troy nodded, a smirk twitching at the edge of his lips. "We'll see about that," he muttered. I rolled my eyes but continued to eat my burger.

We continued to talk when I noticed that it was getting very late. I wiped my lips with a tissue.

"I think we better go before your mom gets too worried," I suggested. Troy glanced at his watch. He started the car and after a couple of seconds, we were back on the road. I sunk in my chair and leaned my head against the window as we went silent.

A yawn escaped my lips as my eye started to feel weary. I noticed Troy glancing at me a couple of times but I didn't pay much attention as I slowly fell into slumber.

144

I felt someone's arm wrapped around me. My eyes went wide as I saw the dark sky spotted with stars. I frowned in confusion but soon saw Troy. He didn't notice that I woke up as he carried me bridal style towards the front doors of the house.

My cheeks went hot at the realization that I fell asleep, causing for Troy to carry me out the car. I immediately shifted, making him look down at me.

"You're awake," he spoke softly.

"I didn't notice that I fell asleep. Sorry." I murmured. Troy shook his head.

"No, it's okay. I just didn't want to wake you up," he explained. "You looked tired."

I nodded but started to squirm in his arms. "Thank you but yo0 u can put me down." He immediately let me down, placing his hand on my shoulder to assist me.

"Your crutches are back in the car," Troy told me as he helped me walk to the door. "I'll take you to your room then I'll come back to give it to you."

I smiled softly at him. "Okay. Thank you." We eventually walked in the house as silently as possible. However, right after we set foot in the house, Rose appeared in front of us. Her eyes went wide as she saw me. She walked up to us with a worried look on her face.

"Oh, God. Ariel, are you okay?" she whispered.

"I'm okay, Rose. It's only a broken leg."

She gasped. "Oh, goodness. What would I have done if something worse happened to you. Your parents put you under our care yet we weren't able to protect you." By now her eyes started to tear up. I felt my stomach sink and a frown to take over my lips. I immediately shook my head and grabbed onto her hands.

"Rose. I swear, I'm fine. Troy was with me all this time," I told her softly. She then looked up at her son.

"How could you let her get hurt?" She narrowed her eyes at him. "How could you put her in such danger?"

145

"Please, don't blame Troy. I willingly went with him. It's not his fault. I was the one who left his side." Her eyes went soft before she pinched the bridge of her nose with her fingers. She then let out a troubled sigh.

"Fine. Just please, be carful next time," she begged. We both nodded in defeat. She took a step back. "Take her to her room so she can rest," she ordered Troy. Troy nodded again and that's when we started to make our way towards my room in silence. Eventually, I was sitting on my bed as Troy stood in front of me.

"Do you need anything else?" he asked. I shook my head.

"No, but thank you," I whispered. He took a couple of steps backwards.

"I'll give you the rest of your stuff that's in the car," he said. I nodded and he walked out the room. I immediately changed into some comfortable pajamas which wasn't easy to do with a broken leg.

I tried not to touch it so it wouldn't hurt as much as it already does. As soon as I laid on my bed, someone opened my bedroom door and walked in. At first, I thought it was Troy but it turned out to be Ozan. I sat up.

"Ozan?" I said as he closed the door behind him.

"Ariel . . ." He slowly sat on my bed. Before I even knew it, Ozan wrapped his arms around me and pulled me towards his chest. I was taken off guard for a moment but soon wrapped my arms around him as well. "God, I was so worried about you," he muttered under his breath. He eventually pulled away and looked in my eyes.

I frowned as soon as I stared at his face. I could see the bags under his eyes. He looked very tired. *What is wrong with him?*

"I was with Rose when Troy called her. I heard everything. Why the hell would you go to a party with Troy? You put yourself in danger. The least you could have done was tell me," Ozan asked, looking quite pissed.

146

I looked down at my hands. Eventually, I looked up at him with guilt. "I'm sorry. I didn't think that this would have happened. It was my fault."

Ozan sighed in frustration. "That was reckless of you. Please don't do that again. Don't make me worry about you. Next time, tell me and I'll come with you. I'm here to be by your side, aren't I?" he lectured.

"Yes, you are. I'm sorry, Ozan. I should've told you. It's just that this whole week you seemed kind of distant. That's why I didn't tell you," I mumbled.

He ran a hand through his hair. "I was tired this whole week. I feel kind of weak. I'm sorry. I didn't mean to," he stated.

"Weak? Are you okay? You do look very tired. Did you see a doctor?" I said.

Ozan shook his head. "No, but I will. Don't worry," he assured, smiling softly at me. I returned the smile.

"That's good," I murmured.

Ozan then glanced at my leg. "Does it hurt?" he wondered.

"Kind of." I shifted in my place as I tried to get comfortable. I winced as I moved my leg so Ozan got up to grab my shoulders.

"Easy there," he said, fixing my pillow as he helped me get into a more comfortable position. As Ozan was helping me, Troy walked in with a plastic bag and my crutches.

"I also got you the med—" Troy stopped and narrowed his eyes at Ozan. Ozan looked back at Troy, raising a brow.

"Troy." I let him in. Troy stood silent for a moment.

"Is there something you need?" Ozan asked. Troy cleared his throat.

"Uh . . . I . . ."—he stepped closer—"I came to give you the crutches," he murmured. He placed the crutches on the floor and handed out the plastic bag. "Also the medicine the doctor prescribed to you. I bought it while you were asleep in the car."

Ozan stepped forward and grabbed the plastic bag from Troy. "Thank you, Troy. I appreciate it," I said.

Troy nodded. He did not say another word. He just glanced at us. Troy then turned around and walked away.

CHAPTER NINETEEN

I swung my bag over my shoulder before carefully leaning down to grab onto my crutches laying on my bedroom floor. I started making my way out my bedroom door and down the hallway. I'm hungry for breakfast. I need to have one before I left for school.

I was quite pleased with myself as I was able to walk with the crutches without stumbling or falling. I guess I was now used to them. After all, it's already been two weeks since I've started using them.

I still couldn't believe two weeks have already passed. They went by like a blur. Not many things have happened. It was quite boring.

Troy and I were talking normally. After that day I broke my leg he was a little distant but he soon started talking to me normally. I couldn't help feel butterflies in my stomach at the thought of him. He has definitely changed his attitude towards me since I first came here and it was an understatement to say that I was happy.

I frowned when I made it to the staircase. I sucked in a breath as I placed my well foot on the first step. I hate this part. It was the most difficult task of the day. I feel so paranoid of falling down the stairs again. I just might break something more than just my leg.

I stopped as soon as I heard someone walking towards my way from behind me. A smile made its way to my lips as Ozan came into sight.

"Oh, thank God you're here," I mumbled as he stepped closer to me, shaking his head at me.

"How many times do I have to tell you not to go down the stairs without anyone to help you?" Ozan immediately wrapped his arm around my waist as he helped me walk down the stairs. "Do you want to fall and break your head?"

I offered him an apologetic smile in return. "But I didn't go down the stairs without anyone."

Ozan rolled his eyes. "But you were about to," he argued, frowning. I chuckled.

"But I didn't," I told him. Ozan rolled his eyes again as we made it to the end.

"And don't ever. I don't want you to fall down the stairs and break something else!" His eyes looked serious so I nodded.

"Okay, okay. I won't." I smiled softly at him. He let out a troubled sigh. I was ready to say something when I saw someone walking down the stairs from the corner of my eyes. I winced when I saw Troy walking towards us.

Ozan looked to where I was looking and then frowned. Troy stopped as soon as he saw us. After a moment, he slowly continued down the stairs. I followed his eyes to Ozan's arm which was still wrapped around my waist. My cheeks blushed. I stepped away from Ozan, offering him an apologetic smile.

Troy soon stood in front of us. His eyes flickered to mine as he gestured his head as a greeting. "Morning," he mumbled.

"Good morning," I said back to him.

Troy looked down to my leg. "How does your leg feel? Is it better?" he asked, placing his hands in his pockets.

"Yes, a little," I assured. Troy took a step forward.

"Go eat something so we could head over to school. We don't want to be late," he stated in a low tone. Troy started driving

Ozan and I to school for a while now. Sometimes, Ozan would just walk as he didn't really mind, but with my broken leg, Troy wouldn't let me walk to school.

Troy glanced at Ozan one more time before walking away. I looked back at Ozan. He had a frown on `his face.

"You're okay?" I asked. He snapped his head towards me.

"Yeah. I'm fine," he mumbled.

"Come on. Let's eat breakfast so we could head off to school." I tugged onto his arm so we could head off to the kitchen. Ozan shook his head.

"I'm not going to school today."

"Why?" I asked, furrowing my brows.

"I have a doctor's appointment today. These days my headaches are getting worse and it's making me nauseous."

I stared at him. "That's good. If you want, I could come with you?" I didn't want to leave him alone at a time that he might need me. Ozan immediately shook his head, offering me a small smile.

"No, no need to. I can go alone."

"You sure?" I wanted to know for sure if he didn't need me. He placed his hand on my shoulders in comforting manner.

"Yes, I'm sure. Now come on, go eat some breakfast."

After I ate my breakfast, I said goodbye to Ozan and made my way towards the exit. I saw Troy leaning against his car, his hands in his pockets as he looked down the ground. I could feel my cheeks heating up.

Unfortunately, I was too busy gawking at Troy that my foot accidentally tripped on a rock. My eyes widened and a small shriek escaped my lips as I stumbled. Good thing I managed to land on my left leg. I let out a groan. Two hands landed on my shoulders. Troy's eyes were filled with worry.

"Ariel." He gripped tightly onto my shoulders as he inspected my body. "Are you okay? Does your leg hurt you?" he asked.

151

"No. I'm fine. I wasn't looking to where I was going," I murmured, quite embarrassed that I fell in front of him. Troy immediately helped me stand on my feet.

"You should be more careful. Your leg could have gotten worse," he said.

I nodded, wincing as pain shot from my other leg. "Sorry," I mumbled.

"Does your other leg hurt?"

"Not really. But I think it might bruise . . ."

Troy shook his head. "You're so clumsy," he said under his breath. "Come on, let's go." He helped me walk towards the car as I frowned at him.

"Clumsy? I'm not clumsy."

Troy snickered as he opened the door for me. "Sure, you're not." I entered the car. Troy closed the door before I could say anything else.

We started driving towards our school. I sat silently, glancing at him a couple of times as he concentrated on the road. After a moment of silence, his phone rang.

I frowned as soon as I saw the caller ID.

Randa.

Every time I thought things were going perfectly fine between us, reality would slap me in the face. I wasn't his, Randa was. It never failed to hurt.

My expression turned into a frown as I watched his phone ring. Troy looked at me and then back at his phone. He then turned it off.

"Why didn't you answer?" I sulked in my chair.

"I'm driving," Troy answered, glancing at me. I looked away from him.

Troy eventually parked in front of the school. He immediately came to my side, but I shook my head.

"It's okay, I can get to class on my own," I assured. He looked quite hesitant, but he eventually nodded his head.

152

"Okay. Be careful," he muttered.

The morning passed, until the lunch bell finally rung. I waited for all the students to exit the classroom so I could walk out with no one rushing. I got up from my seat and grabbed onto my crutches. I then made my way out of the classroom.

A large crowd of boys came walking behind me not too long after I exited the room. I got caught up in the rush and was about to fall. I closed my eyes, bracing for impact against the cold hard floor for the second time today when two hands grabbed onto my shoulders.

I opened my eyes to see eyes exactly like mine, staring right back at me with concern. My mouth opened wide as I stared at Randa.

"Are you okay? You were about to fall," she asked.

"I'm fine. Thank you."

Randa placed her hand on my back. "You're heading to the cafeteria, right?"

"Yeah, I am."

"Then come on, we'll head over there together," she said softly. I stood silent for a while before hesitantly nodding my head. As we walked towards the cafeteria, I glanced at Randa to see her quite off.

"Are you okay? You seem a little off."

She looked over at me, sighing. "I'm just bothered by something," she muttered.

"By what?" I asked. She remained silent for a moment, as if she was debating whether to tell me or not.

"By Troy." She was frowning. My eyes widened.

"Troy?"

"Yes. He's constantly ignoring me. He's not talking to me. He's acting cold towards me. I don't know if I did something wrong for him to act like that towards me. It's been a while since he has started acting like this. I honestly don't know what I should do," Randa explained.

I gulped, looking at the floor. "Maybe you should talk to him. Confront him about it and ask what's wrong. A relationship isn't well without communication," I whispered. I can't believe that I was offering her some relationship advice for her and Troy. It made my head hurt.

She smiled softly at me. "You're right. I'll talk with him. Thank you, Ariel."

I only nodded as we entered the cafeteria. Randa looked over at me. "Why don't you sit with us today? It would be nice to have your company."

I immediately shook my head. "No, it's okay." I gave her an apologetic smile.

"Come on, please," Randa said, tugging onto my hand.

My eyes scanned the cafeteria and I saw Troy sitting on his usual spot, staring at us intensely.

"Fine," I said quietly. Randa's smile widened and started making our way towards their table. Troy's usual friends were also here. Randa sat down and tapped the seat next to her, which I obliged.

I looked at everyone in the group. "Ariel will be sitting with us today," Randa said out loud. Everyone greeted me, and I acknowledged.

Troy was sitting directly in front of me. The rest ate and chatted as I felt extremely awkward. I had to witness Randa trying to have a conversation with Troy, only for him to shrug her off every now and then.

No matter how strong my feelings for Troy was, I couldn't help but feel bad for her. I don't think anyone deserves to be treated that way.

Randa was telling me about something she did over the weekend when someone tapped on my shoulder. I looked up to see familiar eyes staring right at me. A small smile crawled onto my lips as I stared at Rex. "Hi, Ariel. Long time no see."

"Hey, I haven't seen you around for a while," I said.

154

Rex smiled sheepishly. "Yeah, I've been hanging out with my friends in the hallways during lunch. I don't really sit around here, but I saw you so I thought I'd stop by and see how you were," he explained, shrugging his shoulders.

"I'm good. How are you?" I asked.

"I'm doing fine. I was actually meaning to ask you whether or not you're still up for my offer? I didn't forget about it," he said.

I chuckled lightly. "You mean the tour you promised to take me on?" I raised a brow. He grinned.

"Yes, I was actually thinking we could start off on Disneyland . . ." He shrugged his shoulders.

My eyes widened. I have never been to Disneyland, and it was always something that was on my bucket list ever since I was a child.

"Disneyland?"

Rex nodded. "Yes, I mean, if you want that."

"You should totally go. It's amazing. You'll have so much fun," Randa cut in with a wide smile on her face.

I looked around the table to see everyone urging for me to say yes. However, when I made eye contact with Troy, all I could see was the annoyance in his eyes.

"Disneyland with a broken leg? I don't think that's good for her." Troy looked right at Rex with a raised brow.

"Broken leg?" Rex muttered, looking down at my leg for the first time.

"Yeah, I have a broken leg," I admitted, smiling softly at him.

"Oh, I didn't notice that," he muttered, frowning slightly. "What happened? How did you break it?"

"I fell down a flight of stairs," I answered. Rex widened his eyes. "It's a long story. I'm fine. Nothing serious other than a broken leg and a little headache from when I hit my head," I said.

"I'm glad you're okay, hope you get better," Rex stated.

"Thanks." I gave him a smile.

"I guess it wouldn't be good to take you out to Disneyland with a broken leg."

"Exactly." Troy scoffed and crossed his arms against his chest.

"Well, that's okay," he murmured. "I guess we'll just have to wait until your leg heals so we can go to Disneyland. How does that sound?" Rex asked as he grinned.

I glanced at Troy. He was staring at me intensely. I looked back at Rex, smiling up at him.

"That sounds nice."

CHAPTER TWENTY

Finally it's my last class. I paid no attention to whatever the teacher was talking about. All I could see was his mouth moving up and down. I didn't care. I just placed my chin on my hand. My mind is drifting away from the class. I couldn't help it. My mind was thinking about one thing the whole day. About one person.

Troy.

I couldn't help but feel quite frustrated, worried, and upset all at once. It was like a combination of feelings squished altogether. Why isn't Troy sitting with me in class for the third time this week? Why isn't he present for the third time? I was starting to get worried. When I confront him about it, all he would say was that he didn't get much sleep and felt tired, but now for the third time this week? There must be something wrong, and that thought alone was eating my insides.

I made a mental note that as soon as this period finished, I'll rush to Troy's house and get an answer.

I watched the clock anxiously. The moment I heard the bell ring, I jumped out of my seat and rushed out the room before the angry mob of students came rushing my way. I walked out the school campus and straight to Troy's house.

I rang their doorbell. I tapped my foot as I wait for the door to be opened. After a few seconds, I looked up as I heard someone fidgeting with the doorknob. I smiled up at Rose as soon as she appeared in my sight.

"Ariel?" She frowned slightly as she saw me.

"Hi, Rose. Is Troy in there? I was wondering why he didn't come to school today." I looked into the house.

"Yes, he is," she answered stiffly. "He woke up sick, that's why he didn't go to school," Rose explained.

"Can I see him?" I asked. "I was worried about him all day."

Rose looked quite hesitant, which made me a little confused. After a second, she moved aside.

"Yeah, sure," she mumbled. I smiled at her and walked toward's Troy's room. I didn't bother knocking and just walked in as usual.

"Troy, I came over to see you."

Troy's head snapped at me. He was sitting on his desk, writing on something what looked like a small journal. My eyes narrowed at the journal, but Troy shut it harshly without a second thought.

I frowned as he opened his drawer and shoved it in. "Ariel,"—he cleared his throat—"I wasn't expecting for you to come."

I took a couple steps towards him, my mind still at the journal. "Well, you were absent for the third time this week. I was getting worried," I told him.

Troy stood up from his seat. "I felt very tired today, that's why I decided not to come," he explained. I saw the bags under his eyes.

"Did you go to a doctor?" I asked.

He shook his head. "It's not necessary. I'm fine."

"Are you sure? You do look tired. Maybe we should go together," I suggested. Troy immediately shook his head and grabbed onto my hands as he gave me a reassuring smile.

"I'm fine. I swear. There's no need to," he exclaimed

158

I let out a troubled sigh. "Okay then," I mumbled. "What was that journal?" I looked at the drawer he placed it in. His soft smile vanished. "What were you writing in it?"

"Nothing important. Just something I write in when I'm bored," he muttered.

"Like what?" I questioned.

He shrugged his shoulders. "Notes and reminders. Not anything that's important," he said lowly. I took a step towards the drawer.

"Can I see it?" I asked, looking up at Troy.

Troy shook his head drastically and grabbed onto my head. "No," he exclaimed in a hard tone. "I mean, I don't want to bore you out."

"I won't get bored. I'm actually quite curious in what you write in it," I said, taking another step towards the drawer but stopped as Troy pulled me towards him.

"They're just some studying notes and stuff like that. Let's not waste our time. I'm actually very hungry. I haven't eaten all day. Let's go downstairs and grab a bite," Troy suggested.

I hesitantly nodded. "Okay," I muttered.

Troy pecked my lips as he wrapped an arm around my waist. "Come on," he said as he made his way out the room. I walked by him, but before he could close the door, I glanced at the drawer, wondering what really was inside that journal.

*   *   *

As usual, I waited for the crowd of students to disappear so I could exit the room. I grabbed my bag and crutches then got up from my seat. I walked out the class in a slow pace.

I was actually a little disappointed that I had to wait for more than a month for my leg to heal so I could go to Disneyland. There was no doubt that I was happy for the offer. I've never been to Disneyland so that was a no-brainer for me. Besides, who in their right mind would reject an offer to Disneyland? Not me.

I stopped in my tracks as soon as a familiar car pulled up next to me. The windows rolled down to reveal Troy staring right at me.

"Get in," he mumbled. I was a little confused but I opened the door and got in. I placed the crutches next to me then buckled up. Troy started the car as I got comfortable in my seat.

He's concentrating on the road as usual, but with a hard expression.

"You okay?" I raised a brow. He glanced at me.

"Yeah . . ." he muttered.

"You look quite stiff," I stated.

"I'm not," he mumbled.

"Does it have to do with Randa?" I asked him.

He shook his head again. "No."

"Don't you think you're treating her quite harsh?" I looked at him.

He looked back at me. "I'm not treating her harshly."

I scoffed. "Yes, you are. You're an asshole to her. She's a nice girl and she doesn't deserve to be treated that way." I crossed my arms.

His expression went harder. "I'm treating her normally. That's how I usually treat everybody. It's not like she's special."

My eyes widened. "You really are an asshole," I exclaimed. Troy narrowed his eyes at me. "Why are you her boyfriend if she's not special to you? Aren't you just playing with her feelings? Because that's not cool, Troy. No one deserves to be treated that way, especially from someone who they love," I beamed.

Troy looked at me with shock. He turned away and focused on the road with a confused expression.

"You should either treat her with respect or end the relationship if you're only going to hurt her. It's not healthy," I mutteredhead.

He sighed. "Don't worry about it," Troy mumbled. "I'll fix it."

I only nodded. Neither of us adding anything to the subject.

After a couple of minutes of silence, Troy cleared his throat and glanced at me. "So, I'm guessing you've never been to Disneyland?"

"Yeah, never in my life. I've always wanted to go there," I said.

"And you've decided to go with a complete stranger?" He scoffed.

"What do you mean?" I frowned slightly.

"I mean, you don't even know this Rex guy, yet you still agreed to go out on a date with him?" he said.

"It's not a date, and I do know him. He's my friend," I retorted.

"A friend that you've only talked to a couple of times Ariel? Are you that naive? No friend will just offer to take you to Disneyland from the kindness of their heart." He raised a brow.

"Maybe you wouldn't do it, but others would. He seems like a nice person, and I like him," I argued.

He scoffed loudly. "You like him? You don't even know him," he beamed.

"If I didn't know you better Troy, I would have said you're just jealous," I shot back. His expression went hard. His grip on the wheel tightened.

"I—I'm not jealous. I'm only looking out for you."

"Looking out for me? I thought you didn't give a single f*ck about me." I remembered his harsh words when I first reunited with him two months ago.

Troy suddenly stopped the car right in front of the house. He sucked in a breath and closed his eyes as he pinched his nose.

"Ariel," he said lowly as he looked in my eyes. "I might seem like an asshole, but I do care. I actually do."

161

I sucked in a breath. I was caught off guard by his words. Even though they weren't much, they were enough to make my heart go crazy.

He cared about me? That question circled my head.

However, before I could ask any further, he looked away from me. "Come on, let's go. Julia's staring at us." he muttered. He glanced at the window. Julia was waving at us from the house.

I smiled at her then looked at Troy. "Okay," I mumbled. We walked toward the house in silence.

"Hey, Ariel," she greeted.

"Hi, Julia. How was school?" I asked.

She shrugged her shoulders. "It's okay."

"I'll be heading to my room. If you need anything, I'll be in my room," Troy said and left immediately.

"Did Ozan return from his doctor's appointment?" I asked Julia.

"Yeah, he returned a while ago, but he looked quite off," she answered.

"Off?" I questioned. She nodded her head. I wonder why. "I'm going to go see him," I told her.

"Okay."

I turned around and walked towards the Ozan's room. I knocked on the door, but I heard nothing. I knocked again but still, no response. Maybe he wasn't in his room?

I decided to step into his room. Ozan was sitting on his bed, his head burried in his hands. My gut was telling me that something was not right.

"Ozan?" I called out. His head immediately snapped up to my direction.

"Ariel . . ." He cleared his throat.

"I knocked twice but you didn't say anything, that's why I entered." I stepped closer.

"Oh, sorry. I wasn't paying attention," Ozan said.

162

"Are you okay, Ozan? Did the doctor inform you about something bad?" I sat next to him. Just the thought of a bad diagnosis made me feel nauseous.

Ozan immediately shook his head and grabbed onto my hands. "No, don't worry. I was just thinking, that's all," he assured.

"So, what did the doctor tell you?" I asked, waiting to hear something that would put me at ease.

Ozan smiled softly at me. "The doctor said it was all from the stress and studying. He said I'm not getting enough rest, that's why I'm constantly tired. Apparently, all I need to do is sleep and be healthier. That's it," he explained.

"Really?"

Ozan nodded. "Yeah. Everything's fine."

I finally smiled , pulling him into a hug. He wrapped his arms around my waist, placing his chin on top of my head.

"That's a relief. I was worried you'd be sick," I told him.

He chuckled softly. "Don't worry. I'm as strong as a lion," he claimed. I pulled away from him, looking into his eyes.

"That, you are."

CHAPTER TWENTY-ONE

As it got late, I decided to change into my comfortable pajamas and lay on my bed. I occupied myself with some game in my phone as I wasn't able to fall asleep.

I lost in the game I was playing the moment my phone starting buzzing. My mom's name soon appeared on the screen. I immediately answered the call.

"Hello," I said.

"Hi, Ariel. How are you, sweetheart?" my mom asked. Hearing her voice made me frown. I realized I barely called my parents to see how they were doing. It has been a while since I last talked to them. There was no doubt that I missed them so much. I want to see them.

"I'm good. How are you both?" I said.

"We're fine. We just miss you so much," she replied.

"I miss you too. I miss you guys so much." I tried to hide the sadness in my voice. It would surely upset my mom.

"How are you doing there? Is Rose treating you well?" my mom asked.

"Rose and Damon are treating me very well. They are very kind." I could hear my mom breathe out of relief.

"That's wonderful, honey. I knew I could rely on them. What about Troy? Is he giving you a hard time?" she asked this time.

I cleared my throat. "No, he's not. He's fine." I don't want to tell my mom how much he affected me. Hell, Troy was giving me a difficult time. A very difficult time for my heart, and it's driving me crazy.

"That's a relief," she mumbled. "Your dad and I were worried that he'd cause some trouble for you. We did hear from Damon that his attitude drastically changed from before."

"You guys don't worry about it. "I'm taking care of it just fine. He is a huge jerk, but he's not that bad," I said. My mom let out a soft chuckle.

"Do you still love him? I mean, we knew how much he affected you and how much you adored that boy," my mom said after a moment of silence. I was surprised by her question.

I let out a troubled breath, not sure on how to answer her. "Mom, if all these years I still loved him when he was far away, how could I not love him when he's so close?"

"Oh, honey . . ."

"I swear, I'm trying. I'm trying to control my feelings. I really am, but, it's hard epecially when he's showing signs that he cares about me. That makes me hold on to a little bit of hope even if he might not love me," I told her, feeling my heart skip a beat at the thought of Troy.

What I liked about my mother was that I could talk to her about anything and she would listen. She wasn't just my mom, she was my best friend.

"So, he's not a total jerk to you?" my mom said. A soft chuckle escaped my lips.

"He used to, but not anymore. He improved his attitude towards me these past two months," I explained, a small smile taking over my lips. "I guess you could say we're friends."

Friends . . . I was willing to take that. It was better than nothing.

"That's good, sweetheart. I'm happy for that," she exclaimed. "How is Ozan? I haven't talked with that young lad in a while," my mom asked.

"He's good as well. He's taking good care of me. A week ago he was feeling sick so he went to the doctor, but other than that, he's doing fine."

"That's great. We knew we could count on that boy. At least you have a friend with you so you wouldn't be alone," she said.

"Yeah, you're right. I don't know what I would have done without him. I'm happy that he volunteered to come with me," I said.

After a while of chatting with my mom, a question popped in my head.

"Ariel, is something wrong?"

I guess my mom sensed that.

"Mom, did something happen with our case? Did they find anything that had to do with the shooter?" I asked her sternly

I could hear my mom letting out a troubled sigh from the other end. "There is something," my mom finally said after a moment of silence. "We weren't sure if we should tell you because we didn't want you to worry."

"Just tell me. What is it?"

"The shooter escaped from prison."

My eyes widened. "What? What are you talking about Mom? How could he have escaped?" I could feel my voice shaking, but I can't let anyone else in the house hear me.

"The man attempted suicide while in jail, so they took him to a hospital. While he was in the hospital, he escaped. It looked like someone was helping him out because he wouldn't have escaped on his own. I think it was all planned out," she said.

"Oh, God," I gasped.

"But don't worry, honey. "If you really are under a threat, then there is no way that they could know where you are. Besides, the police is tracking him down. They'll surely find him."

No matter how much my mom assured me, I still couldn't help but worry as I thought about all the possibilities. This wasn't good. A shooter was out on the loose, bringing danger to not only me, but to the people around him.

I cleared my throat. "When was this? When did he escape?"

"Yesterday," she responded.

I sighed out. "Okay, but are you guys okay?"

"Don't worry about us. You father has placed high security. I don't think anyone can hurt us."

"I hope so."

After what felt like an hour, I finally said goodbye to my mom and closed my phone. I thought hard about what I found out. I felt anxious. I just prayed that nothing would happen to me or my family.

It was almost midnight. I should sleep so I wouldn't wake up extremely tired tomorrow. However, I heard someone opening the front door.

I ran a hand over my face. Who was possibly getting out at a time like this? I walked towards my window the moment I heard a familiar voice. My room was exactly above the front door. A frown took over my expression the second I saw Troy closing the door. He talking to someone over the phone.

"Randa, I'll be at your place in ten minutes." My eyes widened at what I heard.

I watched Troy step away from the doors. His words kept echoing in my head. I gulped. I was about to step away from the window when Troy raised his head and looked at the direction of my room.

His eyes widened as he saw me standing by the window in the dark. I stepped away from the window and closed the curtains.

167

I slowly walked towards my bed as I thought of his words. His words that twisted my heart. I couldn't think of any other reason on why he would meet up with Randa at a time like this. That thought only made me feel one thing that I hated. Jealousy.

It was no surprise that I couldn't sleep. For the whole night I was thinking of two things: Randa and Troy, and the shooter that was on the loose.

CHAPTER TWENTY-TWO

"What do you mean Troy isn't here?" I asked Rose who was cooking breakfast in the kitchen. She looked back at me and shrugged her shoulders.

"He wasn't in his room. I think he stayed overnight at a friend's house or something. He usually does that," Rose said.

I felt my stomach swirl. Troy didn't come back last night. That must have meant that he stayed at Randa's house. That thought alone made my heart sink. I took a step back from the counter and ran a hand over my face.

"If you're worried about getting to school, Damon will drive you and Ozan to school before heading to work." She offered me a reassuring smile then took out a bottle of orange juice from the fridge.

"That's not a problem. I can walk to school. There's no need for Damon to waste his time," I said.

"Don't say that. Damon won't be wasting his time. His work is in the same direction of your school. Besides, I'm not letting you walk with a broken leg."

"But—"

"No buts." Rose gave a slight glare as she took a step closer to me. "Now go call Ozan and Julia so we can eat breakfast. Go on."

There's no convincing her. I turned away and walked towards the rooms to call everyone for breakfast.

*　　*　　*

I sat in the back of Damon's car next to Ozan. Ozan sat silently with his eyes closed. His window was down, so the wind hit our faces.

I didn't budge a word for the whole ride. My head wasn't with anyone at this moment. The only thing that my mind was focusing on was Troy. I feel haywire. Any moment, my mind could explode from the overthinking. Did Troy really stay over at Randa's place?

I decided to push that thought at the back of my head before I end up going crazy.

I frowned as I looked at Ozan's state. "Ozan?"

His eyes slowly opened. "Are you okay?" I asked.

He softly smiled at me. "Yeah. I'm fine," he assured.

"You look tired," I pointed out. I could see his eyebags.

Ozan shrugged his shoulders. "Didn't sleep last night," he said.

"Neither did I," I mumbled, feeling the energy sucked out of me today.

How could I sleep after what happened last night? The fact that the shooter escaped from prison brought chills down my spine. It made me feel sick in the stomach. It frightened me to my core. Those words still rung in my ear to this day. I just learned to cope with it and brush it off. After I found out that he escaped, his words turned into a siren.

He's going to get you! You're going to die! You can't hide forever.

I let out a troubled breath. I sensed Ozan's eyes staring at me.

"Are you okay? You look like you've seen a ghost." It was his turn to ask questions.

"I'm fine," I muttered. Ozan didn't look convinced.

170

"No, you don't look fine," Ozan argued, narrowing his eyes down at me, telling me to fess up. "Now, tell me. What's wrong?"

I forced myself to suck in a breath then looked back into his worried yet demanding eyes. "Well—"

"We made it," Damon interrupted. I closed my mouth.

"I'll tell you later. Come on, let's go before we're late to class," I said. Ozan hesitantly nodded. I unbuckled then grabbed onto the crutches. Ozan was soon rushing to my side to help me get off the car.

Damon drove away, leaving us standing on the school campus. Without a second to spare, Ozan and I walked to our class.

Time passed, and I'm now sitting in class, spacing off as usual. My mind can't concentrate on what the teacher was saying. I noticed that Randa wasn't present during the first period, so I thought she must have been absent. However, she came late in our second period.

I wonder if Troy came in to school today. I will have to wait and see this afternoon.

I was pulled away from my thoughts when the lunch bell rang. I waited for the rest to leave before grabbing onto my bag and crutches.

It took time for me to walk. I wanted to see whether Troy or wasn't sitting in his usual spot in the cafeteria. I stopped on my tracks when I saw something from the corner of my eyes. More like someone.

Randa was sitting under a tree instead of being in the cafeteria. I slowly made my way towards her. Our eyes connected and I noticed the sadness in her. Her eyes were puffy and red.

"Randa?" I placed my crutches on the ground then sat next to her under the tree. "Are you okay? What's wrong? You look like you've been crying."

She sighed as she shook her head, her eyes watery.

"No Ariel. I'm not okay. I'm not okay at all," she finally said.

171

I don't know what to say. I then placed a hand on her shoulder as she looked back at me. "Hey, hey. Don't cry. It's okay." I rubbed her back in a comforting manner.

"It's not okay. Nothing's okay." A tear slipped from her eye.

"Randa. What happened? What's bothering you?" I couldn't help but feel this had something to do with Troy. She remained silent.

"Randa, what's wrong? Maybe if you tell me, I could help you," I suggested. Randa's eyes soon averted from me.

"You can't help me," Randa claimed.

"Why?"

"Because Troy broke up with me," she finally said.

"What?" I said out of surprise. "He broke up with you?"

"Yes. He ended everything yesterday night."

"Why?"

"I don't know," she muttered. "I took your advice. I tried talking with him all week to know why he was acting the way he was. But all he would do was ignore me. I called him last night and he told me he was coming over to talk." I listened to her in silence, extremely shocked with what she was saying. "And when he did, he broke up with me and left," she mumbled. I could see from her eyes that she was trying to hold in the tears.

I let out a breath. "Oh, Randa." I pulled her into a hug. "Everything will be okay. Trust me. Everything will be fine."

For the rest of the lunch period, I sat with Randa under the tree. I couldn't help but feel sad towards her. She seemed very upset, and I didn't want to leave her alone at a time like this.

Sitting in my last period wasn't so easy. It turned out that Troy actually came to school. Fortunately, Randa went home early. I advised her to return home so maybe she could rest a bit. She looked extremely exhausted.

I didn't know if what Troy did was the best decision, but maybe it was the right one. This had nothing to do with my

172

feelings. Yes, it extremely hurts to see him with someone else. However, I never wished anything bad upon Randa, and I never will.

Yet, maybe this was healthier for the both of them. Maybe in the future Randa will find someone better, someone who will treat her with respect. It didn't take a genius to figure out that Troy was treating her coldly.

As the bell finally rang, everyone rushed to exit the classroom. Troy rushed out the class as usual as I stayed at the back, holding on to my crutches. I was soon walking down the hall and towards the front of the campus. I wasn't surprise when Troy's car stopped in front of me the moment I stepped off campus.

I didn't wait for him to say a word. I opened the door and got in. Troy drove off.

"We're not going to wait for Ozan?" It became a habit for Troy and I to leave together ever since my broken leg. Ozan would sometimes walk home on his own. He told me he preferred to walk, as it gives him time to think about many things.

"He can walk," Troy muttered, leaving me speechless. I decided not to ask any further.

"I'm guessing you know," he blurted out after a moment.

I looked back at Troy to see him glancing at me with a neutral expression. "Yeah. Randa told me. She was very upset. It looked like she cried all night," I said. He went back to concentrating on the road.

Troy's long breath hit my ears. "I tried doing it in the most civilized manner," Troy mumbled.

I raised a brow at him. "At midnight? Really? You decided to break up with her at 12 AM?" I questioned. He glanced at me, a frown taking over his face.

"Okay, maybe that part wasn't civilized, but she called me and she was very angry. When I said that I was coming to talk, she didn't decline. I tried not to hurt her feelings, but she didn't take it lightly," Troy explained.

173

"Of course she won't take it lightly. It's not an easy thing. Besides, why did you decide to break up with her now when she was all attached to you? Couldn't you have done that when her feelings haven't grown too much?" I said.

There was a moment of silence. The air around us was thick as I waited for Troy's answer.

"I guess you were right," he admitted. My brows furrowed. "It wasn't healthy. I realized that too late. I only dated her because she was a close friend of mine ever since I came here. When she confessed to me and asked me out, I saw no reason to say no. I guess I was just being foolish. I never had any feelings towards her and didn't really care that I was dating someone I didn't have strong feelings for. But you made me realize that this wasn't good for the both of us. She deserves someone better. Someone who will love her. I'm not that person."

I listened in silence. He looked over at me.

"I just hope she won't stay upset. I really felt bad for her." I mumbled. I felt bad for her because I knew what she was dealing with. I hundred percent know how she is feeling. It's difficult to endure the misery, to endure a pain caused by someone you loved dearly. I could feel her pain, but as Troy said, it wasn't healthy. The best I could wish for her was to heal and move on. Something that I wasn't able to do.

"Don't worry about her," Troy assured me. "Everything will be fine."

I let out a breath, then remembered something. "Where were you all night then? You didn't return home." I raised a brow at him.

"I crashed at a friend's place that was near Randa's house. I didn't want to return home at a late hour," he answered.

I nodded my head. "Oh."

After a while, Troy parked the car and then unlocked the doors. "Come on, go inside. I'll be right behind you."

I hopped off the car and entered the house, Troy walking right behind me.

CHAPTER TWENTY-THREE

My eyes snapped open. I scanned my surroundings. It was dark. I took a step forward even though I was unsure on where to go.

I sucked in a breath as I continued to walk into the never-ending darkness. A bead of sweat trickled on my face. My heart was beating faster.

My legs are starting to feel numb. I felt like I was walking for hours in nothing but darkness. I was soon out of breath. I frantically looked around, but like the previous attempts, there was nothing, not a single thing in sight.

I got more anxious so I started dashing. Tears threatened to escape as I sucked in a breath. I ran and ran until I wasn't in darkness anymore. I was at another place.

Thank God I was finally let out of the abyss. I took a quick look around. I frowned slowly as I realized where I was. I've been here before.

My eyes widened. I was in my old school. I was standing at the high school I attended for three years. The school I left when that horrific incident happened. The day of the school shooting, a day which I cannot seem to foget.

I slowly began walking around the school campus. "H— How did I get here? Why am I here?"

I searched for any living being, but I saw no one. I felt something pulling me to the school campus. I immediately forced myself to take a step back.

"No, I can't go in there," I argued with the instinct. I tried to turn my body around and run away, but I couldn't. I was fixed in my spot, as if someone was holding me. I gasped as I felt myself slowly getting near the school campus.

"No! No, no, no! I can't go back in there. I don't want to. Please, no!" I continued to yell, but to whom? I did not know.

I closed my eyes, screaming and thrashing to the invisible force that was holding me. When I opened my eyes, I was horrified.

I wasn't outside the campus anymore. I was in the school, right in front of the bathroom I hid in more than two months ago. Right at that moment, I felt the oxygen being sucked out of my lungs. My eyes scanned the place. There were bodies scattered on the floor. My eyes started to feel watery. The sight tore me to pieces and left me speechless. All I did was stare at the motionless bodies.

My head then snapped into the direction of the footsteps coming my way. I gulped as a familiar person came into sight. It was the man who was the cause of all my stress. The shooter.

I saw a smirk crawling onto his face and a gun in his hands. My blood went cold as he stood in front of me, bringing back the memories from two months ago.

"Wha—what—"

"You thought you could get rid of me?" He laughed menacingly which shook me to my core.

"How did you get here? How did you escape prison?"

The man took a step towards me. "No matter where you are, he will find you." His smirk went serious, looking deep into my eyes. "He knows your every move."

I glanced in horror as he raised his gun to my face.

"You can't hide forever."

My eyes watered as he placed the gun in front of my face. "Please, don't. Please. Don't do it."

177

He snickered. "Sorry, orders from the boss."

Then he pulled the trigger. Everything went black.

A gasp escaped my mouth, my eyes jolting open as I woke up in cold sweat. I took deep breaths as I ran both hands over my sweating face while remembering the nightmare I just had.

"Oh God. This is getting to my head." I groaned slightly.

I sat up and looked out the window. The sun was setting. I shouldn't have taken that nap. Maybe then, I wouldn't have had that horrid dream.

I ran a hand through my tangled hair, breathing out in frustration as the dream continued to replay in my head. I didn't even notice that someone entered my room until I heard someone call me.

"Ariel?" Ozan stared at me with a raised brow. "Am I talking to a wall? I've called your name three times already."

"Sorry, I wasn't paying attention. I was thinking about something," I said. Ozan sat next to me on the bed.

"Are you okay, Ariel? You've been quite off since morning. What happened? And don't tell me it's nothing, I know there's something. Come on, spill." He narrowed his eyes at me. I stared into his dark eyes.

"I talked with my mom yesterday," I started.

"Did something happen to your mom?"

"No, nothing like that. My mom told me the shooter escaped," I confessed. Ozan's jaw dropped.

"The shooter? As in the one who came to our school?"

I nodded. "Yes. Him."

A look of disbelief crossed his face. "God," he muttered. "When? And how? How the hell could someone escape prison?"

"I don't know how he escaped. My mom said that it's believed someone helped him out. This happened two days ago. The police are still tracking him down."

"Dammit. Dammit. A f*cking shooter is out on the loose? How the f*ck can that happen?"

I placed a hand on his shoulder. "Calm down. Let's just hope he's found," I said. Ozan looked at me and released a breath as he ran a hand over his face. He then wrapped an arm around my shoulder.

"I know you're worried, but don't be," he said.

"Ozan, I'm very worried. I can't get this thing out of my head, especially since I know he's out there somewhere, maybe looking for me. My parents wouldn't have sent me here if I wasn't in a real threat. That means someone is trying to harm me," I said.

Ozan immediately tightened his hold on me. "No one will harm you. I won't allow that. I'm here to be by your side, and I will till my last breath. I promise you that," Ozan assured.

I laid my head against his chest as his arms wrapped around me. "Thank you, Ozan," I mumbled.

"Mm-hmm."

"I'm glad you're here. I'm glad I'm not alone." I looked up at him and smiled softly.

"You'll never be alone, Ariel. You won't get hurt. You're safe here. We'll stay here as long as we have to," he promised, staring deeply into my eyes.

I nodded, smiling at him.

"I've got your back."

CHAPTER TWENTY-FOUR

I smiled as soon as I saw Clare's caller ID pop up in my phone screen. I immediately answered it. I missed her more than I already do as soon as I heard her voice.

"Hey, Ariel!"

"Hi, Clare! How are you?"

"I'm okay. Everything's fine." She sighed. "It's so boring here without you, Ariel. I miss you," she said.

It left me feeling down. "Clare, I miss you, too. I really do."

"Can you believe that we haven't seen each other in two months and two weeks?" Her voice softer than before. I could sense her feelings. She was feeling the same way as I do. "It feels longer. Feels like a year."

I let out a troubled breath. "Yeah, it's been awhile," I mumbled. "We haven't seen each other since the day I left."

"Yeah . . . It's really lonely without you, Ariel. I miss you and Ozan."

I felt guilty for leaving Clare alone.

"I'm sorry, Clare. I really am. I wish I didn't leave you alone."

"Don't apologize! It's not your fault, Ariel, and you know that. You didn't have a choice," she said

I bit my lip and leaned my head back against the wall. "Yeah," I mumbled. "I didn't have a choice, but it makes me sad to know that you're lonely. I wish I could do something."

"It's alright, Ariel. Everything's fine. Besides, what matters is your safety. That's more important," Clare emphasized.

"I don't know when this will be all over Clare, or when I don't have to worry about anything," I whispered.

"Don't be worried, Ariel. Everything will be fine."

"How can I not be worried when the police has yet to find the shooter?" I sat up straight. "It's been a week, Clare. Yet they still didn't find him. Who knows where he is or what he's planning." I feel so frustrated.

Clare let out a troubled sigh, pausing for a moment.

"The police will find him, Ariel. They will. As long as you're far away from us, then he won't find you. You're safe over there," she said.

I tried to use her words as a motivation to calm my nerves down but it's juts not working. It's already been a week and there weren't any news about him. Nothing at all. I didn't know if he was out there hurting someone else or on the look out for me for whatever reason. My guard was up the whole week. I wasn't able to calm myself down. I bet the whole house noticed my odd behavior, that's why Damon and Rose questioned me about it two nights ago.

When I told them, they tried to reassure me that everything was fine. However, something in my gut tells me that there is something wrong.

Troy was probably suspecting that there was something wrong with me. He hasn't asked me yet though. Just the thought of Troy made me feel slightly better. I felt myself relax as I thought about him.

"Hello, Ariel? Where did you go? Am I talking to myself?" she called out.

"Sorry, I was thinking about something," I muttered.

"You were thinking about what?" she questioned.

"About the shooter." I lied. "That day of the school shooting is haunting me. That day when someone trashed my room is also haunting me, Clare," I told her. "I'm honestly scared—"

My bedroom door opened and Troy stepped in my room. I went silent. Clare on the other end asked why I stopped.

Troy had a confused expression on his face. "Ariel, Mom says that dinner is ready," he said, scratching the back of his head. "Come down to eat. You haven't eaten anything for lunch."

I slowly nodded my head, keeping contact with his dark eyes. He stared at me for a moment.

"Okay, I'll be down there," I assured, smiling softly at him. He walked out of my room and closed the door. I exhaled. "Sorry about that," I mumbled on the phone.

"Was that Troy?" Clare asked sadly. I paused for a moment.

"Yes, that was him."

She went silent for a moment. I could feel her gloom and I didn't question it. Troy and Clare were friends as well, so I know she missed him too.

"It's been so long since I've heard his voice. More than three years. That's a long time," she finally said.

I nodded even though she couldn't see me. "Yeah. Three years is a long time. Enough time to change someone."

"Oh, Ariel," she sighed. "How is he treating you? Are you both okay?" she asked.

"Everything fine, Clare," I assured. "It was difficult in the beginning, but I kind of got used to it. He's no longer a prick to me like how he was when I first came here. He's acting neutral with me. I'm willing to take anything." I'm getting mixxed emotions as I thought about these months.

"Ariel," she mumbled. "You'll never get over him, will you?"

I'm not sure how to answer her.

"I don't think I ever will," I confessed. "The moment I decide to move on, he reappeared in my life, making things way more difficult. When he's so close to me, I can't seem to control my feelings, Clare." I felt teary, but I forced myself to blink them

182

away. "I know I'm weak and foolish for feeling that but I can't seem to control my heart."

"You're not weak for feeling that way, Ariel. It's not easy to erase feelings. It doesn't work that way. I think you're strong for enduring this, especially since you're living under one roof and dealing with a different type of Troy," she stated, which made me smile. "I just hope that everything will be fine with the both of you. You both deserve happiness."

I felt a huge lump in my throat as I listened to her.

"And I hope that one day, Troy will remember the history between you two, because a love like that deserves to be cherished," Clare said. A tear slipped down my cheek.

"I hope so, too," I mumbled, wiping off the tear.

Clare cleared her throat. "Well, go on. I don't want you to keep them waiting. Go eat dinner and we'll talk later."

"Okay, let me know if anything new happens," I made my way to the door, grabbing on to my crutches.

"Okay, I will."

"Bye, Clare," I said softly.

"Take care, Ariel."

I ended the call then placed my phone in my pocket. I started walking towards the dining room.

Everyone was sitting on the table except for Ozan. "Ariel, come on," Rose called out to me. I placed the crutches by my side then sat down next to Julia.

"Where's Ozan?" I asked.

"He said he wasn't hungry," Rose answered, shrugging her shoulders. I nodded and started to eat, making eye contact with Troy as I felt his eyes on me. He was looking at me oddly, as if trying to figure out something. It was like he spaced off, but as soon as he realized that I was staring right back at him, he looked away and played with his food. I could've swore I saw his cheeks flush.

I glanced at him a couple of times as I ate. The air around us was silent for a moment.

"So, Ariel. How's your parents?" Damon the silence. I smiled softly at him.

"They're fine. They miss you both," I answered.

"We miss them too. It's been years since we last have seen them," Rose said, smiling.

Damon nodded. "Let them know that if they need anything or any help, do not hesitate to ask," he stated. I knew that he was talking about the shooter issue.

"Thank you, Damon." I smiled.

"Anyways, how's your leg, honey?" Rose asked.

I drank a cup of water before answering. "It's much better. I have a doctor's appointment tomorrow," I pointed out.

"Tomorrow?" Troy blurted out for the first time. All heads turned to him as he stared at me intensely.

"Yes."

"Oh, that's good. Hopefully you'll get rid of those crutches as soon as possible," Rose said.

It made me chuckle. "I hope, too. They're a pain in the neck."

"Is Ozan coming with you tomorrow?" Damon wondered.

I shook my head. "No. I'm going alone."

"Make sure you be careful then," Damon said. I nodded, glancing at Troy.

"Don't worry, I'll be fine."

After helping Rose with the dishes and cleaning everything up. I excused myself to my room. I stopped dead on my tracks when I saw Troy leaning against the wall near my bedroom door with his arms crossed.

I sucked in a breath and forced my feet to move. Troy immediately stood straight and cleared his throat when he found me.

"Troy, is there something you need?" I said hesitantly. Troy took a step back, placing his hands in his pockets as he stared right in my blue eyes.

"No," he mumbled. "I just wanted to know if you're okay?"

That took me off guard. "Why are you asking?" I tilted my head in confusion.

Troy cleared his throat once again and averted his eyes from mine for a moment. "I heard you telling someone on the phone a while ago that you were scared of something. What are you scared from?" Troy asked.

I averted my eyes from him, debating with myself whether I should tell him or not. He looked at me with persistent eyes. My heart raced when he took a step closer.

"What's scaring you, Ariel?" I need to know what's scaring you. Or I'll keep thinking about it," he said with concern.

I looked down at the floor. "The shooter that attacked our school months ago escaped prison. He's out there, and my parents fear that he wants to hurt me." I told him, watching his eyes widen in surprise.

"He escaped?"

I nodded. "Yes."

His eyes went dark. "Dammit. Dammit. This isn't good," he muttered, running a hand through his hair. I looked back in his fiery eyes. It made me shiver. He forced himself to calm down with me around.

"Don't worry, Ariel." He placed his hand on my shoulder, taking me off guard. "You're safe here. I promise no one will hurt you." I stared into his eyes for long seconds.

"I know," I mumbled. "Thank you."

Troy took a step back. "Go rest. You have a doctor's appointment tomorrow," Troy ordered.

"Okay," I said, entering my room. I turned around and looked back at him. "Goodnight," I told him.

185

"Goodnight," he mumbled back, making me smile softly at him. Troy took another step back as I started closing the door.

"Oh, Ariel." He stopped in his tracks.

"Yes, Troy?" I questioned.

"I'm coming with you tomorrow. No arguments."

Then he turned away and walked down the hall, leaving me petrified by my bedroom door.

CHAPTER TWENTY-FIVE

Sitting by the window was relaxing, especially since I had a book in my hands. I sipped on my coffee, enjoying the rays of light that hit my soft skin. I was in my own little world as I read about a romantic tale which left me feeling satisfied every once in awhile. I continued to sip my coffee, not pulling my eyes away from the pages.

However, I was soon interuped from my little world when someone knocked on my door.

"Come in," I called out, placing the mug on my desk. My bedroom door opened, revealing Troy. I immediately sat straight and cleared my throat. "Troy?" I murmured as he took a step in my room, placing his hands in his pockets.

"I just wanted to ask what time is your appointment so we can get going," Troy said. I glanced at the clock that hung on my bedroom wall.

"It's at 5 PM," I answered. We only have an hour left till the appointment. It's a good thing Troy reminded me. This book was completely distracting me. I shut the book and stood up as I grabbed the crutches.

"We should probably get going," Troy stated. "We don't want traffic to stall us."

I nodded. "Yeah, you're right. The hospital is half an hour away from here so it would be better if we go now. Are you ready to go?" I glanced at his appearance which never failed to make my heart race.

"Yeah. I'm ready. "If you're ready, then let's go." Troy stepped aside. I started making my way out my room, Troy walking right behind me. Troy soon gripped my shoulder to assist me on the stairs.

We saw Rose standing near the staircase, smiling softly at the both of us. "Ariel, are you going to the appointment?" she asked with a raised brow.

"Yes, I am." I returned the smile. Rose looked up at Troy, her eyes twinkling as she glanced at his hand which still laid on my shoulder. Troy seemed to have noticed it so he took it off and cleared his throat.

"Is Troy coming with you?" Rose nudged at me.

"Yes, he is."

Her smile widened. "That's good of you, Troy!" she exclaimed, looking at her son. "Now go on. We don't want you to be late," she shooed us away with her hands. I smiled at her one more time then made our way to the front door. When we were out the house, I glanced at Troy.

"She seemed pretty happy that you're coming with me," I pointed out. He glanced at me as we walked to his car.

"Yeah. I guess she didn't want you to go alone," he said before we got in the car. Troy started the car as I looked at him.

"Why did you decide to come with me?" I asked, biting the inside of my cheek. Troy looked at me.

"Because I didn't want you to go alone. Someone needs to accompany you. Besides, it is my fault that you have a broken leg so the least I could do is tag along," Troy explained.

My eyes were glued to him as his words registered in my head. "Thank you." I smiled. "I appreciate it."

He nodded his head as an answer. I continued to stare at him. He raised a brow, a smirk slowly twitching at the side of his lips. "Is there something you're meaning to ask since you're staring at me like that?"

I blushed. "Actually, there is," I pointed out.

"What is it?" Troy asked as he stopped at a red light.

"Are you and Randa still talking? It's been a week since you've broken up with her and I stopped seeing her around in classes and lunch," I said. Troy let out a sigh.

"No, I don't talk to her. I think she needs time to get used to it," he replied. I nodded.

Troy continued to drive in silence. We didn't really talk much. I kept glancing his way as his eyes were only on the road. I took that as the time to admire him.

His chocolate brown hair looked so soft. It's tempting me to run a hand through it like the old times. I gawked at his appearance and eventually meet his dark eyes which looked at me with a slight amusement.

"I'm guessing staring at me is becoming a habit of yours," he said. My cheeks went red as a smug look took over his face. I sulked in my chair with embarrassment. I heard him chuckle as I averted my gaze away from him.

"Sorry, I spaced off," I murmured. I looked back at him. He still had that smug look on his face, which only made my cheeks hotter. "It's kind of a habit." It was true. It was a habit of mine. I couldn't help but remember the times I'd fool myself in front of Troy as I always stared at him, spacing off as I thought about anything. Mostly about him.

"I could tell. Would you always space off at me like that? I mean, when we were together . . ." Troy cleared his throat.

My eyes widened. I stared at him in silence "Yes," I answered. His facial expression changed as he remained silent for what felt like forever. I could feel the tension in the air. Troy eventually glanced at me, his eyes dark.

"Tell me about myself," he asked, making me frown.

189

"What?" I said. He glanced at me again with determined eyes.

"How was my character before, Ariel? How would I treat you and the people around me?"

Troy had a serious expression onto his face. I gulped. He was actually asking this question.

"Go on," he insisted. "Tell me."

I was in disbelief, but I eventually forced some words out my mouth. "You were outgoing. Kind and funny. You'd always make me laugh . . ." I breathed out as memories flushed in my head.

Troy didn't glance at me, but I knew he was listening closely. "You were foolish at times, but that's what I loved the most." I giggled. Troy stared at me with serious eyes. "You knew when to be serious and when to be childish. You were basically a child at times."

A small, wistful smile crawled onto his lips. "You were a wonderful person, and you still are." I said with a smile. His eyes lightened up with emotions. He soon stopped the car then turned to me.

"I'm an asshole. I'm not nice, funny or kind. I can't bring the old character back, Ariel. I can't."

Our eyes continued to stare at each other.

"You're right," I agreed. "You are a jerkface at times, but I still like you," I murmured, slowly smiling at him. I forced myself to say "like" and not "love." His eyes softened and let out a chuckle.

"Jerkface? Really, Ariel? Is that all you've got?" he mused. He didn't even comment about the "like" part.

"Okay, fine. You're an asshole, a jerk, a prick—"

"Okay, okay. I get it. I get it. I'm a jerk." Troy raised his hands. He started to unlocked the doors. I looked around and noticed that we have made it to the hospital. "Come on, let's go," Troy said, ending the subject.

Troy came to my side. I smiled at him and made our way to the front doors. Troy's hand laid on my back the whole time.

We reached the doctor's office a few moments later. After a few checks, the doctor started to make an assessment.

"You're in good condition," the doctor smile at me. "Your head is completely fine from the impact that you suffered, although your leg needs some more time. Approximately another month until it heals. You can then have another appointment so we can remove the cast. Take good care of it until then," he explained, walking to the door. "You're excused to leave. Take care." The doctor left the room.

I stood up. Troy helped me balance myself, rolling his eyes as the doctor walked away. "It took him that long to see you?" he grumbled, crossing his arms in annoyance.

"It wasn't that long," I mumbled.

Troy looked down at me with a raised brow. "Really? An hour and a half isn't long?"

"Okay, maybe it was but it's over now," I told him as we walked out the room.

"Remind me to bring a blanket and a pillow the next time I come with you. I swear, I was about to take a nap before he walked in the room. 'The doctor will be with you in a minute.' Bullsh*t," he mimicked the nurse. I looked at him with amusement.

I laughed as he opened the car door for me. His annoyed expression was slowly replaced with an amused one. I shook my head at his behavior as he started the car. He kept throwing comments here and there about the doctor and the hospital, which I found amusing.

It was getting dark outside. Troy eventually calmed down and remained quiet as he drove the car. I threw glances at him every now and then. We were on a silent, dark road. There weren't many cars in sight. I felt Troy glance at me. I raised a brow as I caught his eyes, but he quickly averted.

"Is there something wrong?" I asked, shifting in my seat.

Troy went silent for a couple of seconds. "I'm trying to figure you out," he mumbled.

"Figure me out?" I asked. He nodded slowly.

"Yes. I'm trying to figure out how you easily walked into my life," he murmured as I continued to listen. "How you made me confused, and how . . ." Troy stopped. I bit my lips, waiting for him to continue.

"And how?" I asked, wanting him to continue.

He glanced at me for a second. "How you easily affected—"

Troy's words immediately stopped as we started to hear weird sounds coming from the car. Troy immediately drove to the side of the road before the car came to a stop. My mouth opened as Troy struggled to get the car to move. We were stranded there.

"What happened?" I asked.

"Shit," Troy cursed, hitting the wheel. "Looks like something's wrong with the engine," he said, unbuckling then opening his door.

Great timing.

"Where are you going?" I asked, my eyes widening.

"I'm going to see what's wrong with the engine," he answered. I immediately shook my head and grabbed onto his hand. He was surprised as he glanced at our joined hands.

"Don't," I said.

Troy raised a brow. "Why?"

"Have you ever seen a horror movie, Troy?" I hissed, looking at our surroundings as we were the only cars in sight. "You'll either end up killed or . . ."

"Or what?" Troy questioned, an amused expression forming onto his face.

"Or killed!" I threw my hands into the air. "Please don't be that dumb person in every horror movie."

Troy laughed out, shaking his head. "Those are only in movies, Ariel. You're overreacting."

192

"I'm not," I argued. "You don't know who could be lurking in those trees."

Troy rolled his eyes. He looks amused. "I'm going to go check the engine. If it bothers you so much, lock the doors," he insisted. He hopped out the car and closed the door. I bit my lip as he walked to the front of the car. He started inspecting the engine with the flashlight from his phone on.

I sucked in a breath and grabbed my crutches. I stepped out from the car and walked towards his side.

If he's going to die, might as well have his back.

Troy smirked at me. "How brave of you for not leaving me to be killed all alone." He chuckled.

"Troy!" I hissed, rolling my eyes. He laughed then stepped away from the car. "Did you find the problem?" I asked.

"No. I can't seem to find the source of the problem." He turned the flashlight off and placed his phone back in his pocket.

I frowned. "What are we going to do now? Please don't tell me we're going to walk. We all know what happens to people when they walk at night in the middle of nowhere!" I exclaimed.

"We have no other choice, Ariel. Unless you want to stay here for the rest of the night."

"I'd rather stay in the car and lock the doors. That's the smartest thing," I claimed, pointing at the car. Troy rolled his eyes.

"You've been watching too many horror movies," he said.

"I'm just being smart!" I stated. Troy placed a hand on my shoulder.

"Ariel. We have to find someone to take us home. If we stay in the car till morning, then mom will go crazy. The car isn't moving anywhere," he explained. "Don't worry. No one will hurt you," he mused. "If someone does try to, then you have those to defend yourself. I'll take one and you take the other." He pointed at my crutches.

I looked down at my crutches. I know that he was only kidding but maybe they can actually work. Might as well hold onto them for dear life.

I opened my mouth to say something when we saw a car driving our way. Troy immediately stepped forward and waved his hands in the air to make them stop. The car eventually started to slow down.

"I guess there's no need to walk anymore," Troy mumbled. "We got lucky."

I squinted my eyes as the car stopped in front of us. We immediately walked to the window. The window slid down to allow Troy to speak. As soon as Troy opened his mouth, he shut it after he looked inside the car.

I frowned. I stepped to his side, then looked into the car. My eyes widened when I saw who it was.

Rex.

CHAPTER TWENTY-SIX

"Rex?" I said as Rex looked at us. His eyes widened.

"Ariel? What are the both of you doing here? Did your car break down?" Rex asked, glancing at the car parked on the side of the road. I nodded, glancing at a stiff Troy who was eyeing Rex with caution.

"Yes. It broke down while we were on the way home," I said.

"I was already driving to your place." Rex unlocked the doors as he looked at Troy. "Hop on. You'll come back for the car first thing tomorrow morning."

I smiled at him and opened the door to the passenger seat. I glanced at Troy who stood in his place. "Come on, Troy. Get in," I muttered. His eyes remained on me for a second then slowly got in the backseat of the car as his eyes remained on Rex.

I got in and buckled up as Rex drove away. "Thank you, Rex. I don't know what would have happened if you didn't pass by."

Rex glanced at me with a toothy grin. "Don't thank me. Anyone would have done the same."

I glanced at Troy from the mirror. He was so silent. Our eyes met, making him shift in his seat as he glared at the back of Rex's head.

"Why were you driving toward my place?" Troy finally said, narrowing his eyes at Rex.

"My dad sent me some papers to give to your dad. Something that has to do with work," he answered. Rex grabbed onto a file of papers and raised it in the air. He placed them next to him. Troy nodded his head but kept his glare on Rex. I couldn't help but notice the attitude he had towards Rex. Did he ever do something to Troy?

I shrugged the feeling off. "So, how's school?" I looked back at Rex to ease the awkward tension in the air. Rex glanced at me, shrugging his shoulders.

"It's fine. It's quite boring. I'm counting the days for graduation."

"Tell me about it," I said.

"Where were you both coming from?" Rex questioned, raising a brow.

"Why do you want to know?" Troy asked. My eyes widened at his attitude. I gave him a glare, urging him to behave. Rex looked back at Troy.

"Just curious," he replied.

"We were at the hospital," I said. Rex looked concerned.

"Hospital? Are you okay? Did something happen?" he asked. I saw Troy roll his eyes.

"Everything's alright. I just had an appointment for my leg." I pointed down at my leg. Rex glanced at my leg then went back to concentrating on the dark road.

"Oh. How is it? Is it better?" Rex asked.

"Yes," I answered. "The doctor said it's almost healed. Needs about two weeks."

"That's good. You better be careful till then," he pointed out. "If you need any help, don't hesitate to ask."

"She's capable of taking care of herself," Troy blurted. My eyes widened at his behavior but Rex only looked amused.

"I know. I'm just offering my help whenever you need it." He looked at me.

"Thank you, Rex. I won't hesitate if I ever need something," I said.

Rex's smile reached his ears. I glanced back at Troy. Troy looked like this was the last place he wanted to be in. He rolled his eyes out of annoyance every time Rex spoke. I only decided to brush off his attitude. I guess Troy didn't like Rex for some kind of reason.

"So, how about we go to Disneyland after you take off your cast? Are you still up for it?" Rex suggested, raising a brow at me. I remembered our agreement a month ago. I have completely forgotten about that.

"Yes. Of course I am," I said estatically. "I've always wanted to go there so I won't let this opportunity slip by." This was always something on my bucket list, and the child in me wanted to go badly.

"That's great! I was a little worried that you would change your mind." He chuckled, scratching the back of his neck.

"No. I just kind of forgot about it since it's been more than a month, but I'd love to go," I said.

"Then as soon as your leg heals, I'll take you," he exclaimed.

"Sounds nice," I giggled. I glanced at Troy from the mirror who had his arms crossed. He was staring at me with an intense expression. I immediately looked away and stared back at Rex who seemed to be in a happier mood.

Rex and I chatted on the way back while Troy remained silent. Not too long after that, Rex was parking in front of the house. Troy immediately got out of the car as if staying in there was only bothering and suffocating him. I hopped out, the cold wind hitting my skin and blowing my hair off my shoulders.

Rex got out the car with the file in his hands. He soon walked to my side. "Come on, let's go inside. It's pretty cold out here," I said. Troy didn't wait for another second and walked off, leaving Rex and I standing alone.

I stared at his retreating body with a frown on my face. I snapped out of my gaze as Rex placed a hand on my back. We saw Rose talking with Troy, probably explaining why we were late. Rose looked back at us with conern.

She placed a hand on my shoulder. "Oh, honey. Are you okay?"I was wondering why you both were late. Were you scared?"

I offered her a small smile. "Don't worry, Rose. I'm fine. I had Troy with me . . ." —Troy looked at me—". . . and thankfully, Rex found us on the way here."

Rose looked at Rex, smiling at him. "Thank you, Rex. I appreciate your kindness," she gushed, placing her hand on his shoulder.

"It's nothing, Mrs. Rose. I actually came here to give this to Mr. Damon," he stated, showing her the files. "I have to get going, but I'd appreciate it if you handed this to him."

Rose took the file from him. "I'll give it to him, but how about you stay for dinner?" Rose said. Rex looked quite hesitant but Rose looked persistent. "I was just about to put dinner on the table. Stay and eat with us. It will only take a short time."

Rex nodded, smiling at her. "Okay, why not."

"Great." Rose clapped her hands, stepping aside. "Go to the dining room. The food won't take long." Rose shooed us with her hands towards the kitchen. Rex and I started walking towards the dining room when I noticed Troy walking the opposite direction.

"Troy?" I called out. He stopped and looked back at me with a raised brow. "Where are you going? Aren't you going to eat with us?" I asked as Troy stared at me.

He placed his hands in his pockets. "You go eat. I lost my appetite."

He turned around and walked away.

CHAPTER TWENTY-SEVEN

"Come in," I yelled. I grabbed my crutches and took one last look in the mirror. Troy was waiting for me by the bedroom door.

"Are you ready? We have to get going before we're late for class," Troy said. I threw my bag over my shoulders and walked towards him.

"Yes. Let me just go call Ozan," I said, passing him by. I frowned at his blank expression, but proceeded to walk to Ozan's room. I felt a sinking feeling in my stomach as I walked out.

I couldn't help but feel quite disappointed with his behavior. It all started when Rex came and helped us when the car broke down. Troy didn't change dramatically, as he was never really jolly towards me in the first place.

However, I could still see that he's acting different. The little things caught my attention. He avoided eye contact at all times. He seemed more distant. It bothered the heck out of me. I couldn't help but feel hurt as he avoided me.

I eventually knocked on Ozan's door.

"Come in," he called out.

As I entered his room, Ozan grabbed his bag and looked at me. "Are you ready?" I asked with a raised brow.

"Yeah. Let's go," he replied.

We walked out the house and waved Rose. Ozan held my shoulder as we hopped in the backseat of Troy's car.

Troy stood silent the whole ride. I wasn't surprised. What took me off guard was that Ozan was silent too. He was just looking out the window the whole time. I narrowed my eyes at him. He must've felt my gaze.

"Are you okay?" I asked. He nodded.

"Yes, I am. I'm just thinking about something," Ozan answered.

I raised a brow at him. "What were you thinking about?" He stared at me through the mirror then placing his attention back on the road.

Ozan frowned, scratching the back of his neck. "Uh . . ." He muttered under his breath, averting his gaze away from my eyes. "Well, I wanted to . . . Forget it. It's nothing important."

"Are you sure?"

Ozan smiled at me. "Yeah, I'm sure," he murmured.

I bit the inside of my cheek. Ozan averted his eyes away from mine. I forced myself not to ask any further.

I met Troy's eyes once again. The whole ride was just tensed.

*　　*　　*

After classes, I went towards the cafeteria to meet up with Ozan. As usual, I avoided the large crowds and walked slowly. I was about to open the cafeteria doors when I caught something from the corner of my eye. It was Randa seating under the same spot I sat with her two weeks ago.

Ever since she and Troy broke up, I haven't seen her a lot. I've only seen her a couple of times and when I'd try to approach her, she'd disappear.

I took slow steps towards her. She looked up at me, her eyes wide as I took her off guard.

"Hi, Ariel." She gave me a smile as I sat next to her.

200

"Hi, Randa. Are you okay? I haven't seen you a lot lately," I said. Her soft smile turned into a sad one. She looked away from me for a couple of seconds then met my eyes once again.

"I'm fine. Thank you for asking, Ariel," Randa whispered. "It's hard, but I'm getting used to it. I guess it will be easier once I'm gone."

"Once you're gone? What do you mean by that?"

"I'm moving away," she answered, her eyes filled with sadness. "My dad has a new work in Philadelphia. So we're moving there. I think what Troy did was bound to happen. Maybe it was for the best. Hopefully, I'll move on and find someone better."

My eyes widened. I stared at her with sad eyes, placing my hand on her shoulder. I hoped she'd do what I couldn't do, and that was to move on.

"When are you moving?" I asked.

"Tomorrow morning," Randa replied.

"Oh," I murmured. "That's so soon."

"Yeah. The sooner I get out of here, the better," she said. I could hear the pain in her voice.

"I wish the best for you, Randa. And I'll miss you," I said. She gave me a wide smile.

"I'll miss you too. Thank you for being such a good friend, Ariel. I appreciate it." She pulled me into a hug. I hugged her back.

We eventually pulled away from the hug as I smiled at her. "Don't thank me, Randa. If you ever need someone to talk to, call me. Hopefully, you'll be happier there."

"I will. And I hope so too."

Heartbreaks are painful, and I know that very well. Maybe this was a new start for her. A new start that I wasn't able to do.

*　　*　　*

Another week has passed. It felt like a month to me. I was really eager for the week to end so I could finally take my cast off.

It has been around my leg for what felt like a whole year. It bothered me and I really missed walking without crutches.

Yesterday, I went with Ozan to take off the cast. I was so relieved once it was finally off my leg. It felt as if my leg was free from it. I made a mental note to never fall down the stairs ever again so I wouldn't end up like that.

Stairs. Bad. Broken leg. Bad. Going to a party with Troy and ending up falling down the stairs and breaking my leg. Worse. Yeah. I drilled that in my head. I have to be more careful next time. I have to tame the clumsy child in me.

I was finally free to walk normally for the first time after a month and a half. I couldn't be happier.

I was currently sitting in my English class, the class I shared with Troy. Troy sat a couple of seats in front of me, giving me a perfect view of his back side. I couldn't stop myself from glancing at him every now and then.

I was drifting off, something I usually did when I was too bored or not in the mood to concentrate on the teacher.

"Okay, everyone. Listen up!" The teacher exclaimed as he clapped his hands.

Well that snapped me out.

"I have good news and bad news. Which one would you like to hear first?" The teacher raised a brow.

"The good news!" a good amount of students answered.

My English teacher looked around the class as he cleared his throat.

"Okay, then," he mumbled. "As I informed you in the beginning of the school year, we have a senior trip to Hawaii about three weeks from now. For those who are planning to go, you'll have to hand in the fee a week before the trip," he explained. Many students started to grin and whisper to each other. They were excited. "I'll hand out the permission slips the week before but for now, this contains more information about the trip. I already let everyone know about the fee for the trip at the beginning of the

202

year as a heads up for anyone willing to save up. It's also mentioned in the paper. For those who are going, I'd say to get the money ready since it costs a lot." He made two students pass out the papers.

The class was starting to get noisy. "Calm down, everybody! You still didn't hear the bad news," oour teacher blurted.

Almost everyone in the class started groaning. I could've sworn I saw a smirk crawling onto the teacher's face. Not a surprise. Teachers took satisfaction from our misery.

"Please, don't tell us you're going to make us read Shakespeare again!" a boy yelled from the back of the class. This made some students laugh.

"No, not that." The techer shook his head. "As you all know. The finals are coming. You will have a project to do within this week which will take up 50% of your final grade. Meaning, if you fail the project, you fail your finals."

Everyone was obviously disappointed. The teacher shook his head again as he distributed another set of papers. Most of us glared at it like it had murdered someone.

"Oh, stop your whining!"—He waved his hand in the air—"You're lucky I made it very easy for you. The papers you all have right now in front of you will tell you exactly what you need to do."

I scanned the paper. "You need a partner to work with. I feel nice enough to let you choose your own," he said with a smug smile. The bell rang and I frowned, thinking of who to work with. Unfortunately, Ozan was not with me in this class so I had limited options.

Immediately, many people started to find their partners. I glanced at Troy to see a couple of girls surrounding him. Guess he already had many options for partners.

"Remember. It's due next week. This coming Monday! "You're all excused," the teacher said as soon as the students got up from the seats to leave. I grabbed my bag and walked out the class,

203

not sparing another glance at Troy as he was too busy talking with a group of girls.

I let out a sigh as I walked towards my next class. I wonder who can I work with for the project? I then stopped the moment I heard someone calling my name.

"Ariel." Troy caught up with me. "Do you want to be my partner?" he asked, placing his hands in his pockets. My eyes widened.

"You want me to be your partner?"

"Yes."

"Why me? Why didn't you pick those girls back there?" I asked. He started to smirk and leaned his head towards mine.

"Are you jealous that those girls wanted to work with me, Ariel?" He raised a brow.

"What? No!" I was just asking. You seemed pretty occupied."

Troy let out a chuckle. "No. I declined their offers. I would rather work with you," he stated.

My heart skipped a beat. "Yeah. Sure. I'll be your partner. It will be easier anyway since we live in one house." I said that but I know in my heart that this wasn't the case.

Troy nodded. "Okay. Good."

Since Troy and I shared our last period, we started making our way towards the class. All the sudden, someone else called up on me. I turned around to see Rex jogging towards me.

"Ariel." He waved his hand. Troy stopped and turn towards him. Rex was catching his breath before looking at me with a smile. "Hey. How are you?"

"Hi, Rex. I'm good," I said.

"I can tell. You finally removed your cast." He pointed at my leg.

"Yeah. I finally did." I chuckled, ignoring the glare Troy sent him.

Rex scratched the back of his neck. "I don't want to make you late for your class, but I was wondering since your leg healed. Do you want to go to Disneyland this Saturday? " he asked, smiling at me.

"I would—"

"She can't," Troy stated. My eyes widened. Rex and I looked at him doubtfully. "We're busy this week. We have a project to deal with."

Rex frowned. "Oh," he muttered.

I offered Rex a smile. "I'm sure Troy and I could finish the project before Saturday," I said, glancing at Troy who had a frown on his face.

I looked back at Rex. "I'd love to go."

CHAPTER TWENTY-EIGHT

I rolled my eyes at Troy. He's been trying to balance the pencil on the tip of his nose. He looks like a complete fool at the moment. I held the urge to laugh as I crossed my arms under my chest. I had to take my eyes off my book.

"Troy?"

"Yes, babe?" Troy didn't even spare me a single glance. He was trying his ultimate best to keep the pencil balanced as if the world relied on it.

"What are you doing?" I asked.

A small grin slowly made its way on his lips. Eventually, the pencil fell right on his lap. He let out a groan and picked it up, looking back at me with apologetic eyes. "I was trying to balance a pencil on my nose. It's harder than it looks."

I shook my head as I leaned against the chair. "I can see that, Troy, but I'm wondering why you're doing that when we're supposed to be doing this." I pointed at the opened book that was laying on my desk.

Troy sulked in his chair before letting out a huff. "I'm too bored. We've been studying for like two hours," he whined, crossing his arms across his chest.

I narrowed my eyes at him, holding back the urge to grin.

"Two hours, Troy? We've only started ten minutes ago."

"Ten minutes?" he exclaimed, making me nod.

"Yes. Only ten minutes. We've barely even opened the third page."

"I swear, it feels like hours to me," he groaned, glaring at the book. "Can you remind me why we're even studying in the first place?" Troy huffed out.

I swear, at times I mistake him for a child.

"Finals. Because of finals. They're only two weeks away."

He stood silent for a moment to process what I just told him about. A smirk made its way on his face.

"What?" I murmured. "What's with the smirk?"

Troy scooted his chair closer to mine. "You know . . ."— his eyes lowered to my lips—"We could finish many things in two weeks. Instead, why don't we do something else?"

My eyes were wide, but I forced myself not to fall for his tricks and move my head away from him.

"No!" I exclaimed, as I placed the book in front of him. "Studying comes first."

His shoulders sagged as he looked at the book. He started to pout and I couldn't help but chuckle.

Troy frowned. "What's so funny?"

"I swear, you look like someone who dropped your ice cream. There's no need for that long face."

"Okay, okay . . ." he muttered, scooting himself closer to me. "Do you enjoy seeing me suffer?" he asked, making me roll my eyes. *Drama queen.*

"Kinda." I'm really enjoying his dramatic behavior.

He crossed his arms. "Okay. I'll give you something to laugh about."

My smile dropped. "Wha—"

I squealed as Troy attacked me with his fingers. Troy smiled goofily as he tickled my sides.

"T—Troy! Please stop!" I gasped but I was also laughing.

"Sorry, my little mermaid. You wanted something to laugh about? I'll give you something to laugh about."

Memories of the days when Troy and I were so close flooded in my head. Troy and I were young, foolish and most of all, happy. They hit me like cold water.

I couldn't help but replay them over and over again as I stared at Troy right in front of me. His eyes remained on the laptop screen as mine fixed on him. My heart raced at the thought of what we once had. Those pure and good times stung me. I looked away from him to ease the pain. I glanced back at Troy, but to meet his eyes this time.

"Are you okay?" he asked with a raised brow.

I snapped out of it. "Yes. I just spaced off," I muttered.

"Right. That habit of yours," he chuckled. "Anyway. Did you find anything?" Troy asked. I looked at my laptop, completely forgetting that it was there in the first place.

I shifted in my seat and cleared my throat. "No. I'm still looking," I muttered. "We have to finish this today," I stated, glancing at Troy who was looking at me with a raised brow.

"What's with the rush? We still have two days."

"I'm going to Disneyland tomorrow Troy," I stated. "Besides, we're almost done. We just need to search for a few more things then that's it. I want to be fully done so I won't have to worry about it tomorrow."

"Oh, right. You have a date tomorrow," he muttered as he leaned against the chair with crossed arms.

It was my turn to frown. "It's not a date," I exclaimed. "We're just friends hanging out with each other. That's it. Besides, I've never been to Disneyland before and I'm dying to go."

Troy snickered. "Sure," he muttered. "You say yes to a guy you don't even know that randomly asks you out to Disneyland. Right. Real smart, Ariel."

My frown deepened. I placed my laptop on my desk, looking at him confusingly. "What so bad about it? Why don't you like Rex? What did he ever do to you?" he asked.

Troy looked at his laptop, completely ignoring my eyes as the research I was looking for on my laptop was long forgotten.

We were moving perfectly fine. Troy was working on his laptop while I searched for the information on mine. We were almost done. We only needed a couple of things to look for on the internet, then that was it.

Troy met my eyes coldly, sending shivers down my back. "What's wrong, Troy?" I asked.

He let out a huff. He suddenly grabbed onto his laptop which got me confused.

"Nothing's wrong," he said. "Do whatever the hell you want, Ariel. I don't give a f*ck."

I did not expect him to burst out like that. Troy marched towards my bedroom door. "Where are you going? What about the project?" I asked loudly.

Troy opened the door. "I'll finish it. You don't worry about it. You worry about tomorrow."

He slammed my door, leaving me shocked as ever. There was one thing I was so sure of. Troy was not enjoying the fact that I was going to Disneyland with Rex tomorrow.

The day passed. It was finally time for the Disneyland trip! I looked down at my phone when I heard a ring. A small smile appeared on my face.

You ready? I'll be at your place in ten minutes.
~ Rex

To say that I was excited was an understatement. I was finally going to check something off my bucket list. I know I might seem like exaggerating, but it was something that I truly looked forward to.

209

I knew that Troy was bothered that I was going with Rex. I didn't know if it was just because he didn't like him, or if it was because of another reason,. It could also be that he was actually concerned for me. Nonetheless I was still going. In the end, I'm not doing anything wrong. Rex and I are friends and I don't see anything wrong in that.

I bit the inside of my cheek when I remembered yesterday. I debated with myself whether I should go see Troy or not before I leave. I sucked in a breath and shook my head. Maybe after I came back.

I grabbed my purse and looked at the mirror one more time before I walked out my room. I walked towards the kitchen to grab a glass of water before Rex arrived.

I saw Rose finishing off with the dishes. She turned towards me, smiling. "Ariel? Well, don't you look pretty today."

I giggled. "Thank you, Rose," I said, filling a cup with water before drinking it.

"Are you going somewhere?" she asked, raising a brow.

I nodded. "Yes. Rex offered to take me to Disneyland since I've never been there," I replied, placing the cup on the counter. Rose stood silent for a moment, soon smiling softly at me. She then placed a hand on my arm.

"Oh. Well, I hope you have fun," Rose said.

"She's not going anywhere," Troy blurted out of nowhere. Our heads snapped towards him.

"What do you mean? I am going," I said.

"No." Troy shook his head. "We have a project to deal with."

I narrowed my eyes at him. "What do you mean by that? We finished it yesterday."

Troy shook his head once again, looking at me seriously. I could've sworn I saw a look of satisfaction flash through him.

"About that," he muttered, stepping closer to me. "Everything was deleted. We have to start all over."

210

CHAPTER TWENTY-NINE

I walked down the hallway through the crowed area as lunch finally started. I walked towards our usual spot in the cafeteria, completely ignoring someone else's eyes.

I sat down next to Ozan.

"Ariel," he greeted, giving me a side hug.

"Hey. How were your classes?" I asked, taking a fry from his tray and popping it into my mouth.

Even though I had Ozan in most of my classes in the beginning of the year, they eventually changed his schedule so I saw him less. It bothered me. I only had him in two classes, and we barely even spoke in those two classes as his desk was all across the room.

"They're fine," he sighed out, shrugging his shoulders. "Tiring," he added. "What about yours?"

I have an urge to look at Troy from across the cafeteria, but held myself back. I thought of what happened over the weekend, which made me frown.

"They're okay," I muttered, shrugging my shoulders. "I have a project to present in a couple of classes and I'm a little nervous," I said, rubbing my arm.

Ozan smiled. "Why are you worried?" he asked, raising a brow. "You were able to finish it yesterday. There's nothing for you to worry about."

I sucked in a breath. I met Troy's hard dark eyes for a couple of seconds then looked away. I told myself to not do that again. "I'm nervous that this won't turn out good as the previous one," I confessed, a frown taking over my features.

"It will," Ozan assured me. "You'll get a good grade. I know it."

I smiled softly at him, happy that he was trying his best to comfort me. "I hope so," I said softly.

Ozan glanced towards Troy. His smile was replaced with a frown. He then looked back at me, clearing his throat.

"Are you angry at Troy?" he asked, shifting in his seat.

My frowned deepened. I remained silent for a couple of seconds. "Yes. I'm upset that he put my grade on the line. What he did was selfish," I answered.

Ozan slowly nodded his head. "What if it was all deleted by accident? How do you know he did that on purpose?"

I bit the inside of my cheek and crossed my arms as I recalled the last two days of stress that I had to endure. Cramming a week-long project into only two days wasn't something that I wished to repeat at all.

"He deleted it on purpose," I said without a single doubt. "How can a project get accidentally deleted from the laptop and from the pen drive? It can't be a mere coincidence!"

Ozan nodded his head, popping a fry into his mouth as he though about it. "You're right," Ozan admitted, nodding. "What an asshole. But why would he do that? It's his grade too."

I shut my mouth, deciding in not telling him about the Disneyland issue. I didn't feel like explaining to him about it because for the most part, I had no idea on why he did that too.

I knew he didn't like Rex and he didn't want me to go with him, but that was no excuse to ruin my grade and my opportunity of a trip I always wanted to go to.

I was upset at him for two reasons. One, because he put my grade on the line, and two, because I missed out an a trip to Disneyland.

Just by the thought of those two days made me feel terrible.

*   *   *

My eyes were glued to the screen. I tried my best to concentrate on what was in front of me, and not on the sulking person that sat next to me. I kept my eyes off him to show my displeasure and disappointment. Troy searching the topics for the second time as I typed away.

Troy would try to make a conversation every now and then, but I'd only ignore him. What he did yesterday made me furious. I had to apologize to Rex and tell him that I couldn't come because of what Troy did. It was very upsetting and embarrassing at the same time.

I missed out on an opportunity to go on a one of a kind trip. Troy had to ruin that. No only that, but he messed with my grades. Now we had to cram the work that took one whole week finish into two days. I have to finish this project before tomorrow.

I was angry at him. I didn't remember when the last time was that I got this angry at him. I've reached the point of giving him the silent treatment.

Ever since yesterday, Troy and I have been working nonstop to get this done. For the whole time, I avoided eye contact and making a conversation with him. However, I could kind of tell that this was actually bothering him in a way.

He didn't even try to make an excuse on why he did that. He admitted himself that he deleted it both from the laptop and from the pen drive. He didn't try to justify his actions. That's what bothered me the most. He had no excuse. Thankfully, we were almost done.

213

I yawned but I forced myself to continue typing. As usual, I felt Troy's eyes on me. "If you're tired, go sleep. I'll finish it off," he said after a long moment of tensed silence.

I finally narrowed my eyes at him. "The last time you said that, I ended up with a canceled trip and a deleted project." I turned back to the screen.

I heard him suck in a breath. "Ariel," Troy breathed out, his voice in a low tone. "Don't do this."

I scoffed loudly, shaking my head. "What am I doing, Troy?" I asked, looking back at him. "All I'm trying to do is finish something you couldn't finish." I averted my gaze away from him.

"I'm sorry," he let out after a moment of silence. "I'm sorry for doing that. I didn't want you to go. I don't trust this Rex guy."

I held back another scoff which threatened to come out. I glanced back at him, shaking my head. "Since when do you care about me, Troy?" I questioned, standing up. "The last time I checked, you didn't give a single f*ck of what I did."

His frown deepened as he looked down the floor. Troy's fist clenched tightly.

"I—I . . ." He shook his head in frustration.

"Save it," I mumbled as I grabbed my laptop. "I don't want to hear anything." I turned around and walked towards his bedroom door.

"Ariel," he called out. I turned to him to see him staring at me with dark eyes. "Where are you going? We still didn't finish."

"I'm going to finish everything off this time! Don't worry. I won't put your grade on the line." I slammed the door and walked away, leaving a shocked Troy standing behind. I didn't care if what he did was justifiable or not. I was so upset to the point of ignoring him for days.

*   *   *

214

Troy and I stood in front of the class. We finally finished presenting our project to the class. I stood stiff as Troy stood so close to me. I didn't make eye contact with him till now. I watched my English teacher nervously as he scanned our project. He then stood up. "Good job, Ariel and Troy. You did good. You can now take your seats."

I let out a relieved sigh, thanking God that it didn't go bad. I took out the pen drive and inserted it in my pocket. I then rushed towards my seat.

Troy sat down, glancing at me one more time before sitting in front of me. The English teacher soon called for someone else to go up and present their project. I'm just relieved that this was finally over. For the whole class I was spacing off, not paying attention to the others.

As soon as the bell rung, I grabbed my bag and walked out the class with the group of students. I rushed so I wouldn't have to interact with Troy. Out of nowhere, someone placed their hand on my shoulder. When I turned around, I met Troy's eyes.

"Ariel."

I shrugged his hand off my shoulder. "What?"

"Please, don't do this," he whispered, looking at me with serious eyes. "The project was well and the teacher like it. It's all over. Stop being angry at me."

I scoffed at him. "I don't have time to talk with you, Troy," I said, stepping away. "I have a class to get to." I turned away and walked off.

"F*ck." I heard him say from behind me. I completely ignored him but was caught off guard when he grabbed my hand tightly and pulled me away from the crowd. My eyes went wide as I tried to release my hand from his tight grip.

"What the heck, Troy? Let go of me!"

He shook his head and opened a door to what looked like a janitor's closet. He pushed me inside the dim, small room then closed the door. My mouth hung open. "What the hell?" I yelled as

215

I tried to exit. Troy stood in front of me, not letting me get to the door. "What are you doing? I'm going to to be late for class!"

"F*ck your class," he spoke out, anger present in his tone. "I'm not going to let you out until you stop with this f*cking silent treatment that's going to make me insane."

My mouth hung open, shocked from his words. I then cleared my throat, shaking my head. "I'm not doing anything," I spoke, meeting his dark eyes that stared down at me intensely. "You were the one that started it. Now let me out of here." I took a step forward.

"F*ck!" he said to himself, running a hand through his hair. He blocked my path, making me collide to his chest. "I'm sorry, okay? I'm sorry for doing what I did. Just please, stop acting as if I don't exist."

"Sorry won't work, Troy. Because of you, I had to restart the project and miss out on a trip," I said.

"But you heard the teacher. We did good. You shouldn't worry about the project anymore," Troy huffed out. "I'm sorry for doing that. I'll keep apologizing, Ariel. I just didn't want you to go with him. As I said, I don't trust that guy."

"But—"

"And I do care. I worry about you and I do give a f*ck," he admitted. "Just stop with this. It's driving me crazy."

I stared at him, trying to comprehend his words. I averted my gaze away from him. I bite my lip. I haven't seen Troy making this face in a long time. A look begging me to forgive him. I remained silent for a couple of seconds.

"But—"

"If you're angry because you weren't able to go to Disneyland then I'll take you," Troy suggested.

"What?"

Troy sucked in a breath. "I said I'll take you. This Saturday," he added.

216

I bit my lip, looking up at him with wide eyes. "You'll take me?" My mind can't process his words.

"Yes, Ariel," he whispered, stepping closer to me. "I'll take you to Disneyland. Just forgive me."

CHAPTER THIRTY

I glanced at my appearance through the mirror one more time, offering myself a satisfied smile. I ran a hand through my long wavy hair and sucked in a breath as I walked towards my bedroom door. I glanced in my bag to make sure everything was with me.

To say that I was nervous was an understatement. I was biting my nails for the whole night. Going to Disneyland was something big for me, something that I dreamt about ever since I was a small girl. Going with Troy however was a completely different thing. Never have I ever thought that Troy and I would go to a place like that together.

Nervousness wasn't the only emotion I was feeling. Excitement has been eating me up as well. Troy sent me a text message an hour ago saying to get ready.

I tried to hide my smile as I thought about him. What he did last week really upset me, but after I saw that he was willing to make it up for me, I forgave him. Besides, we both got a good grade in our project so I saw no reason to continue giving him the silent treatment.

I was about to walk down the stairs when I heard someone call my name from behind me.

"Ariel." I turned around to see Ozan walking towards me, smiling nervously at me as he scratched the back of his neck.

"Hey," I greeted, smiling warmly up at him.

"Are you going somewhere?" Ozan asked, running his eyes over my appearance. I glanced to the floor. I looked back at him with a smile.

"Yes," I answered. "Remember I told you last week that Troy promised to take me to Disneyland?"

His smile dropped. "Oh," he murmured, rubbing his arm. "So you're going on a date with him to Disneyland?"

My eyes widened. "It's not a date," I stated. "He just wanted to make up for what he did. That's all."

His lips went into a thin line. He soon made a small smile. "That's good," he muttered to himself. "I actually wanted to ask you something important."

"What is it?"

Ozan sucked a breath, shaking his head. "I can't ask you now. It's not the right time," he claimed, scratching the back of his neck nervously which only made me more curious. "Maybe after you come back."

"Okay, sure. When I come back you'll ask me," I told him.

Ozan nodded, smiling softly at me. "Okay," he agreed.

"I better get going," I pointed out. With one last smile, I walked down the stairs, wondering what he wanted to ask me. I guess I'll find out once I come home.

I took out my phone to see a text from Troy, which made me smile.

I'm outside. I'll be waiting in the car.
~ Troy

I put my phone back in my bag then made my way outside the house. I saw Troy's sitting inside the car. I ran a hand through my hair and cleared my throat as I hopped in the passenger seat. Troy turned to look at me.

"Hi," I greeted softly, putting on my seatbelt.

Troy started the car. "Are you ready?" he asked.

219

I smiled. "Yes," I answered as neutral as possible. I didn't want to show him my excitement. "Is Disneyland far away from here?" I questioned.

Troy shook his head. "No, only twenty minutes from here," he answered, keeping his eyes on the road. "It will be your first time, right?" Troy asked, glancing at me.

"Yeah," I replied. "What about you? Have you ever been to Disneyland?" I wondered.

Troy shook his head. "No, this is my first time too," he answered, which only surprised me.

"Really? When you live so near?" I asked him.

He chuckled lightly. "I didn't really see the point in going there. You're the only reason why I'm going," he stated. I smiled at him, feeling my cheeks heat up with his words.

Troy stared at me for a second then turned his attention back to the road as he cleared his throat. "Oh, and Ariel?" he murmured.

"Yeah?"

"I should probably tell you something," he said lowly.

"What is it?"

Troy remained silent for a moment. I could tell that he wasn't sure. He then shook his head. "Never mind. I'll tell you later," he finally spoke out.

I furrowed my brows at him. "You sure?" I asked, raising a brow.

Troy nodded. "Yeah. Don't worry about it," he assured.

"Okay."

We remained silent in the car. I laid my head against my seat, enjoying the view. Before I knew it, Troy was parking the car. He turned to look at me, offering me a crooked smile.

"Come on. Let's go." He opened the door. I smiled and got out of the car. "Let's go buy the tickets," Troy said. I nodded. We walked side by side towards the gate. "I'll go get the tickets.

You wait here," he said before walking away. I stood at my spot, looking at my surroundings in astonishment.

After a few moments, Troy came back. "You ready?"

I smiled at him and nodded.

Ready as I'll ever be.

A couple of hours passed and I was having a blast.

"I'm not going back in there!" Troy exclaimed. I let out a chuckle as we exited the "Pirates of the Caribbean" ride.

"Don't tell me you were scared?" I teased, raising a brow at him. Troy immediately shook his head.

"I wasn't scared. It's just those moving people creeped me out," he argued.

"They're robots." I laughed out. He shrugged his shoulders.

"They're still creepy," he muttered under his breath.

We went on simple rides and had some walks around the area. I had a really good time. I felt like I was a kid again. I could also tell that Troy was having a good time, even though he was trying to show me that it was no big deal.

We continued to walk through the crowd of people. Troy soon glanced at something. "Stay right here. I'll be right back," he ordered, taking a couple of steps back. I furrowed my brows but I did what he said and stayed put.

After a while, I saw Troy walking towards me, but this time, with something in his hand. I couldn't tell what they were, but soon smiled as he stood in front of me, handing me cotton candy.

"Here. I figured that you'd be hungry," he said.

"I am." I took a piece and popped it in my mouth. "Thank you."

Troy only nodded as we walked towards a bench. I slowly ate my cotton candy. He stared into my eyes as if he was thinking about something.

I gulped, feeling my cheeks heat up. "Cotten candy?" I offered. He glanced at it and chuckled lightly but he still took a piece.

"Thanks," he said lowly. I smiled softly at him.

"Are you having fun?" I asked. Troy looked hesitant, but eventually nodded.

"Yes. I haven't been this amused in a while. What about you?" Troy asked.

"I'm having fun. I'm happy too. I'm also glad you came with me," I said. Troy's eyes widened. "If you asked me who I'd rather come with, you or Rex. I'd pick you."

Troy looked me straight in the eyes. I was worried if what I had said wasn't a good thing. However, all those thoughts were thrown out of my head the moment I saw his lips twitch into a smile. Troy looked away to hide his face from mine. He then cleared his throat, looking back at me with soft features.

"I'm glad I came with you too. It's nice having you around," Troy said, making me grin.

I could've sworn that I heard my own heartbeats. His words made me feel something, something that I was trying to hold in for a long time. I sucked in a breath and looked away to tame my heart. After a moment, I turned back at him to see him looking at me intensely. I slowly let out a chuckle. Troy raised a brow at me, a frown taking over his lips.

"What's so funny?" he said. I pointed to his head, completely forgetting that I made him wear the Mickey Mouse ears which I couldn't help find amusing. He looked so serious, but with those ears, it made him look like a kid.

Troy touched the ears. "I completely forgot about these," he muttered, taking them off.

"No," I whined. "Keep them on. You look cute with them."

"No. I look like an idiot with them on," Troy said. I slightly pouted, which made Troy roll his eyes. "Here," he muttered, putting on the Mickey Mouse ears on my head. "It looks cuter on you."

I felt my cheeks blush as his face lowered near mine. I caught him glancing at my lips but he immediately cleared his throat and backed his head away. I hid my disappointment.

"So, what's the next ride you want to go on?" Troy said.

I looked around the place before landing on a roller coaster. My eyes widened and I immediately pointed at it. "That." So far we haven't been on a roller coaster with really high twirls. "Let's go on that."

Troy's eyes widened. "You want to go on that?"

"Yes," I replied, pulling him along. "Come on. Let's go." Troy's eyes immediately glanced at our joined hands. He looked hesitant but Troy stood up to follow. I let go of his hand so I wouldn't embarrass myself further.

We waited in line for the roller coaster. I was thankful that the line wasn't that long. I glanced at Troy who was looking elsewhere except me.

Time flew by and we were finally buckled on the ride. We held onto the metal handle that was in front of us as the ride started. I was smiling from ear to ear, excited like a little kid.

The ride was moving slowly at the beginning, nothing too exciting. It started to increase its speed and go upwards on the railroad tracks. I glanced at Troy to see him stiff. "Why are you frowning? Are you okay?" I asked.

"Ariel, about that thing that I was going to tell you in the car . . ."

"Yes? What were you going to tell me?" The ride soon came to a stop as soon as we were at a high point of the tracks.

"I'm afraid of roller coasters."

We immediately descended down the tracks in a rush, the wind hitting our faces. I let out a squeal, looking at Troy who had his eyes completely shut, his hands gripping tightly on the metal handle. His words took me off guard, but I immediately placed my hand on his, gripping it tightly in a comforting manner.

His eyes opened and stared at my hand on his, looking a bit relaxed.

For the whole ride I kept my hand on his to comfort him. After the ride came to a stop, we exited the ride and I breathed in, running a hand through my tangled hair. I looked up at Troy, seeing him look away in embarrassment. "What didn't you tell me?" I asked him. "We could've avoided that ride."

Troy shrugged his shoulders. "It's not important," he muttered, breathing in. "I just don't like rides that are extremely fast." I offered him a comforting smile, not asking further so I wouldn't embarrass him.

We continued to walk through the park. I soon noticed that it was getting dark. "What ride do you want to go on before we leave?" Troy asked.

"You pick one this time," I stated. "I've already picked enough."

Troy nodded his head. His eyes roamed our surroundings, eventually stopping at something from the distance before pointing at it. I followed to where he was pointing at, my eyes landing on a Ferris wheel. "How about that?"

"Sure," I agreed. "Let's go."

We waited in line for the Ferris Wheel. Not too long after, we were entering the small cabin. We sat down next to each other and we started to move up. I looked through the window.

"Do you remember the last time you've been on a Ferris wheel?" I smiled wistfully at him.

"No," he replied lowly. "I don't think I have ever been on one."

I glanced to the window as the Ferris Wheel took us higher. I looked back at him, not knowing if what I was going to say was good or not.

"You have. With me. Three years ago," I stated. His eyes widened.

"With you?" he muttered.

I nodded. "Yes," I replied softly. "We went to a carnival. And at the end, we went on a Ferris wheel." Troy's eyes looked at me, not moving away from mine. He sucked in a breath.

"Did we kiss at the top?" Troy blurted. My eyes widened at his question. I could still remember that moment.

"Yes," I whispered. Troy glanced at my lips. He looked at me with a serious expression plastered onto his face. I glanced out the window, realizing we were at the top, letting us see the amazing view of California and the stars that lit up the dark sky.

I looked back to met his eyes, seeing his face closer to mine. "Ariel," Troy murmured. "Can I ask you something?"

"Yes." I nodded.

"Can I kiss you right now?" he whispered. My eyes widened. I remained silent for a second but eventually nodded.

Troy cupped my cheeks with his hands then placed his lips on mine. I closed my eyes feel the moment. This is bringing back memories from the past. I gripped onto his shirt as I embrace the moment I was in. His lips were soft, kissing me so gently.

Our lips parted. We looked at each other for a moment. My eyes shut again as Troy went in for another kiss but harder this time. He gave me a couple of pecks before pulling away. I opened my eyes to see him staring at me deeply, his forehead laying on mine. At this point, our cabin has started to descend.

Troy ran a hand through his hair. "I couldn't resist," he admitted. "I couldn't resist you, Ariel."

"It's okay," I whispered.

Troy glanced back at my lips. "I was holding myself back for too long," he admitted. "I've wanted to kiss you for so long. You make me so confused."

225

My heart raced. I couldn't believe that Troy was admitting this to me. "You make me feel something that I have never felt," he whispered, closing his eyes in an attempt to calm himself down.

"I do?" I bit my lip.

"Yes," he answered. He opened his mouth to speak once again, but stopped when the door to our cabin opened. We snapped our heads towards the man who was standing by the door. Troy cleared his throat before standing up. I stood up and walked out the cabin in silence.

Troy placed a hand on my back. "Come on. Let's go home," he whispered. I nodded and walked towards the exit as I replayed what happened back there.

We made it to the car and entered it. I looked at Troy who was already staring at me.

"Ariel—"

"I love you, Troy. I never stopped loving you," I blurted. I needed to get that out. Those were words that I haven't said in three whole years. Troy's mouth hung open in surprise.

"Ariel—"

"For three whole years I never once stopped loving you, Troy. I never stopped missing you." My eyes were locked on his.

"Please—"

"I miss you, Troy. I miss you so much." I wasn't able to hold it back, not after what happened back there. I had to let it out my chest. It was a huge weight that was on my shoulder for so long. I can't lie to myself anymore.

"Ariel," he whispered. "I—I . . ." He sucked in a breath. "I'm sorry for causing you pain. I can't remember what we had, but you do make me feel things, things I haven't felt in three years."

I smiled softly at him. "I'm bringing back your old feelings," I said, grabbing onto his hand. He looked at our joined hands before looking back at me. "Maybe I can bring back your memories if you let me back in your life? Let me back in your life, Troy. Take me back," I said

Troy remained silent for what felt like an hour, staring at our joined hands. I waited for him to say something. After a moment, Troy slipped his hand out of mine.

"I can't, Ariel."

My heart sank. "Why?" I whispered.

"Because . . ." He avoided my eyes. "I just can't."

I closed my eyes, holding back the tears. "You admitted that you have feelings for me. What's holding you back?" I asked, hoping that my voice wouldn't crack.

"Forget what I said, Ariel," he said lowly, avoiding my eyes.

"What do you mean forget, Troy?" I questioned loudly. "Why don't you want me in your life? What are you scared from?"

"I said enough!" Troy snapped, turning his head over at me. "I can't remember you, Ariel," he spoke harshly. "I'll never remember! I can't."

A tear slipped down my cheek. "I don't need you to remember me, Troy," I argued softly. "I just want you. I'll take you the way you are." Troy looked at me with hard eyes, shaking his head from side to side.

"We can never work out, Ariel," he stated, turning his stare away from me. I felt my heart break, feeling myself suffocate from the inside.

"Why?" I asked.

Silence.

"Why, Troy?" I asked him again. Like the last time, no response. "For God's sake, Troy! Answer me!"

"F*ck, Ariel! It's because I can't remember you! And if I ever do, I have a 50 percent chance of forgetting you all over again!"

My eyes widened.

"Do you understand now? I'll never remember anything. I'll keep forgetting and forgetting! I don't want to be attached to anyone, and I don't want to form strong relationships with anyone. So when I forget, I won't have someone to forget about."

"But—"

"We can never work out, Ariel. I can never love you," he said as he looked me dead in the eye. "Give up on me."

CHAPTER THIRTY-ONE

I sat silently in my seat as the car traversed on the silent dark road. I kept my eyes out the window as Troy drove. It's like we were driving on a never ending road that doesn't take us anywhere.

We weren't far, yet I felt like I have in the car for hours, slowly suffocating me from the inside.

I felt speechless and shattered. I begged my heart to stop this pain and give me relief, but it was too difficult. A tear slipped out my eye and trickled down my cheek. It felt as if someone stabbed my heart in a torturous way. No, this pain hurts more than a stab. I would have thought I'd get used to it, but foolish me wasn't capable of doing so. I was an idiot—a huge idiot—for going after something that was no longer mine in the first place.

I was being greedy to actually think that Troy and I had a chance to go back to what we were. It was only a childish dream of mine that I had to eventually wake up from. This was reality. Troy was right. We could never work out. He could never love me.

Another tear slipped down my cheek at the thought of that. I shifted further towards the window. I didn't want Troy to see me like this. I didn't want to show him that his words affected me so much.

I wiped the tear, hoping that I wasn't making it obvious. I continued to forced the tears away. I can't cry in here, not in front of him. No matter how painful his words hit me, I have to hold it in, just for this moment.

I forced myself to take steady breaths. My mind continued to replay his words till I was begging for it to stop even just for one second, but it was surely impossible.

I can never love you. Give up on me.

I glanced up at Troy. His eyes were hard on the road. He looked unaffected with his words or from what happened today. It was as if nothing happened a moment ago. It was as if we weren't in Disneyland. It was as if we didn't kiss. He was unaffected, completely the opposite of me.

I must have been staring at him for quite a while because Troy eventually met my eyes. I immediately avert my eyes from him. I didn't want him to see my wet eyes.

I reminded my self of his words. He has a chance of losing his memories all over again. A huge chance. That alone made me let go of the little hope I was holding on to. It crushed me. I thought that we'd have a chance, that we'd be able to rebuild what we once had. However, if he continues to forget me, why should I even try?

Troy was right. We'll never work out.

It was difficult to believe, difficult for me to actually do, but maybe I have to do it to finally move on and forget. Maybe it was finally time to give up. Maybe this will be better for the both of us.

I opened my eyes as soon as the car abruptly came to a stop, jerking my body forward that would have flew out of my seat if my seatbelt wasn't secure. Troy gave me a hard look, a look which made my stomach turn.

I glanced around to see us parked in front of the house. I must have been spacing off for a while. Troy looked away from me, his grip on the wheel tight. "Go inside," he ordered, his voice low as ever.

"Are you coming?" I asked softly, avoiding his eyes as well.

230

"No." He didn't utter anything else. I got out of the car and walked away. I stopped in my tracks the moment I heard the car drive away, leaving me standing there in the cold night.

I didn't know what happened but the moment I got out the car, everything I was holding in bursted. I sobbed as my mind kept replaying his words.

I walked towards the main doors, placing a hand on my lips as I tried to muffle myself. I started to slide down against the wall with my head buried in my hands. I let out all the emotions I held in the car.

I didn't know how long I stayed like that but I soon tried to regain my strength. I wiped my cheek and stood back up. I told myself that the moment I'd enter the house, I wouldn't cry anymore. I have to be stronger than this, not this weak girl who's only solution was crying.

I sucked in a breath. The moment I enter this house will be the moment I try to move on. I need to do this, at least try to.

I was giving up.

I opened the door and walked in. Thankfully I didn't meet Rose. I didn't want her to worry about me. Anyone who would see me would surely know that something happened.

I dashed to my room and slammed the door shut. I walked towards my bathroom and looked at myself in the mirror. A sad girl looked back at me, looking through my soul. Her blue eyes looked dead from the crying.

I took a step towards the mirror. I hated how I felt. I hated how I looked miserable. This wasn't right. I have to change.

I turned on the sink and splashed water on my face. I looked back at the reflection and sighed, wiping my face with a towel. I continued to stare at myself, thinking about how I was going to move on.

I walked out the bathroom. I remembered I promised to talk with Ozan, so I headed to his room right now. Maybe I could occupy myself with something and take my head off of things.

I knew Ozan could make me feel better. He always does.

His door was slightly open. I stood in front of his door, ready to push it open when I heard him speak in a hushed tone from inside. My brows furrowed.

"Dad." Ozan huffed. "I'm fine. If I knew you were going to act like this I wouldn't have told you in the first place."

That made me more curious.

"No. Of course I'm not coming back," he stated. "I want to stay with Ariel. I don't want to leave her alone here. She needs me."

He paused for a moment. "I'm already on medication," Ozan spoke even louder, taking me off guard. "The doctor said my condition is stable for now. The tumor isn't big. I can continue normally."

My breath got stuck in my throat, not able to process his words.

"Dad," Ozan sighed out after a pause. "I'm okay. I promise you I'll start doing therapy but over here. I'm not leaving Ariel alone so I could get treatment. I'll do that right over here."

My eyes widened. I couldn't believe it. Ozan was sick?

Many unanswered questions ran in my head, making me feel weaker than before. I placed my hand on my mouth to prevent any gasp from escaping.

"No. No one knows," he whispered lowly. "I—I don't know when I'll tell her, but I will, eventually. I just need time." He paused for a couple of seconds. I could hear my rapid heartbeats. "Okay. I'll talk to you later," Ozan said. "Don't worry. I'm taking care of myself. Ever since I've been on the brain tumor medication that the doctor prescribed for me, I've been better than before."

Shock took over me. I can't breathe. I can't comprehend what I just heard. Ozan had a brain tumor? The same tumor that took away Troy from me?

I placed my hand on my chest. I felt sick. How could I not notice? How could I not notice his weary features from before?

There were numerous signs in front of me, yet I hadn't seen any of them.

"Okay. Bye, Dad."

Before I could even snap out of it, the door flew open, revealing a shocked Ozan in front of me. "A—Ariel? Were you standing there for long?"

My mouth hung open, unsure on what to say. I forced myself to plaster a normal expression on my face. "No. I came because you wanted to talk to me." I wasn't sure if my tone sounded normal.

I saw relief flash through his eyes. Ozan opened the door wide for me. "Yeah. Come in," Ozan said.

I sucked in a breath. Should I tell him that I heard him? Should I demand him to tell me everything?

I was hoping he wanted to talk about the thing I heard just now but I know that he wasn't planning on telling me any time soon, and that gave me a sinking feeling.

"Ozan—" before I could even continue, he cut me.

"Please, listen to me. Let me talk," he stated. "I need to tell you something."

I sucked in a shaky breath. I couldn't speak. I felt my words disappear into thin air.

Ozan took a step forward. "Ariel. I know we've been friends for so long. I know that you care about me, but there is this thing I have to tell you, something I should have told you from the beginning. I can't keep holding it in." Ozan took a huge breath. "Ariel," he whispered, grabbing onto my hand. "I have feelings for you. I mean strong feelings. I've had them for a while now."

"Wha—"

"I like you, Ariel. I can't hold them in anymore," he blurted out. "I don't know if you feel the same. I know this might be a shock to you, but I want you to know that I have feelings towards you."

"O—Ozan . . ." I whispered, too shocked to say another word. My mind was about to burst from all the shocking news that I received today.

"Ariel. I don't want to lose you," he whispered. "Please, give me a chance."

I see nothing but sincerity in his eyes. I feel breathless. Before I could say anything, Ozan beats me to it.

"Be my girlfriend."

CHAPTER THIRTY-TWO

My mouth hung open at his words. I was in disbelief as Ozan stared at me with hope in his eyes, something that tore me to pieces. He looked so happy, his eyes glinting with emotion I never knew saw before.

I was too flabbergasted to say anything. It was too hard to take in. Too much happened today.

Ozan's hopeful eyes dropped. "Ariel, please. Don't be silent. Say something," he murmured, tightening his hold on my hand. I glanced at our joined hands.

"O—Ozan . . . I—I don't know what to say."

"I know it's a shock for you," he started, giving me a comforting smile. "But it's the truth. Ariel, don't you see? I can't get you out of my head. I was a coward to keep it in for so long but these days I came to realize that I have to let them out. I can't keep them locked in. You never know what could happen, and I don't want to regret not ever telling you," he said lowly.

I'm getting teary. His words hit me so deep. I understood what he meant. I sucked in a breath. Ozan was sick. The friend that was with me through a hard time, the one who offered to come with me, the one who is refusing to return to New York for treatment so he could stay by my side, is sick.

What have I ever done to deserve someone like him? What have I ever done to deserve someone who cares so much about me? What have I done to deserve somone who pushes his own well-being for my own? I always knew he had some sort of feelings towards me, but I never thought it would be to this point.

Ozan took a step closer. "Give me one chance, Ariel. Just one. I promise, you won't regret it. I'll make you happy."

"I . . . I don't know. I'm confused," I said. His smile dropped. He remained silent for a moment.

"Is it because of Troy? Do you still have feelings for him?" Ozan asked.

"No!" I shook my head. "Its not because of him. I'm just a little surprised."

His face relaxed a bit. "I know you still have feelings for him, but I can make you forget him," Ozan stated. "You deserve someone better. Someone who can make you happy. And I want to do that. I can heal you."

I bit my lip, shutting my eyes for a moment as I listened to his words. I did want to forget. I wanted to heal so badly. I can't take this pain but is this fair for Ozan?

"Ozan, I love you so much. You mean so much to me but I don't want to lead you on. Yes, I want to forget everything about Troy, but you don't deserve to go through this. You deserve better," I said.

"I want you. I'm willing to take anything. I'm willing to help you forget. I'll do my best to make you forget about him and fall for me. Just give me one chance. That's all I'm asking for," he blurted out, serious as ever.

That's all he was asking for. How could I say no? How could I say no when I knew he was sick? He's willing to help me forget, but is this a bad thing? I want to give up on Troy but I don't want to put Ozan through the pain.

"Ozan. You do know that I don't see you that way," I spoke honestly in a soft voice.

Ozan nodded. "I know but I can make you see me that way soon. If you just give me a chance."

I then recalled his conversation with his dad a while ago. Ozan's sick. You never know what could happen, and I don't want to upset him. I care for him so much that it broke my heart. I shouldn't be selfish. I want him to be happy too.

I remained silent for a couple seconds. He looked at me with determination. It was a look telling me he wasn't giving up. He was willing to help me.

Maybe I needed this. Ozan cares for me, and I care for him. Maybe we could be a good match? I sucked in a breath.

"Okay," I whispered, seeing his lips turn into the biggest smile I have ever seen. "I'll be your girlfriend but let's take this slow?" I suggested. Ozan immediately nodded, pulling me tight into his arms.

"Okay. Whatever you say. I promise, you won't regret it. I'll make you happy," he said. I could hear the happiness in his voice which gave me a sense of relief. I'm willing to try. I'm willing to start new with someone else. He pulled away, smiling from ear to ear. I smiled back at him, happy to see him this joyful.

I noticed his weary features. I remained silent but I made a mental note to ask him about his tumor. Sooner or later but not now. This wasn't the right moment. He looks too happy, and I didn't want to ruin that.

However, it didn't stop the fear that crawled in me, the fear that I had a chance of losing Ozan to this tumor. It was a reality and it scared me to my core. I don't want to upset him. I want us both to be happy. Maybe we can offer happiness to each other?

Maybe I can eventually love him?

It has been two days since Ozan and I started dating. It felt so weird to say that. Never have I ever thought that Ozan and I would be a thing. I was surprised with myself. It was hard to comprehend but it was real.

I was nervous that I'll end up hurting Ozan. I was also worried that this wouldn't turn out good but I was willing to give it a shot. He meant so much to me.

He was so kind and caring these two days. He kept his distance, though. He was taking it slow just like what I asked him to do. I was happy that he was willing to do that. I actually was hoping that Ozan would make me happy.

Troy was still in my mind. He left a hole in my heart and it hurt. Now, I was in the process of trying to forget. These two days were quite easy since Troy didn't return home. I overheard Rose saying that he was staying at a friend's house. I was thankful for that. It gave me time to rethink what happened two days ago.

His words didn't leave my head. It never did. He wanted me to give up on him, and that's exactly what I was doing. I might sound weak. Maybe I am but I was tired. I wanted peace. Troy made it clear that he can never love me. He didn't want me, so I was finally giving up.

After three long years of holding on, I was ready to move on.

Ozan and I didn't inform anyone in the house about us. We decided to keep it quiet for these two days but we'll have to tell them sooner or later. I was also hoping that Ozan would soon tell me about his tumor. I wanted him to tell me himself. It hurts knowing that he was keeping this to himself.

I have to do something about it if he doesn't tell me himself soon. He can't keep this hidden.

I pushed those thoughts out my head so I wouldn't ruin my mood. I looked up from my phone when I heard my bedroom door open. Ozan came walking in.

"Hey," I said. He planted a kiss on my cheek.

"Are you hungry?" Ozan asked. I nodded.

"Yes. I am," I said. Ozan grabbed onto my hand, pulling me off my bed and onto my feet.

"Then, come on. Rose prepared dinner." We started walking towards the door but I stopped him, making him turn to me with a raised brow. "What?"

"Ozan . . ." I muttered. "Don't you think it's time for us to tell them? I mean, we can't keep this hidden. If we want to give each other a chance, then we have to be open about it."

Ozan's lips turned into a smile, one that made me want to continue to bring happiness to him. "Of course. I was just waiting for when you were ready," he stated, smiling down at me. "We could tell them at dinner, if that's ok with you."

I nodded in agreement. "Okay. We'll do that," I murmured, smiling softly at him. His eyes lit up with excitement, letting go of my hand and cupping my face with his hands. He brought his face closer to mine and kissed my forehead.

"Thank you for giving me a chance Ariel. I know you don't love me yet but I promise, I'll do my best to make you happy. I know it will be hard at first, but we'll get used to this. Just give us time and maybe you'll fall for me," he whispered.

I nodded, offering him a reassuring smile. "I will, and I know you'll make me happy. You always do."

Ozan's smiled grew. He grabbed my hand and pulled me out my room. My hand was still in his as we walked down the hall. I was nervous of what to say and do but we had to do this.

I was kind of relieved that Troy wasn't here. It made it easier even though he was bound to find out. It doesn't matter, anyway.

Damon, Rose, and Julia were sitting down on the table. I bit my lip as we walked forward. Julia smiled at us but her eyes widened as she saw me and Ozan holding hands. Damon and Rose eventually looked our way.

"Oh, there you are," Rose spoke out, not noticing our joined hands. "Come on. Let's eat before the food gets cold."

Damon's smile slowly disappeared as he eyed our hands, blinking in surprised. I glanced at Ozan and he offered me a reassuring smile, pulling me towards the table. Rose glanced back at us, her eyes widening as she finally looked down at our hands.

Julia's mouth hung open. "Wait . . . are you—"

239

"Is there something you both haven't told us?" Damon interrupted Julia, standing up as he walked towards us. I gulped and Rose took a couple of steps towards us. I didn't know if they were upset. I couldn't read their emotions, but I was sure they were surprised.

Rose looked between Ozan and I, a frown taking over her lips. "What's going on?" Rose asked in a low tone.

"Yes. There is something we haven't told you," Ozan admitted. "We wanted to tell you—"

The front door suddenly slammed. I frowned as we all turned our heads. Just as I expected, it was Troy who walked in.

He soon stopped dead in his tracks. I looked away immediately. This was the first time I've seen him since that day. It was hard to look at him normally. I look at him to see his eyes fixed on my hand and Ozan's. Troy gave me a hard look. His jaw clenched, making me look away.

"As I was saying," Ozan cleared his throat, glancing back at Troy. "Ariel and I have something to tell you."

"Well. Go on," Julia said. Rose's frown deepened as she stared at me and Troy.

I sucked in a breath as Ozan tightened his hold onto my hand in a comforting manner.

"Ariel and I are dating. She's my girlfriend now."

CHAPTER THIRTY-THREE

"Girlfriend?" Julia blurted out. Her mouth hung open, her eyes holding disbelief in them. She looked at Troy who was still giving me a hard look. "Since when were you two a thing?"

All eyes were on us. I couldn't tell how they were feeling. I saw confusion and a hint of sadness in Rose's eyes. I couldn't read Damon's expression and Julia's face held shock. I didn't glance to see Troy's reaction. I couldn't make myself do it. I avoided him as hard as I could.

"We've been a thing ever since Saturday night," Ozan answered, smiling down at me for a second before returning his stare back at Rose and Damon. "We wanted to tell you, but we decided to give it a little time."

"Are you kids sure on what you're doing?" Damon finally spoke out, raising a brow at us with a questioning look. Ozan glanced down at me, making me nod.

"Yes. We are," I answered in a soft tone. Damon stared at us in silence for a moment. I glanced at Rose who gave me a sad look. I offered her a small smile as an assurance that I knew what I was doing.

"So, like . . ." Julia spoke out. "You both like each other?"

Ozan wrapped an arm around my waist, smiling as he nodded his head. I saw Julia's eyes glance to Troy again. I finally tried to look at Troy. I sucked in a breath as I saw a hint of sadness. I immediately concentrated back on Ozan.

"I've liked her for a long time," Ozan confessed. "I guess I was late to tell her that but I don't regret anything."

My heart sank when I heard his words. Knowing that he was hurting brought pain to me. It hurts that he was suffering on his own. I don't want to leave him on his own.

I pushed those thoughts at the back of my head. I glanced back at Rose who was ready to say something but Damon cut her off.

"How about we start dinner?" he suggested, placing a hand on Rose's shoulder. Damon was giving her a look which told her to behave. "I bet we're all hungry," he continued. He eventually looked at his son. "Come on."

Rose sighed reluctantly and walked towards the dining table to lay out the spoons and napkins. Ozan grabbed onto my hand and led me towards the table. We were all ready to sit down but Troy was not moving an inch.

His fist clenched as he looked at Ozan's and my joined hands. He looked back into my eyes, making me hold the shiver that threatened to crawl down my spine. I sucked in a breath, moving my eyes away from him.

"Troy. Come on. Aren't you going to eat with us?" Julia said. All heads turned to him.

"Come on, son. The food will get cold," Damon said softly.

Troy shook his head and took a step backwards. "I'm not hungry," he finally said, the first since he came here. I glanced at Ozan to see him glaring at Troy. Troy did the same. I tightened my hold on Ozan's hand. "You enjoy your meal."

When Troy said that, his eyes met with mine. I looked away. "Where are you going?" Rose called out.

"To my room." That was all he said before he left. I let out a breath of relief. I felt weird being stared at like that. I couldn't tell what exactly he thinks about this, but I could tell he wasn't happy.

It doesn't matter anymore. He has to get used to this.

242

Ozan sat down. I was about to follow.

"Oh. I forgot the juice in the kitchen," she said, looking at me. "Ariel. Will you help me get the juice?"

"Rose, honey. I'm sure you could get them yourself," Damon told her, giving her the same look he gave her a while ago. Rose offered him another look, making me wonder if I actually wanted to go with Rose.

"It's okay. I can get them," I said. I made my way towards the kitchen. I know that Rose was going to follow me in here. I guess I was bound to talk with her.

Just as I thought, Rose walked in with a frown. "Ariel," she whispered. "Sweetie. What the hell are you doing?" I could hear the displeasure in her voice.

"Rose—"

"Why did you accept to be his girlfriend? We all know that you don't feel that way about him. We all know how you feel about Troy and we know that Troy feels the same. So, why would you do that?"

"Rose. Please, listen to me," I whispered. "I want to start off new. Troy and I will never happen. We can never be the way we used to be."

"So, you're leading Ozan on?" she asked, her frown deepening.

I shook my head. "No, I'm not. I told him honestly how I feel about him. We're both willing to try this relationship. I want to move on," I told her.

"Why? Why would you want to move on?" Rose questioned.

I raised my voice. "Because Troy doesn't want me."

Rose shook her head. "I know my son and I know what he wants. He wants you," she said.

"Well, that's not what he told me a couple days ago."

Rose looked at me with confusion. "What do you mean?"

I sucked in a breath. "I confessed to Troy and he rejected me. He told me he could never love me. He told me to move on and that's what I'm trying to do," I explained. "Rose. How come you never told me that Troy has a 50 percent chance of losing his memories all over again?"

Her eyes went wide. "He told you? Oh, honey. He didn't want anyone to know. Ariel, don't you see? He's just afraid to start new. He's afraid to lose everything he already has. That's why he's pushing you away."

I sucked in a breath. "Rose. I can't keep running after him," I said to her. "I also don't want to keep living with the pain and fear of him constantly forgetting me. I don't want to live through the pain I had to hold for three long years. I don't want to be in hell forever. I think it's time for me to move on."

Rose opened her mouth to speak, but I interrupted her. "Please, just accept it. I know you're worried about your son, but this could be the best for both of us."

"I'm not only worried about him. I'm worried for the three of you," she stated, shaking her head. "What if you end up breaking Ozan's heart?"

"I'm going to try my best not to." I offered her a small smile. "We both know what we're getting ourselves into. Besides, Ozan means so much to me. I would never hurt him intentionally."

Rose stared at me for a good second, sucking in a breath as she nodded. "I don't like what you're doing Ariel. Maybe it's because of the fact that I was hoping for you and Troy to get back together but I also know he's giving you a hard time. I just hope you won't end up hurt or hurting someone with the decision that you've made."

I only nodded. Rose placed a hand on my shoulder, smiling softly at me. "If you need some advice, come to me," she suggested.

I smiled at her. "Thank you, Rose."

She pulled me for a hug. I forced myself not to cry. We soon pulled away and Rose looked back at me.

"Come on. Let's go back before Damon thinks I'm giving you a hard time." I nodded and we walked out the kitchen and towards the dining table. All heads turned to us as Julia raised a brow.

"Where's the juice?" she asked. I glanced at Rose, knowing she was mentally face palming herself.

"That's not important," Damon stated, eyeing us. From his expression, I could tell that he knew what happened back there. "Just sit down so we could begin." We both nodded and walked towards our seat. I sat down, seeing Ozan giving me a questioning look.

"What happened back there?" he asked. I smiled softly at him.

"It's not important," I assured. He hesitantly nodded, taking a bite from his food.

Glancing at Ozan one more time, I turned to my food and took a bite.

After helping Julia and Rose clean up, I excused myself and walked towards my room. Ozan was chatting with Damon so I left without him. I made my way towards my room. I glanced at Troy's room as I walked past it.

I sucked in a breath and shook my head. As I made it to my bedroom door, I opened it and walked into my room, closing the door behind me. Before I could even notice it, a gasp escaped my lips the moment I laid eyes on Troy.

He was in my room, standing against the wall and crossing his arms against his chest, giving me a hard look. I placed my hand on my chest to calm myself down, seeing Troy take a couple of steps towards me.

"What are you doing here?" I asked him, hoping my voice would be strong but it turned out soft. "What are you doing in my room?" I question again, louder this time.

245

Troy remained silent, taking a more steps towards me. I sucked in a breath and took a step back, but failed to do more as Troy gripped my arm, making my eyes widen. "Troy," I said. "What are you doing? Let go of my arm."

He snickered, shaking his head. "Shouldn't I be the one asking you that?" He questioned lowly, his eyes hardening. "What the hell are you doing, Ariel? Why the f*ck are you his girlfriend?"

"That's none of your business," I stated, trying to step away from him but winced when his hold on my arm got tighter.

"It is my f*cking business," he stated. "Why are you his girlfriend?" Troy asked louder.

"You have no right to ask that," I hissed. "I'm moving on from you. I'm starting new."

"That's why you immediately jump into the arms of another man?" He scoffed. "You're using him to forget me? You're leading him on."

I shook my head. "I'm not leading him on."

"You're doing the same thing I did to Randa."

"No. I'm not," I argued, trying to step away. "Ozan knows how I feel. He's helping me move on. You played Randa while I actually care for Ozan. This is nowhere near what you did."

"You're doing this to make me jealous. You're trying to hurt me," he stated hardly.

I shook my head. "I'm not. I'm doing this for myself. You said it yourself, Troy. Give up. And that's what I'm doing," I explained, staring right in his eyes. His jaw clenched.

"You're making a mistake," he said, stepping closer to me.

"No. I think I should have done this a long time ago," I whispered. "I could have saved myself the heartbreak."

Troy took a step back, staring at me with angry eyes. I could see the frustration in them, the fury and the jealousy. I knew that this would have bothered him, and I couldn't help but feel a bit satisfied but that wasn't my intention. He pushed me away, and I didn't want to keep running back to him. I would never hurt him the way he hurt me intentionally.

Troy looked at me before aggressively letting go of my arm. He walked past me without uttering a single word. I sucked in a breath as Troy walked out my room. I stiffened the moment I heard my door brutally slam shut. I wasn't able to hold back the tear that fell down my cheek.

I had to do this. A new start was what I was hoping for. I was hoping that in the future, just maybe, it wouldn't hurt like this. I was praying that I'd finally heal.

CHAPTER THIRTY-FOUR

I snapped my eyes open, meeting the boring white ceiling. I frowned, wondering why I woke up at this time. I stiffened the moment I saw a body standing in the corner of my room.

My eyes widened. I drastically sat up, squinting my eyes so I could make out the person standing there. It made a shiver crawl down my body as a gasp escaped my lips. At first, I thought my eyes were playing tricks on me but the more my eyes adapted to the darkness, the more I knew I was staring right into Troy's dark eyes.

"Troy?" I croaked out. "What are you doing in my room?" I asked. I glanced at the clock that hung on my wall. "What the hell are you doing in my room at 5 AM?" I asked louder this time.

Troy didn't utter a single word. He just stood there, staring right at me as if he was paralyzed. The way he was staring at me only made me feel creeped out. I gulped the moment he made a move. Troy took a step closer without taking his eyes off me.

"Troy?" I said louder. "What the hell? What are you doing?" I demanded.

Like the last time, Troy remained silent. I sucked in a breath as he continued to take small, slow steps towards my bed. I wanted to get up and move, but no matter how hard I tried, I couldn't. I wasn't able to move an inch. It was as if I was paralyzed from the neck down.

My breath accelerated as Troy soon stood in front of me. The darkness that surrounded us didn't make this situation any better. It only made me more anxious.

"What's—"

"Ariel," Troy finally said. "Oh, Ariel. You won't do it." His hand reached my face, caressing my cheek softly as his eyes made contact with mine.

"Won't do what?" I managed to let out, somehow feeling as if something wasn't allowing me to speak.

"You won't get over me," he whispered, his face expression as serious as ever. "You can't. You love me so much."

"What are you saying? Get out of my room!" I urged. Troy shook his head, his hand now running down my hair.

"You love me. You won't ever forget me," he stated.

"I will," I muttered. "I will forget you."

Troy shook his head again. "You can't. I made my way deep down in your heart. It's impossible to dig me out now," Troy whispered. "You weren't able to forget me for three years. What makes you think you could forget me now?"

"Stop!" I demanded, trying to move away from him. "Get out of here."

"Ozan won't help you. He won't do anything," Troy claimed, the side of his lip twitching. "You think you can use him to forget me? You won't. You'll only realize that you won't ever get over me."

"I will get over you," I argued. "And I'm not using him. I care for him."

Troy snickered. "Ariel. Admit it," he whispered as he brought his face closer to mine. "You love me. You won't ever stop loving me." Troy's face was extremely close to mine. His eyes went down to my lips.

"See the affect I have on you, my little mermaid?" Troy questioned, running his thumb over my bottom lip.

"Stop. Step away," I said softly. Troy shook his head from side to side.

"No matter what you do, I'll remain in your heart. I'm imprinted and I won't ever escape your mind," Troy claimed. "You won't ever stop loving me."

Before I could even argue, his lips were on mine.

My eyes snapped open. I immediately looked around my room. I sat up and let out a breath.

"Oh, God," I muttered. "What the hell, Ariel?" I took my head out of my hands. I was surely going crazy. Why would I dream of something like that?

I glanced at the clock and got out of my bed. I have little time to get ready for school. As I walked towards the bathroom, the dream I had not too long ago replayed in my mind. I couldn't believe that I dreamed that.

I know that what happened yesterday with Troy in my room had an effect on me. That surely caused the dream. I have to get my mind off of this. I shouldn't think too much of it. It was merely a dream.

I turned the sink on and splashed cold water on my face. I let out a breath and ran a hand over my hair. I couldn't help but feel like I was missing something. I told myself I'd get used to this. I'd get used to forgetting Troy.

Sooner or later, I'll have to leave this place. I'm not staying here forever. When the time comes, things will be much easier but for now, I have Ozan by my side.

I was so grateful for that. I was thankful for having him in my life. He was not leaving me all alone. I only wished that I wasn't making a mistake. I hope that in the end, no one will get hurt. It was getting harder and harder by the day to keep quiet about what I overheard. It felt as if I was slowly suffocating as I played along that I didn't know anything. I don't want him to go through misery. I also don't want to be the cause of his misery.

Pushing those thoughts away, I started getting ready for school. After I took a quick shower and got dressed, I grabbed my bag and walked to the kitchen. Troy standing by the door.

I stiffened the moment his eyes were on me, bringing the dream back to my attention. I averted my eyes away from him and walked in the kitchen. Rose was standing there. "Good morning," I said. She looked at me and smiled.

"Morning, Ariel. I'm almost done with breakfast so go ahead and sit down," Rose said. I smiled at her and nodded.

"Thank you, Rose." I drank a cup of water before walking out the kitchen. Troy was in the same spot. I sucked in a breath and walked towards the dining table, smiling softly as I saw Ozan walking in.

"Good morning, beautiful." He grinned.

My smile grew. "Morning. How are you today?" I asked, running my eyes over his features. He's looking better.

"I'm better the moment I saw you." Ozan stepped closer and pecked me on the cheek the same time Troy came walking in. I felt his eyes on us, which brought me discomfort. Ozan then glanced at Troy, his smile disappearing. He cleared his throat as Troy started walking away from us.

Rose came out of the kitchen and frowned as she saw her son's retreating body. "Troy? Won't you stay for breakfast?" she wondered.

Troy shook his head. "No. I'm heading to school." He didn't wait for a response and walked out. Rose shook her head and returned in the kitchen. I looked up at Ozan and he smiled softly at me.

Eventually, everyone sat down and started to eat. I sat next to Ozan in silence as Julia excused herself. When Ozan and I were done, Damon got up and looked at us.

"I'll be driving you both to school," he stated. Ozan glanced at him and shook his head.

"There's no need to. We can walk," Ozan said.

251

Damon shook his head. "Don't argue with me. Come on. Let's go before you're late."

We nodded and got up from our seats, saying our goodbye to Rose before walking out with Damon.

*   *   *

Ozan and I walked side by side towards the cafeteria. I listened as Ozan complained about the teacher in his previous class. Ozan opened the door for me. I offered a smile in return.

"Thank you," I chuckled. He grinned and grabbed onto my hand. Ozan and I walked to our usual table.

"I'm going to go get our lunch. You stay here," he ordered. I nodded and he got up. I ran my eyes over the large room. I flinched the moment I saw a particular person walking in the cafeteria.

Troy sat alone on the table in front of me, meeting my eyes.

I frowned as I noticed that he stopped sitting with his usual friends. These past few days he's been sitting on his own, not interacting with people. I noticed he'd always walk off when some people would sit on his table.

I looked away, forcing my eyes not to glance back at him.

I was interrupted from my thoughts the moment I heard my name being called out.

"Ariel? Hey."

I looked up to see Rex smiling at me. My eyes slightly widened as I remembered what happened recently. I didn't really talk to him after I canceled the trip. I must have sounded rude.

"Hey, Rex," I greeted. "How are you?"

"I'm good. I haven't seen you much after you canceled the trip," Rex stated.

"I'm so sorry, Rex. I must have seemed like an asshole for doing that," I murmured. He chuckled.

252

"No. It's fine."

"I'm honestly sorry. I had a project to do that day, that's why I couldn't make it," I explained, hoping he'd believe me.

"It's fine, Ariel. I understand," Rex exclaimed. "We could always go on another day?"

"She can't," Ozan came out from behind me, sitting down as he glared at Rex. "As her boyfriend, I'll take her to wherever she wants."

Rex's eyes widened. "Boyfriend?" Ozan nodded. "Oh. Well, okay. It was nice talking to you but I have to go," Rex said. He smiled apologetically at me. "Bye, Ariel." He turned around and walked away. I frowned at his behavior and looked at a pleased Ozan.

I raised a brow at him. He grinned, putting his hands up defensively at me. "What? He has to know," he claimed. Oh well, I didn't really care that he told Rex. I then noticed Troy standing up and walking away. My eyes followed him until he disappeared from my view.

Lunch ended and a couple of periods passed. I was currently sitting in my English class, listening as the teacher discussed about a book. I glanced at the clock to see that the period will soon end. The English teacher soon shut the book that was in his hands and clapped his hands for attention.

"Okay everybody, listen up! As you all know, the senior trip to Hawaii is on Monday. For those who are going, make sure you sign these papers and bring the money on or before Monday," he explained, passing out the permission slips to each students. "Make your guardian sign them as well. We'll be staying two nights in Oahu. There will be tours, hiking, and many other activities."

The teacher gave me a paper as he walked by me. "Oh . . ." he said loudly. "Don't even try to bring anything that's not allowed. That goes for drugs and alcohol."

Loud whispers emerged in the air. I looked down at the paper. I didn't really decide whether I was going or not.

253

The bell soon rang and the teacher excused us. I looked up and saw Troy walking out with the paper in his hand. I got up and grabbed my bag, wondering if Troy was going or not.

I sighed and shook my head, telling myself it didn't matter.

CHAPTER THIRTY-FIVE

I ran my eyes over the group of students rushing to get home. I continued to look around until my eyes stopped on Ozan. He was walking towards me with a smile. When Ozan stood in front of me, he wrapped his arms around me and kissed my cheek.

"How was your last class?" he asked as we started walking off the school campus.

I shrugged my shoulders. "It was okay," I answered, looking back at him. "How was your class? You had a quiz, right? How did it go?"

"It's was fine. I think I did good," Ozan replied. "Come on. Let's go home."

"You want to walk?" I asked, stopping in my tracks.

Ozan raised a brow at me. "Isn't that what I usually do?"

I couldn't help but feel worried about him walking a long distance. What if it tire him?

Ozan soon chuckled. "Oh, don't be such a lazy pants."Come on, we're walking," he teased. I reluctantly nodded as he pulled my hand.

We started walking down the street in silence. Ozan would say something about a class or a teacher every now and then. We were now five minutes away from the house.

"Did you receive the permission slip for the trip?" he asked, raising a brow. I looked up at him and nodded.

"Yeah," I replied. "The trip to Hawaii?"

"Yes. My chemistry teacher passed them out," Ozan stated. "Doesn't the trip sound interesting?"

"Well, it's a trip to Hawaii. Of course it sounds interesting," I chuckled. "Why? Do you want to go?"

"Are you planning to go?" Ozan asked.

I shrugged my shoulders. "I don't know. I haven't thought about going but it does sound nice."

Ozan then stopped in his tracks. "How about we go? It's a nice opportunity and we could make some memories over there," Ozan suggested, his smile growing. "Please, Ariel. Come with me. It will be nice and we can have some fun. I want to be able to make some memories with you," Ozan continued, his smile turning into a soft, sad one. I felt my heart sink from his words. I could hear the meaning behind them.

What if something happens to Ozan and I didn't have any big memories with him? Ones to look back at and smile at. We were friends for years, but we never went on a trip like this. I wanted him to be happy, and I want him to spend the best time he could have.

"Sure. It's only for two nights," I murmured. "We could go. It will be nice but I have to talk with my parents so they can send me the money for the trip," I said.

We continued walking back to the house as he commented about the trip. I could feel his excitement growing like a little child, which made me chuckle.

Every time I remembered his illness, I'd feel a sickening feeling in my stomach. I kept hoping that my ears were playing tricks on me and that what I heard the other day wasn't true. I didn't want to accept it. Maybe I have to ask him about this soon. I can't keep this hidden for too long.

I was pulled out of my thoughts when we made it to the house. "I need to take a shower and change. Then I'll make Rose or Damon sign the slip," Ozan said.

"How about you give me the slip? I let her sign for the both of us," I suggested. Ozan nodded and opened his backpack, handing me the slip. "Okay. I'm just going to put my bag in my room first," I said.

We soon walked off to our rooms. I entered my room and placed my bag on my bed. I then turned around and walked towards the living room with both slips in my hand. I saw Rose sitting on the couch, switching through the channels on the TV.

"Hi, Rose," I greeted. Her head turned towards me, a smile growing on her lips as she patted the seat next to her.

"Hi, sweetie. How was school?" she asked.

"It was good." I shrugged my shoulders. "Actually, we have this senior trip to Hawaii on Monday. Only for two nights." I never really brought up the trip to her because I didn't think I was going.

Rose raised a brow. "To Hawaii? Wow. There are schools who offer trips like that?" she asked. I smiled and nodded. "Well, that seems like a nice opportunity. Are you planning on going?" she said.

"Yeah. Ozan and I decided to go. We could have a nice time over there," I answered her. It sounded like a nice place to go and relax. Maybe if I go over there, I can get my head off of things, especially from Troy. "We wanted you to sign this. We need a guardian's permission."

I handed the papers to Rose and offered her a pen. She looked at them and nodded. "Of course." She looked through the papers. "What about the money? Who are you going to get them from?"

"I can ask my dad to send me some. It's no big deal," I answered, shrugging my shoulders. Rose narrowed her eyes.

"There's no need. We'll lend you both the money for the trip," Rose answered, looking back at the papers. I drastically shook my head.

"No. I can't," I argued. "I'll just call my mom—"

"Ariel, do I look like a stranger to you?"

257

My mouth hung open. "No."

"So, it's not a big deal. We'll pay for the trip. You shouldn't feel embarrassed. We've known each other for so long, right?" Rose stated.

I nodded. "Yes but . . . I don't what to be a burden. It's bad enough that I'm already staying in your house," I said. Rose immediately shook her head.

"Honey. You're never a burden. Trust me, your parents did many things for me when I was young. So, it's the least I could do," Rose explained, smiling at me. "You're welcome to stay here as long as you want. This is your home."

I smiled at her. "Thank you, Rose."

"Besides, it's not like we don't have the money to pay for the trip," she chuckled, shaking her head. I laughed lightly, my smile growing.

It was true. They had plenty of money. Damon and my dad used to work in the same business while they were still in New York. They are both wealthy men. What caught my attention was how things were different here for Rose and Damon. It wasn't like the way they lived in New York.

I could remember them living in a huge house with maids, security and drivers. They were pretty wealthy. Even though they still are, it was completely different here. They lived in a big house, but a comfy one that fit perfectly for everyone. There were neither maids nor drivers. I noticed that Rose and Julia did all the work. They didn't rely on anyone and I found that nice. They were humble and didn't show off the money they had. I remember asking Rose about it once and she said that after they moved here, they realized that money wasn't important, but family was. Damon took on a smaller business than the one he had in New York. They didn't see the need to spend more than what they need. Rose told me that the most important thing was to live as a normal family and to be responsible. They didn't need to rely on money.

Rose looked back at the papers and grabbed the pen. I sat silently, waiting for her to sign them when Troy walked in. I went stiff. Troy's eyes met mine for what felt like minutes.

Rose glanced up at him, looking between him and I. "Is there something you need, son?" She wondered. Troy took a couple steps, glancing to the two papers in her hands. His eyes slightly widened as he looked at the permission slips before glancing at me.

"No," he answered.

"Are you planning on going to the senior trip?" Rose asked, glancing at Troy.

Troy glanced back at the slips. "I wasn't planning on going," he muttered.

"Oh," Rose mumbled, sounding a little disappointed. She then looked back at the papers and quickly signed them. "You can give this back to Ozan and let him know we'll pay for it."

I nodded and took the papers. "Thank you, Rose." I didn't glance back at Troy and walked out of the room, exhaling the air I was holding. I shook my head and told myself it didn't matter that Troy wasn't coming. This was a chance to forget and have fun.

I ran a hand through my face and walked towards Ozan's room with the papers in my hand.

The night passed and I was already in bed but I suddenly woke up. I stretched in my bed as I squinted to make out the number on the clock. I frowned as I realized it was 1 AM. I sat up and glanced around the dark room. I didn't know what woke me up at this time.

I laid back down and closed my eyes. I tried to fall asleep but I wasn't able to. I let out a groan and opened my eyes. I was definitely waking up tired tomorrow.

I stood up and ran my hands over my face. My throat was dry, so a glass of water could help me at the moment. I silently opened my bedroom door and walked down the hallway. I tried my best to not make a sound. The least thing I wanted right now was to wake the whole house up.

I proceeded to make my way to the kitchen, not bothering to turn the lights on. The lights of the hallway was enough to allow me to make out everything in the kitchen. I filled a glass with cold water and immediately drank it.

As I placed the cup on the counter, I heard some movements behind me and turned around to see a dark figure standing by the kitchen entrance. My eyes widened as Troy walked into the kitchen, his eyes staring back into mine.

"Troy?" I spoke out, biting the inside of my cheeks as he took slow steps towards me. "I . . ." Clearing my throat, I continued. "I came to drink water." I didn't know why I said that. I felt like I had to justify myself. Troy nodded, placing his hands in his pockets. I averted my eyes away from him. I decided to leave.

I was about to make my way past him when he grabbed onto my hand. Troy's eyes were looking at me but since darkness surrounded us, I couldn't read them.

"What are you doing?" I asked, trying to pull my hand away from his tight grip. He then pulled me to him.

"Ariel," he finally said in a low and serious tone. "When are you going stop with this game?"

My eyes widened. "Game? I'm not playing a game," I argued, making Troy snicker.

"You are. You're going to drive me crazy," he whispered. "Stop with this game. End it with Ozan."

My brows furrowed. "This is not a game, Troy," I argued. "I'm not ending it with Ozan."

Troy started backing me against the wall, making me anxious. "Ariel. You're making me angry. End it with Ozan. I know you're not serious." His voice was low, but I could sense the anger in them.

"I am serious!" I tried to walk past him but his hold on me was tight. "Besides, this is none of your business. Now, let go of me."

"Are you going to the senior trip with Ozan?" he asked out of nowhere. I narrowed my eyes at him as I desperately tried to pull my hand away from him. "You're going, right?" He scoffed. "Of course. You want to spend some alone time with your boyfriend."

"That's none of your business but yes. I am going. Is that a problem? You shouldn't care, right?" I asked. Troy lowered his face to mine, allowing me to see his dark eyes.

"Don't go, Ariel."

My eyes widened. "I've already decided."

His face got closer to mine. I could feel his breath fanning my face. "I said don't go. Don't go with him," he demanded. I shook my head and pushed him away.

"Don't tell me what to do, Troy. You have no right at all." I hissed.

"Ariel—"

"Stop, Troy." I raised my hand in between us. "You can't tell me to give up on you then act as if you care. You pushed me away yourself. You also can't tell me what to do. I'm going with Ozan and there's nothing you can do to stop me."

I pushed past him and rushed out of the kitchen. I closed my bedroom door. I placed a hand on my chest, sucking in a breath as I shook my head.

This wasn't fair.

One moment, he'd tell me to give up on him and another moment he'd act as if he cared about me. He's making me feel many unwanted emotions.

How does he expect me to forget about him when he acts this way?

CHAPTER THIRTY-SIX

I walked towards my window and looked out the sky, meeting the large moon that stared back at me. I let out a sigh as I continued to stare at its beauty before closing the curtains and walking towards my bed. I got in the covers and stared at the ceiling, my mind starting its usual daily thinking.

It was a little early to go to bed but I was too tired so I got ready to fall into the darkness. All the sudden, I heard my phone ring. I grabbed my phone and looked at the caller, smiling as I saw my mom on the screen. I immediately answered the call.

"Mom." I breathed out.

"Hi, sweetie," she greeted. I finally heard her voice for the first time in a while. "How are you?" she wondered.

"I'm good. I miss you," I said softly.

I heard my mom let out a soft sigh. "We miss you, too. As a matter of fact, there's someone here who would like to say hi."

"Who?"

"Ariel!" a familiar voice yelled in the background. I sat up with a grin on my face.

"Clare? Oh my God. I miss you so much," I said. Hearing her chuckle in the background made my grin wider.

"I miss you too. I really do!" she exclaimed.

"Clare came over to eat dinner with us. She's such a nice girl," my mom said.

I chuckled. "Of course she is. Thank you for keeping my mom and dad company."

"Oh. It's no big deal," she stated. I heard my dad in the background, which made me smile.

"How are you? I hope you're not facing some trouble out there," my dad asked.

"I'm fine, Dad. I got used to it," I assured. After a moment of talking with them, I bit the inside of my cheek, debating with myself whether I should tell them or not.

Well, they had to know.

"Mom, Dad, Clare?" I murmured. "I need to tell you guys something."

"What is it, honey?" my mom said. I took a deep breath, playing with my blanket to ease my anxiety.

"Well, since you're all together, I've decided to tell you now. You guys should know," I continued, waiting for a response.

"Go on," Dad said.

"Ozan and I are dating," I blurted out, wishing I could see their reaction. My eyes widened the moment I heard chocking noises in the background. I heard gasps and the phone was put down.

"Oh, dear! Clare, are you okay?" my mom gasped. "Hold up. I'm going to go get you water." Hearing my mom rush out of the room and Clare's coughing made my jaw drop. I didn't know what to say.

"Clare. Are you okay?" I asked out of concern. My mom then came back as I heard her sooth Clare. I waited for a moment before I could speak. I felt my cheeks blushing.

"Did you actually mean what you said?" she asked.

"Are you really serious?" I finally heard Clare's voice. "You made me choke on a cookie."

"I'm sorry," I whispered. "And yes. Ozan and I are dating."

"Since when?" Dad asked, his voice getting louder.

"Since Saturday," I answered, silence hitting me.

"Well, wow," Clare muttered. "I don't know what to say. I guess that's good?" Her voice didn't sound so sure. Clare always tried to make me forget about Troy when I was still back in New York. She didn't like seeing me suffer through this heartbreak so she constantly tried to make me date someone. She even tried to tell me to date Ozan. However I think ever since I came here, her mind might have slightly changed.

"Are you sure on your decision?" Mom asked.

"Yes. I am," I answered.

"Are you happy?" Dad asked.

I bit my lip. I took a few moments. "Yes." I wasn't too sure on the answer, but I was hoping that I was sincere about it.

"Is Ozan treating you right?" It was Clare's turn to ask.

I chuckled lightly. "Yes. He is."

"Well, as long as you know you're not making a mistake, I'm happy for you," Mom said, making me smile softly. "Just be careful. I don't want you to end up hurt Ariel, nor do I want Ozan to end up hurt."

I let out a long breath. "I know, Mom. Thank you."

With a couple more questions and chatting, Clare had to leave. My mom remained on the phone with me before heading up to her room. As soon as she went to her room, I finally asked.

"Mom. I wanted to ask you something," I whispered.

"Yes?" she wondered.

"What happened to the shooter? The police didn't find him yet?" It's been weeks and we still have yet to hear about him. I was getting worried and nervous as the time passed. It was still in the back of my head but I tried not to think much about it as I didn't want to continue to worry.

"No, Ariel. They didn't," mom answered, her voice low. "They're still looking for him."

"Oh, God. When will they find him? It's already been too long." My voice got a little louder due to the concern. "There's a shooter out there and the police still didn't find him?"

"Honey, they're trying their best," she assured me. "Don't worry. They'll find him."

"I'm worried, Mom. I'm worried for you guys too," I confessed, closing my eyes as I tried to calm myself.

"Don't worry, Ariel. We have security with us 24/7," she assured.

"Okay. Be careful. I don't want anything to happen to you guys," I said.

"Don't worry, honey. You be careful too." We said our goodbyes and closed the line. A worried breath escaped my mouth as I thought of the situation. I laid back down on my bed as I closed my eyes.

I really do hope everything will be okay.

It was finally the day of the senior trip. I grabbed the small suitcase that was filled with everything that I needed and walked out my room, meeting with a grinning Ozan in the hallway. He pecked me on the cheek.

"Are you ready?" he asked.

I smiled and nodded. "Yeah. We should get going. We don't want to be late for the bus that will take us to the airport," I said as we walked down the stairs. Ozan helped me with the bag as we walked towards the main doors. Rose was standing by the door.

"I'll put the bags in Damon's car," Ozan said, grabbing onto my bag. "Take care, Rose. I'll see you in three days."

"You too, Ozan," Rose replied. With that, Ozan offered her one last smile before walking off.

"See you in three days," I told Rose.

She hugged me for a moment. "Take care, honey. Oh, and Ariel. I think you need to know something . . ." I raised a brow at her, knowing something was behind that smile of hers.

"What is it?" I asked.

Her grin widened as she remained silent for a moment. "Never mind. I'll leave it as a surprise."

I stared doubtfully at her. "Okay . . ."

265

"Have fun!"

"Thank you." I nodded at Rose before walking towards the car. I sat next to Ozan as Damon smiled at us and started the car. During the ride to school, Damon and Ozan chatted a bit. I glanced at Ozan, hoping this trip would make him happy and not wear him out.

I was nervous of going. I didn't want anything to happen to him over there. However, I realized that he needed this. I also double checked his bags to see if he took his medication and I was relieved to see that he was still taking them. I acted as if I didn't know though.

We eventually made it to the school and started to walk to the front of the campus where we could meet with the bus. I saw many students out there, excited to go on the trip.

There was a large bus with teachers scattered everywhere. When Ozan and I walked up to them, a teacher started to tell us rules. They informed us to stick together and that misbehaving students will be suspended.

They started to allow the students to go on the bus one by one. The teachers were counting each student that got on. After a while, Ozan and I finally climbed on it, sitting next to each other.

I stared out the window, waiting for the last student to get on the bus.

Numerous teachers were with us. As the last student got on, the bus doors were about to close.

"Hold on a second. There's one more student left," a teacher said, glancing at the paper in his hand.

At that moment, someone walked in the bus. My eyes widened as I saw Troy walking in, meeting my wide eyes. I held my jaw from dropping.

I can't believe he was actually coming. What the hell? I thought he wasn't coming.

As he passed my isle, I saw a satisfied smirk on his lips and amused eyes twinkling back at me.

CHAPTER THIRTY-SEVEN

My body immediately went stiff as I watched Troy slip to the chair exactly behind mine. I felt very uncomfortable. Ozan stared behind me, meeting the eyes of an amused Troy who felt like this situation only brought joy to him.

"What's he doing here? I thought he wasn't coming?" Ozan whispered. I shrugged my shoulders. Ozan let out a sigh.

Ozan and I stared at each other for a moment before he grabbed my hand. He gave me his soft, comforting smile that made me ease a bit. His eyes told me that everything was going to be okay and all that mattered was that we are going to have fun.

I tried my best to ignore the person behind me and smiled back at Ozan. He glanced back at Troy one more time before looking forward. I glanced at the glass window that was next to me to see Troy's reflection from behind me.

That amused smirk was wiped off his face. He was staring—more like glaring—at something in front of him. I followed his eyes and glanced at our joined hands. I looked back to Troy's reflection to see him glaring at my hand in Ozan's grasp. Troy met my eyes through the window. I immediately turned away. I let out a breath, trying to shrug him off.

The bus soon started moving. A teacher stood in front of the bus, telling us the rules and what to do as we make it to the airport. He told us that there will be people with us to help us through the process and that we should behave on the five-hour flight to Hawaii.

Ozan and I listened carefully. After giving the details, the teacher sat back down in his seat. The way to the airport was going to take a while, especially with all the traffic.

Ozan kept glancing at me and smiled, rubbing his thumb over my hand in a comforting motion. "Are you excited?" he asked.

"Yeah. It's my first time going to Hawaii," I confessed.

"Me too. I've been to other countries and states but I've never been to Hawaii," Ozan said.

"I've never even been outside the country and I don't know if I ever will," I chuckled lightly.

Ozan laughed lightly, shaking his head. "That doesn't matter. What matters is that we have each other. Right?"

"Of course," I replied. Ozan's smile grew. He placed a quick kiss on my hand, making me glance at Troy's reflection. Troy soon met my eyes with a glare. I immediately looked back at Ozan. I smiled again at Ozan as he looked at me happily, completely forgetting the fact that Troy sat behind us.

We were still on the road when the bus soon came to a stop near a gas station. A teacher stood up, clapping his hands to get everyone's attention. "We still have about half an hour to reach the airport. The bus needs to be filled up with more gas so if you want, you can get out to buy a snack or to use the bathroom. But make it quick."

A couple of students got out the bus with two teachers.

I looked up at Ozan. "I'm going to go get water. Do you want something?" I asked.

"Just water," Ozan stated. I nodded and walked to the small store. The cool air in the store hit my skin. A couple of students were buying snacks. I walked to the back where the water bottles were.

I grabbed two water bottles. When I turned around, I faced Troy's chest. I stumbled backwards met Troy's hard eyes.

"What the heck, Troy?" I mumbled. I tried to slip through him but failed to do so as he gripped my hand.

"Ariel," he cautioned.

"What?" I frowned. "Let go of me," I whispered. I didn't want anyone to see us. I pulled my hand from his grip.

"What you're doing is pissing me off," he said lowly. I do not want to go through this again so I walked past him, ignoring his warnings.

"Stop it, Troy. Don't do this," I told him as I turned to glance at him. He was staring at me but I ignored him and walked to the cashier to pay for the water. I walked back to the bus, seeing a worried Ozan.

"Is Troy bothering you?" Ozan asked as I sat next to him. "I saw him follow you in. Ariel, if he's not leaving you alone then tell me."

I smiled softly and shook my head. "No. It's fine, Ozan. He's not bothering me," I assured

Ozan sighed. "I'm just worried, Ariel. I want you to be happy . . . with me," he said.

I placed my hand on top of his. "I am. Don't worry," I comforted. However, I couldn't help but feel like I was comforting myself more. I was trying to tell myself that I was happy.

Ozan nodded and went silent as Troy came walking in the bus. I saw Troy glancing at my hand on Ozan's. His once amused eyes when he first walked in here completely vanished. I pulled my eyes off him.

The bus eventually started moving again. During the ride to the airport, Ozan opened his backpack and took out something. I saw him take out the medicine that was for his tumor.

Ozan saw me looking at it and gave me a fake smile. "Painkillers. My head is getting dizzy from the ride," he muttered. I slowly nodded.

"Do you feel sick?" I asked, worry laced in my tone.

Ozan shook his head. "No. My head just hurts. That's it. But this will make the pain go away for a short time," Ozan stated, trying to assure me that nothing was wrong. I bit my lip to prevent myself from saying anything. I soon placed my hand on his, looking him straight in the eyes.

"You know, Ozan. You could tell me anything, right?" I told him. I saw him take a deep breath, nodding his head hesitantly.

"I—I know . . ." he murmured. He then looked away from me, staring forward. I tried to hide the frown that was plastered on my expression.

For the whole ride, Ozan and I would talk briefly before we finally made it to the airport. As we got off the bus, many people helped us through the airport and with all the process. For the whole time, I tried my best to ignore and stay far away from Troy. After a while, we were sitting in the airport, waiting to get on the flight.

The teachers were helpful and stood by us as we waited. Ozan and I were sitting next to each other, talking as we waited. I glanced around the cluster of students. I didn't see Troy. I shrugged it off and looked back at Ozan.

"I'm going to go to the restroom before we board the plane," I told him, getting up from my seat.

Ozan nodded. "Okay, but be quick."

I walked to the restroom to do my business. After, I walked out the bathroom. I stopped on my tracks and placed my hand on my chest.

"Oh my God," I whispered, meeting Troy's eyes. "Can you stop scaring me like that?"

"Can you stop ignoring me?" he asked.

I gulped as I tried to step away from him. Troy grabbed onto my hand. "Troy. I said stop this. Let go of my hand," I whispered, pulling my hand away from his.

"Will you stop acting as if I don't exist? You're doing this on purpose. You're pissing me off."

271

"I'm not doing anything on purpose, Troy," I stated. "Why did you even come? You said you weren't coming."

"I told you not to go to the trip," he started, stepping closer to me. "But you didn't listen to me."

"Because I don't have to. You can't tell me what to do. Why do you even care? Why did you come?"

Troy sucked a breath. "I'm not letting you go on this trip with Ozan alone. I told you not to go, but you didn't listen. That's why I came."

"Are you serious, Troy?" I scoffed. I managed to slip through him and shook my head. "Please. Stay away from me. You're making this harder for me."

"Ariel—"

"Don't, Troy. You're making me very confused," I told him, stepping away. "Don't play with my feelings like this." I walked away from him, letting out a frustrated sigh.

I walked back to Ozan and sat next to him, trying to push Troy out my head and forced my thoughts on something else.

"How much until we board the plane?" I asked Ozan.

"Ten more minutes," Ozan replied, grabbing my hand and rubbed his thumb over my skin. I noticed that Ozan did that quite often as it was his way to bring comfort to himself and I didn't mind. If he was comfortable then I was happy. "The last time we've been on a plane was four months ago," Ozan said. I remembered the day we flew from New York to California.

"Yeah." I smiled, thinking back at the day I first saw Troy after three long years. "It feels like yesterday. I can't believe it's already been four months."

"I know." Ozan nodded. "You know, I don't regret one bit that I came along with you," Ozan pointed out, smiling innocently at me which made me return a smile.

"Oh, Ozan. Thank you," I whispered.

"Don't thank me, Ariel. It was the least I could do for you," he exclaimed. "I knew that you needed someone to stay by

272

your side and I wanted to be that someone. I want to be someone that can take that load off your shoulders. I truly want to make you happy."

I remained silent.

"When we first came here, I noticed how you felt towards Troy. I knew it wasn't easy after all these years but that's why I'm here. I want you to heal and I want to be the purpose of your healing," he continued to explain as his words hit me right in my heart. "You can always rely on me, Ariel. You mean so much to me, since the moment we first met."

I smiled at him. His eyes were filled with hope and sincerity. "You mean so much to me too, Ozan. I'm glad I have you by my side," I said in all honesty. His smile grew.

I saw Troy again. He sat down in front of us. I tried my best to ignore his presence and focus it all on Ozan.

Not long after, we were boarding the plane. Ozan soon found his seat and sat down.

"My seat isn't next to yours," I stated, showing him the small paper. He frowned but nodded anyway.

"Oh. That's not a problem," he mumbled, giving me a crooked smile. "Go find your seat." I smiled back at him and continued down the aisle, looking at each seat. Finally, after a couple seats later, I sat down by the window and looked at the other students finding their seats.

Teachers were helping everyone settle down and buckle up. I glanced out the window, feeling more excitedd as I thought about the trip. A trip which I hoped would be something to remember.

That all went away when I saw Troy approaching me, amusement in his eyes all over again. I stared at him in confusion. He raised his paper which indicated where his seat was. A smirk soon crawled on his lips.

"Oh, would you look at that. My seat is right next to yours."

273

CHAPTER THIRTY-EIGHT

"Troy," I groaned, rolling my eyes as we sat in my room like any other day. My brows furrowed at a bored Troy who was playing around with the world globe that laid on my desk. He was spinning it around and giving me a headache. "Remind me why do I even try with you?"

He glanced at me as foolish grin made its way on his lips. I rolled my eyes once again. He continued to spin the world globe. "Um, maybe because you love me?" He scooted his chair closer to mine.

"Or maybe because I don't want you failing your classes?" I suggested, trying to hold back the smile that threatened to come out. Troy lost the grin, showing me his displeasure.

He let go of the globe and leaned against his chair, scratching the back of his neck. "I'm not failing my classes . . ." he mumbled.

I crossed my arms. "Yeah. Getting an F in two of your classes isn't failing?" I wondered out loud, smiling as his face dropped. I laughed the moment his lips pouted. He rolled his eyes.

"Okay. I might be failing a couple of classes, but that's why I have you as my tutor." He smiled softly

"And that's why you need to concentrate and not play around with that thing," I stated, pointing at the world globe that he kept playing around with.

"Okay. You're right. I'm sorry," he mumbled, shrugging his shoulders. "But you can't blame me. Math is too boring. Besides, look at this." He looked back at the work globe and continued to spin it fast.

His eyes stuck to the world globe. Well, I guess it brought him a tiny bit of joy when it came to math.

"I'm eventually going to throw that out," I muttered to myself, making him stop and laugh.

Troy scooted his chair closer to mine and placed the world globe on his lap. "Look," he murmured, grinning. "One day, we're going to travel around the world. Together." He smiled, spinning the globe.

A small smile grew on my lips, completely forgetting about what I was lecturing him about.

"One day, when we grow up, I want to take you to places. Other countries and states around the world," he exclaimed, pointing at a couple of countries.

"Really?" I asked, staring up at him with hopeful eyes. His grin widened and he nodded.

"In the future, I'll take over my dad's business. I'll have enough money to show you the world," Troy stated. "I'll take you anywhere you want to go."

I felt my eyes water at his words. Him talking about our future made me feel all types of emotions. We were still young, but I was excited for what the future held for us. I was excited for my future with him.

"Where would you want to go first?" he asked, looking down at the globe. At this moment, I placed the studying at the back of my mind and glanced at the globe that sat on his lap.

"I don't know," I mumbled. "There's so many beautiful places. I want to explore many places."

Troy nodded, placing a kiss on my forehead. "What about you?" I asked, looking up at him. "Where would you want to go to?"

Troy looked down at the globe, shrugging his shoulders as well. "There's so many places I want to go to," he started, smiling as he spun the globe until he stopped at a point. "But first, I want to explore this place with you. This should be our first destination."

I looked down at where his finger was pointing at and smiled.

"You want to go to Hawaii first?" I asked.

"Yes. That will be our start. Once we land foot on Hawaii, our journey begins."

*   *   *

My eyes opened, snapping me out from the dream. I stiffened. It was a memory that I tried to keep at bay. It was an innocent memory of Troy and I three years back. It hit me hard.

I tried not to remember that memory, but it all came rushing down to me the moment I set foot on the plane. I let out a shaky breath. I glanced at the person that sat next to me, the person I tried my best to avoid this whole ride.

"You're awake," he murmured lowly as I met Troy's dark orbs. "Good. We're about to land."

I ran a hand over my face, glancing out the window. "I fell asleep?" I wondered loudly.

Troy nodded. "Yes. You've been asleep for three hours," he answered. I slowly nodded, taking the information in. I was kind of happy that I fell asleep. It made time go faster. Ever since he sat down next to me, I went stiff.

I expected him to say something but surprisingly, he remained quiet and so did I. The person that sat next to Troy would talk every now and then but would remain silent for most of the time. I'd feel Troy's eyes on me every single moment, but I try my best to ignore it.

I was sort of embarrassed that I fell asleep in front of him. I ran my hand over my face to hide the embarrassment.

"Oh," I muttered.

Just then we heard the pilot's voice announcing that we were landing. I kept staring on the window, gawking at the beautiful view.

I was astonished and amazed. The view caught my breath.

I didn't know for how long I was staring, but I eventually snapped out of it and looked back to the front. Before I knew it, we were landing safely and walking out the plane. As soon as we were off the plane, teachers started guiding us as I looked around for Ozan.

He came walking towards me with a smile. He then grabbed onto my hand. "How was the flight?" he asked as we started walking. Troy was walking right in front of us. He took glances at us from time to time.

"It was good. I slept for the majority of the time," I answered.

He nodded. "That's good."

After a while, we were outside of the airport. The heat hit our skin. I wiped my forehead, feeling the sweat roll down my skin.

A large bus stood before us. "Now, we'll be boarding this bus. It will take us to the hotel we'll be staying at. Each person is assigned to a room with a partner. You'll be lead to your room once we get there," he explained. "We'll take a two hour rest before we head off to our first activity. Be smart and don't get lost. There will be people around that will help you. We don't want to face any problems. Please cooperate so we could have a good time," a teacher said.

Everyone nodded which made him smile. "Good. Now come on." He allowed everyone to enter the bus and settle down. I sat next to Ozan, the same as before before the bus started moving. Another teacher soon stood up, repeating the rules they once told us about.

"The hotel isn't far away so we'll arrive shortly," he said before sitting down.

Ozan and I kept glancing at the window, taking in the beautiful view. Ozan commented about how beautiful this place was.

It was mesmerizing.

Twenty minutes went by and we were exiting the bus. Troy got off last. He met my eyes which eventually traveled down to where Ozan was holding my hand. I glanced away. The teacher began to speak as we started to grab our bags.

"Okay. Everyone will be accompanied to their room. Please don't be rude and respect the people that's staying in this hotel. After two hours, there will be people that will accompany you to this same spot in case you get lost so we can head to our first destination," he explained. "I'll talk about our first destination once we board the bus but for now, you can all go to your rooms and settle down."

It wasn't a difficult process to find our rooms. The teacher passed our room numbers. After I said goodbye to Ozan, I walked to my room with the help of some employees. I soon found my room and scanned the number card. The door opened and a girl was already inside checking out the place.

I immediately recognized her as a girl I shared my English class with. She smiled kindly at me, which was a relief. It's a good thing that I was paired with her. I didn't really know her well, but she seemed to be a kind girl.

"Hi, Ariel. It's nice to see that you're my partner."

I placed my suitcase on the floor and smiled back. "Hey, Layla," I greeted. "It's nice to see that you're my partner too. Thankfully, I did not end up with someone I didn't get along with."

There were many girls on this trip that I didn't get along with. They just didn't seem friendly so it would have been a bit of a problem if I was paired with them.

Layla chuckled, nodding. "I feel the same."

I adjusted my bag near the bed I chose and saw Layla do the same. "So, we have two hours?" I spoke.

"Yeah. I'm just going to relax until then," she said, laying on the bed. "If I fall asleep, can you wake me up after two hours?" Layla mumbled, stretching as she yawned.

"Sure. Don't worry about it," I assured her.

"Thank you." She went silent, assuming that she was drifting off. I breathed out and sat on the bed, staring off into space. I didn't feel tired because I already took a nap on the plane so sleeping was not an option.

I guess I'll just sit around for two hours.

After two hours of doing nothing, I woke Layla up so we could get ready. I changed into something more comfortable before we walked back to where we were supposed to meet up. Eventually, everyone was in sight, including Ozan who was waving at me.

"Is he your boyfriend?" Layla asked as we walked towards the group.

I nodded. "Yes." She nodded slowly with a weird expression plastered onto her face. "Why? Is something wrong?" I asked.

"No," she murmured. "I just thought you had a thing for Troy." She shrugged her shoulders as if it was nothing. My eyes widened and I shook my head.

"No. Why would you think that?" I asked.

Layla shrugged her shoulders again. "I don't know. I just noticed how you guys always stare at each other," Layla said, waving her hand in the air. "Forget it. I must have thought wrong."

I only nodded and the next thing I knew, Ozan was standing by my side, smiling at me. "Hey," I said. "How's your room. You like it?"

"It's okay. My partner is pretty cool," Ozan replied.

"What are we waiting for?" We were just standing here.

"For the bus. It still hasn't arrived yet," Ozan replied. The moment he said that, a bus came into view. The teachers allowed us to enter it. The minute we were settled, another teacher stood in front of the bus and began speaking.

"Okay, everyone. Attention all on me." He clapped his hands, making all heads turn to him. "We're now heading to a mountain nearby. We'll hike our way up until we reach the top. There, you'll enjoy the view and grab a bite. I don't want any problems, so please, no running off or exploring when you're not supposed to."

Everyone in the bus nodded, making him smile.

"Great. We can get going."

CHAPTER THIRTY-NINE

Today was a hectic day. I let out a breath as I stretched my legs across the smooth, warm sand, making my muscles relax at the nice sensation. I hummed in satisfaction and let my hands roam through the sand as I watched Ozan play in the water with a couple of his friends. I could hear his loud laughter.

It's been a couple of hours since we have arrived in Hawaii and we already did a couple of things. First, we went hiking in this mountain which wasn't so hard. The most beautiful and amazing thing about it was once you reach the top. You get to see this magnificent view of the ocean and the island. It was just amazing.

We then ate and stayed there for a while before it was time to go down. A man gave us a tour around the beautiful area which made many students snap pictures at the spectacular view.

After that, we returned to the hotel and walked to the shore with a couple of lifeguards keeping an eye on us. They allowed us to swim and relax on the beach and that's what we were doing. Many of the students were out in the water, playing around and splashing the others while some only sat on the sand and enjoyed the sunlight hitting their skin. That's what I was doing. I wasn't really fond of swimming so I decided to just sit around and enjoy the view. The sunlight hit my skin, spreading the warm feeling all over my body. The warm sand only made it better.

I waved at Layla the moment I saw her waving at me. She was playing around in the water with a couple of friends. She gestured for me to come over but I shook my head, offering her an apologetic smile in return.

She nodded nonetheless and continued with what she was doing. I scanned the beach and saw many familiar faces scattered around on the shore and in the water. However, there was one person in particular that's missing, which made me frown.

Troy.

I tried to push him out my thoughts. I couldn't help but be slightly worried. I noticed something, but I wasn't too sure if it was just my head playing tricks on me or if I was actually noticing his weird behavior.

Ever since we came here he was acting a little weird. I expected him to talk to me, to say something. However, he stayed rather quiet and off. After we boarded the plane, he remained silent. After we landed foot on Hawaii, I noticed weird expressions on his features. It was as if he was trying to comprehend something. I couldn't pull my eyes away from him.

When we went up to the mountain, he remained silent and spaced off. He didn't really interact with anyone but would only walk around and stare at the place. When we first came to the beach, which was only five minutes away from the hotel, he came along and stood with a couple of guys. Now, he was nowhere in sight. He must have wandered off somewhere.

We weren't allowed to wander off too far from the group but it was okay to walk around the vicinity as long as we weren't getting lost.

I was pulled out of my thoughts the moment I saw Ozan walking back towards me, running a hand over his wet face. His smile disappeared and was replaced with a thin line.

Ozan sat next to me. "Are you okay? Did something happen?" I asked worriedly.

He nodded, looking me in the eye with a small smile of assurance. "I'm okay," he mumbled, placing his hand on his head. "My head just hurt. I'm going to go back to the hotel to rest."

My eyes widened and when he stood up, I stood up as well. I placed a hand on his arm, looking up at him with concern. "Are you sure you're okay? Do you need us to call someone?" I asked. Ozan immediately shook his head.

"No. There's no need. Just a small headache," he insisted, rubbing my arm in a soothing manner.

"Okay. Then let's go back to the hotel," I said, stepping forward. Ozan grabbed my hand and shook his head.

"No, there's no need to. I can go alone," he exclaimed.

"No—"

"Ariel. It's okay. Just a headache. I'm going to go back and relax," he assured, yet it did nothing to ease my worries. "You stay here and enjoy this while you can. Go play in the water or something."

I opened my mouth to speak but was cut off when he placed a kiss on my forehead. He took a step back, smiling softly at me. "I'll see you later." With that, he turned around and walked back to the hotel, leaving me standing there with a worried expression plastered on my face.

I was debating with myself on whether I should follow him or not. He didn't want me following him, but I couldn't help but feel worried.

With a sigh, I looked away from where he walked to. He wanted to be alone so I shouldn't go after him. Hopefully after he relaxed, he'll feel better.

I started walking on the sand barefooted, trying to take my mind off of Ozan. I started walking away from the group. I didn't think much of it and walked along the beach with my feet in the cool water.

I continued to walk away from the group. Maybe if I walked around I'd feel a little better.

As I was walking, I could make out someone sitting on the sand not too far away from me. I continued to take small steps towards the sitting figure. I came to a stop the moment my eyes made out Troy's appearance sitting calmly on the sand, spacing off at the sunset.

I frowned as I watched Troy stare intensely at the water with a weird look on his face before he buried his head between his hands. My frown deepened as he stayed like that for a while.

My feet were walking towards him without my consent. He has yet to notice my presence. I sucked in a breath as I notice him go stiff.

Troy slowly turned to me. I tried to speak but the words were clogged in my throat. I closed my lips as he only stared at me, forcing my feet to step closer to him.

"Troy?" I whispered. "Are you okay?"

Troy opened his mouth but no words escaped his lips. He reluctantly looked away from me, staring off into the ocean. He stood like that for a moment.

"Troy? What's wrong? You don't seem okay," I said. Troy's eyes soon met mine. We were just staring at each other for what felt like minutes before he stood up, stepping towards me.

"Ariel, I—"

"You kids over there!" A familiar voice called out. A teacher was waving his hands at us. "Come on. We're heading back to the hotel."

I looked back at Troy and our eyes met again. This time, he shook his head. "It's nothing." He then walked past me. I looked at him in confusion, wondering what he was going to say. I knew that it wasn't nothing. There was something off and I didn't know what.

I started making my way back to the hotel with confusion still present in my mind and worry plastered on my face.

A few moments later, I was back in the room. Layla and I were sitting and talking as I held my phone in my hands. I listened to her silently as she basically complained about a teacher that was with us on this trip. I nodded every couple of seconds to show her that I was listening as I texted Ozan, checking if he was okay.

The moment I heard a ringing sound, I opened my phone and saw a reply from Ozan, telling me that he felt okay and that he was going to sleep. I let out a sigh of relief.

"Did you hear what I said?" Layla asked, raising a brow. I offered her an apologetic smile and shook my head.

"Sorry. I was texting Ozan," I told her. She smiled but shook her head.

"It's fine," Layla assured. "So, you're chatting with your boyfriend?"

"Not really. Just wanted to see if he was okay," I answered, shrugging my shoulders before replying to Ozan's text. I told him to text me if he felt tired. Layla nodded. After a while of not hearing from Ozan, I assumed that he fell asleep.

It wasn't late but from all what happened today, I could only assume that many were tired and wanted to sleep. We were going to wake early tomorrow.

Minutes of Layla and I talking passed and she soon got in her covers. "I'm going to sleep," she yawned and stretched as she closed her eyes. "I'm so tired."

"Okay. Goodnight," I said back to her.

"You're not sleeping?" she wondered, her eyes still close.

"I'm not that tired. I'll stay up for a bit," I replied. She only nodded. Her breathing became steady, telling me that she was falling asleep.

I sat in my bed, staring out the window and at the silent ocean which caught my attention. I didn't know for how long I was staring at its beauty. After what felt like an hour, I couldn't bring myself to sleep, so I got up and walked towards the door, opening it silently so I wouldn't wake Layla up.

I sighed when I saw the empty hallway. Maybe a walk on the beach could sooth me? I know it might have seemed like a bad idea to get out of my room without permission, but it wasn't so late and no one really prohibited us from exiting our rooms. All they would say was don't make trouble and don't get lost.

I shrugged it off and walked towards the lobby. The person at the desk didn't seem to care that I was exiting the hotel. I continued to walk out the hotel, inhaling the cool air that hit my skin, forcing a shiver down my body.

I walked towards the beach, the one I was at hours ago. This time, the ocean was calm and quiet. I stared at the stars and closed my eyes, breathing in. I started walking along the beach, my feet hitting the soft sand. It brought me comfort.

However, just like the last time, I stopped dead in my tracks when I saw a body laying on the sand, staring up at the stars. Immediately, I knew it was Troy and my eyes slightly widened. What was he doing here?

Like the last time, he didn't notice my presence until I started walking towards him. His face soon turned to me, dark eyes meeting.

As I took more steps towards him, he sat up. "What are you doing here?" he asked.

"I was going to ask you that," I stated. He stared at me for a moment, soon pulling his eyes away from me.

"Couldn't sleep. I needed fresh air," he murmured.

I nodded. "The same reason why I'm out here," I confessed. His eyes remained on the ocean and I reluctantly sat next to him, staring at him with confusion.

"Troy? Are you okay?" I asked him.

"Why do you ask that?" he questioned lowly.

"Because you seem off," I mumbled. Troy finally turned and looked at me, his eyes staring at me so intensely that I held in the shiver that threatened to escape.

"I'm fine," he mumbled.

"You're not," I argued softly, shaking my head.

His eyes softened. He ran a hand through his hair as he let out a frustrated sigh.

"Troy," I whispered. "Tell me. What's wrong?"

Troy turned over at me. "I don't know," he mumbled.

287

"What do you mean?" I asked, looking at him with confusion clear on my face.

"I don't know what's wrong, Ariel. I feel weird," he grunted. "There's something in the back of my head trying to tell me something."

My brows furrowed. "I don't understand."

He snapped his head at me. "Nether do I. I didn't want to come here but the moment I came, I felt like I wanted to be here," he confessed in a low tone. I sucked in a breath, listening carefully to his words. "It feels like I was meant to come here."

My eyes widened. I was speechless. Did he remember something? Did he remember what he once promised me?

"T—Troy? Did you—"

"Ariel I don't remember anything but I think I wanted to come here three years ago." He looked away with a hard expression on his face. I continued to stare at him, waiting for him to continue. After a couple of seconds, Troy looked back at me.

"I think that I wanted to come here . . . with you."

CHAPTER FORTY

I let out a hum of satisfaction the moment I felt his hand run through my hair. He was twirling strands around his finger as I stared at the dark sky that was lit up with thousands of stars bringing light and beauty to the darkness that surrounded us.

I remained laying on the soft green grass as my eyes stared at the countless shiny white dots that played a beautiful pattern in the black sky. Troy laid next to me, but his body wasn't facing the sky. His body faced mine as his one hand went underneath his head to give him support while the other played with my hair softly. I closed my eyes at the comfort he brought.

I could feel his eyes on me. His hand soon let go of my hair and move down to my arm which laid down on the grass motionless. He ran his finger on my bare skin as his eyes continued to bore into me.

I shivered at the sensation. I heard him chuckle lowly, then another moment of comfortable silence. That silence was soon interrupted when Troy's voice hit my ears.

"Ariel?" he murmured.

"Hmm?" I mumbled, my eyes still close.

"Do you love me?" he whispered. My eyes slowly opened to meet his serious yet calm eyes. A soft smile tugged on my lips and I nodded.

"More than anything," I answered. That answer brought a smile to his lips, but his eyes said something else. It had a hint of sadness in them which only piqued my curiosity.

"Will you love me till the day we die?" he wondered. I smiled at him again, nodding as I stared back at him sincerely.

"Death won't stop me from loving you," I replied, making his smile grow. He chuckled a little. His eyes were twinkling with happiness.

"Will you still love me even if I hurt you?" Troy asked, his eyes back to being calm but serious.

"Yes. I will," I answered softly. Troy remained silent, staring at me for what felt like minutes. Smiles tugged on our lips as he held my hand softly. His thumb rubbed my skin. His breaths were soft, yet loud enough for me to hear.

"Would you still love me if you ever forgot about me?" Troy finally said. His smile disappeared and was replaced with a sad one. I stared at him for a moment, taking in his words.

"My mind might forget you, but my heart never will."

His dark orbs stared at me with so much emotion I couldn't point out. There was love, hope, and faith but somewhere in there, I could make out sadness. It tore my heart.

"What about you?" I asked, raising a brow. "Would you still love me if you ever forgot about me?"

His mouth closed, not uttering a word as he slowly took his eye off me for the first time. His eyes looked up at the sky, soon closing them for a moment before turning back to me and smiling, shaking his head.

"You already answered that question, Ariel," he mumbled softly, grabbing onto my hand once again as his eyes twinkled with sincere love. "My mind might forget you . . . but my heart never will."

*　　*　　*

290

My eyes snapped open. I met the dark ceiling. I immediately sat up on the bed and pulled my knees under my chin, trying to remain silent so I wouldn't wake Layla up. I placed my hand on my mouth, recalling the dream I just had. I closed my eyes to hold back the tears.

He gave me so many signs. How did I not notice? How did I not notice the times when he gave me so many signs? I was so blind. So stupid.

I remained in that same position. I felt so many emotions within me. I have so many unanswered questions that I couldn't seem to find the answers to.

What happened a couple hours back replayed in my head. Was he starting to remember?

I feel that him coming here triggered something. He didn't remember everything, but he remembered one thing, one thing that held so much meaning to us. That alone made my heartbeat race.

I couldn't ask him further because he got up and left, leaving me sitting on the shore shocked and brimming with tears.

What if Troy was beginning to remember? What if Troy actually remembered something?

Tears fell down my cheek as I kept my hand on my mouth. I was starting to question my actions. I was starting to wonder what I was doing. I was questioning whether Ozan and I would ever work out. I doubt if I could ever remove Troy from my heart and forget him. I didn't know if what I was doing was wrong and useless.

I felt like a coward. I felt stupid. What if I can never forget Troy? Most importantly, what if Troy soon remembers? What do I do then?

* * *

"We made it back to the hotel," a teacher said, catching everyone's attention that was in the bus. "Everyone go rest. We'll wake up early tomorrow and at the evening we'll head to the airport."

The bus soon opened its doors to allow us to exit. This was our second day and it was quite hectic. We did many activities which were actually fun. It would have been better if my mind wasn't distracted. My whole head was going haywire and was soon to burst.

I had so many thoughts on my head that I didn't know what exactly to do.

I glanced at Ozan who smiled at me. I smiled back at him but turned away. I was so confused at the moment.

I said goodbye to Ozan and walked to my room with Layla. It was dark outside, but not too late for me to actually fall asleep. However, staying up last night kind of got me tired, yet I still know that I won't be able to sleep.

We eventually entered the room and sat on the bed. Hours soon went by and Layla got in her covers, yawning out. I glanced at her, seeing her get comfortable.

"Going to sleep?" I wondered.

Layla nodded. "Yeah. What about you?" she asked.

I shrugged my shoulders. "Not yet. I don't think I'll be able to sleep," I told her. She nodded and went quiet, her breaths soon turning into soft snores. I sighed and turned to the window to staring at the beach, the same one I sat on with Troy yesterday.

A ringing sound caught my attention and pulled me from my thoughts. I glanced at my phone to see a text message.

Meet me at the shore.
~ Ozan

I stared at the message for a moment, confused why Ozan wanted to meet me at this time. I shrugged my shoulders and silently got up. I quietly walked towards the lobby, doing the same thing that I did yesterday.

As soon as I exited the hotel, I was immediately hit by the cool wind. I sucked a breath and walked to the beach. The moment I arrived, I scanned my eyes around the beach and stopped at a figure not too far away from me.

I started walking towards the body the moment I realized it was Ozan. His face was looking at the silent ocean. I was soon standing in front of him.

"Hey, Ariel," he whispered. I smiled softly at him.

"Hi, Ozan."

"I'm sorry that I called you out here. You were probably sleeping," he muttered, scratching the back of his neck. I shook my head.

"No. It's okay. I wasn't sleeping," I assured him. "Is there something wrong? Are you okay?"

"There's nothing wrong. I'm okay," Ozan said. "I just wanted to talk with you. I wanted to be alone with you for a moment."

"Oh . . ." I murmured softly. "Okay."

Ozan's smile grew and he placed his hand in his pocket. He took out something. He revealed a bracelet. "While we were in the local store, I saw this and couldn't help but buy it," Ozan spoke, meeting my eyes. "I know it's not something big, but I want to give this to you."

I stared at the beautiful bracelet that laid in his hands. "You bought this for me?"

Ozan smiled and nodded. "Yes. It's for you."

"Ozan. You didn't have to. There's no need to," I said softly.

Ozan immediately shook his head. "No. I wanted to. Please, take it."

I looked back at Ozan, his eyes twinkling with hope. "I want you to wear it. I want you to have something from me, to remind you of me."

I blinked, trying to hold the tears. I took it and wore the bracelet in my hand. "Oh, Ozan. It's beautiful," I whispered. "Thank you."

Ozan's smile grew and his eyes stared back at me with happiness, yet a hint of sadness present in them. I immediately pulled him in my arms and hugged him. Ozan hugged me back and I couldn't stop the tear that trickled down my cheek. I feel so bad. He was so sweet. I didn't deserve him at all.

I heard Ozan chuckle lowly. "Thank you. It's beautiful," I whispered again as we pulled away. Ozan grinned at me.

"Don't thank me. It's not something big but I'm glad you like it." He shrugged his shoulders.

I smiled thankfully at him and was about to speak when I saw someone walking towards us from the corner of my eye. I glanced at the person and immediately went stiff as I saw Troy walk on the sand. Troy must have noticed us because he stopped dead in his track, meeting my eyes from the distance.

I glanced back at Ozan to see him staring intensely at me, unaware of Troy watching us. I was about to open my mouth to speak when Ozan's face got closer to mine. Before I knew it, Ozan's lips were on mine.

My eyes widened as I felt Ozan kissing me softly. The kiss didn't last for long since Ozan pulled away, smiling apologetically.

"Sorry. I must have surprised you," he whispered, scratching the back of his neck. "I just wanted to kiss you for once." He then ran a hand over his face. "Sorry. Maybe you weren't ready."

I immediately shook my head. "No. It's okay," I assured. "It surprised me a little but it's okay."

Ozan smiled at me. I looked back to where Troy was standing but he was gone. He must have seen us. I couldn't help but feel guilty, even though I knew I shouldn't.

Dammit, Ariel. What the hell are you doing?

"Let's head back, it's late," Ozan said, pulling me out of my thoughts.

We slowly started walking back to the hotel, my eyes scanning the area to see if I could catch a glimpse of Troy. He was nowhere in sight.

I let out a breath as Ozan placed a hand on my shoulder. We remained silent as Ozan took me to my room. I smiled softly at him when we finally reached the door. A few moments later, he suddenly groaned and placed a hand on his head.

"Ozan?" I whispered, placing my hand on his arm. "Are you okay? What's wrong?"

Ozan let out another groan, but louder this time.

"Ozan, what's wrong? Does your head hurt?"

It all happened so fast. I had no time to register what was happening.

Ozan soon fell to the floor. His body was shaking and his eyes looked like they were rolling back. The next thing I knew, I was on the floor holding him as I yelled for help.

CHAPTER FORTY-ONE

I sat on the chair for what felt like a very long time, staring at Ozan's sleeping figure. I could hear his heart monitor. My puffy red eyes remained on him as I waited him to wake up. I felt like hours had past and I was still in the same position.

When I saw his body shake and fall to the floor, I immediately started calling for help. We took him to the nearest hospital. That experience was horrifying. I don't think I'll ever forget this night.

I was so scared that I'd lose Ozan. I tried to be strong and hold in the tears but it was no use. I couldn't hold back the sobs that escaped my lips as I held an unconscious Ozan in my grasp. It was heartbreaking. I hope that I'd never experience that ever again.

My eyes were glued on Ozan. He should be awake any second now. It has already been a couple hours and I was getting nervous by the minute.

The doctor told me that Ozan had a seizure due to the tumor. His tumor was growing and was affecting his health. Ozan has to have surgery as soon as possible. That was not a choice.

They put him under medication to keep him sleeping. I was so thankful that the seizure didn't end his life. However, the doctor warned me that another seizure could cost him his life. It could take Ozan away.

Another tear slipped down my cheek as I watched Ozan's steady breathing. I wasn't alone in the hospital. A couple of teachers are waiting outside. Thankfully, we only had a couple of hours left till we left Hawaii. As soon as we reach California, Ozan has to see a specialist to determine when he should do the surgery.

I sucked in a breath and closed my eyes, listening to his heart monitor. I immediately snapped my eyes open the moment I heard a movement in the bed.

I immediately stood up and made my way to his bed, my heart thumping. "Ozan?" I whispered, making his eyes glance towards me with confusion. "Oh, God. Ozan." I grabbed onto his hand and kneeled to the floor, another tear slipping down my cheek as Ozan tried to comprehend his surroundings. "I was so worried about you. You scared me to death."

"Ariel?" He grasped out, worry present in his eyes. "Where am I?"

"You're in a hospital, Ozan. Do you remember what happened?" I asked him, my thumb rubbing over his hand in a soothing manner.

"A hospital?" He questioned in a louder tone. "I'm in a hospital? Why?"

"Because you had a seizure, Ozan. You had a seizure due to the brain tumor," I answered his question, staring at his eyes to see shock and sadness. His eyes widened and his mouth opened, not knowing what word to utter. "Why didn't you tell me, Ozan? Why did you keep it a secret?"

"A-Ariel..." He murmured before stoping for a second. "I'm sorry."

"Why did you keep this to yourself? Why couldn't you tell me?" I asked him again. His eyes lowered in sadness and he sucked in a breath, closing his eyes.

"I'm sorry, Ariel. I didn't want to worry you," he replied, opening his eyes. "I came with you to look after you, not to be weak because of some tumor.

"A tumor which could cost you your life," I stated softly. "You could have told us. We could find a solution. You didn't have to stay silent."

"You're right," Ozan whispered, meeting my eyes with sadness twinkling in his. "I'm sorry for making you worry. I should have told you."

I sighed out and ran a hand over my face. "I was scared that I'd lose you," I whispered, another tear slipping out of my eyes. Ozan grasped onto my hand and offered me a soft smile.

"Don't be. As long as you stick by my side, you won't lose me."

*   *   *

Ozan, Julia, Rose and I sat silently in the living room as we watched Damon walk back and forth. He was clearly frustrated. He ran a hand over his face as he tried to comprehend Ozan's words.

Rose was shedding tears while Julia tried to comfort her mom. They were not expecting to hear that Ozan had a brain tumor, the same tumor which changed their son and took away his memories. It was the same tumor that created a deep hole in their family. It was the same tumor which separated Troy and I.

Damon soon came to a stop. "Do you know how worried we were when we heard from a teacher over the phone that you were hospitalized? And now we find out that you have a brain tumor? Why didn't you tell us this, Ozan?" Damon beamed, trying to calm down.

Ozan looked at the floor. I grabbed on to his hand as Damon waited for his answer. With a deep breath, Ozan looked back at Damon.

"I'm sorry. I should have told you guys," he whispered, shaking his head. "I was going to tell you guys but I guess I was too late."

Damon ran a hand over his face and sighed. "Do your parents know about this?" he asked.

"Yes. I already told them," Ozan answered. "My dad wanted me to return to New York to seek medication but I declined. I'm not leaving Ariel."

"Ozan. This is your health we're talking about. A brain tumor is a serious thing." Damon stated.

"I know," Ozan claimed. "I can do all that here. I don't want to leave Ariel." Ozan looked at me. His eye began to tear up. I tightened my hold on his hand. "Besides, I'm already on medication and I've already been prescribed to antiseizure medication to help control the seizures." Ozan looked back at Damon.

Damon stared at him in disbelief.

"Fine. Very well," Damon mumbled as he finally sat down. "You will stay here but I'm going to make an appointment for you to meet a specialist. The faster we go to one the faster you can go to surgery."

Ozan nodded and Damon placed a hand on his shoulder. "Don't worry, everything will be fine," Damon stated, pulling out his phone from his pocket as he stood up. "I'm going to go make an appointment."

Damon left the room to make the call. Ozan was frowning. I held onto his hand and Ozan turned to me, smiling softly.

"Everything will be okay," I stated. Rose only remained silent. I could understand her pain. She was scared and hurt. This was the second time she'd witness something like this in her lifetime. It wasn't something easy to take in. I already knew that she saw Ozan as her son so this dug up the memories of her past. It was clear on her face.

Ozan nodded and placed his head on my shoulder.

It has been a couple days since then. It has been a while since Rose and Damon found out that Ozan had a brain tumor. These days went by so slowly. Today was Ozan's appointment and we prayed that everything will go by smoothly.

Rose and I silently sat down in the living room. She kept glancing at her watch every minute. I took a breath and tried to be patient so I wouldn't add much stress on Rose.

She was very worried. She didn't really speak much on the subject but I could tell that this was a sore subject for her. We were now waiting for Ozan and Damon to arrive from the appointment. They've been gone for a couple hours now. We just keep getting more tensed as the time went by.

I stared off into space, trying to occupy my time until they arrived.

Troy didn't come home these past few days. Once we arrived from Hawaii, he came and placed his bags then left. Rose was quite worried but she decided not to question him as he did it often. Her mind was mostly on Ozan right now.

I couldn't help but feel my heart sink at the thought of him. The plane ride to California was tense. Troy didn't even make eye contact with me. I kind of knew that was because he saw Ozan kiss me.

I shouldn't feel guilty, but I do. I tried to keep my mind off him, but it was too hard. I felt many unwanted emotions and I didn't know how to control them. However, my first priority right now is to make sure Ozan is okay. I don't know what I'd do if I lose him.

I was immediately pulled out of my thoughts when we heard a car stopping in front of the house. Rose's eyes immediately perked up. She stood, eagerly waiting for them to make their appearance. I took a deep breath as I heard the front door opening and footsteps coming our way.

I frowned as soon as I saw Damon walking into the living room with a frown on his face. Ozan was also nowhere in sight.

"Where's Ozan?" I asked loudly.

"He went up to his room," Damon stated lowly, running a hand over his face in a frustrating manner. "He needs some time alone. What he heard today wasn't something easy to take in."

I stood up, gulping at Damon's words.

"What do you mean, Damon?" Rose asked, frowning as she took a step towards her husband. "What did the doctor say?"

Damon looked between Rose and I. "Surgery is out of the question. He can't do the surgery."

"Why?" I asked, mustering the strength to find my voice. "Why can't he do the surgery?"

"It's too dangerous. The tumor is located in a place of his brain near a vital structure," Damon answered. "The surgeon won't be able to reach it. It could bring major side affects to his health. He could die from the surgery."

Rose gasped and sat down. Damon walk over to comfort her as tears streamed down her cheeks. I feel choked. I blinked to try to regain my control, but his words made me weak.

"What do we do now?" I finally asked after a moment.

Damon rubbed Rose's back. "Radiation therapy and chemotherapy is his only option. He's already been prescribed to the drugs and now, Ozan has five sessions a week for a month of radiation therapy. That will either stop the growth of the tumor or decrease its size."

I sat down, running a hand over my face as I listened to his words. I could see the sadness in Damon's eyes.

"Let's just hope that this will be enough to keep him stable," Damon whispered. "But if that doesn't, then there's nothing we can do to keep him alive."

I was reluctant to enter Ozan's room. I didn't know if it would be a good idea to see him. What if he needed space? What if he needed some time alone?

I sucked in a breath and hesitantly knocked on his bedroom door. I did not hear a single sound from him. After a couple seconds, I knocked again but like last time, I heard nothing.

"Ozan? Are you okay?"

My frown deepened as I heard no response. I sucked in a shaky breath and knocked once again. "Ozan. I'm worried about you. Can I come in?" I asked. After a moment, I decided to do it. "I'm going to enter." I slowly opened his bedroom door and looked in the room.

I squinted my eyes at the dim room. The curtains were drawn. I gasped as I glanced to my right. Ozan scrunched in the corner of his room with his head in his hands.

"Ozan . . ." I whispered. He raised his head to look at me. His cheeks were wet with tears and his eyes were red and puffy.

Immediately, I kneeled next to him, placing a hand on his cheek.

"Ariel . . ." he whispered then pulled me in his arms. I hugged him back as he placed his head on my shoulder. His breaths were calming down.

"Don't be scared, Ozan. You're going to be okay," I murmured, rubbing his back. "We're here for you."

"Don't leave me, Ariel," Ozan finally spoke, his voice low. "As long as you're by my side, I'm not afraid."

CHAPTER FORTY-TWO

I closed the book I was reading when I heared a knock on my door. I got up to answer it. I smiled as I looked up at Ozan who was smiling, reflecting my own.

"Hey," he said.

"Hey. Are you going?" I asked, glancing at the clock.

"Yeah . . ." he murmured. "Rose is waiting for me downstairs. I just wanted to see you before I get going."

I stepped foot out my room and closed the door, standing by his side. "Okay. I'll walk with you to the front," I said. We started walking down the hall, Rose was already standing by the door.

It has been around two weeks since Ozan started doing his radiation therapy. He went there five times a week. Since the hospital wasn't close, he'd leave at 6 PM and return at 8 PM. Sometimes, Damon would take him, but if Damon was at work, Rose would be the one to accompany him.

We were so thankful for them both. They worked so hard for Ozan's treatment as if he was their own son. I was sure Ozan was grateful for that.

Rose smiled at us and opened the door. "You ready?" she asked Ozan. Ozan only nodded, making her glance at me. "Will you be okay on your own again?" Rose wondered, looking at me and raising a brow.

"Yes. It's alright," I assured her.

Rose stared at me for a moment before taking her phone from her pocket. "If you want, I can call Julia to come home. She's been staying at her friends house for some time now," Rose stated, glancing down at her phone.

Shaking my head, I smiled reassuringly at her. "It's fine, Rose. Let her stay at her friend's house," I insisted, waving my hand in the air. "I'm okay all alone. There's no need for her to return."

Rose nodded, sighing. "Okay then," she murmured. "We'll be back around 8 PM. The usual. If you need anything, make sure to call us. But I think Damon will leave early today so he might be home before us."

I nodded as Rose and Ozan stepped outside. Ozan smiled at me one more time and with a wave, he walked to the car.

"Take care," I said, waving my hand. Rose waved back before walking to the car, making me close the door behind them. I locked the door and walked to the living room, getting comfortable on the couch as I let out a long breath. I grabbed the remote and flipped through the channels, staring at the tv screen for what felt like a long time.

After a while of flipping through the channels, I let out a bored sigh and turned the TV off. I leaned my head against the wall and closed my eyes.

I tried to listen for something, but the air around me was quiet. This was the third time this week that I was left alone in this house. Julia would be out with her friends and Damon would be at work.

Troy, however, I didn't know where he was. For these two weeks I only saw him a couple of times. He'd return home, do something then leave without saying a word. I could notice that Rose and Damon were worried but Rose claimed that Troy did this often. I guess he was staying at a friend's house.

I could tell that he was trying to stay away from me, that's why he wasn't returning home. I didn't know if that was a good thing or not. It gave me some alone time with Ozan, but I couldn't help but feel empty when days went by and he wasn't here.

I groaned out of frustration and placed my head in my hands, trying to pull myself out from those thoughts. I couldn't lie to myself. I missed him and my feelings for him were still there but I know that Ozan needed me more. I don't want to leave him. It's difficult.

Deep down, I knew that I was doing Ozan wrong, but I don't have the strength to leave him, especially when he's sick. Ozan needed me more than ever, and I needed him too. I was just hoping that Troy would soon leave my heart, giving me the peace that I want.

It's too hard.

I pulled my head from my hands and stood up, heading towards the kitchen.

Ozan was so nice and kind to me. He made me feel a sense of happiness and I was thankful for that. At times however, I couldn't help but compare that happiness with the one that Troy offered me three years ago. I felt guilty every time I do that. Ozan deserves better. He deserves someone better than me but I know I can't leave him now.

I didn't know what I'd do if something happened to him, especially if it was because of me. Deep down, I knew what I was doing was wrong, but I was too weak to let him go. I didn't want to be selfish and hurt him. I didn't want to break him like what Troy did to me.

I still couldn't brush off the fact that Troy remembered something when we were in Hawaii, even if it was something small. It still held so much meaning. That alone made me doubtful with my actions.

I was afraid that I'd regret my decisions and end up hurting someone. However, I found it too hard to believe that Troy would end up remembering. It could have been just a one time thing. It didn't seem like he was going to remember. All these years, he didn't remember anything, so what makes me think that he'll remember now?

Admittedly, I wished that he'd recover his memory and remember the years we've spent with each other but another part of me was afraid of the fact that he'd forget me all over again. If that happens, I would be reliving the hell that I was in.

I was a coward. I was terrified to relive those same days that I felt lonely and hopeless. That's why another part of me wanted Troy to forget, so I wouldn't have to go through that all over again. It's so I wouldn't break all over again.

I ran a hand over my face, forcing those thoughts out my head as I opened the fridge. I pulled out a bottle of juice and closed the fridge before grabbing a glass cup. I filled the cup with the juice and returned the bottle back in the fridge before drinking a bit.

I leaned against the counter and stared at the cup that was in my hands, spacing off. I guess I was in my own world that I didn't notice someone entering the house. I gasped as Troy's figure randomly appeared out of nowhere. I dropped the glass that was in my hands and it shattered on the floor.

"T—Troy?" I did not pay attention to the glass across the floor. "When did you—"

"Be careful," Troy cut me off, his voice low. "Don't move."

However, I didn't pay much attention to his words and winced as I felt something sharp stab me in my bare foot, making his eyes widen. I gasped as I glanced at my foot, seeing blood drip from it.

"Shit, Ariel. I told you not to move." Troy walked into the kitchen, ignoring the shattered glass as he was wearing footwear. "Does it hurt? Are you okay?"

I glanced at my foot and winced. "Well . . . yeah," I muttered. Troy shook his head and carried me off my feet.

"W—what are you doing?" I asked in shock, seeing him walk out the kitchen. He had a serious expression plastered onto his face.

"What does it look like I'm doing? You have glass in your foot and I can't let you step on more. I told you not to move yet you did," he said. I frowned and looked away from him.

"Sorry. I wasn't paying attention," I muttered.

Troy nodded and placed me on the couch, standing in front of me with a stern face. "Stay here. I'm going to go get the medical kit," Troy ordered, running a hand through his hair. I nodded obediently as he walked off.

Stupid Ariel. Clumsy Ariel.

I glanced at my foot, wincing as I saw the blood. I tried to force my mind off from the pain. Not too long after, Troy came walking in with the kit. He knelt in front of me, examining the cut.

"Does it hurt?" he asked, opening the box.

"Yes," I admitted. "But I could take care of it myself. You don't have to do anything."

"It'll be easier if I do it," Troy said with a stern look. He carefully grabbed on to my foot and looked at the cut. "Don't argue."

I stared at him for a moment. I decided not to argue and looked away.

"The glass isn't too deep. I'll be able to take it out but it might hurt a bit," Troy said, cutting the silence. I bit my lip and nodded.

"Okay," I whispered. "Just do it quickly."

I looked away as he started to treat my foot. I winced when I felt him pull the glass from my foot.

"Got it," he said, throwing the glass away in the trash. He then took out a cotton ball and opened a small bottle. "I need to clean the cut."

I nodded, remaining silent as he proceeded to clean my cut in silence. I tried to hold in the pain.

"Thank you," I whispered as he dabbed the cotton on my open cut.

"There's no need to thank me," he mumbled.

I bit my lip, turning to him. "You haven't been home for a while," I muttered, meeting his eyes. He eventually looked away, shrugging his shoulders.

"Yeah . . . I needed some time alone," he said.

"Did you remember anything else?" I asked after a moment of silence. Troy met my eyes before pulling them away from mine.

"No."

"Oh . . ." I whispered, looking down at my lap.

"Would it matter to you if I remembered anything?" he asked. My eyes widened, staring at him in disbelief.

"What are you talking about, Troy?" "Of course it matters to me." I asked in a whisper.

"Even when you're dating Ozan?"

I sucked in a breath, pulling my eyes away from him. "Yes . . ."

I heard him let out a breath. "Are you happy with him? Is Ozan making you happy? Or are you only with him because he's sick?" Troy asked. I do not know what to say.

"No . . .I like Ozan," I whispered, staring at my hands that were on my lap.

"But you don't love him," he claimed as we met eyes. "You're trying to forget me by using him. You still love me."

I sucked in another breath, blinking to prevent any tears from falling down my cheeks.

"You hurt me many times," I whispered, finally mustering the strength to speak. "All I'm trying to do is heal from you. Ozan and I need each other."

Troy threw away the cotton before looking at me, his face clear with frustration. "What you're doing is wrong," he said, bringing his face closer to mine. "I don't like seeing you with him. I didn't like seeing him kiss you."

That day in Hawaii returned to my head. "Could you ever love me, Troy?" I asked. Troy's eyes windened but remained silent. "See. You said it yourself that day. You won't. You never will. So you have no right to say that. I have the right to try to move on."

Troy didn't look back at me. His eyes remained on the floor as I spoke.

"Especially at this time, Ozan needs me more than ever."

Troy grabbed a band aid from the box. He then patched it on the cut. He got up, avoiding my eyes. "Make sure to not step on it," he muttered. "And don't be clumsy." Troy then turned around and started to walk towards the door.

I glanced at my foot before looking at his retreating body.

"Troy," I called out. Troy turned his head to look at me. "Thank you. "I appreciate it."

He continued to stare at me for a moment before nodding his head. And with that, he walked out, leaving me sitting there with a cut on my foot and a confused heart.

CHAPTER FORTY-THREE

I silently sat on the couch, letting out a comfortable sigh as I stretched my tensed limbs. I placed my phone right next to me as I took hold of the remote. I began to switch through the channels out of boredom. The house was quiet.

I waited for Ozan to come down from his room so we could put on a movie to watch to occupy our time. Ozan and I were the only ones in the house at the moment. Damon, Rose, and Julia were out visiting a relative. Ozan remained in the house since he had no radiation therapy on a weekend. I wanted to take this as an opportunity to spend some time with him. Rose also said that they might come home late. She didn't want to leave me but it was urgent so I told her it was fine since Ozan was with me.

Ever since Ozan started with the radiation therapy, we have not spent that much time together. We'd return from school, and a couple hours later he'd be on his way to his appointments. Ozan needs two more weeks with his radiation therapies. Hopefully by then, his tumor would have decreased. If not, then he might need some more sessions. However, I have started to notice some improvements in his health which put my heart at ease. He did not look that tired though his body was getting weaker because of chemotherapy. Most of all, his mood changed. He seemed more hopeful to live and to keep going which was my motivation to keep holding on.

The doctor had also informed us that the chance of Ozan getting another seizure was low, so that was a huge relief to us. However, he warned us not to let our guards down as anything could occur at any moment.

I let out another sigh as I felt my nerves tense just by the thought of Ozan being in danger. I forced those thoughts completely out of my mind and back on the TV.

That didn't last long when I heard the front door open.

I had a gut feeling that I knew who was about to enter the room. I sucked in a breath and moments later, Troy came walking in.

I pulled my eyes away from him. It has been a couple days since I have last seen Troy and that was the day I stepped on glass. After that, who knows where Troy went. I figured that he'd return home very late at night and leave the house for school before I even woke up. I only saw him in my classes.

I couldn't help but feel that I was the reason on why he wasn't coming home. That made me feel guiltly.

Troy tood in front of me, staring down at me with an expression which made my insides flip. Troy eventually sat next to me, not bothering to hide the fact that he was staring right at me.

"Ariel," he murmured softly under his breath.

"Are you ok?" I asked, finally turning to him. "I haven't seen you for a couple days."

Troy nodded, running a hand through his hair as he closed his eyes for a moment before looking back at me.

"Does your foot still hurt?" He asked out of the blue, catching me off guard.

"My foot?" I murmured as Troy glanced down to where he aided me the last time. My eyes widened and I nodded my head, surprised by the fact that he was worried if my foot still hurt me. "Oh, no. It doesn't hurt anymore. I'm fine."

Troy nodded, opening his mouth to speak before someone cutting him off.

311

"What doesn't hurt you anymore?" Ozan's voice made me look away from Troy and right at Ozan's confused expression as he walked in, making me go stiff. Ozan had a frown on his face as he glanced at Troy sitting right next to me, stepping towards us.

Troy looked at me before looking at Ozan, his expression visibly tensing.

"We were talking about my foot," I answered softly as Ozan stood in front of us, staring down at Troy.

"What's wrong with your foot?" Ozan asked, finally turning to me with confused look in his eyes.

"I stepped on glass, remember?" I stated, glancing towards Troy for a split second.

Ozan nodded his head. "Oh, right," he muttered, glaring at Troy for a couple seconds before looking down at me, a soft smile appearing on his lips. "So, did you find a movie to watch?"

I shook my head. "No, I was waiting for you to come down so we could pick out a movie," I replied, seeing Troy tense. Ozan sat down next to me on the other side, completely ignoring the fact that Troy was in the room.

"Ok, what would you like to watch?" Ozan murmured as he tried to find a suitable movie. Inhaling a breath, Troy stood up and took a step away from us, making me snap my head towards him. I didn't reply to Ozan's question but looked up at Troy who was walking away without saying another word.

I frowned, not liking the fact that he was leaving too soon.

"Troy," I called out. Troy stopped and looked back at me, seeing his eyes in a hard glare. "Where are you going?"

"I'm leaving," he stated, his face expression hardening.

"But you just came," I said, staring up at him in worry.

Troy shook his head, making my frown deepen. "Don't worry about me. Worry about your movie," he spoke lowly. "Sorry to disturb." And with that, he walked out of the house and slammed the door behind him. My eyes were wide, turning my attention to Ozan who had a frown on his face.

He met my eyes, showing me his dissatisfaction before looking back at the tv as he continued to search for a movie, not once commenting about Troy's behavior.

Throughout the whole movie, my mind wasn't on the screen but on someone else. Troy.

An hour or so passed. I assited Ozan to his room after we finished the movie and got him ready for bed. I brought the covers over his. body. He fell asleep quite easily. I made sure he was comfortable on his bed before I stood up. I watched his sleeping figure as his chest rose with every breath he took.

I could tell that he was getting tired while we watched the movie. It wasn't that late but Ozan has been sleeping a little early recently. I frowned at that thought. It was obvious that his body was getting weaker.

I couldn't do anything to help him. The only thing I could do at the moment was to stay by his side and hope for the best. I know that Ozan needs me. I don't have the strength to leave him. He helped me through all these years so this was the least I could do.

I glanced at him one more time. I turned off the lights and walked out of his room quietly. I made my way towards my room.

The house was so quiet which made me tense. I couldn't help but feel uncomfortable being alone at this time.

Even though I knew I was safe out here in California, I couldn't stop my mind from replaying those scarring memories every time I was alone. I felt as if every time I'd let my guard down, something was going to happen.

I still fear that someone is out there looking for me. I don't know why. I don't know who but it scares me to the core.

I desperately tried to comfort myself. I told myself that they didn't know where I was. I was out here in California, a place far away from that incident. I was brought here in the first place for my safety. However, even with all that, I'm still worried. We don't even know whether if he's looking for me or if he knew where I was. That's still in the back of my head.

It has been more than four months since I left New York, yet I still feel like it was yesterday. I still feel scarede every time I'm alone and every time these came into my thoughts.

I laid on my bed and tried my best to pull these thoughts out my head. I groaned and decided to fall asleep since I had nothing better to do. It was better than staying alone.

My body relaxed, slowly pulling me into the darkness.

Not so long after, my eyes snapped open. It was still dark. I glanced at the clock to see it was almost 11 PM. I immediately sat up when I heard some noises from downstairs. Rose and Damon must have returned. I grabbed my phone to see a text message from Rose. My body went stiff as I read that Damon and Rose would be home in half an hour, meaning that they had yet to return.

My mind went back to the noises which were coming from downstairs.

I calmly opened my bedroom door and walked down the stairs, hoping that I wasn't putting myself in danger. I noticed that the sounds were coming from outside the front door.

I was taken off guard the moment someone banged on the door. I placed a hand on my mouth, trying to calm myself down. I looked through the peephole but all I saw was a black figure banging on the door repeatedly.

I grabbed my phone to dial the cops. It couldn't be someone who lived in this house as we all had extra keys, meaning it had to be someone else.

I got so frightened when I heard groans from the other side. I was about to dial 911 when I heard a familiar voice.

"O—open the door. Lost keys . . ."

My eyes widened and I immediately opened the door to see Troy. He stumbled towards me.

"Oh my God, Troy," I gasped at his appearance. "What happened to your face?" I glanced at his bruised lips. Ther was dried blood as well. He also reeked of alcohol. "Are you drunk?"

Troy entered the house closed the door behind him. He kept stumbling so I grabbed on to him.

He shook his head, groaning. "A little. I had a . . . few drinks," Troy slurred.

"Oh God," I murmured as I assisted him to the couch. "Why were you drinking? And how did you get that bruise?"

Troy laid on the couch, closing his eyes for a moment.

"Wanted to get my mind off of things . . ." he murmured. Troy then placed a hand on his chest, letting out a sigh. "It hurts," he tapped his chest. "Here . . . hurts."

I sucked in a shaky breath. "Did someone punch your chest?"

Troy let out a chuckle. "N—no . . ." he managed to say. "It hurts . . . more than a punched chest."

"Stay here, I'll go get the medical kit." I was about to walk away when Troy pulled me towards him.

"W—what are you—"

"You keep hurting me. Why do we keep hurting each other, Ariel?" His voice was softer than before. Troy let out a couple of groans.

"I'm sorry," I whispered gently.

"It's not your fault," Troy mumbled. "I pushed you away . . . I hurt you. I'm paying the price," he slurred.

I closed my eyes, trying to hold in the tears. I pulled my hand away from his and cleared my throat. "I'll be right back. Don't move."

I walked towards the kitchen and opened a cabinet, pulling out the kit. After, I kneeled in front of the couch and opened the kit. Troy's eyes remained on me.

"This might sting a bit," I mumbled as I cleaned his bruised lip. Troy didn't faze one bit.vI prepared another fresh cotton with oitment.

I cleared my throat once again. "How did you get this bruise?" I asked one more time.

"Fight . . . in the bar. Must have lost the keys then," Troy answered lowly, trying to gather his words.

"Bar? How did you get in a bar?" I asked him.

Troy shrugged his shoulders. "Have my ways."

"Goodness," I whispered, applying the oitment on the bruise. "You have to be more careful. There's no need to go drinking. What if something bad had happened?"

"I wanted to forget," he said sternly. My eyes softened. I don't know if my heart is able to take this. "Ariel," he said gently as he grabbed my hand. "I wanted to forget how much I want to remember you."

Our eyes connected for what felt like a long time. "I want . . . you, but I can't have you," he mumbled. A tear slipped through my eye unwillingly. Troy lifted his hand and wiped it away. "It hurts to want you but not to remember you."

I tried to hold in the tears. "It hurts," he mumbled again. His eyes had pain written in them. "But . . . I bet, seeing you with another man would hurt less than forgetting you all over again." His hand was still on my cheek.

I closed my eyes. Another tear trickled down my cheeks. His words hit me right in my heart.

"Forgetting, forgetting, and forgetting . . . would hurt more," he mumbled, placing his hand to his side. "It would hurt you . . . but would hurt me more," Troy said softly, closing his eyes.

Right then and there, I started to cry in front of a sleeping Troy.

CHAPTER FORTY-FOUR

I rushed to my room to place my bag the moment I stepped foot in the house. I immediately headed towards Ozan's room to see if he felt any better than before. I couldn't concentrate in my classes as my mind was wandering off to Ozan's health.

Ozan stayed home today. He woke up tired so Rose made him stay in bed. I also agreed with her when I saw his condition, which definitely gave me a bad feeling. Ozan woke up to vomit, looking weaker than before.

I was scared for him, but Ozan assured that he was fine. The scene replayed in my head throughout the day. Ozan seemed to be in a better shape for the past few days now. However, seeing him like that today made me doubtful about his progress.

Rose reassured me that everything was going to be fine and that this was normal. This was the side effect from the chemotherapy. Ozan has an appointment today and hopefully things will get better. I tried to throw away any negative thoughts as I did not want to even think about the possibilities.

Ozan had two more weeks of radiation therapy and that will determine how his health is. I pray that he will get better.

I knocked on his bedroom door.

"Ozan? It's me, Ariel." I hope I wasn't waking him up or disturbing him. "I'm coming in." I entered his dim room. My eyes followed to where his bed was and landed on Ozan.

317

Our eyes met and a smile lit his face. "Ariel," he mumbled. I immediately rushed to him the moment he tried to sit up.

"Lay down. You need to rest," I ordered. Ozan nodded. "How do you feel? Are you still tired?" My eyes flickered with worry. I sat down on his bed.

"I feel slightly better. Don't worry about me," Ozan answered, grabbing onto my hand.

I glanced at our joined hands. I was relived. "It's hard not to worry," I murmured. "You looked completely fine yesterday. It took me off guard."

"It's normal," Ozan claimed. "I have an appointment today, so hopefully I'll feel better."

I reluctantly nodded. "I hope so," I whispered as Ozan offered me a comforting smile. "I know you're strong enough to get through this but I can't help but worry at times."

Ozan's grip on my hand tightened. I cleared my throat and looked back at Ozan.

"What did I tell you, Ariel?" he asked, raising a brow.

"What?" I wondered.

"As long as you're by my side, I'll be fine," Ozan stated, his smile growing.

I nodding my head. I glanced towards his desk when I heard a ringing sound coming from his phone.

"Can you get my phone?" he asked. I nodded and picked up the phone. It washis father calling.

Ozan's parents would call every now and then to check up on him. I know it was hard for them to be apart at this difficult time, but Ozan refused to return. We owed so much to him. His dad and mine were friends for a couple years now and they worked together. When we were back in New York, he helped our family with many things.

Ozan and I became friends because of our parent's meeting. If it wasn't for that, then I wouldn't have met him.

I sat back down on his bed and offered him his phone.

318

"Dad. Hi. How are you?" he said.

I stared at Ozan in silence. "I'm fine. Don't worry . . . I feel a little better than before . . . Yes, I have an appointment today. I need two more weeks of radiation therapy."

I was about to get up to give them some privacy but Ozan grabbed my hand. "Stay," he told me. "I was talking to Ariel. She's with me right now." I nodded and stayed put. "She's good. Ariel's with me all the time. We're both doing great." He then looked at me, smiling. "My dad says hi."

I smiled back at Ozan. "Tell him I said hi, too."

I sat there for a couple minutes as Ozan's dad talked with him. After a while, Ozan closed the call and turned to me. "My dad said that if there's anything you need, don't hesitate to ask," Ozan exclaimed, rubbing his thumb on my hand.

I smiled at him. "That's kind of him. That reminds me, I need to call my parents to check up on them. You rest before heading to your session. I'll see you before you go. Okay?" I then stood up,

Ozan nodded. "Okay. Don't worry," he reassured me. "Go on. Tell them I say hi."

"Will do." I turned around and walked out of his room.

I slowly came to a stop along the hallway when my eyes landed on Troy. He was walking towards me.

Every time I remember what happened when he was drunk, it tore my heart to pieces. It was too painful to remember. I didn't know how to react after that. I didn't even know if Troy remembered what he said to me. I tried to act natural though.

I knew he was hurting. He looked hurt that day but there was little I could do. I had to take care of Ozan. He needs me more than ever, and I didn't want to be selfish and abandon him.

I would be lying if I said I have never doubted my relationship with Ozan but I couldn't bring myself to hurt him. In the end, I do care for him. I know it wasn't to the extent of how I cared for Troy. Yet, Troy and I can't go back. We have so many obstacles in front of us, and I was a coward to face them.

Troy's eyes met mine for a few seconds. The moment we stood in front of each other, he came to a stop. His eyes softened and emotions flickered through them. "Ariel," he whispered, clearing his throat. "How are you?"

"I'm good. What about you?" I asked.

"I'm okay." Troy nodded, scratching the back of his neck. "Ariel, I . . . I don't exactly remember what happened that day. I don't remember what I said to you. I only remember you cleaning my bruise." Troy took a step closer to me. "Thank you for doing that. And I'm sorry if I said something that bothers you."

"Oh, no. It's fine. You made me worry when you came back like that. I hope you're fine now," I said.

I could see the sadness in his eyes which surely mirrored mine. "I'll get used to it," he mumbled. I don't know what exactly to say. "You were in Ozan's room?" he asked, frowning.

"I was," I said gently. "He's tired. I was checking up on him."

His eyes hardened a bit then he looked away. "Well, that's good of you. He's your boyfriend, after all. Take care, Ariel."

Troy then walked past me. I couldn't help but feel sad.

After a while of gathering my thoughts. I walked back to my room and laid my head against the wall, trying to keep my tears at bay.

Troy was right. We do keep hurting each other.

Time passed, and it was already late in the evening. I stared out the window for a while, admiring the twinkling stars and the cool breeze that hit my skin. I closed my eyes, enjoying the feeling.

I know I'm going to regret this tomorrow morning. I glanced at the clock to see that it's already past midnight. I look back out the window. Surely, everyone was asleep by now.

A thought came to my mind as I stared out the window but I was reluctant about it. A few seconds later, I shrugged my

320

shoulders. Sleep wasn't coming to me anytime soon, so maybe walking out would get me to relax. Besides, it wasn't like I wasn't safe. The house was surrounded by a gate.

I could just take a stroll around the house. The cool breeze could relax my nerves. Maybe then, sleep would overcome me.

I exited my room silently and made my way to the front door. I unlocked the door and opened it, allowing the wind to hit me. I let out a breath before stepping outside and closing the door behind me. I calmly walked around the house, taking my time as my feet toouched the grass.

The wind that brushed my skin brought me comfort and eased my tense muscles. Before I even knew it, I was already at the backyard. I took a look at my surroundings. I didn't really come here often so I admired the place. I was about to walk back when something caught my attention.

It was a ladder which lead to the roof. Why is there a ladder here in the first place? I stared at it for a moment. I decided to get back but came to a stop when I heard shuffling and noises. Someone was on the roof. I debated on whether I should let someone know or investigate first. I bit my lip and before I could even stop myself, I was quietly climbing the ladder.

As soon as I made it to the top, I took a peek, not knowing what exactly I was going to see. However, my mouth opened in shock the moment I saw Troy laying on the roof, his hands under his head as he stared up at the stars.

"Troy?" I called out, causing for his eyes to snap to me. His eyes widened and he immediately sat up.

"Ariel?"

I was taken aback and my foot slipped. I let out a gasp. Before my hands could let go of the ladder, Troy grabbed onto them. He pulled me on the roof and I stumbled on top of him. Our eyes were wide.

It took me a moment to realize our position. I immediately got off him and sat up. "Uh, sorry," I mumbled.

"What are you doing here so late at night? You could have fell," Troy stated, his eyes roaming over my body to see if I had any injuries.

"I wasn't able to sleep so I decided to take a walk. I then saw the ladder and wanted to know who was up here," I explained. "But I could ask the same. What are you doing here so late at night?"

Troy laid on his back, his eyes staring up at the dark sky.

"This is my thinking spot," he said, flickering his eyes at mine.

"Thinking spot?"

Troy nodded. "I come here often when I want to think," he started. "Usually when everyone's asleep. It's relaxing and I could gaze up on the stars."

"Oh," I whispered.

"It's my secret spot," Troy said, turning his head to me. "Well, not anymore, that is."

My eyes widened. "Oh. I'm sorry. I didn't mean to disturb," I said, scooting away. "I'll go back." I started making my way towards the ladder when he grabbed onto my hand.

A soft gasp soon escaped my lips the moment he pulled me towards him. My head landed on his chest. "No. Since you're already here, stay," he whispered. Our eyes met and a soft smile appeared on his lips.

"We'll watch the stars together. Like how we did three years ago."

CHAPTER FORTY-FIVE

A frustrated groan escaped my lips as I turned to the other side. I shoved my face on my pillow. I closed my eyes for the hundredth time, forcing my thoughts to calm down so I could sleep.

My body, however, refused to sleep and forced me awake. I stared at the ceiling that was barely visible in my dim room.

It was almost midnight yet I still couldn't sleep. I was starting to feel even more frustrated. All the sudden, my phone beeped.

Who was sending me a message at this time? I sat up and reached over for my phone. I smiled the moment I saw a message from Troy asking whether I was asleep or not.

I immediately called him. It didn't take long before Troy answered my call.

"Ariel.

"Troy. Why are you awake at this time?"

"I couldn't sleep," Troy answered. "What about you. Why are you awake?"

"I couldn't sleep either," I said. I could hear him chuckle from the other line. "I tried for hours but it's no use."

"I figured, that's why I'm outside your house," Troy stated. I bolted up.

"You're outside my house?"

"Yes."

"At this time?"

"Yes. Come outside. I'm taking you somewhere," Troy said.

"Somewhere? Where? It's so late," I said as I got up to take a look outside. Troy was indeed right outside my house with his bike. A smile crawled onto my lips.

"Just get down. We won't take long," Troy ordered playfully.

"Okay." I closed the line and quietly made my way out the house. I hope I wouldn't wake my mom or dad or I'd surely get into some kind of trouble. Gently, I opened the door and the cool breeze hit my skin. A shiver ran down my spine and I closed the door behind me.

Troy's smile grew and he grabbed onto my hand.

"Hey," I whispered. "Where are we going?" I asked, glancing at his bike. "You know if my parents find me gone I'll surely be in trouble."

"Don't worry," Troy spoke. "We won't be gone for long. I just want to take you to a place that might relax you. You might be able to sleep then."

I couldn't find the nerves to say no.

"Okay. Then let's go," I said. We both got on the bike.

"Hold on tight."

I did as he said and wrapped my hands around his waist. The wind blew through my hair as Troy paddled. We rode through the dark night with the streets almost empty. I made a big smile. I wasn't worried about anything because we lived in a quiet and safe neighborhood.

I wondered where exactly Troy was taking me at this time of night. It didn't take long for Troy to come to a stop, allowing me to take in the surroundings. My eyes roamed through the park that was in front of us.

We were in front of a park I usually pass by. I have never entered it at night. It was quiet and calm and there was no person in sight. I looked over to Troy, raising a brow at him.

"Why are we here?" I asked. He grinned but pulled my hand, walking through the trees that surrounded us. After walking for a couple minutes, we came to an empty spot filled with soft grass and trees surrounding the area in a circle.

"This is my favorite spot," Troy finally said as he sat down. Troy then grabbed my hand and pulled me, making me fall next to him. I was taken off guard the moment Troy laid on his back, staring up at the stars. "The stars are beautiful at this time of night. Our surrounding makes it better."

I stared at him for a moment, taking in his words. A small smile soon appeared on my lips. "You took me here to watch the stars?"

"Yes," he answered, pulling me once again and forcing me to lay down on my back. My eyes were met with the twinkling white dots in the sky which with no doubt were beautiful. "This might relax your nerves. And it's very beautiful, isn't it?" Troy turned to me.

I nodded. "It sure is. Do you come here often?" I wondered, looking back at the sky.

"Only a couple times. Only when I need to think about something or feel bad. Staring up at the stars never fail to ease my tension." Troy said, shrugging his shoulders.

My smile grew and I glanced at him. "I can see why. We should come here often. It's nice."

Troy met my eyes, smiling as we stared at each other for a moment. "Sure. We could," he stated, glancing at the sky. He then looked back at me. "We will always watch the stars together."

*　　*　　*

We stared at one another for a while. I feel choked. My eyes were wide.

"H—how? How do you remember?" I said.

Troy was silent as his eyes remained on the dark sky lit up with stars. I waited for him to say something, anything.

How did he remember?

"Troy," I called as he continued to admire the beautiful sky as I laid next to him. "Please, answer me. Do you remember?" I asked.

Troy's eyes finally left the sky and met mine. I sucked in a breath as his eyes were filled with so many emotions. A sad smile soon crossed his lips.

"No," he whispered. "I'm sorry, Ariel. I can't seem to remember."

His words made my heart sink. I couldn't help but feel disappointed. Something in me was hoping for something. Something inside of me wanted him to remember me but, another part of me knew it as too good to be true.

"But . . ." Troy said.

My eyes perked up as Troy looked away from me.

"But I see memories. Little memories," he said, looking back at me. "I don't remember completely but ever since you came here, I've been seeing memories for split seconds."

My eyes widened.

"I—I see stuff at times. They come and go so quickly. It hurts my head, Ariel," Troy said. It looked as if bringing this subject up was hard for him. I blinked away the tears. I listened to him continue. "At first, I thought they were fake scenarios my head was playing. I thought they were someone else's memories. But, I then saw you. You are in them. A younger you, Ariel."

Troy's eyes met mine. "It pains me to see them and not know what is actually going on. It hurts not seeing the whole picture. I see scenes but they go by too fast I cannot comprehend what I actually saw and when I see you, you're gone before I could see anything else."

"This started after I came?" I asked after a moment of silence.

Troy stood quiet for a second. "A while after you came," he answered. "It happened a lot more often after the Hawaii trip. It's confusing. I wondered why I was attracted to you but after seeing those memories, I knew why."

A tear fell down my cheek as Troy smiled wistfully at me. Troy raised his hand and wiped the tear off my cheek.

"Ariel. You don't know how much I wish to remember everything, to remember what we had together but, I fear if I ever do, I'll forget you all over again." Troy whispered.

"Troy," I whispered, trying to find my voice.

"And that would surely hurt the both of us."

*   *   *

I brought the covers over Ozan's sleeping figure. After a moment, I started making my way out his room.

I feel as if a huge weight has been lifted off my shoulders. I felt so relieved after I found out that Ozan's health was getting better and that the tumor began to decrease its size. Ozan only had a week left of his therapy. I hoped by then, he'd be much better. He looked better as well, but the chemotherapy was tiring him out.

Ozan and I were chatting before he fell asleep. It wasn't late, but he looked quite tired.

I started making my way downstairs when I saw Julia and Damon sitting down in the living room watching TV. I walked up to them and smiled.

"Hey, Ariel," Julia greeted. Damon smiled at me.

"Hi," I said. "Do you know where Rose is?"

"She's in the kitchen," she answered. "Mom's preparing dinner."

327

I nodded and walked to the kitchen. Rose was by the sink and Troy was drinking a glass of water. Our eyes met and he smiled softly at me. I smiled back.

It has been a week since the day on the roof. After that day, I noticed that we have gotten closer. I bet Rose also noticed because she was smiling from ear to ear.

"Hey, Rose."

"Ariel, dear. Come in," she said.

"Do you need any sort of help?" I wondered.

"Oh, yes. If you don't mind, why don't you chop these vegetables?" she asked, putting the vegetables and a knife in front of me.

"Sure," I said as Troy's eyes remained on me.

"Troy," Rose called him.

"Yeah?" he mumbled. Rose walked up to him, handing him a knife. Troy then raised a brow.

"Here," Rose said.

"What's this for?" he asked, holding the knife in his hands.

"How else will you help Ariel?" Rose raised a brow at her son. His eyes perked up and went to me. I looked at Rose and shook my head.

"No. It's fine," I exclaimed. "I can do this by myself."

"Pass me some vegetables." Troy stood by me, holding the knife in his hand as I looked up in surprise. Rose smiled delightedly.

"But—"

"It's fine. We'll finish it faster if we both do it," Troy said.

I nodded and passed him some vegetables. We chopped in silence as Rose continued to chat. She kept glancing towards us, smiling to herself.

"You finish up. I'll go set up the table." Rose eventually walked away, carrying spoons and plates in her hands. Troy stood beside me as he continued to chop the vegetables, slower than me.

I couldn't help but chuckle as I noticed him struggling. He was surely not used to this. Troy glanced at me before looking back in front of him. My head soon snapped towards him as I heard him gasp. My eyes widened the moment I saw his finger with blood dripping from it.

"You cut yourself?" I stated, grabbing onto a paper towel.

"I usually don't do this," Troy grunted, looking a little embarrassed. I handed him a towel. He took it and wiped the blood off his finger. I opened the sink and turned to him.

"You should wash it," I suggested. He nodded and placed his finger under the rushing water. "Does it hurt?"

"It's only a cut," he said. I chuckled as I saw him blushing. Troy glanced over at me, raising a brow. "What's so funny? Do you find amusement from my pain?"

Humor was laced in his voice, making me chuckle one more time. "Kind of. You're so clumsy," I said. Troy also began to chuckle.

"I'm not clumsy. I'm just not used to this," he defended.

I rolled my eyes. "Yeah, yeah. Sure."

I went back to chopping the vegetables as Troy dried his hands. Suddenly, my phone rang. I stopped and pulled it out from my pocket.

I looked up at Troy, seeing him raise a brow. "It's my dad," I said.

"Hey Dad," I greeted. There was a pause. "Dad? Are you there?"

"Ariel," Dad whispered seconds after.

"What's wrong Dad? Did something happen?" I said. Troy noticed my tone and forgot about the vegetables that we had to chop.

"Ariel. I need to tell you something," he said, his voice low. "What is it?"

"Your mom was stabbed. She was stabbed by the man who ran from jail."

CHAPTER FORTY-SIX

There are times in a person's life when you feel as if everything has stopped around you. The voices that surrounded you are in slow motion. It's a never ending headache.

I was experiencing that at the moment. I felt breathless. I took a step back and placed my hand on my mouth, trying to hold in any sound that might escape.

"Ariel? Are you there?" Dad asked, his voice laced with worry.

"W—what did you say?" I whispered after a moment of silence. This caught Troy's attention, making him take a few steps towards me with a frown on his face.

"Ariel, honey. Your mom was stabbed," Dad repeated softly through the other line.

I failed to hold back my tears. I sucked in a breath and Troy's eyes widened as he saw my state. He immediately stood by my side and placed a hand on my shoulder.

"Ariel. What's wrong?" Troy asked.

"Mom was stabbed?" I repeated Dad's words. Troy was shocked.

"Yes, but calm down. She's not in any danger," Dad reassured. What a relief. Rose stopped in her tracks when she saw me crying. She immediately came to my side.

"Ariel? What's wrong? Why are you crying?" she asked.

I wasn't able to concentrate on Rose's question as many unanswered questions roamed through my head.

"Really? She's not in danger?" I asked.

"Don't worry, honey. Your mom is alright," he said, trying to calm me down. Tears of relief fell down my cheek.

"Did something happen?" Rose asked.

I nodded. "My mom was stabbed by the shooter who ran from jail," I finally answered. Rose gasped as her eyes began to tear up.

"Oh, Lexi," she whispered. "Oh, God. Is she alright?" she asked. I wiped the tears off my cheeks and nodded. Troy then placed his hand on my back.

"Let's go sit down in the living room," he said as he helped me walk to the couches. I heard my dad's worried voice from the other line, but I was too overwhelmed to answer. Rose, Troy and I sat down as Julia and Damon looked at us in confusion.

Damon sat straight and immediately placed his hand on his wife's back the moment he saw her glossy eyes. "Did something happen?" he asked, turning to his son. "Why are they crying?"

"Oh, Damon. Lexi was stabbed," Rose said.

"Stabbed? By who?" Damon said. Rose then started explaining to him what she already knew. I remained quiet.

Troy sat beside me in silence as I tried to comprehend everything. For a moment, I completely forgot that my dad was still on the line. He's probably worried. I placed the phone back on my ear.

"I'm here, Dad. Sorry. I'm just taken off guard," I said. Everyone in the room turn to listen.

"Don't be worried, Ariel. Your mom is alright," he reassured for the second time. "How about you hand me Damon? I'll explain everything to him."

"Okay," I said and handed the phone to Damon.

"Xavier. Is Lexi okay?" Damon said. After a few seconds, Damon nodded and sighed. "Okay. That's good but how did this

331

happen? Did they catch the man?" Damon remained quiet for a while. I'm so tensed. The worry was building up in me. I was praying that they caught him for what he did to my mom.

Damon's frown deepened, a look which I didn't like. He listened to my dad as we all sat there in silence. "Goodness, Xavier. This isn't good. You should tighten up the security."

I gulped. I felt a hand rub my back. It was Troy who was trying to comfort me. He smiled softly at me.

"Okay. Be careful," Damon said. He was about to take the phone off his ear. "Yeah?"

Damon listened to whatever my dad was saying through the other end. I felt like these seconds were going by so slowly. Damon nodded. "Don't worry. She's safe over here . . . Okay. I won't let her. You have nothing to worry about. Bye, Xavier. Take care."

Damon handed me back my phone. I immediately took it. "Dad?" I whispered.

"Ariel. I explained everything to Damon. He will tell you everything, okay?" he said. "Don't be frightened. You're both safe but I have to deal with some stuff so I have to go. I'll call you back in half an hour. Okay?"

"Okay. Bye, Dad."

"Bye, honey. Take care."

I then closed the line and placed my phone on my lap, looking up at Damon.

"What did Dad tell you? Tell me everything," I asked, a little worried to hear the answer. We all looked at Damon, waiting to hear his response. The air around us was tense and thick.

"Ariel, apparently, that man was following your mom for while," he started, causing my back to go stiff. "From what they saw from the surveillance cameras, the man was watching your house from afar for a couple days. And a couple hours ago, when your mom was exiting her car to enter the house, he popped up and stabbed her."

I placed my hand on my mouth to hold in the sob. I couldn't help but feel worried and guilty. I didn't know that this would happen. I thought they were perfectly safe and sound. "Did they catch him?" I asked, blinking the tears away.

That's when Damon's frown deepened for the second time, and when he shook his head, my heart sank. "Your mom was alone at that time. He stabbed her then ran away. They caught his face from the cameras and clarified that he was the one who escaped prison," Damon explained calmly as I tried my best to register everything in my head.

"He's still out there?" I whispered, placing my head in my hands. Troy continued to comfort me in silence as Damon continued to talk.

"He is. But don't worry. Your dad said that he's going to tighten the security," he stated. I pulled my head from out of my hands and looked back at Damon. "The police is trying their best to catch him."

"But why would he stab my mom? What does he have against us? Oh, God. I have to go see her." I stood up. Damon immediately walked over me, placing his hand on my shoulders to calm me down. "Damon. I have to book the nearest flight to New York."

Damon shook his head. "Ariel. Sit and calm down," he ordered softly. I was hesitant but soon sat down. "You won't be going to New York. Your dad specially told me to keep you here. You can't visit your mom. She's safe, awake and healthy. She won't stay in the hospital for long."

"But why?" I questioned. "I want to see my mom. I won't relax until I see her."

"Your mom specifically told your dad to tell you not to come. She wants you to stay here," he explained.

"Why?" I said weakly.

"She's worried that the man targeted her for that reason, for you to come to New York. She's afraid that this is what they

333

want, for you to visit your mom and to finally get to you," Damon explained. Troy then nodded his head.

"Dad's right, Ariel. You should stay here," he said calmly. "Your mom is healthy. You'll be safer over here. You shouldn't take the risk."

"They're right, honey," Rose spoke. "It's better if you stay."

I inhaled a shaky breath, running my hand over my face. I soon looked back at Damon who was still standing in front of me. "I still don't understand why someone would want to get to me," I whispered. Damon frown and shook his head.

"We don't know, but all we know is that man is definitely working for someone. Your dad is trying his best to figure out who," Damon explained. "But for the meantime, staying here is the best option."

"Okay." I nodded. "If that's what my parents want, then I'll stay."

Damon smiled softly before patting my shoulder. Rose then stood up and walked over at me. "You should go get some rest. I know what you've heard must have tired you out," she stated, glancing at Troy as the dinner was long forgotten. "Troy. Why don't you take her to her room?"

We both stood up. I turned to Rose and Damon. I nodded and they both smiled at me as Troy placed his hand on my shoulder. "I'll get some rest. Goodnight," I said.

"Goodnight, Ariel," Rose said, rubbing my arm before I walked to my room with Troy. I felt like my head was spinning and the only solution was to get some rest. It was so hard to hear something like that and do nothing, but I know my mom would feel better if I was here and not by her side.

Troy and I remained silent as I walked to my room. I could sense the worry off him. He seemed concerned for me. We finally stood in front of my bedroom door. When I opened it, I looked up at Troy.

"Thank you, Troy. You can go now," I whispered calmly.

Troy took a step towards me. "Ariel," he spoke my name. "Don't be afraid. I'm here with you." Our eyes met for a long second as we remained quiet. Sucking in a breath, I nodded.

"Thank you." I looked down to the floor. My eyes widened when he placed his hand gently against my cheek. Troy smiled gently at me then pulled me in for a hug. It took me off guard.

"You don't have to worry. Everything will be alright," he whispered as my head laid against his chest. "I won't leave you again to suffer on your own."

His arms were around my waist and my breath hitched. I soon relaxed in his arms as he calmed me down.

I let out a breath as I closed my eyes, hoping that this moment wouldn't end.

CHAPTER FORTY-SEVEN

I turned to my other side and opened my eyes. I was immediately met with the window, allowing me to see the dark sky filled with stars which lit my dim room. The opened window allowed the cool breeze to hit my skin, forcing me to bring the covers under my chin.

I gave up trying to sleep, as it was dawning to me that sleep wasn't going to overcome me anytime soon. I've been like this for almost a week now. Ever since that incident with my mom, I've been feeling restless and on the edge.

Being like this was definitely tiring me out. I didn't know if I was supposed to be worried or if I was suppose to relax. I felt as if any moment now someone was going to barge in and get me.

My mind has been more awake than ever. I kept thinking about what that man did to my mom and it frightened me to my core. Mom was right. He must have done that for a reason. Why else would he be after my mom?

I was more aware than ever that there was someone out there trying to hurt me and my family. I couldn't put my guard down as this was a critical moment for me.

I have many questions I wanted answers for. Yet, the biggest question that never failed to leave me was who and why? Who would be after me and who would that man be working for? Most importantly, why?

For now, I was only thankful that my mom was doing alright. Thankfully, the stab wasn't deep enough to cause anything major and my mom will soon leave the hospital tomorrow. That brought me the little comfort I needed.

I was upset that I couldn't see her at this time. However, I know that both my parents didn't want to risk it. It was best for me to stay here.

It's almost going to be five months since I first came here. Yet, we still didn't find the person we needed to find. That meant, I was not leaving. I have so many feelings about the thought of that. I didn't know what I was going to do if I had to leave.

Leaving meant not seeing Troy. I don't know if my heart is able to take parting from him for the second time, whether he remembers me or not.

I let out a breath and closed my eyes, trying my best to tame my thoughts and fall asleep.

*   *   *

As soon as I returned from school, I went to my room and pulled out my phone, calling my mom. I placed the phone by my ear and waited. I smiled the moment I heard her answer.

"Ariel, honey," she spoke.

"Hi, Mom," I greeted, sitting down on my bed. "How are you today? Do you feel better?" I wasn't able to control the worry in my voice. No matter how many people told me that my mom was fine, I couldn't help it.

"I'm fine, Ariel," she chuckled, which allowed me to relax. "I told you not to worry. How many times did you call to ask me that question?"

"I'm sorry," I mumbled. "I can't help but worry."

"Don't worry, honey. If I wasn't alright, then I wouldn't be leaving the hospital today," mom pointed out, trying to lighten up the mood.

"That's right," I agreed. "Any news about the man?" I was quite nervous to ask that question. I'm afraid to get an answer I didn't want to hear. It bothered me more that the person who hurt my mom was still out there.

A sigh from her brought me the answer. "No. Not yet," she replied, her voice in a serious tone. "They don't know where he could possibly be. But they're trying their best to catch him and whoever is behind this."

"Mom, please be careful. You and Dad. I'm honestly worried about you both." I said.

"We are, Ariel. Don't worry," Mom stated, trying to assure me that everything was fine. "Your dad tightened the security and the police will be watching over us for a few days. So there's nothing to be worried about. Relax."

"Okay. That's good," I said. "When are you leaving?"

"In an hour," she answered. "I'll be leaving with Clare and your dad."

"Tell her I said hi," I said, smiling as I thought about Clare. It has surely been a while since we last talked and told each other about what exactly was going on in our lives. Yet, due to the circumstances, we have no time to talk a lot.

Clare was so sweet to keep my parents company. She knew them for a long time, so she considered them as her second parents.

"Will do," Mom said. "How's Ozan, by the way? Is his treatment going fine?"

"He's a lot better," I answered. "Today's his last session and hopefully after that, he won't need more radiation therapy. I can tell that he's getting better."

"Oh, that's great," she said out of relief. "Are you both doing well together?"

I bit my lip at her question. It wasn't like we weren't doing well. We were actually fine but lately, I've been feeling more doubtful about this relationship. I wasn't feeling what I was hoping

338

to feel especially with Troy still in my mind. I felt extremely guilty and didn't know what I should do.

I cared so much for Ozan and I didn't want to hurt him. However, I knew that this relationship might not actually work out. Yet, I didn't have the strength to tell him that. I was afraid that he'd get upset at me. Or worse, he'd be badly affected because of me.

I knew that he needed me by his side more than ever. Yet, I wanted to be by someone else's side. I was surely conflicted, but I knew that I had to stay by Ozan's side for now.

"We're fine," was all I answered.

"Just fine?" Mom wondered. "What about you and Troy? Are you both doing fine?"

"Yeah.." I mumbled quietly. "We've been closer lately. He also comforted me when I heard you were stabbed," I explained to her, a grin growing on my lips. "Even though he can't remember me, I can tell that he cares for me. He was at first hard to read, but after he got used to me, I was able to see past him."

"Oh, honey," mom whispered. "I hope things will get better for you both. I know you're still in love with Troy. And it's clear that Troy has some affection towards you. Yet, you're also with Ozan. Why are you with someone else when you could be with the one you like?"

"But Troy and I can't work out. He rejected me when I wanted to start over. There's so many things stopping us. Mom, I'm honestly afraid," I said.

"Afraid of what, Ariel? What's possibly stopping you? Not only are you hurting yourself and Troy, but you're hurting Ozan by letting him think that there's a chance for you two. What's so hard about starting over?" she asked.

"Mom, Troy has a 50 percent chance of forgetting all over again," I exclaimed, finally telling her the reason. "What if he forgets about me all over again? What do I do then? I don't think I can take losing him for the second time. It'll be too hard for me."

My mom was silent for a moment. "Oh, God. I didn't know that," she said. She was clearly shocked. "I understand what you mean. It's a scary thing. But if you both love each other, why don't you take the risk?"

"But—"

"Ariel. If Troy truly loves you then no matter how many times he forgets you, his heart won't."

Her words lingered in my head even after the call ended.

*   *   *

Since Damon was at work, Rose took Ozan to his appointment. Julia accompanied them while I stayed at home. Rose was reluctant to leave me alone because of what happened recently and because she knew I was on edge. I told her it was fine since Troy was also home.

I felt a little nervous but not too much. I decided to stay in my room and lay under my covers as I waited for their return. The lights in my room were on. I played games on my phone for a while to distract myself. Out of nowhere, the lights went out.

My eyes immediately widened as I was surrounded by darkness. I let my eyes roam the dim room. I got up and walked to the switches, flickering them. I frowned when the lights didn't turn on.

I then opened my bedroom door, taken off guard when I saw the hall lights also off.

"What the heck?" I whispered.

My nerves tensed and the air got stuck in my throat. I couldn't help but feel afraid at my situation. I started walking down the hall, not knowing what I was to expect.

I gasped the moment a hand touched my shoulder from behind.

"Ariel. Are you okay?" Troy asked.

His voice hit my ears and the fear disappeared. I looked up at him but could not see his features.

"Troy . . ." I said, letting out a breath. "I'm fine. But what happened? Why is the electricity out?"

"I don't know," he answered. "The moment it went out I came to look for you." Troy then grabbed onto my hand, catching me off guard. "Come with me. I'll go check." Troy pulled me down the stairs. He then stopped in front of a window and peeked outside.

Troy turned to me. "The electricity for the whole street is out," he answered, opening his phone and allowing me to see his face. "Let me make a phone call. Looks like there's a problem with our block. Go sit down on the couch."

I nodded and silently sat down as Troy placed his phone by his ear. I watched his figure talk to someone on the phone. After a couple minutes, Troy ended the call and walked to me with his phone supporting us with a little light.

"There were some workers working on our street and caused an electricity shortage," Troy explained. "The electricity will be back in twenty minutes. We'll have to wait till then."

"Oh. Okay."

"Just wait here. I'm going to get something," Troy said before walking off. I watched him disappear with the light, forcing me back into the darkness. I waited until he returned, holding a lit candle in his hands. Troy then sat next to me, placing the candle on the table.

"This will do for now," he murmured.

"It's better than nothing," I said, smiling at him. I saw him smile back before I turned to the candle. We sat in silence, waiting for the electricity to return. I didn't want to leave him because I was too afraid to be on my own.

"Were you nervous?" Troy said. I glanced up at him.

"Yeah," I mumbled. "For a second, I thought someone broke into the house."

He chuckled, which made me grin. I sucked in a breath when he wrapped his arm around my shoulder, pulling me to him. I could hear my heart beating rapidly as my head laid against his chest.

"Don't worry. I'm here beside you. You're safe here."

CHAPTER FORTY-EIGHT

I opened my eyes to see nothing but darkness, a darkness which never ended. I squinted my eyes, rubbing them a few times to scan over my surroundings. Like the first time, I failed to see anything. I was engulfed by a blackness which was as cool as death. There were no signs of warmth to be found.

I turned to the other direction only to see the exact same thing. I could feel my anxiety as I searched for a way out of this nightmare. My feet finally started moving on their own accord but it was bringing me to the same spot no matter how hard I ran.

At that moment I could hear my own heartbeat. My face started to sweat and I wanted to scream. However, the words were stuck in my own throat.

My vision blurred with my own tears as all I could do at this moment was break and fall to the ground. Before I could even do so, I saw a bright light in the distance. It wasn't too bright but I could make it out due to the blackness surrounding me.

All my fear suddenly vanished as I started running towards it. I felt relieved. I smiled from ear to ear as I was finally engulfed by light. That soon vanished when I laid eyes on two people.

One of the them was the cause of my nightmares. A gasp escaped my lips the moment I saw Ozan being strangled by the man who haunted my dreams. The man who escaped from prison had his arm wrapped around Ozan's throat as he held a gun in his hand, directing it at Ozan's head.

In shock, I placed my hand on my mouth as the shooter looked me straight in the eyes as Ozan struggled to be released. I took a step back.

"O—Ozan?" I whispered, my voice cracking. Ozan stopped struggling and met my stare.

"Ariel . . ." he mumbled.

"What's going on?" I asked in a louder voice, stepping closer. "Let go of him," I demanded, speaking to the man who soon smirked at me. He chuckled as his grasp on Ozan tightened. "Please. Let go of Ozan. You're after me, not him."

The gun soon got closer to Ozan's head as the man remained silent, staring at me with a creepy glare. My fear grew even more. I stared taking more steps towards them. "Please, let go of him," I begged as Ozan stopped struggling in his hold. "Don't hurt him. Please let him go."

A snicker soon took me off guard, and that was because it came out of Ozan's mouth. My eyes went to him and he was giving me a stare which brought a shiver down my spine. "Since when do you care, Ariel?" he asked loudly.

I remained silent for a couple seconds. "What do you mean, Ozan? I always cared about you."

Another snicker escaped his lips. "You never did. All you care about in this world is Troy," Ozan said, taking me off guard. "You don't love me. You love Troy. If I died, you wouldn't even care."

"Of course I'd care. I really do care about you, Ozan," I argued.

"But you don't love me," he spat. "And you'll never love me. You'll always love Troy."

A few tears rolled down my cheek as I listened to Ozan's words. He was right. In this lifetime, I'll only love Troy. I was stupid to think I'd ever forget him. I was horrible for leading Ozan on.

I looked down at the ground as I sucked in a breath. "I'm sorry, Ozan. I really am," I whispered loud enough for him to hear. When I looked up, the man was ready to pull the trigger. "No!" I yelled, running up to them. "Don't. Please!"

The next thing I heard was a loud bang. Everything else went black.

I then jolted out of my bed. I gasped for air as my skin was drenched in sweat. I placed my hand over my heart, closing my eyes as I recalled the nightmare I just had. I opened my eyes and laid back on my bed, running a hand over my face in frustration.

I glanced out of my window to see the sun rising, allowing a bit of light to enter my room. I let out a long breath and stared up at my ceiling, the dream replaying in my head on repeat. I wasn't able to brush it off as it scared me to my core.

Two weeks has passed since Ozan stopped with his radiation therapy. He has been getting a lot better and healthier. Fortunately, the tumor decreased in size dramatically. He was showing good improvement and it was a relief. However, he was still doing his chemotherapy so the tumor wouldn't regrow and cause problems. The doctor still has yet to decide when to stop his chemotherapy and Ozan had to go in a couple times for checkups.

However, they have been saying that Ozan is not in any danger at the moment. It was like a miracle that the tumor was shrinking rapidly.

The thing was, ever since he was getting better, the thought in my mind only grew. I came to realize that the relationship we were in was not healthy for the both of us. I came to realize that by doing this, I was hurting the both of us. Maybe that's why I had these dreams.

My mom's words rung in my ears everyday now. She had a point. Troy and I were just scared, but we weren't taking the risk.

I really care for Ozan. He's my best friend. I don't know if I am able to continue with this, whether or not Troy was willing to start all over. I came to know that I would never love Ozan more

345

than a friend. When I agreed to be his girlfriend, I was scared, scared of being alone and abandoned. I thought if I tried, I could fall for him. Now I think I was stupid for thinking like that.

I was also scared to reject and hurt him, especially in his condition. If I had told him that I didn't want to be with him while he was sick and something happened to him, I would never forgive myself. However, ever since he was improving, the thought grew and grew in my head.

I couldn't hide it anymore. It was wrong of me to be his girlfriend in the first place. The thing was, I didn't know when was the right time to break it off. I was too scared to do it the wrong time.

I'll always love Ozan as a friend and I'm thankful for having him in my life, but I couldn't have him as a boyfriend in my life while my heart still beat for someone else, whether or not he was willing to accept me.

I have come to realize my love for Troy for a while now. I also know that he feels the same for me, but I didn't know what would become of us. Only time could tell.

For now, I have to find a solution for this problem. Maybe when his health becomes better I can talk to him and we can resolve this. I only hoped that Ozan would be understanding and wouldn't hate me for it. I wouldn't blame him if he did, though.

I ran my hand over my face one more time, my head aching by the thought of all of this. I let out a breath as I pushed those thoughts out of my head and fell back asleep, hoping that soon all of this would be resolved.

The day passed. I was walking down the hall, making my way towards Ozan's room. Ozan came back from a doctor's appointment so I wanted to see how he was doing. I stopped when I saw Troy walking the opposite direction.

I smiled as soon as Troy stood in front of me, reflecting my own smile.

"Hey," I mumbled. I haven't seen him for two whole days since he was staying at a friend's house.

"Hi, Ariel," he greeted back. "You're heading towards Ozan's room, right?"

"Yeah," I answered gently. "Ozan came back from a doctor's appointment. I'm going to check up on him."

Troy nodded, his smile turning into a sad one as his eyes softened. He scratched the back of his neck. "Oh, okay," Troy murmured. "Also about the physics quiz on Monday, I wanted to know whether you need help studying."

My eyes widened. "You're offering to tutor me?" I smiled. The corner of his lips twitched upwards as he nodded.

"Well, I know how bad you are on that subject. I don't want you to fail," he pointed out with amusement.

"Oh," I chuckled lightly, rubbing my arm in embarrassment. "Sure. Thank you."

"Let me know when you need help," Troy said.

"Okay. I will."

With a nod and a soft smile, Troy went past me. I watched him disappear before continuing my way towards Ozan's room. I walked in after knocking on his door. Ozan was sitting down on his bed as he talked to someone on the phone. He smiled when our eyes met.

"Yes, I feel better," he said. "Okay. I'll talk to you later. Bye." He then kept the phone. I sat on the edge of his bed. "Ariel," he said.

"Hey," I said gently. "How are you feeling?"

"Better," Ozan answered with a wide smile. "The doctor said I'm getting better."

"That's great. Who were you talking to?"

Ozan placed his phone on his lap. "I was talking to my dad," he replied. "He wanted to check up on me."

I nodded. "That's good."

347

I stayed in Ozan's room for a while, chatting with him and keeping him company. I soon got up, smiling gently. "It's almost dinner time. I'm going down and see if Rose needs any help," I said. Ozan nodded.

"Okay. Go ahead," he said. I nodded and took a couple steps back.

"I'll call you down for dinner when it's ready." I turned around and walked out of his room. The moment I descended from the stairs, I saw Rose struggling to hold two boxes while walking into the living room.

I immediately walked by her side. "Do you need help?" I asked. Rose smiled and nodded, passing me a box.

"Yes," she gasped. "These boxes are heavy. Thank you, dear."

"They are," I agreed as Rose started walking up the stairs. "Where are we taking them?"

"Up to my room," Rose answered. I nodded and we walked up to her room, soon placing the boxes on her bed. "Thanks again, Ariel."

"You're welcome," I said, glancing at the boxes. "What's in them?"

Rose sat down on her bed and started opening one box. "These are some old stuff we left behind in New York three years ago," Rose said.

"Really?" I asked, sitting next to her.

"Yes. When we left New York, we left some stuff in our old house. Like pictures, photo albums, antiques, books and many others stuff," Rose explained as she looked down at the opened box which was filled with exactly what she told me about. She looked at it in awe. Memories were surely rushing back to her. "Damon made some old friends mail them back to us. We almost completely forgot about them."

"That's nice. They can bring back some nice memories," I exclaimed as Rose emptied the box. She was taking out photo albums.

"They are," she gushed. I watched her explain about every single thing she held in her hand. She then opened the second box, repeating the same process. I saw a few pictures of Troy and I when we were young.

Rose handed me some childhood pictures of us with a soft, sad smile. "Here, honey. You can keep them. I know those days mean a lot to you," she said gently. I felt my vision blur and with a nod of my head, I took them and stared down at them.

"Thank you, Rose," I whispered.

I couldn't help but be in awe at the young Troy that I missed deeply. It was the Troy I loved dearly and till this day still has a place in my heart. I continued to adore the pictures as Rose emptied the box. My attention wasn't at the box anymore, but was at the old pictures in my hands of Troy and I.

However, something caught my attention from the corner of my eyes the moment Rose emptied the box completely. I glanced at the pile of books, photo albums and antiques that laid on the bed and my eyes landed on something. My eyes widened the moment I realized what it was.

A familiar journal. Troy's old journal.

CHAPTER FORTY-NINE

It was the journal I have not seen in years. After a couple of seconds of staring at it, my head registered the fact that it was the journal Troy wrote on before his surgery.

That was the journal that got me suspicious a few times with Troy's behavior around it. Three years ago, he wouldn't let me near it so I always had my suspicions. After the incident, I had completely forgot about it. It was always in the back of my mind, but I had more stuff to worry about.

I never really thought about where it could be after all these years. However, after laying eyes on it for the first time in three years, questions ran through my mind. I thought of what to do. I had to see what was in it. Maybe it could be helpful.

I cleared my throat and looked up at Rose who was not paying attention to me. She continued to explain everything that laid on the bed. I guess Rose must have noticed that I wasn't paying attention because she soon looked at me, raising a brow.

"Ariel? Are you listening?" she wondered. I immediately pulled my eyes away from the journal.

"Oh, sorry," I murmured.

"What were you looking at?" Rose asked. I bit my lip the moment she fixed her eyes on the journal. She grabbed it and looked at me. "Were you staring at this?"

I slowly nodded my head, glancing at the journal before looking back at her. "Yeah," I confessed. "It looks pretty. It caught my attention."

Rose looked at it and nodded. "It sure is." She frowned a second later. "But how come this is the first time that I have seen this? I don't remember having a journal." Rose continued to stare at it.

"Can I see it?" I asked, hoping she wouldn't open it. "Would that be okay?"

Rose let out a chuckle. "Of course, honey. Here, you can have it," she stated before handing it to me, smiling comfortably towards me. "It doesn't look important. I don't even remember someone in the family owning a journal."

I smiled widely at Rose, grabbing onto it and looking down at it before raising my head up to meet Rose's eyes. "Thank you, Rose," I said, standing up. "If you don't mind, I'm going to head back to my room."

Rose nodded her head, offering me a warm smile. "Okay, Ariel. Go ahead."

I held the journal and the pictures Rose gave me of Troy and I in one hand and waved at her with my other. I made my way towards the exit and rushed to my room. I sucked in a shaky breath the moment I entered my room and locked the door. I didn't want anyone disturbing me.

I sat down on the bed and put the pictures aside. I feel nervous. I stared down at the journal in between my hands. I closed my eyes as I opened the journal. I let out a breath and told myself I had to do this, even though I felt like I was violating Troy's privacy.

I opened the first page and roamed my eyes on the paper.

I never thought that I'd ever buy a journal. I never in my whole life have thought that I'd need one to write in it for a purpose. I never thought that it would be necessary, but after two days ago, I knew I had to have one. I had to get one.

351

Two days ago was like cold water splashing on to me. It was like a slap back to reality and I never thought that I'd have to face something like this. For the past few weeks I have been having a bad headache and was feeling nauseous, but I didn't think it was that serious. I thought it would soon fade. But after passing out, Dad took me to the ER to find out something. I had wished that I'd hear relieving news, news that would bring me comfort. But unfortunately, that was not the case.

Two days ago I had found out that I had a growing tumor in my brain, one that could kill me. Mom and Dad were very upset but I didn't know what to think. It was as if time had stopped right then and there. I was still young. I had many things I wanted to do but thinking of dying at this age gave me a sickening feeling.

I'm not ready for this.

I still have many things to do. To go to high school, to graduate and to get married. It was as if all those pictures in my head was getting burned down. How could this all happen suddenly? How can all my dreams fall down to my feet all at once?

But the most thing that lingered in my head was a specific person. Ariel. My little mermaid.

Ariel and I are best friends. But I have been in love with her for the longest time. I have always wanted to confess my feelings to her, but I knew that if I did, it might ruin our friendship. But after finding out that I could die two days ago, I knew I had to make a move. That's why yesterday, on our first day of freshman year at prom, I said everything that was in my heart. I told her how I felt about her. I know if I died without telling her, I'd regret it deeply.

I'm happy that I could finally be with the girl that I love, even though it could be for a short period of time. I made Mom and Dad promise me that they won't tell anyone, especially Ariel. I want us to be happy for a short period of time. For now, I was getting treatment until I could do a surgery.

The purpose of why I'm writing in this is because if I do get to live, there is a big chance that I will lose my memories. I will forget *everything that has to do with my life and the people around me. I will forget Ariel. That's why I'm hoping if I could write about my life now, in the future if I do forget, this journal will bring back my lost memories.*

It will help me remember.

I let out a shaky breath as I finished with the first page. A tear fell down my cheek. I closed my eyes and remembered the day at prom when he confessed to me. I always thought that it was so sudden, but now everything made sense. He knew at that time he had a tumor, that's why he did that.

I flipped to the next page.

It's been a couple days now and Ariel and I have been doing very good. I have never been this happy before. We kept walking towards the park we usually went to and sitting under the bridge, a spot only for us. I was able to hug her in my arms and hold her, hoping that I wouldn't ever let her go.

Ariel has always been beautiful, but it was like at this time, I've been noticing her beauty even more. Her ocean blue eyes always called out to me and mesmerized me. I could stare at them all day. They were the prettiest eyes I have ever seen.

It makes my heart sink at the thought that I chose the wrong time to finally tell her my feelings, to finally appreciate her and love her wholeheartedly. I wish I could have done this sooner.

Ariel is the sweetest girl I have ever met. She's always been by my side. And I hope that I'll always remember her, even if my mind forgot her.

Another tear fell down my cheek as I read over the second page. Reading this was making me feel so much. I scanned my eyes over several other pages. He talked about his family and friends.

The other few pages were him talking about his life with his family, bringing a smile to my face. He wrote about several

353

events he went to with his little sister and what he did with Rose and Damon.

I couldn't stop the tears that's making my vision blurry. So many memories came to my mind. I turned to the next page.

> *It's been a week now and I didn't feel so good today, that's why I skipped school. For the past week I have been doing a few radiation therapy sessions, keeping it a secret from Ariel. There were many times that I wanted to tell her everything, but I chose not to.*
>
> *I'm too afraid to tell her. Dad has been trying to find an appointment for the surgery, but unfortunately, there was no room for me. All I could do at this time was wait. I had to wait until I could do the surgery, but I feared that before I could even do the surgery, it would be too late.*
>
> *So much stuff was on my mind today. That's why I went to the park near us and sat under the bridge to relax my thoughts. I thought that it would help me think and calm down. I could tell that Ariel was catching onto something because she kept calling me. But I chose to turn off my phone.*
>
> *I didn't know how to answer her so I stayed there for a few hours until Ariel popped up in front of me, looking worried. I smiled as I thought how well she knew me. She asked me many questions. I didn't fail to notice her worried look. But all I could do was tell her that I was fine.*
>
> *Lying to her hurt me. But this was for the best.*
>
> *But the moment I held her in my arms, everything else flew out of my head and the only thing I thought about was Ariel. I thought about how I'd never want to forget her.*

I wiped the tears as memories flew into my head. Reading through Troy's pain hurt me. He suffered a lot and I wish I had known to comfort him. I inhaled before flipping a few more pages as he continued to write about other events in his life.

I read through every page which made me emotional. I sniffed as my vision blurred once again.

Two weeks went by so fast. I have been getting worse. I could tell that Ariel is catching on to it, yet I'm trying to convince her that everything is fine. I have been more determined to write in this journal as the doctor informed us that the chance of forgetting was a huge percentage.

The tumor continued to grow, but at the mean time as I was waiting for surgery, therapy was the only thing I could do. The doctor warned us that at this rate, I had to do the surgery soon or it would be too late.

I would be lying if I said I wasn't scared. I am. I couldn't be brave. I'm terrified and nervous. I'm scared for many reasons, and the most was forgetting. I don't want to forget. I want to remember and live happily. If I forget, it will be lonely. I will forget about all the stuff that happened to me. It will be like everything that I lived through never happened.

I'm determined to spend more time with Ariel. That's why last night, very late at night, I took her to the park and to a place which was surrounded with trees, leaving a small empty circle of grass. We laid down there and watched the stars. It was relaxing as she laid next to me, enjoying the view.

I then promised her that we'll watch the stars again. I just hope I'll be able to keep that promise.

I smiled wistfully as I read the last line, knowing that he did keep his promise even though it took him three whole years to do so. I ran my hand over my wet cheeks. I sucked in a breath and flipped more pages.

Yesterday Ariel and I hung out at the park after school. We laid down on the grass as she closed her eyes. The only thing I did was stare at her and play with her smooth hair. We talked about everything. We remained like that, enjoying our surroundings. Moments like these soothed me. It brought me comfort.

Today Ariel came over to study. I didn't have the strength to study. I felt too tired. But I didn't want her to notice that. That's why I tried to be my normal self and act how I'd usually act when we were studying. I made jokes, made her laugh and we went off the topic many times.

I distracted myself as she tried to teach me. Ariel was always like this, the nerd who liked to study while I was the complete opposite of her. And that's what I love about her.

There was also another promise that I made to her, hoping that one day I'll be able to keep that promise. And hoping that whether I forget or not, I'll be able to fulfill it.

And that was to go to Hawaii together.

I sobbed as I read the last line. I put the journal to aside for a moment and placed my head in between my hands. I cried quietly at his words. Reading how much he didn't want to lose me and wanted to stay with me hurt me.

It hurts knowing that he never gave up on me, yet I gave up on him. It hurts to know that he was suffering so much. He never wanted to forget me. Troy didn't want to lose me.

I looked back at the journal and grabbed it, continuing to read. I read through the many pages of him talking about me, his parents and what he did for the past three weeks. My vision blurred again and again as I kept roaming my eyes at the pages.

I noticed I was on the last page. My heart was pounding. I wiped my teary eyes and started to read.

It's been a month now. I always liked it when time flies by so quickly. But this time, I hated it. This month went by so fast that I feel like I didn't even have the time to comprehend everything. I wish that it went so slow for me to enjoy everything. But it didn't.

356

I'm getting worse. The tumor kept growing and I couldn't wait anymore. Therapy wasn't doing anything. Surgery is a must, or else it will be too late. Dad has been doing everything he could to make me do the surgery, and after a whole month, he finally did.

But the thing was, I'm not doing it in New York. I'm doing it in California. Dad has an old friend in California which helped us with the surgery appointment. But I don't want to go. I want to stay, but they assured me we were coming back after the surgery. I decided to not tell Ariel. I wanted her to know after the surgery so she won't worry.

Tomorrow we're leaving to California. Tomorrow is finally my surgery day. I feel relieved but scared. I could finally be better and recover. I could finally go back to my normal life. I will live. But the huge chance of me forgetting makes me worry.

I don't want to forget Ariel. I want to continue loving her till I get old. I want to cherish her in my memories forever. But I am afraid that I will forget everything and live without these memories. These memories, I wish to never forget and hold them with me forever.

That's why, I hope if something does go wrong, this will help me remember.

I hope this will help me remember Ariel.

Tears fell down on my lap as I read his final words written on this journal. I cried silently. It brought so many emotions to me. I started sobbing the moment I read the final paragraph.

And Ariel, if this journal ever falls into your hands, if you ever get a chance to read this, then know that I love you so much. And if you're reading this and I don't remember you, then don't give up on me.

Ariel. Don't give up on us.

CHAPTER FIFTY

I didn't know what to do or how to act. Times like this shuts down my brain. I tried to figure out a solution. I felt as if my whole body gave up on me as I sat lifelessly on the floor of my dim room.

My head would swirl just by the thought of what laid inside this journal, the journal which could help Troy. What I had read made me fall back to realization. It was like a slap to the face as I finally read what was inside Troy's journal.

Troy's journal was like cold water splashing onto me, waking me up from my nightmare.

I didn't know how long I was sitting here in my room. I sat on the floor as I held the journal tightly in my hand or it might disappear.

My eyes began to hurt because I haven't slept all night. My head is pounding and begging me to let it rest. I let out a long breath. All I could think about was this journal and what I had to do. The questions swirled in my head.

Thinking of the last line in the journal alone was making me emotional. I felt terribly bad. All this time, deep down, Troy didn't want to lose me. He didn't want me to give up on him.

Yet I did.

I closed my eyes and laid my head against the wall, letting out a sigh as I tried to calm down. I didn't know how long I stayed like that, but the next thing I knew, someone was knocking on my door, forcing my eyelids open.

I glanced at my door and sucked in a worried breath the moment I heard Troy's voice.

"Ariel?" he called out. "Are you awake?" I remained silent, glancing at the journal that was in my hand. My breath hitched the moment my bedroom door opened and Troy walked in. "Mom said that breakfast is ready—"

Troy stopped dead in his tracks the moment he saw my state.

"Ariel? What's wrong?" he asked, worry laced in his tone as he took steps towards me. "Why are you like this? Did something happen to your parents?" Troy kneeled down. I gulped, glancing at the journal.

"No. My parents are fine. It's just . . ."

"It's just what? What's wrong? You look like you haven't slept all night," Troy said.

I closed my eyes to calm myself down. I felt teary, knowing that the moment I hand over Troy's old journal, everything will change.

"It's just . . . this . . ." I raised the hand that was holding onto the journal. His eyes lingered at it for a moment before finally grabbing it.

"This?" he murmured. "What is this? What's in here to cause you to be like this? Is it something bad?" I could clearly see the worry written on his face. I smiled softly at him.

"No," I answered. "It's not bad. Just open it and read it."

Troy stared at me for a moment before nodding and bringing all his attention on the journal. He reluctantly opened the first page and began reading. I sat in front of him, my heart pounding as all the possibilities rushed into my head.

What if he doesn't remember?

I gulped as Troy read, his eyes widening. He brought his shocked eyes to me after he finally finished with the first page.

"This . . . this . . . was mine?" he whispered. Troy didn't even give me the chance to answer as he immediately flipped to the next page.

I sat in silence. Troy continued to flip the pages one by one as his eyes watered with emotion. I held myself back from asking him any questions. I had to have him read the whole thing. Troy didn't even utter a word as he turned the pages. Tears started to flow down his cheeks as he read the last couple pages.

Seeing him tear up made me tear up as well. The moment he flipped to the last page, I began to worry. Troy read in utter silence as I stared at him. When he finally finished reading the entire journal, he calmly shut it and stared at it before finally looking back at me.

The moment our eyes met, I saw eyes that I haven't seen for three long years. Tears continued to flow down his cheeks as he remained speechless for moment. When he finally spoke, I broke out into tears.

"My little mermaid . . ." he whispered. "Oh, Ariel." The next thing I knew, I was being engulfed into his arms. I took no second thought and wrapped my arms around him as well. The tears didn't stop falling.

"Troy," I whispered. "D—do you remember?" I asked.

"I'm sorry, Ariel," Troy spoke. "I'm so sorry. I'm sorry for forgetting you." His arms tightened around me and his face laid on my shoulder. "I'm sorry for leaving you for three years. You suffered because of me. I gave up on us."

I pulled myself from his hold and shook my head, smiling up at him. "It's not your fault, Troy. You couldn't do anything," I assured him as he stared back at me. "You didn't give up on me. I was the one that gave up on you. It's all my fault."

Troy then cupped my face and wiped the tears off my cheeks. "I hurt you so much. I forgot all about you," he whispered. "Ariel, I missed you."

I smiled at him as my eyes watered for the second time. "I missed you, too." Troy and I hugged again as I laid my head comfortably against his chest.

"Ariel," Troy murmured. "Don't ever give up on us."

I smiled and nodded, letting out a comfortable breath. "I will never give up on us."

Then, my eyes opened as a tear rolled down my cheek. My eyes widened and I immediately sat up, roaming my eyes around my room.

No signs of Troy.

I ran a hand over my face, still holding the journal in my other hand.

The sun finally came up, allowing a bit of light to make its way into my dim room. I looked around my surroundings and let out a sigh. I fell asleep on the floor. The dream was something else. I smiled softly to myself as I recalled the dream. It was a beautiful dream.

I immediately stood up and looked at the journal, telling myself I had to go tell Troy. I had to show him his journal. I washed my face and brushed my hair before walking to my bedroom door. But before I could even touch it, I realized something.

Ozan.

I had to break it off with Ozan first. I immediately started to worry but I know I have to do this. I can't go to Troy first without talking with Ozan. I have to tell him everything. I have to let him know how I really felt. I only hope he'd take it calmly.

What if he hates me afterwards? I also feared that this would affect his health but he was getting better each day. That comforted me. I'll have to assure him that I'll remain by his side. I just couldn't remain by his side as his girlfriend.

I let out a breath before opening the door. I placed the journal on my desk and told myself I'd be back for it. I then walked out my room and slowly made my way to Ozan's room. The closer I got, the more nervous I became.

I really do care for Ozan but I know that staying with him in this relationship would hurt all of us. If only I figured that out sooner . . .

I hesitantly knocked on his door. "Come in," Ozan yelled. Opening the door and stepping into the room was quite hard, yet I forced myself to do so. The moment I closed the door behind me, Ozan's eyes met mine.

His lips turned into a smile as he sat up. "Ariel," he called out. "Come over here." Ozan waved his hand for me to walk towards him. I nodded and walked to his bed, sitting down.

"Ozan," I murmured.

"What's up?" Ozan wondered, placing his hand over mine. I glanced at his hand before taking a large breath, looking back at him. His eyes roamed over my body, worry lingering in them. "You look tired. Did you not sleep well?"

I shook my head. "No," I whispered softly but continued before he could ask anymore questions. "But I need to tell you something."

Ozan must have picked up that it was something serious. He slowly nodded. "What is it?" Ozan questioned. Closing my eyes for a brief second, I finally spoke.

"Ozan. You and I have been very close for three years and you must know that I do really love you," I started, feeling extremely nervous. "But I can't love you like this. I don't think I can continue with this relationship."

Ozan was shocked. "A—are you breaking up with me?" Ozan was in disbelief. "You're not breaking up with me, right?"

I averted my eyes from him for a moment then willed myself to face him again. "I'm sorry, Ozan. I tried to give you a chance. I really tried but I can't keep lying to the both of us," I confessed. Ozan drastically pulled his hand away from mine like it burned him. He then got out from his bed and stood in front of me.

"You're really ending it off with me?" Ozan asked.

I shook my head. "I won't ever end it off with you. You're still my best friend," I said, trying to calm him down. "And it will remain like that. I really do care for you. I just cannot care for you as my boyfriend."

Ozan remained silent for a while before shaking his head. "It's because of Troy, right?" Ozan asked, his voice louder than before. "You're breaking up with me because of him? The person who completely forgot about you?"

I stood up and took a step closer to him. "I'm sorry, Ozan. I tried to forget him," I confessed. "But I couldn't. Troy will always be the one that's in my heart. I can't keep lying to the both of us."

Ozan continued to shake his head, his eyes growing angrier. "He's still in your heart?" Ozan asked. "After all this time, you couldn't forget him?" His voice became louder.

"Ozan. Please, calm down. It's not good for your health," I said. Ozan then snickered.

"You don't care about my health," he snapped.

"That's not true," I disagreed. "I swear I care about you."

"The only person you care about is Troy! You never cared about me. And now, you're throwing me away!" He was taking rapid breaths.

I shook my head. "No, I'm not." Tears began to roll down my cheeks. I never thought I'd ever see Ozan like this. "I would never. Please, understand me."

"You are!" Ozan snapped. I took a step closer, trying to calm him down. Ozan opened his mouth to say something else, but before he could even do so, his eyes rolled to the back of his sockets and his body started to shake. My eyes widened as I saw Ozan fall to the floor.

A gasp escaped my lips. This can't be happening again. I immediately fell to the floor and grabbed on to his shaking body. I yelled for help as shock overcame me. The next thing I know, Rose, Damon and Troy came running into the room. Everyone was gasping as I held Ozan's body in my arms.

"He's having a seizure," Damon said, looking at Troy. "Help me get him to the car." They both carried him to the car as Rose and I followed them. Rose was too shocked to ask anything while I prayed that everything was going to be okay.

Troy and Damon finally placed him in the backseat before Damon ran to the driver's seat. "I'll take him to the hospital. You all stay here," he ordered. I immediately shook my head and stepped towards the car.

"No. I need to come," I said.

"Okay. Just get in. We have to be fast," Damon said. Without a second thought, I climbed in and sat in the back as Damon started the car. I placed Ozan's head on my lap as Damon drove away from the house, leaving a shocked Troy and Rose behind.

I sucked in a breath and placed my hand on Ozan's face. Tears beginning to fall down my cheek as I thought of the worst. "Please, Ozan. Wake up," I whispered. "I'm sorry. I'm so sorry." I cried softly, staring at his lifeless body. "This is all my fault."

Ozan opened his eyes. "He opened his eyes," I told Damon. "Hurry, Damon." Damon only nodded as he tried his best to get us to the nearest hospital.

I looked back at Ozan. "I'm so sorry, Ozan. Please forgive me," I exclaimed.

Ozan shook his head. He held my hand. "I was a bit harsh on you," he whispered. "I'm sorry."

"No. It's fine." I shook my head, my vision blurry. "I'm the one to blame."

"I shouldn't have shouted at you," Ozan murmured. "I should have been understanding. I'm sorry, Ariel." Tears fell down as I continued to shake my head.

"Don't be sorry. I should be sorry. I hurt you, Ozan. I hurt you," I said as Ozan's head laid on my lap.

"Don't be sad," Ozan said. "We both hurt each other. But I'm happy that you remained by my side." Ozan then took his hand off mine and raised it to my cheek. He calmly wiped a tear and smiled at me. "Don't cry. Be happy." Ozan then placed his hand to his side, his eyes comforting me. "I give you my blessings."

After that, Ozan slowly closed his eyes. He was motionless in my arms. My eyes widened and I placed my hand on his shoulder. "Ozan, open your eyes," I begged. "Please, wake up." Ozan did not move a bit as I tried to hold in the sob.

"Ozan, please don't leave me." Tears fell down onto his face as I checked his pulse. My eyes widened in horror and I grabbed onto his face. "No. Don't, Ozan. I'm sorry."

Damon remained silent, yet I could tell he was worried. He continued to drive while I sat in the back and held on to Ozan's body. I was crying and begging for him to wake up but it was no use. Ozan wasn't going to wake up.

Ozan was already dead.

CHAPTER FIFTY-ONE

I silently made my way towards the cafeteria to grab some food. It was a bit difficult because of the many students bumping into each other. I took a breath and forced my way through the line.

I felt sort of lonely today. Clare was absent due to a cold and I had to go through the school day all alone. I wasn't used to this and it made me feel sad. This was the first time that Clare was absent ever since Troy had left, and it just brought the lonely feeling back to me.

It has been a hard few months living without Troy. I didn't know how I was doing this. I didn't know how I was living. All I could feel was sadness and loneliness no matter how hard I tried to forget him. It was no use. I could never forget him.

It hurts that he left. I miss him. Yet, I don't even know if he misses me back. I was scared to think that right now, I had no meaning to him. It's like I don't even exist in his world. I always thought about him and wondered how he was doing but it only made me suffer even more.

Clare has always been by my side. I could tell she was trying to fix the hole that was left in my heart and I usually felt better when she's with me but since she wasn't here today, those unwanted feelings were coming back to me.

I let out a sigh and made my way out the cafeteria as soon as I got my food. Clare and I usually ate inside the cafeteria, but since she wasn't here today, I won't be eating there.

I walked away quietly from the large group of people and sat under a large tree. I placed the tray of food on my lap and stared at it for a moment. I grabbed my bag and pulled something out from it.

A smile made its way on my lips as I stared at the picture of Troy and I. It's a picture we took a few months ago. My eyes continued to linger at the photo in silence as many memories rushed back to me. I always carried this picture in my bag. It always made me smile whenever I looked at it, even though I'd feel sadness afterwards.

I closed my eyes to prevent the tears from slipping and leaned my head against the tree. However, my eyelids snapped open the moment I felt someone snatch the photo from my grip. I saw a boy standing in front of me with a smirk, holding onto my picture.

I frowned and looked up at the boy called Alex, a boy I dislike a little too much.

"What do we have here?" he asked out loud, looking at the picture.

I stood up and stepped towards him. "Alex. Give me back the picture," I demanded. His smirk grew and I got more anxious that he'd do something to the picture.

"Who's this?" Alex asked, completely ignoring what I said a couple seconds back. "Wasn't this your boyfriend before he completely left you?"

I clenched my fist to control the anger that was seeping through. I took another step towards him, annoyed by his expression. "I'm not in the mood of your games. Now, give me back my picture."

Alex's eyes lingered at me before looking back at the picture. "What would you do if I ripped it?" Alex asked, raising a brow. My eyes widened and I shook my head.

"You wouldn't," I whispered, feeling more nervous than ever.

Alex let out a chuckle, shaking his head. "Oh, I would." I took a few steps towards him the moment he started ripping the picture slowly from the top. My eyes widened in shock and I shook my head.

"Please, Alex. Don't," I begged him, which only brought him more amusement. But before he could even continue, someone snatched the photo from his hands, making him frown. My eyes immediately looked at the person who took the photo from Alex's grasp and I let out a sigh of relief.

Alex and I stared at a boy I have never seen before, a tall boy who was glaring down at Alex.

"Hey!" Alex snapped. "Give it back."

"Get out of here before I rip your hair from your head," the boy demanded in a serious tone. Alex stared at him for a moment, fear passing through his eyes as he looked up at him. "Leave," he demanded another time as I stood silent, thankful that someone was helping me out.

Alex looked back at me and gave me a glare, glancing back at the unknown boy before turning around and walking off. The moment he was out of sight, I turned back to the boy.

"I believe this is yours?" He handed the photo to me. I smiled and took it from him.

"It is. Thank you," I said, sitting back on the ground as I stared at the picture. "I don't know what I would've done if you didn't take it from him." The boy sat down next to me as I smiled back at him.

"It's not a big deal," he chuckled, glancing at the photo. "It seemed like an important photo."

I nodded. "It is," I confirmed. My smile soon turned into a frown as I saw a rip at the top of the photo. "But now there's a rip." I let out a frustrated breath.

I glanced at the boy to see him pulling out tape from his backpack. "Can I?" he asked. I glanced at the piece of tape. I handed the picture to him.

He grabbed a hold of it then placed the tape on the the small torn part of the picture, smiling up at me. "There, new as ever." He handed it back and I smiled back at him.

"Thank you, it means a lot to me," I said.

"You're welcome. I'll always try to help," he said. I chuckled.

I glanced at the picture of Troy and I before looking back at the boy. "By the way, what's your name? I've never seen you here before. Are you new?" I asked.

The boy nodded. "Yes, I'm a new student here," he confirmed. He reached out his hand towards me and smiled from ear to ear. I grabbed his hand and shook it, returning the smile.

"I'm Ariel," I said.

"And I'm Ozan. It's nice to meet you."

*   *   *

I stood lifelessly, surrounded by many people. I didn't know for how long my eyes were staring at the new grave. It brought many memories back to me. Tears fell down my cheek as I heard people crying. The tears continued to fall as it started to sink in the more I looked at the grave.

Ozan wasn't here anymore.

It was hard for me to believe. I didn't want to. I didn't want to accept the fact that Ozan was gone for good.

I miss him already.

Everything went by like a blur. I didn't know how I was dealing with this and how I made through two whole days. I was breathing, but I felt dead inside. I felt a hand on my shoulder, pulling me into a hug as I cried. I looked up to see my mom hugging me tightly.

I hugged her back, missing her hold. It has been a long time since my mom has hugged me like this and comforted me.

Two days ago when Ozan passed away, everything in my head shut down. I didn't want to believe it but it was true. I felt like my world fell down. The doctors confirmed that he had already passed away. The rest was like a blur. I don't remember the rest.

All I remember was crying. I remember seeing tears fall down from everyone's faces as we acknowledged that Ozan was gone. I then remember Rose packing my stuff and Damon making phone calls. I insisted that I wanted to return to New York to watch his funeral. It was the least I could do.

I knew it wasn't safe, but that was the least of my worries. Ozan did many things for me and went through many sufferings because of me. The least I could do was say a proper farewell to him.

I returned to New York yesterday with Damon. Damon came on the behalf of everyone to watch Ozan's funeral. I remember meeting with my parents and with Clare for the first time in a long time. I couldn't exactly recall what exactly happened these two days as my mind wasn't paying attention to anything. I was trying to cope with the loss.

Now, I was in my mom's hold as we both cried. People were starting to leave as Damon, Mom, Dad, Clare, and Ozan's parents were the only ones left. My heart broke even more as I saw Ozan's mom sobbing by the grave while her husband tried to comfort her.

It hurt even more realizing that they never said goodbye to their son. Time passed and we had to leave. My dad and Damon remained with Ozan's parents while me, my mom and Clare went inside the car. I sat silently as mom started driving off while I looked outside the window, the graveyard disappearing from my sight.

I stared at my hands as my tears dried up. We all remained silent as Mom drove us back to the house. I had no strength to say

370

anything as many thoughts circled in my head. My emotions were everywhere.

I felt sadness and guilt. I felt like I was the cause of Ozan's death, and that broke me. I don't know how I was going to cope with this feeling.

I also felt disappointed. Disappointed by the fact that I never gave Troy his journal. When Ozan died, that was the least of my worries but thinking about it now, I felt like I've missed my chance. I left that journal in California and I didn't know if I'll ever see it again.

I still didn't know whether I was going to return to California or if I will be staying here. I didn't really try to find out whether I was going to return or not. I had so many things going on in my head.

We eventually made it home. The moment I walked into my house, I made my way towards my old room. I heard my mom calling my name but I ignored her and entered my room, closing the door behind me. I let out a breath, slowly sitting on the floor before reaching for something that was in my pocket.

I smiled softly as I stared down at the bracelet.

The bracelet that Ozan gave me in Hawaii.

My eyes began to tear up as I recalled the memories that we made together. A tear fell down my cheek as I placed the bracelet around my wrist, smiling softly. "I miss you, Ozan," I whispered. "I'll never forget you."

I looked up the moment my door opened, revealing a worried Clare. She walked in with my mom behind her. I could see the same pain in their eyes. They both sat next to me on the floor. My mom wiped my wet cheek.

"It's okay, honey. You'll get used to it," she said calmly. "Everyone has to go someday. With time, the pain will lessen."

Clare was rubbing my back in a soothing manner. I could tell she was trying to be strong for me even though she was feeling horrible on the inside. "Your mom's right," Clare stated. "With time, everything will get better."

"What about the guilt?" I asked, looking up at my mom. My mom's frown deepened as I began to tear up again. "It's my fault that Ozan is now gone. I took him from his parents and I hurt him. How will this guilt disappear?"

"Don't say that, Ariel. You know Ozan wouldn't want you thinking that way," Clare exclaimed. She smiled at me yet her eyes were full of sadness. "Ozan wanted to go with you. He also knew how much you cared for him."

My mom nodded in agreement. "That's true," she said. "What happened wasn't something in your control. I'm sure Ozan wouldn't want you feeling guilty when you remember him."

"He'd want you to smile when you remember him," Clare added. "So don't blame yourself. Death isn't something we can control. That's how life is."

I closed my teary eyes for a brief moment. I know that this all happened because of me, and nothing would change that. I know I will carry this pain with me for as long as I live, and it would be a reminder of the mistakes that I have commited.

"I'll miss him," I cried. "I'll miss him so much."

"We'll all miss him," Clare said, a tear rolling down her cheek. "He was a friend to all of us. He suffered from his illness. I'm sure he's now in peace."

Clare and my mom pulled me in a warm hug. I took in their words and let out a breath. I sure hope he's now in peace.

After a moment in their grasp, Clare stood up. "Let's give Ariel some time to rest. I'm sure she's very tired," she suggested. My mom nodded and got up.

"Okay. Get some sleep," Mom said. "You need to rest."

I nodded, knowing that some alone time would be better for me. "Okay. I will."

372

Clare and Mom soon walked out my room, closing the door behind them. I let out a long breath and laid on my bed. I fell asleep with the image of Ozan in my head.

A buzzing noise woke me out of my sleep. I immediately thought of Ozan. I opened my eyes and felt my phone buzzing in my pocket. I pulled the phone out and was shocked to see Troy calling me.

I sat up straight and stared at the phone. Why is he calling me?

Ever since I left California, I haven't contacted him. We didn't talk much either before I left. He only said a few words of comfort when I was leaving. There was no doubt that I surely missed him. However, I felt sad that I wasn't able to give him his journal and I wasn't able to brush off that feeling.

Sucking in a breath, I answered the call.

"Troy?" I said, waiting to hear his voice.

And after a long second, I heard him speak.

"My little mermaid . . ."

CHAPTER FIFTY-TWO

It was like at that moment I felt all the air got stuck in my throat. I think my heart skipped a beat. It took me seconds to register the words that hit my ears, and when I realized the importance to those words, I froze.

"What did you just say?" I asked. Troy went silent for a moment. I got anxious.

"Ariel," he whispered softly. "My little mermaid . . . I missed you."

I placed my hand against my mouth to muffle my gasps. All sorts of emotions hit me all at once. I closed my eyes and took deep breaths.

"Troy. Do you remember?" I asked, fearing that the answer I was going to hear might disappoint me.

I heard a chuckle coming from his end. He took a second to answer again.

"Yes, Ariel," he answered, his words hitting me right in my chest. "I remember."

I jolted up from the sudden shock that slapped me in the face. This was too good to be true. "You actually remember?" I asked again, my voice cracking as I tried to hold in my cries. "You remember everything? Our past? Our memories?"

"I remember everything," Troy responded, his feelings seeping through his voice. "I remember our past and our memories. I remember our love."

I couldn't stop the tears that fell down my face as I tried to comprehend everything. All of this was too sudden, and it made my feelings go haywire.

"How?" I asked, gripping onto the phone for my dear life. "How is this possible? After three years, how do you remember?"

"I read the journal," Troy answered. "It brought me my memories and my past. It also made me realize how much I missed you."

"Oh my God," I whispered to myself, placing my hand over my rapidly beating heart. I was trying to calm it down as the river of tears continued to fall down my cheeks. "You actually remember."

"I do, Ariel," he whispered. "I finally do."

"I missed you, Troy," I cried, placing my hand on the wall to help me balance my body before I fell to the floor. "I missed you so much."

"I miss you too, Ariel. I really do," Troy said painfully.

"It was so hard, Troy," I said, wiping my tears from my cheeks and trying to calm my feelings down. "Living with you but you not remembering me was so hard. It was painful being close to you, yet you do not even know who I was."

"I'm sorry, Ariel," Troy exclaimed, regret seeping through his voice. "I really am. I wish I could've remembered sooner. I really do. I'm sorry for hurting you. I'm sorry for bringing you pain."

"I still can't believe you remember," I whispered, smiling to myself as I comprehend everything. "I only wish you were here, with me."

"Ariel"

"Yes?"

"Look out the window," Troy ordered.

"The window?" I asked, taking a few steps towards my bedroom window.

"Yes. And look down," Troy ordered once again. I did what he said. I opened the window and looked down. I lost grip of my phone as I looked down to see a smiling Troy waving at me, right in front of my house.

A gasp escaped my lips and I took a few steps back. When everything finally made sense to me, I dashed out my room. I ran as fast as I could, ignoring Clare and Mom who were asking me what was going on. I swung the door open to see Troy right in front of me, holding his arms out for a hug.

It took no second thought for me to jump into his arms. His arms tightened around me, something that I longed for a long time. I cried silently as we stayed in each other's hold.

"Ariel," Troy murmured. "My little mermaid. I missed you."

"I missed you too. I missed you a lot," I said, trying to calm down.

When we finally broke apart, I saw from the corner of my eyes my mom and Clare appearing into sight. I heard gasps as Troy stared warmly at me. Troy grabbed onto my hand then we turned to Clare and Mom, whose eyes were both wide in shock.

"Troy? Is that you?" Clare asked.

Troy nodded, smiling at them. "Yes. It's me. And I finally remember everything."

Clare and Troy hugged each other for a moment, bringing a smile to my face. Clare and Troy were close friends as well. When Troy disappeared, Clare tried her best not to show me how much she missed him because she knew I was suffering as well. However, I could always tell she missed their friendship.

They broke apart. My mom hugged Troy. When they pulled apart, she looked at him in astonishment. "Oh God. You grew up very much," she stated, making him smile. "Come in. Don't just stay standing there." Mom lead Troy into our house.

Troy immediately started looking around the house, his eyes sparkling. "Exactly how I remember it," he said as we walked to the living room. We all sat down while I sat next to Troy.

"How did you remember everything?" Clare asked. Troy grabbed onto his backpack and opened it, pulling out the familiar journal.

"From this," he answered.

"What's that?" Mom asked.

"This was a journal I used to write many things in it before I lost my memories," Troy answered. "And when I read it, everything came back to me."

"How did you find it?" I asked, looking up at him. Troy looked down at me and smiled softly.

"When you left, I felt very lonely. So yesterday, I entered your room and stayed in there for a while," Troy claimed, clearing his throat as he scratched the back of his neck. "I then saw this laying on your desk. At first, I wasn't going to touch it but then it looked very familiar to me. So I took it and read it."

Troy grabbed onto my hand, looking down at me with sincerity. "And when I remembered everything, I booked the nearest flight to New York," Troy stated. "I just had to see you. Especially with Ozan's death, I knew you were feeling horrible and I didn't want to leave you alone."

My heart sank as I heard Ozan's name. I sucked in a breath and looked down at my hands. I felt horrible that I was happy for a moment. Troy immediately placed his hand on my back, rubbing it in a soothing manner.

"It's okay, Ariel. Everything will be better with time," Troy spoke softly. "You just have to be strong."

"Clare, how about we let them spend some time alone?" Mom asked Clare.

Clare nodded. "Okay. Let's go prepare something to eat."

They both got up and walked away, giving Troy and I some alone time. I looked up at Troy with sad eyes. "I feel bad that I was happy a moment ago," I told Troy. "Ozan is gone now. I shouldn't have been all happy."

Troy shook his head. "Don't feel bad," he stated, rubbing my back softly. "It was his time to go. With time, you'll get used to it. I'm sure Ozan is in a better place now."

I looked up at him, my eyes wet with tears. "You really think so?" I asked, a tear rolling down my cheek. "Do you think he's now in peace?"

"Suffering from an illness is painful. I know how that feels," Troy claimed. "I'm sure he suffered a lot. I bet he's now in peace."

"I hope so," I whispered.

Troy raised his hand and wiped my wet cheek with his thumb, smiling softly at me. "So don't be sad," Troy said in a comforting tone. "Because Ozan wouldn't have wanted you to cry. Remember him in happiness."

I looked down at my hands, not knowing what to say. I knew I would forever remember him. I knew that I would forever try to repent for what I did to him. I wished dearly that I could make it up to him, in this life and the next.

A whole day has passed since Troy came to New York and I still felt as if it was too hard to comprehend. I couldn't help but feel emotional as Troy and I talked about our past. I sometimes worry if I was dreaming, if all I was experiencing was all fake. However, it wasn't. This was reality and Troy was actually here with me.

Damon and Troy were currently staying at our house for a couple of days. I didn't know when they were returning to California and I didn't want to think about it. I wanted to savor the moment with Troy without wondering and worrying when we were going to part.

I also didn't even know if I was going to be staying here or returning. These few days have been very hectic so I didn't bother ask. I honestly didn't know what I wanted. I wanted to stay because

378

I truly missed my family and it has been months since I have last spend time with them. On the other hand, I also liked California and now since Troy remembered all the lost memories, I didn't want to apart from him.

I let out a sigh as I looked at my hands.

"What's with the sigh?" Troy asked. I brought my head up to meet his eyes. Troy and I were currently sitting in my room as Troy wrapped his arms around me, my head laying against his chest. I shrugged my shoulders.

"It's nothing. I'm just thinking," I murmured. Troy nodded, playing with a strand of my hair.

"What are you thinking about?" he asked.

"About everything," I replied. "I've got many things that I'm wondering about. You alone is taking up all my thoughts."

Troy let out a deep chuckle. "I am?" He raised a brow.

I nodded. "Yes. I find it too good to be true that I'm actually in your arms," I said, smiling softly up at him. "I missed you a lot. Even though you were a prick."

"A prick?" Troy questioned.

"Yes. You were a jerk to me while I was in California," I claimed. "I loved you, yet you kept pushing me away."

"I was a jerk, right?" he said. I smiled in amusement and nodded.

"Yeah. A huge one. And that day in Disneyland, you even confessed that you had feelings for me. Yet you still pushed me away," I reminded him. Troy's arms tightened around me as he nodded his head.

"I was afraid that time," Troy confessed. "You suddenly appeared into my life and made me feel unwanted feelings. I felt lonely and what scared me the most was forgetting all over again." Troy let out a sigh. "Ariel. One day, I could forget you all over again, and that scares me."

379

"Don't worry," I said, grabbing onto the journal. "If you forget ten times, I'll show you this journal every time. You can't escape me."

Troy let out a chuckle. "Okay. That's fine with me," Troy said. "You just have to handle me being a jerk to you at first."

"Oh, I handled it once, I can handle it again."

Troy's smile grew and he brought his face closer to mine, his breath fanning my skin. "That's good," he whispered, placing his lips onto mine for a second before pulling away.

"You jerk," I muttered, making him smile from ear to ear before he placed his lips onto mine, kissing me again. It didn't take long for us to pull apart when someone knocked on my door.

"Ariel. Your dad wants to see you downstairs."

"Okay. I'll be right down," I yelled, running my hand through my hair. Troy stood up as well and grabbed on to my hand.

"Come on. Let's go see what your dad wants," he said, pulling me out of my room. We walked down the stairs and towards the living room to see Damon and my dad sitting down, talking. They both turned to look at us. My dad patted the seat next to him.

I sat next to him while Troy sat next to his dad. My dad smiled at me and pecked my forehead. "How are you feeling today?" Dad asked.

"I feel okay," I answered.

"That's good." he nodded. "Damon and I have been talking, and we decided that we're going to send you back to California," he said. My eyes widened and I slowly nodded my head.

"I'm going to go back? When?" I questioned.

"Tomorrow. Troy and Damon are leaving tomorrow so you'll be returning with them," Dad answered. I frowned and looked up at him.

"Tomorrow? That's too soon. I barely got to see you and Mom," I said, feeling a little disappointed. My dad sighed and grabbed my hand.

"I know honey but we can't forget that there's someone out there who wants to hurt you and still hasn't been caught," Dad pointed out.

"Your dad's right," Damon agreed. "It's not safe here. You've already been here long enough. It would be better if we leave tomorrow."

Troy nodded. As I thought about everything, I realized the danger. "I promise, the moment that man gets caught, you'll come back. I just can't risk you being here," Dad continued. I looked up at him and let out a breath.

"Okay. I'll do as you say," I said.

They all smiled and my dad kissed me on my forehead. After a while of talking with my dad and Damon, Troy and I went back to my room. Before we could enter the room, Troy grabbed my hand.

"There's something I've got to do before we leave tomorrow and I want you to come with me," Troy said.

"What is it?" I wondered.

Troy smiled. "Pay my respect to Ozan."

CHAPTER FIFTY-THREE

A smile soon appeared on my lips as I registered what Troy meant. I took a step closer to him.

"You're saying you want to visit Ozan before we leave?" I said.

Troy nodded. "Yes. Let's go visit him before we leave. I'll pay my respects and we'll say goodbye to him so you can be in peace."

"But you've never liked Ozan. So why would you finally want to make peace with him?" I said as I rememebed what happened in California. It brought back a frown on my face. I only wish that things turned out for the better. Yet, I knew that no matter how much I regretted it, nothing was going to change.

Troy gently grabbed onto my chin and raised my face to look up at him. His smiled disappeared but his eyes were still comforting, the same eyes that used to look at me three years ago. These were the eyes that I truly missed.

"Ariel. I've never hated Ozan," Troy said, placing his hand to his side as he tried to form the right words. "I never personally had something against him. It was just . . . I didn't like you two together." Troy scratched the back of his neck, averting his eyes from mine. "It bothered me. That's why we never had a good relationship."

I grabbed his hand. "I get what you mean," I said. He smiled at me, but this time, it didn't reach his eyes.

Troy took a breath. "I admit, I sometimes felt anger towards him but other times, I felt bad towards him. He was suffering the same illness that I have suffered. I knew how he felt but the outcomes were different," he said, looking away for a moment. I could tell he was trying to cover up his sadness.

I frowned and closed my eyes for a moment.

"I survived . . . yet, he didn't," Troy murmured, looking at our hands. "Even though we never had a good relationship, I still feel hurt. Hurt over the fact that I was lucky to make it through, yet he didn't."

"This world is cruel, isn't it?" I asked softly as we looked back at each other.

Troy nodded, letting out a sigh. "Very cruel," Troy agreed. "That's why I want to make peace with him and ask Ozan to watch over us. That way, I can be in peace, too."

A small smile made its way onto my face. "That would be very nice," I said. "I would love that." I also wanted to see him. I wanted to talk with him, hoping that somehow he was hearing me. Truthfully, a little closure would make me happy, although the guilt wouldn't completely disappear.

Troy's smile reflected my own and he then pulled me into a hug. I reseted my chin on his shoulder as he ran his hand through my hair.

"And after that, we'll return to California and live in peace," Troy said. I nodded my head as an answer. "We'll have our peace that was taken away from us three years ago."

The next day came, our time to return to California. Before that however, Troy and I will go through our plan to visit Ozan's grave.

I immediately knew who was knocking on the door. I opened the door, seeing Troy standing right in front of me. A smile crawled on my lips and he reflected my own. Troy took a step towards me before grabbing onto my hands.

"Are you ready?"

383

I nodded. "Yes," I answered. "Let me just go grab my phone before we get going." Troy nodded and I walked back to the desk before grabbing my phone in my hand.

We only had a couple hours before we start heading towards the airport but we still have time to visit Ozan. I was a bit nervous but mostly felt good that we were doing this. The last time I was in front of his grave, I was a mess. This time, I'll be able to talk to him properly while Troy makes his amends.

That brought me comfort.

I closed the door behind me. "Okay. Let's get going," I said. Troy nodded and led us towards the car after we told our parents that we were going. I saw a man dressed in black standing in front of the car.

"Who's that?" I asked Troy.

"That's a bodyguard that your dad assigned to watch over us," Troy explained. "We can't forget that there's someone looking for you."

"Oh, okay."

The bodyguard got into the back seat silently as Troy and I sat in front. I input the destination in the GPS before Troy started driving. I glanced at the bodyguard that sat behind us in utter silence. I was thankful that my dad assigned him to us. That way, I didn't have to worry much.

Troy drove in silence as we got closer to our destination. He stopped at a local flower shop. I raised a brow at him and he smiled softly. "We have to get flowers," Troy said. I nodded and smiled.

"Okay. That would be nice," I said. Troy got out of the car, leaving me alone with the bodyguard.

I glanced back at the bodyguard through the mirror. I turned my head to him. "So . . . Do you carry a gun with you?" I wondered.

The man looked at me with a neutral expression but nodded.

384

"Are you allowed to?" I asked again.

The man nodded once again. "It's licensed," he finally said. "It's also for your safety."

"Oh," I mumbled, nodding my head. "Okay." I didn't really ask anymore questions and sat straight, waiting for Troy to return. The moment Troy returned with flowers in his hand, he started driving. I held the flowers in my hands and smiling at it.

It didn't take long for us to finally arrive at the graveyard. I sucked in a breath as Troy parked the car a little far away from Ozan's grave. The three of us got out of the car and walked towards his grave. The guard walked behind us. When we got closer to his grave, the bodyguard stopped in his tracks.

"Go on," he said. "I'll watch from here." We both nodded and walked to the grave while the bodyguard stood in the distance.

The moment we stood in front of Ozan's familiar grave, I felt my heart sink like the previous time. I closed my eyes to calm myself down. Troy placed his hand on my shoulder. I looked up at him. "It's alright," Troy said. "Take a deep breath."

I did so before placing the flowers on the grave. "Hi, Ozan," I whispered. "I'm back. You didn't think that you've gotten rid of me, did you?" I teared up as Troy stood by me. "Look who also came with me. It's Troy. He said he wanted to pay his respects and make amends for being a jerk."

We both smiled softly and Troy took a step closer. "I'm sorry," he mumbled, continuing after a moment of silence. "I wasn't the nicest person. And for that, I'm sorry. We could have been good friends. We could have gotten along if it wasn't for the circumstances."

"He also finally remembers me, Ozan. Isn't that great?" I asked softly. "I know you've always wished for my happiness even though I hurt you. I'm sorry I hurt you. I was very selfish, and I will forever live with this guilt." A tear fell down my cheek as I tried to clear my voice. "But I still wish for your blessing. Please watch over us, Ozan."

"We're going back to California today. We're going to start over, " Troy claimed. "And we hope you're in peace."

A tear fell down again but I wiped it away, inhaling as I stared at Ozan's grave. "I'll miss you. I won't ever forget you, Ozan," I said. "For all those times that you've helped me and comforted me, for those times that you were such a good friend to me even though I hurt you, thank you. I will never forget your favor."

I glanced up at Troy who smiled at me before I looked back at the grave. "In the future, I will surely come back to visit you."

After that, Troy and I had to leave. We bid our farewells and with one last glance towards his grave, we walked towards the bodyguard. The moment we were on the sidewalk, Troy turned to look at me. "You both stay here. I'll go get the car since it's a little far away."

I nodded. "Okay. Go ahead." I watched him walk away while we waited, the man standing behind me to give me space. We stood there in silence.

Someone suddenly appeared in front of me.

Someone familiar.

I gasped and went stiff as I saw the man who haunted my dreams, the man that ran away from jail. The same man who entered my old school with a gun.

The bodyguard soon stood in front of me as the man walked closer to us with a sickening smirk on his face. "That's the man," I told the bodyguard. "He's the one who ran from prison."

He immediately pulled the gun and pointed it at the man who didn't even look afraid. "Stop right there," he ordered. "Don't move."

The man didn't even acknowledge the person pointing the gun at him, but only turned to me, his smirk growing. "So we finally meet again," he spoke lowly. "After five months and two weeks, I've finally got you."

386

I felt a chill run down my body, feeling my head start to stir from his words. I remained silent due to the fear while the unknown man remained put, not moving due to the gun pointing at him. I reached into my pocket to grab my phone to dial 911, but my blood went cold when I realized that I had left it in the car. "What do you want?" I finally mustered the strength to ask. "What is it that you want from me?"

He shook his head. "It is not me who wants you. I'm just following orders."

Before I could even ask another question, I heard a car coming from behind us. At first, I thought it was Troy, but I was soon proven wrong when the car came to a stop and someone else came out from the car. I immediately felt a sense of relief the moment I saw Ozan's dad walk out.

"Mr. Senan," I called out. Help us. Call the police," I said. He took a step towards us as the man remained put in his place. "He's the man that escaped prison. Fast, call 911."

Ozan's dad remained silent for a moment, and the sense of relief soon disappeared the second a smirk made its way on his face. I immediately felt confused, but didn't have the chance to ask anything.

"Oh, Ariel," he said. "I finally have you in my hands. Do you know how hard it was to do so?"

My eyes widened and I felt the air clogging up my throat. "What are you talking about?" I whispered. "What do you mean?"

He took a step closer to us, his smirk growing and the gun pointed to him this time as the bodyguard stood stiff. "I mean it took five whole months to finally continue where we left off," Ozan's dad stated. "It surely wasn't easy."

"No," I whispered in shock. "It can't be you. You can't be the one behind all of this."

"Oh, but I am," he confirmed. "I have been wanting to catch you for so long. The anger is to its highest."

"Why would you want to hurt me?" I asked, feeling my fear only grow as I also felt a stab of betrayal. "My dad is good friends with you. You both are co-workers. Why would you want to hurt me?"

"It's not you who I want to hurt. It's your dad," he said, anger seeping through his voice. "I've been wanting to for a long time now. Xavier made my company go bankrupt. My family and I went through poverty and suffered. We were at our lowest point in our lives and it was all because of your dad."

"I don't understand," I murmured.

"Five years ago, your dad stole a project from me because he was almost going bankrupt, a project which could have helped us financially. My company was the one to go bankrupt," he snapped. "I had debts growing because of him. Two years later, he thinks he can solve everything by taking me into his company. As if that could make amends for his mistake."

"My dad wouldn't do that," I disagreed hesitantly. I always knew that Ozan and his family suffered from poverty previously, but I never would have thought that my dad would be linked to it. I didn't want to accept it.

"But he did!" he snapped again. "He tried to lessen his guilt by taking me into his company and befriending our families. But I have never once forgotten what he did. After all these years, I have been plotting my revenge. I even sent Ozan with you to watch you."

My eyes widened. "Was Ozan on it too?" I asked.

"Ozan didn't even know anything. He was unintentionally spying on you. He was madly in love with you to even question my intentions," Mr. Senan answered. "And even after his illness, he refused to return home. But what did you do? You killed him. That gave me a second reason for revenge."

I shook my head. "That's not true. I really loved Ozan. He was my best friend," I argued.

388

"Bullsh*t! Now it's Xavier's turn to feel what I've suffered. I want him to feel misery and anger after losing something, just like what I felt."

That was the moment that Ozan's dad looked at the shooter. With the bodyguard still pointing the gun to Ozan's dad, he didn't have the time to point it back to the shooter. The shooter pulled out a gun and pointed it at me.

Before he could even do anything, a car crashed into him from behind us. The gun flew out of his hand. My eyes widened in relief when I saw Troy opening the door.

"Get in," Troy yelled. "Fast!"

Ozan's dad immediately pulled a gun from his pockets, forcing me to run towards the car. I heard a gunshot in the air, making my body go stiff and drastically turn around. My eyes widened as I saw the bodyguard's shoulder bleed as he took the bullet for me.

"Oh my God," I gasped. "Are you okay?"

The man raised his hand in the air. "Don't worry about me. Get out of here," he snapped. He then raised his gun and shot Ozan's dad in the leg, making him fall to the ground. I heard Troy yell for me to get in the car, forcing my legs to move.

I heard several gun shots from behind which missed me. The moment I got into the car, Troy started driving. I looked behind me to see Ozan's dad taking down the guard who was severely bleeding. He then ran to his car with an injured leg.

I immediately grabbed my phone and dialed 911 frantically, telling the operator what happened. I let them know to send an ambulance to the graveyard, but stopped as I noticed a car driving behind us.

"Troy, he's right behind us," I said in fright.

"Don't worry. I'll try to lose him," he stated, gripping tightly onto the steering wheel.

"Troy," I said frantically. The car behind us drove in full speed. Troy then grabbed onto my hand. I forgot about the operator on the phone as the car got closer to us.

"Calm down, Ariel. You'll be alright," Troy assured. "No one will hurt you. I'll protect you."

Tears fell down my cheek and I nodded my head, trying to control my fear. Everything happened too soon for my head to wrap around. The car that Ozan's dad was driving in was right next to us, and before we even knew it, he crashed his car into ours.

The last thing I saw before blanking out from the impact was Troy wrapping his arms around me, covering me with his body.

*   *   *

Darkness. That was all I saw. I didn't know for how long I was in there, but it was painful and scary.

My eyes soon slowly opened. I winced as I made eye contact with the light. I grunted as I felt pain all over me. My head was pounding severely. Right after that, I heard familiar voices.

The first thing I saw were my parents's worried expression, making me frown. "When will she wake up?" My dad asked my mom. "She's been asleep for a while now. I'm getting very worried."

"Don't worry, honey," my mom said. "We have to be strong for her."

"I'm just still shocked. I can't believe what happened." My dad's eyes began to tear up. "The culprit was right in front of us all this time, and we didn't even notice."

"Xavier . . ."

"This is all my fault. I brought him into our lives. I made him hate us like that," my dad. "And now because of me, this happened to Ariel."

Before my dad could continue blaming himself, I called out to them with my croaky voice, "Dad . . . Mom."

"Oh God," my mom gasped, both of them rushing towards me. "Ariel. Are you okay?" She then looked to my dad in worry. "Xavier. Go call the doctor." My dad nodded and dashed out of the room. "How are you feeling, honey? What hurts you?"

It was then that I recalled everything. I remembered the incident. My eyes widened in fear. I sucked in a breath, looking at my mom.

"Mom."

"Actually, don't speak," she stated, grabbing onto a bottle of water and helping me drink from it. "You've been asleep for a couple of days now. Your body needs rest."

I had so many questions I wanted to ask.

"Did anyone—"

"No," she claimed. "I know what you're going to ask. No one died," my mom assured me. "Only the shooter and Senan. He died from the impact." She let out a sigh, pausing for a moment. "It's such a shame. We all thought we were truly friends. We've never suspected for that to come from him. We've never doubted him. We're still in shock that he was behind all this. Your dad did do something wrong in the past, but we thought that he has already made it up for him."

"Tell Dad not to blame himself, no one was expecting this," I said, not wanting my dad to feel the burden.

My mom nodded, pausing for a moment. "Even the guard is okay. The ambulance was able to make it on time," Mom explained. "You also have minor injuries thanks to Troy. If it wasn't for him covering you, I don't know what would have happened."

My eyes widened as I heard his name and my body stiffened. "Is he alright?" I finally asked. "Please tell me he's okay."

My mom remained silent for a moment, averting her eyes away from me for a second. "He's fine. It's just . . ."

I gulped, not liking the sound of her voice. "It's just what?" I asked in a louder tone. "Did something happen to him?"

My mom looked back at me. She grabbed onto my hand in a comforting manner.

"Ariel," she whispered. "Troy doesn't remember anymore. He lost his memory again."

EPILOGUE

"Damn it," I snapped, frustration seeping through my voice as tears streamed down my cheek. "I can't find it," I yelled, falling to the floor and landing on my knees. The more I thought about it, the more tears flowed down my cheeks as I looked around my room. "I can't find it . . . I can't find it . . ."

I let out a loud cry as I buried my face in my hands. I felt terrible, worse than I have ever been. I sobbed into my hand as I sat lifelessly on the floor, bringing my knees under my chin.

The next thing I heard was my bedroom door flying open and someone rushing in. My mom's scent immediately hit my nose as she took me in her warm embrace. "Oh, Ariel," she whispered, rubbing my back with her hand in a soothing manner. "Everything's going to be alright. I promise."

I shook my head and took my face away from my hands before looking up at my mom with teary eyes as I held in another cry. "No, it won't be, Mom. It won't. Troy will never remember me," I claimed, my voice cracking. "Troy forgot me for the second time. He forgot me."

"Shh, don't say that," Mom stated. "Troy remembered you once, he could do it again. He just needs time."

"That was because of the journal," I explained. "He remembered me because of his journal. But now, I can't find it." I felt the tears fall down my face as that thought registered in my head. My heart sank. "I can't seem to find it. It disappeared, Mom. It disappeared."

My mom took me in another hug before wiping my cheek. She held my face and made me look up at her. She stared at me with warm comforting eyes. "Ariel, did you forget that you were recently discharged from the hospital? You're in no shape to be looking for it. I understand you're upset. But you need to rest first so your injuries could recover," she said.

I shook my head. "I'm fine. I've been in the hospital for a week," I claimed. "I have to find that journal so I can give it to Troy. I won't rest till I do." It has been one of the hardest week in my life. Waking up to hear Troy has lost his memories once again was a stab to my heart. It tore me to pieces. I don't think I can handle the same pain all over again.

Troy was still in the hospital and Rose and Julia came from New York to see him. I bet they were also suffering due to this problem. It was like we all started from the beginning and that hurt me the most. I entered his room a couple times but it was no use, he wouldn't even recognize me and that would make me rush out of his room before he saw a glimpse of my tears. I didn't want him to see me like that.

This was breaking me. I was feeling the same pain that I felt previously, but this time, I didn't know if I was willing to take it. I didn't know if my heart was strong enough to take the hit for the second time.

My mom placed her hand on my shoulder, pulling me out of my thoughts. "Please, Ariel. Don't do this to yourself," she begged. "I'll look for the journal. I'll search the whole house, just please stop crying."

I sniffed and averted my eyes for a moment, nodding my head right after. I hugged my mom one more time as I let out a troubled breath. "Okay, Mom. Don't worry," I whispered. "I'll get some rest. But after I do that, can I go back to the hospital to see Troy?"

I raised my head to look at her. She hesitantly nodded. I smiled softly and laid my head on her shoulder for comfort.

I wanted to be near him this time, even though he didn't remember me.

Even though it broke me.

Time passed by. I took my mom's advice and rested. When I woke up, I realized that I slept till it was dark. I jolted out of my bed in panic and checked the time.

My brows furrowed in disappointment as I saw it was way past Troy's visiting time. My shoulders sagged and I ran a hand over my face, letting out a sigh.

I opened my bedroom door and walked out. I was wondering whether my mom was asleep or not. As I walked down the stairs, the journal crossed my mind. I continued to think about where I could have possibly placed it.

I stopped when I saw my mom sitting alone on the couch. The worry on her face concerned me.

"Mom?" I called out. She turned to look up at me. Seeing the look in her eyes made my heart pound. "What's wrong? Did something happen?"

She patted the seat next to her. "Sit down."

Hesitantly, I sat next to her, bracing. "Did something happen to Troy?" I asked. My mom shook her head, grabbing onto my hand.

"No, sweetie. Don't worry," she assured, allowing a breath of relief to escape my mouth.

"Then what is it?" I asked. "You look off . . ."

Mom nodded. "I know this is going to worry you . . . a lot," she started. "But you need to stay strong. This isn't the end."

"I'm listening. What is it?" I pressed again.

"It's the journal, Ariel. I was looking for it, but I can't find it," Mom explained. I felt my heart sink. "I think it's gone."

"G—Gone? How?" This can't be.

"Remember the maid I told you about? The one we hired to clean the house while we stayed with you in the hospital," she asked me. I nodded. "I called her today to see if she placed it somewhere. She told me she might have thrown it away by accident. She said it was right next to your trash bin in your room."

My vision began to blur as I processed what my mom was telling me. I shook my head in disbelief. I didn't want to believe it.

"Why? How could this happen?" A tear fell down my face and my mom immediately wiped it away. "How will I make Troy remember this time?"

"You still can, Ariel . . ." Mom stated. "You can do it without the journal. You need to believe in yourself."

I shook my head. "The journal was my only hope." I began to cry. "And now it's gone."

"Ariel, look at me," my mom urged, holding my face in her hands. "The journal was one way to help Troy, but not the only way. You need to stay strong and find that way if you want to help Troy again."

I remained silent. My mom sighed. "Now tell me, Ariel. Are you going to give up on Troy?"

I shook my head. "No."

"Then you will find a way. There is always an answer. You just need to hold on to that hope," she exclaimed, pulling me into a hug. I only nodded as I rested my head on her shoulder. "You'll go visit him tomorrow, okay? Try talking to him this time."

I nodded again. "I'll try."

I didn't know what to say. I didn't know what to do. What scared me the most was, I didn't know if I'd ever get Troy back.

*   *   *

My eyes landed on Rose who was sitting outside Troy's hospital room. I noticed the bags under her eyes. She looked worn

396

out. The moment I got closer, she turned to me and smiled wistfully. I sat down beside her.

"Are you okay? You look tired. You should probably get some rest," I asked in concern.

"How can I rest when my son is in there and doesn't remember anything?" She whispered, shaking her head. "He doesn't even remember his own mother. I can't leave him and let him be in pain and confusion."

I looked away from her in sadness. My shoulders sagged. "I'm sorry," I murmured, blinking to prevent the tears from leaking. "It's all my fault. If Troy hadn't covered me in the crash, he'd probably be fine right now." I looked at Rose, seeing the sadness in her eyes. "I should have been in his place."

Rose shook her head. She placed her hand on my shoulder and let out a breath. "That's not true. You know if that would've happened, Troy would have suffered in misery and sadness. You know your safety comes first to him. I bet if he remembered, he wouldn't have regretted a single thing."

I lowered my eyes, remaining silent. "Troy loves you very much, whether he remembers you or not," she claimed. "I don't blame you. No one should. This was all Troy's decision and we should support it."

"Will Troy ever remember again?" I asked, looking up at Rose. Even though she looked incredibly sad, her lips turned into a soft smile.

"Troy remembered once and that was all because of you," she stated. "So, I'm sure he will for the second time, as long as you don't give up on him."

I remained silent as I remembered the journal. Rose then placed her hand on my shoulder, letting out a breath. "Why don't you go in there and see him?" she asked, pointing to his room. I shrugged my shoulders.

"I don't know if that would be a good idea," I mumbled.

"He's asleep at the moment," Rose claimed. "Go see him before he wakes up." I looked at her then back to his room. I soon nodded my head and stood up.

"Okay. I will," I said. She smiled at me and with that, I walked towards his room. I gently opened the door and stepped in. Troy was sleeping on the hospital bed. A small smile unintentionally came onto my lips as I saw his sleeping form.

I walked quietly towards him. I immediately missed him even more as I got closer. I watched him quietly in comfort, sitting down on the edge of the bed. My eyes lingered on his relaxed face, a face free from all worries. I let out a sigh, wishing that he'd wake up and remember me.

Although, that was too hard to happen.

I averted my eyes away from him after a moment. "I miss you, Troy," I whispered. "I miss you so much." I raised my hand and gently touched his hair, cautious of waking him up. "If only you'd remember me. If only you'd save me from this heartbreak."

I placed my hand on my lap, keeping my eyes on him. "Are you going to live your life not remembering me?" I wondered, a tear falling down my cheek. "Will you never remember our memories? Our love? Is this our fate?"

I wiped the tear off my cheek before standing up after a moment, glancing at him one more time. "Troy. I don't know if my heart is strong enough to take that pain one more time," I said softly. "I don't know." I then turned around and walked towards the door, grabbing onto the doorknob.

"Who are you?" he asked. I immediately turned around and made eye contact with him. He was looking at me with confused eyes, but I could also see sadness in there.

"A—"

"Why do you look sad every time I see you?"

"Troy," I whispered.

"How do we know each other?" he asked. I bit my lip and looked away from him. A moment of silence went by. "Were we lovers?" he blurted out.

"I—I . . . We were," I confessed. "We were friends too."

He took in my words, nodding his head slowly. "You must be in pain," Troy said. "This must hurt you a lot."

I took a step towards him, smiling sadly. "It does," I answered. "But this is not the first time."

Confusion passed through his eyes. "What do you mean?"

"This is your second time forgetting me," I claimed softly.

"My second time?" Troy told himself. "But how did I remember?" he asked, looking up at me with a curious expression. "Did you help me?"

I nodded. "Yes. Kind of," I replied.

Troy sat up, staring right at me with an intense look. "What's your name?" he asked me.

"Ariel," I answered.

He nodded. "Ariel," he whispered. "Will you come back?"

My eyes widened, taken off guard from his question. "Do you want me to?" I wondered. He looked a little hesitant before nodding.

"If you were able to help me the first time, then you could do it again for the second time," he explained.

My eyes lowered to the ground. I didn't know how to tell him that the only thing that could have helped him is now gone.

"Is there something wrong?" Troy asked.

"What if I lost the thing that helped you remember the first time?" I asked, looking up at him with a frown. "Would you still want me to come back?"

He looked confused but after a moment, he nodded. "I don't know what you're talking about, but I'd still like you to come back. Will you?"

His words brought me comfort, and before I knew it, a smile was on my face. "Then I will," I said, walking back to the door. "Goodbye, Troy."

He gave me a smile, and I swore I saw something in his eyes. I saw a hint of his familiar gaze staring back at me.

"Goodbye, Ariel."

Do you like romance stories?
Here are samples of other stories
you might enjoy!

Tyler's Gem

Rua Hasan

PROLOGUE

I looked at my reflection with dull eyes while drops of water were dripping from my hair. The steam from the shower was fogging the mirror, but I could still see myself through it. I sometimes thought that maybe, just maybe, one day I would see a different person with happiness and confidence.

I looked in the mirror to see my flaws that I have grown to accept. The flaws everyone used against me, but why should I care?

Yes, I could be a better person. I could walk to school every day with so much confidence that would bring everyone to their knees.

But why haven't I done that yet? Why did I keep on staring at myself every morning as if it would make things better or make a difference for everyone to like me?

My chubby cheeks and fat belly were one of the reasons why nobody liked me. I was the chipmunk of the whole middle school. I would walk around while everyone called me names, emphasizing why I stood out so much.

It had been like this since elementary school. Probably because I was not much of an active person. I would usually stay home all day and watch TV. I didn't like most things except eating. I mean, who wouldn't? It helped ease the stress. My dad owned a pizza shop that was quite known in our little town of Strawberry Forest in California.

Yes, I knew it was a weird name. Our town was known for growing strawberries in the old days that covered our land like a forest.

I used to go to his pizza place every Friday just to have a bite of heaven, which was probably another reason why I became chubby.

I wrapped the towel tighter around my body as I let my short, straight hair fall down to my shoulders.

I really needed to let it grow.

Walking out of the bathroom, I then headed to my closet. I grabbed a pair of baggy jeans and my favorite sweatshirt that my mom bought me on my twelfth birthday. My fashion sense was another thing I needed to fix.

But should I really care about what everyone would think of how I dress?

I put the clothes on, let my wet hair fall down naturally, and climbed down the stairs to smell the scent of my mom's amazing pancakes. I inhaled it happily and skipped towards the kitchen to see my dad sitting down, reading a book while my mom works at the stove.

My dad was the first to notice me and gave me a smile as he put his book down. He then motioned me to come over.

"Good morning, pumpkin," my dad said, catching my mom's attention. She put the pancake she had on the pan into a plate and turned the stove off. She wiped her hands on the towel next to her and turned to look at me.

"Good morning, mom and dad," I said as I kissed each of them on the cheek. I then grabbed the chair next to my dad and sat down, licking my lips as I stared at the plate in front of me with hungry eyes.

"Is my little girl excited to finish school today?" my mom asked.

Who wouldn't be? School was a living hell because of the constant bullying from none other than Tyl—

No! I promised myself I would never bring up his name as long as I'm alive!

Okay, maybe I was exaggerating a bit. Could you blame me when everyone constantly picked on me just because of how I looked, especially if it was only because one person started it?

"Mom, I'm not a little girl anymore." I groaned playfully as I cut a little piece of my pancake and shoved it in my mouth. The delicious taste in my mouth made me want to moan.

My mom took a seat in front of me and smiled as she pinched my cheek.

"Oh, but you'll always be my little girl," she said, attracting my father's attention. He put his book down again and glared at my mom.

"Hey, that's my line," he said.

I rolled my eyes at them, knowing what they were about to start.

My mom leaned against the table as she put her fist under her chin and smiled teasingly.

"Well, I stole it. *Whatcha* going to do about it?" She teased.

"Why, you!" my dad said.

That was my cue to look away. I ate my breakfast quickly before it got cold. It was obvious that I preferred to watch the pancakes over my parents smooching.

I ignored my parents' little playful argument which would lead to a make out season right here in front of me because trust me, it would always make me want to gag. I finished my plate and placed it in the sink. I turned around and found my parents eating each other's faces.

Ew, couldn't they get a room?

"Mom." I whined.

"Dad!" I said a bit louder and heard a knock at the front door.

"I'll get it," I muttered and headed to the door. I looked through the peephole and smiled when I saw who it was. I opened it and jumped into my best friend's arms as I ruffled his hair and messed it up.

I pulled away and smiled seeing Matt's annoyed face. He was probably the only reason I wake up every morning to go to school. He was practically my rock who was always there for me when I needed a shoulder to cry on, and defended me from all the bullying.

It wasn't like he could stop it in general, but his presence would help me cope with it.

We met somewhere in elementary school and clicked instantly. Matt was like the big brother I never had, supporting me through both the ups and the downs.

"What?" I asked with a smirk. He glared at me and pointed at his hair.

"Really? It takes me forever to fix this." He whined as he tried to fix his hair. Sometimes, I thought he cared about his looks more than I cared about mine.

I grinned and shrugged my shoulders.

"Oh, don't be such a grouch! It's the last day of school, lighten up," I said, punching his shoulder. He gave me a small smile and nodded his head.

"Are you ready?" he asked.

"Yeah, just give me a second," I said and ran back into the kitchen. "Mom, dad, I'm leaving." They smiled and engulfed me a big hug and wished me good luck.

My parents knew that I was being picked on, but they didn't really know that I was being bullied every single day by Ty—

No! Not again.

As I was saying, I thought it was best that they didn't know for them not to worry. Besides, they have already reported it to the principal countless times, but nothing happened. It just wouldn't stop.

I went to the front door where Matt was waiting and closed it behind me. The chill of the morning hit my face as the breeze quickened. It was still early, about seven something, but classes wouldn't start until eight.

I was actually excited to finish this day without problems. Matt and I walked to the school which wasn't too far away and talked about summer. Time went by quickly and the next thing I knew, I was in front of the place I hated the most. I started walking down the hall with Matt at my side as I tried to ignore everyone including the snickers made by some girls hanging by their lockers. As long as I wouldn't bump into him today, I would be fine.

When the bell rang, I sprinted out of my seventh period class and down the hall to head to the school gates at the edge of the school's parking lot. I would usually head towards that direction to meet Matt and walk home together afterwards. Surprisingly, this day just went by simply. I mean, I got called with names a few times, but there was nothing new. I guess everyone was too busy to go home from school and begin their summer vacation, so I wasn't their priority today.

Matt and I usually took our lunch together, and as I went between my classes, I would hide in the mass of children who were bumping into each other to avoid being spotted by my enemy.

Luck was on my side for not seeing him today. I stepped out of the door at the end of the hallway, walked to the parking lot, and looked around for Matt but couldn't see him. I assumed that I was early so I waited under a tree that was planted on the side of the gate. After all, it wasn't the first time he was late.

Suddenly, my vision blurred as something cold hit my head. I squealed in surprise and wrapped my arms around me. When I opened my eyes, I heard laughter echoing through the air and found myself soaking wet.

I wiped the water blurring my vision and looked up in the branches to see two boys, holding empty buckets and laughing their butts off. I was embarrassed, and I felt tears run through my cheeks, but I held them back.

Why would they do this to me? All I wanted was to go home and forget about the worst seven hours of my life that I had to repeat five times a week. All I wanted was to have a normal life like everyone else.

I pushed those thoughts away and was about to shout at the boys when someone else called my name. Shivers ran down my spine as I feared what I was about to face.

Taking a deep breath, I looked upon the face that I hated the most—the one who made my life a living hell.

Tyler Grey was holding something in his hand which I thought a water balloon.

"Just a little reminder of me throughout your summer," he said with a smirk, and threw the balloon at me before I could even move.

Paint. It was paint.

The boys up in the tree climbed down and walked over to Tyler. They were barely able to contain themselves from laughing and gave him a pat on the back. It was then that I could no longer control the tears in my eyes from running down my cheeks. I saw Tyler's eyes glaring at me, and clenched my fists as I watched them walk away with taunting smiles as if they had just won the lottery.

I took a shaky breath as the tears blurred my vision. My day spiraled from ten all the way to a zero because of him. I was freaking wet and my favorite grey sweatshirt now turned pink. I fell to the ground as I sobbed with my knees on my chest and hid my head.

I heard Matt call out from a distance, but I didn't pay attention. My mind was clogged and overflowing with hateful thoughts toward Tyler Grey.

My eyes were blinded from any light that I could have seen. My ears were plugged with his words. He got what he wanted; I was never going to forget him this summer. His face would forever haunt my mind.

CHAPTER 1

I stepped out of the taxi and paid the driver his tip. My long, tan legs resembled like hotdogs that were being heated under the bright, shining sun. I pulled the sunglasses away from my eyes and rested them on my head, looking around the place I used to call home where I lived many years ago.

Once I was completely alone in the quiet, familiar streets, I made my way to the house, and could instantly tell that not much had changed. The grass was as green as ever, and the birds were flying from branch to branch. It was as if I had never left. Although, it did look like it needed some dusting and a few plants in the front yard. But other than that, everything was fine.

I had argued with myself countless times about whether to buy a new house or just come back to this place. My childhood wasn't quite the best, but I would always choose my heart's desire. It wanted to go back home—to the place where I was raised.

I decided to come back to this small town everyone called Strawberry Forest. Was going back to the same house that hold good yet disturbing memories a good idea? Would I enjoy my life here? Or would I just end up regretting my decision?

I walked to the front door and stared at it for what seemed to be hours but were only seconds. Was I ready to face the past? Coming back here after so many years could be a good thing. I may had been away for so long, but it wasn't enough to help me erase and forget the dreadful memories of what this house and town gave me. Nevertheless, I couldn't exactly stop now. I was here for a reason, and that was to stop running away. I had to face reality.

I looked around to see that the house next to us was a bit different than I remembered. Its paint was in a different color and had a different vibe radiating from it. The decorations were of a different taste than that of the previous owner.

New neighbors perhaps?

I finally gathered all the courage that I had and grabbed the keys in my pocket. I opened the door and it creaked as I opened it slowly. Dust flew in the air as the house had not been touched for years. I took a step into the house, and looked around to see memories of the past flood my mind.

The interior and furniture were untouched. I didn't want anything removed when I moved away. I didn't even let my grandma sell it, knowing that I would be back one day.

I closed the door and realized that I would need help in cleaning this place; I didn't think I could do it alone. I grabbed my phone from my bag to send my best friend a text message on my arrival, telling him that I would be expecting his presence in a couple of minutes. I rubbed my eyes to prevent the tears from falling. I was done running away and was going to start a new life now that I had returned. A life that would make my parents proud.

$$* \qquad * \qquad *$$

Three years ago

I walked up to the front door as I wiped the water off my face with the napkin Matt gave me. Matt had been furious throughout the entire walk. He was ranting about how people could be so cruel, especially on the last day of school. Well, we were talking about Tyler Grey so I wasn't surprised.

He also blamed himself for being late. In his mind, if he was there sooner then maybe he could have prevented it. I disagreed and told him that it was fine. My life had been like this for years so I was pretty used to it.

After saying our 'goodbyes' a couple of blocks away, I stood right outside the front door, too afraid to face my parents. What would they say if they saw me like this? They would definitely freak out.

What would I tell them?

I could just lie and say that it was a goodbye prank from a couple of friends. Or, that there was this activity in school where we fought with water balloons. But of course, that would be such a lame lie, and they would not believe me. They knew me too well, and would be suspicious of the pink paint that stained all over my sweatshirt.

I decided to just tell them the truth and get it over with.

I rang the doorbell, waiting for the door to open. Moments passed as I stared at the door and rang the doorbell again, assuming they may have just not heard the first attempt. I waited another minute or two until I figured out no one was going to open the door. I rolled my eyes and guessed that my parents were probably up in their room making out because this wasn't the first time they've been getting it on while I waited outside.

Sighing, I grabbed the pot that had a plant in it and dug for the emergency key to open the door. I walked in to see no one. I took the risk of going upstairs to my parents' room and was surprised to hear nothing and thought that maybe they have fallen asleep.

Pft, come on. Who sleeps at this time?

I knocked on the door and waited for an answer, but nothing happened. I knocked again but this time, I opened the door to stare at nothing. There was no one in the room. It was completely empty as if it haven't been touched since I had left for school.

I ran down stairs to the kitchen and saw that my mom haven't made dinner at all. Well, that was strange. My parents used to leave something for me to eat before going somewhere else. It wasn't that I was always hungry; I just found it strange.

I walked into the living room and grabbed the house phone. I dialed my mom's number, but no one answered. I dialed dad's number, but he didn't answer either.

I was just about to go upstairs to my room when the doorbell rang. I skipped toward the front door thinking it might be them. When I peeped through the peephole, it wasn't my parents standing outside but two men wearing police uniforms.

I opened the door and stared up at the strangers who were standing in front of me, both of whom gave me sympathetic looks for some unknown reason. I lifted an eyebrow in confusion.

"Can I help you officers?"

They both glanced at each other then looked at me.

"You must be Crystal Clare," one of them said.

I nodded my head slowly, wondering why and how they knew my name.

"Yes, that's me. Is there something wrong?" I asked nervously.

"Yes. Unfortunately, your parents were in an accident, and we need to take you to the police station for some information."

My eyes widened, and my heart started to beat so fast that I could feel it hitting my chest. I felt a lump form in my throat as his words sunk into my brain and my world started to spin.

"An accident?" I gasped softly.

I felt tears form in my eyes, and my palms began to sweat.

"Are they okay?" I asked.

I couldn't imagine living without my parents. They were one of the reasons I stayed positive in life. They were amazingly supportive and always gave me warm hugs when I needed them.

If something were to happen to them, then I would be in this life all on my own. I didn't have anyone else here in this small town to take care of me. My life would become way worse than it already was.

One of the policemen took off the cap he was wearing and looked down at me with tender eyes, shaking his head.

"I'm sorry for your loss," he said.

After hearing those words, I couldn't stop the tears from flowing. My parents were dead.

*   *   *

I snapped out of my thoughts when I heard the doorbell rang. I took the sunglasses off my head, placed them on the counter, walked over to the front door, and took my shoes off. I looked through the peephole and smiled.

I quickly yanked the door open only to face the sight of Matt holding a broom.

"Matt!"

I jumped into his arms, causing him to drop the broom as he wrapped his arms around my waist. He picked me up off the ground, and our laughter filled the air.

He put me down on my feet and smiled, showing me his straight white teeth. He then looked at me from head to toe and whistled as he gave me a wolf grin.

I laughed as I punched his shoulder playfully.

"Oh my god! It's been ages," I said, letting him in before closing the door behind me.

"Yeah, I know, right? How have you been?" he asked.

"I've been good. What about you?"

It's been a very long time since I've seen Matt. But ever since I've moved to my grandparents' house in New York four years ago, we have been keeping in touch by using *Facebook* and *FaceTime*. Later on, I bought my own phone, and we called each other every day.

"Better now that you're here," he answered, as we walked toward the living room.

"You look the same like I never left," I said.

He still looked and felt like the Matt I knew many years ago, except that he had grown much taller and broader with facial hair.

"You…well, you look—"

"Different?" I asked.

He shook his head and gave me a smile wrapping his arm around my shoulders.

"Beautifuler," he said.

"That's not even a word, idiot." I chuckled, punching his shoulder again.

"It is for me," he said.

I smiled at his compliment.

Now, don't get me wrong. It wasn't like in the past four years I've been trying to change myself and get skinnier so that everyone would like me. No, that's not what happened.

I got depressed when my parents died and lived in a place I'm not familiar with. I had to meet new people which I wasn't a big fan of, but I found a solution to deal with it.

No, it wasn't drugs or alcohol. It was exercise. I would go out for a run and feel free. I wouldn't stop until I was panting for air and soaked all my clothes with my own sweat.

Doing the same routine every day, running became a hobby and made me into how I looked today.

"I hope you're ready because this place needs some cleaning," I said, as I grabbed his broom and threw it at him.

"Some?" he asked, as he grabbed the broom. "You mean, a lot. This place hasn't been touched in ages."

I cleaned the kitchen while Matt got to work in the living room. My house didn't seem huge when I lived here with my parents. We had two bedrooms upstairs and a bathroom. But now that I was going to live here all alone, it seemed so big and lonely.

I thought about it a lot and came to a conclusion that I wouldn't be moving out anytime soon. This place was sentimental, and I couldn't just let it go. I was pretty sure this was what my parents would have wanted, and I booked the nearest flight ticket to return home, the minute I turned eighteen. I've been planning that ever since I've left.

I was never close to my grandparents. I appreciated them for taking me in though, but I knew that once I turn eighteen, I'd be on my own.

After an hour and a half later, Matt and I were done cleaning the first floor. I walked out of the bathroom after cleaning myself up and saw Matt in the kitchen drinking some water.

"Let's take a break and have something to eat. I'm pretty sure you're hungry," he said.

I watched as Matt took his phone out and ordered pizza. I took two cups and a bottle of *Pepsi* to the living room and placed them on the coffee table in front of the couch. I sat down and grabbed my phone out since the TV wasn't working, and it needed some fixing with the wires and stuff.

Matt walked into the room and sat next to me. We spent time talking about everything that happened in the past four years and how the people at school were sorry for me and my loss. I wasn't planning on holding grudges against anyone, but I could never forget what they have done to me.

I told him about New York and how awesome it was. But I guess I was just a Californian girl who could never trade California for any city. I was born here after all.

Twenty minutes later, a knock was heard on the door. Matt got up to open it while I sipped on the Pepsi I had in my hand. I wasn't such a big fan of soda and preferred juice more, but there wasn't any in the fridge at the moment. I needed to buy groceries.

Matt came back with a box of pizza in his hand. I licked my lips as my stomach grumbled in hunger. When the box was opened, we dug in and ate until we were full. We pretty much finished the box, but you can't blame us. It's been a long day.

We sat in silence, gathering our thoughts until Matt spoke.

"You ready for school on Monday?" he asked.

I sighed. I knew this topic was going to be brought up. Besides, I still had to go to school.

I wished I could delay the time of me having to go to school sooner.

"Yeah," I said, nodding my head. Let's just hope that some things have changed while I was gone.

If you enjoyed this sample, look for
Tyler's Gem
on Amazon.

How to Save a Bad Boy

KAIRY AGUAYO

PROLOGUE

MORGAN COLLINS

You know that angsty teen in your school? The boy with tattoos? The one who started sh*t for absolutely no reason? You know, the bad boy? Every school had one. You either knew him, had an unpleasant interaction with him, or heard about him at least once.

Whichever it was, you probably wanted nothing to do with him.

I had never really bothered talking to the bad boy in my school mainly because he skipped class most of the time.

Until today.

"I need your help." He was obviously drunk, and I was obviously confused.

"What the fu—" Mason pushed a hand to my mouth and looked at me with wide eyes, almost as if he was afraid to be heard.

"Shhh. Someone is gonna hear us, Maddy. I-I need you to be really quiet, Maddy," he slurred as he tossed his leather jacket to the side. I furrowed my eyebrows at him. To be honest, I had no idea who Maddy was and I also didn't know what Mason Hunter was doing in my room this late at night or how he managed to get in.

Actually, now that I was thinking about it, how did he know where my room was? Did he just choose randomly? If so, what would have happened if he had chosen my mom's room? I shook my head, scolding myself for overthinking. It probably wasn't even that deep.

"I'm going to let go. Promise you won't scream?" He giggled when I nodded and carefully removed his hand.

I hissed at him. "What the f*ck are you doing here?" He looked rather attractive even in the darkness of my room. Tousled brown hair, big golden eyes, and a jawline that could grate cheese. *Yummy, cheese. I should try to test that theory.*

Mason giggled once again and shushed me. "You don't swear, Maddy. You're a good girl."

I rolled my eyes at him and let out a breath. "What are you doing here?" I asked again, a bit irritated with his current state.

"I'm running from the c-cops." He chuckled as his eyelids started to flutter. "I beat up a guy," he whispered the last part as if there were a lot of people who might hear him. My eyes widened and I looked at him in disbelief. I suddenly turned my focus on his clothes, which were stained red.

"Mason!" I called out, hoping to catch his attention.

"Shhh, don't scream." His eyes closed completely as he passed out on my carpeted floor; mine widened further as I stared in horror. There were red splotches all over his white shirt. I hoped it was Kool-Aid.

His jeans were torn, and nope, it wasn't Kool-Aid.

I turned to look at the alarm clock and nearly cried out in despair. It was 3 AM. What would my parents do if they found a delinquent in my room at this hour? Not just any delinquent, a f*cking bloodstained delinquent.

"Screw me," I hissed as I further inspected his torn jeans. I couldn't really see a lot, but I could tell he had an open cut. I washed my hands, then retrieved the first aid kit from my restroom. I then sat next to Mason's unconscious body.

I can just let him bleed out.

Shaking my head at the idea, I unbuckled his jeans and hesitantly pulled them down to his knees.

"This is wrong in so many ways," I muttered as I caught sight of his underwear. Good thing he was unconscious or this would have been very awkward for the both of us.

I bit my lip as I saw the gash on his thigh. With shaky hands, I wiped the crusted blood off his leg and applied antibacterial ointment on the cut. I then reached for the bandages.

Mason hiccuped. "If you wanted to get in my pants, you could have just said so." I snapped up. He watched me mischievously with his golden eyes. Mason was quite the casanova, which wasn't a surprise considering his looks. He had a sharp jaw, high cheekbones, and a perfect strong nose. Although it was his confidence that really got the girls.

I pushed his head back down slowly and continued working. I did not bother to say anything. I could feel my face burn with embarrassment.

He chuckled and picked his head back up, observing every detail. "Don't worry, Maddy. I probably won't remember this tomorrow." I sighed when I heard his low snore and shook my head. *This can't be happening.*

CHAPTER ONE
Don't Punch Him in the Face

By the time morning came, Mason was already gone. The rest of that morning sailed on quickly, and before I knew it, I found myself sitting next to my best friend during lunch.

Dee raised her dark brow at me as she shook her head. "Girl, I knew you had a few screws missing when I met you, but I didn't know that it was this bad."

I hissed as I fiddled with the food on my plate. "I'm being serious, Dee. He was in my room."

Dee scoffed and turned to look at Mason, who was sitting alone with his head down. "You want me to believe that that hot piece of ass sat in your room last night?" I nodded and took a note from my pocket that had a messy handwriting sprawled all over it.

"I don't know when he left but look."

Thanks, Maddy

-M.

"Who the heck is Maddy?" Dee questioned as she took the paper in her hands. "And why does he have such a messy handwriting?"

"I don't know, Dee. That doesn't matter," I groaned as I threw my hands up for effect. Dee shook her head and set the paper down, grabbing onto my hand. She smiled apathetically.

"Honey . . ." she trailed off. "I know you're all riled up, but there's no need to make up stories. There is no way Mason freaking

Hunter was in your room last night because he was too busy getting it on at Richard's party."

I ripped my hand away from hers and stood up. "I'll prove it," I stated stubbornly. Before Dee could utter another word, I darted towards Mason's table and sat next to him. I could feel the stares of the other students at the back of my neck. Not everyone had the f*cking balls to approach Mason when he was in a sh*tty mood.

"M-Mason," I said shakily, then cleared my throat. I repeated myself with a more confident tone. "Mason."

His head shot up, revealing a pair of sunglasses. He probably had a bad hangover judging by his physique—messy hair, clenched jaw, and bruised knuckles. He wasn't having a good day, and I wasn't making it any better.

"You left your jacket at my house."

I expected him to smile at me after last night. "Who the f*ck are you?"

I looked at him in disbelief and felt anger coursing through my veins. *I wish I actually threw him out of the window.*

"I—"

He sighed. "Look, if I had sex with you last night, don't get the wrong idea. I have sex with everyone. It doesn't mean we're dating."

My mouth fell open and I searched for the right words to say. What could I say in response to that? "No, you didn't. You don't remember anything?"

He lowered his sunglasses and narrowed his eyes. "If I remembered, I still wouldn't be here playing charades with you."

I hissed through gritted teeth as I clenched my fist. "I have your jacket." This boy made my blood boil.

"Do you have it right now?" He raised his dark brow.

I shook my head. He rolled his eyes, adjusting his sunglasses on the bridge of his nose. "Then stop wasting my f*cking time."

Before I could realize what I was doing, my hand flew past me and straight to his face. The cafeteria grew quiet as I drew my aching hand back. His sunglasses flew off his face. He slowly advanced towards me, his golden eyes bore into my dull green ones.

"Run, b*tch, run!" I heard Dee curse from the other side of the cafeteria.

Mason had never hit a girl, but he also had never been assaulted by one, so who knew how he would react! His face neared mine until it was a few centimeters away. His eyes flashed with anger, but his lips quirked up to a sarcastic smile.

"Get the f*ck out of my face."

Don't need to tell me twice.

I lurched up at his words and stumbled to run to the other direction.

He was going to assassinate and screw me. I was too young. There were so many things that I needed to do like . . . Okay, I couldn't think of anything right now, but I was pretty sure I had a bright future ahead of me.

Maybe not, but I still want to live!

"Girl . . ." Dee trailed off.

"I know," I simply responded.

*   *   *

Later that night, I found myself awakened by the sound of my window clicking shut. I searched frantically for the sound. My blood ran cold when I caught sight of Mason sitting on my windowsill with a cigarette in his hand.

I need to call the cops. I need to scream for help. I need—

"You should really lock your windows. I'm sure you don't want a psychopath breaking into your house."

Maybe if I just jump out the window . . .

Mason stood up and kneeled next to my bed. He reeked of cigarettes, soap, and alcohol.

"Don't hurt me, please," I murmured as I inched away from him. "I'm sorry I hit you. I didn't mean to—"

"Don't worry, Maddy. I'm not going to hurt you." He smirked as he put out his cancer stick on my nightstand. "Not physically anyway."

Wait, what?

I turned to look at my alarm clock and winced at the time, *11 PM.*

"Then why are you here?"

He smirked boyishly and inched his face closer. My heart sped up as he halted dangerously close to my face, our noses were touching.

I instinctively closed my eyes, waiting for him to close the space.

Then he was gone.

"I came here to get my jacket," he stated as he took the leather jacket from the chair positioned next to my desk.

I stared at him dumbfounded, no doubt my cheeks were flushed. Did I really close my eyes? What kind of a f*cking idiot was I?

I heard my window open again. "And Maddy, please lock your f*cking window."

I stared at him as he began to climb out of the window gracefully as if he had done it many times before.

"My name's Morgan, assh*le."

If you enjoyed this sample, look for
How to Save a Bad Boy
on Amazon.

CHAPTER ONE

The worst part about losing someone is losing them when you least expect it. It's not every day you have your parents break the news to you that your best friend has committed suicide. It's one of those days where I just have that gut feeling that something is bound to go wrong—and trust me, I've had more than one of those days—but never in my life could I have imagined something going this wrong.

The memory of hearing of my best friend's death is as fresh in my mind as ink on a sheet of paper. The days after hearing of her death are a blur of tears and locking myself in my room all day, convincing myself that this is all just some cruel joke. I soon learned this to be the first stage of grieving—denial. I'm not ready to move on, but I know I have to try because even if she isn't here to live her life with me, I know that she will want me to live mine for the both of us. Even if I'm still angry and confused about why hers ended.

*   *   *

I sit in my car and stare up at my high school. The lawn is littered with teens conversing about what they did over break, going on as if absolutely nothing has changed when it feels like my whole world has changed. Taking a deep breath, I grab my things before opening the car door and stepping out. Putting my head down, I try to walk briskly into the building without having to run into anyone.

"Alexa!" *Just my luck.*

"Paige, hi." I force some enthusiasm into my voice, but it just ends up falling flat. "I heard what happened, and the girls and I just wanted to say sorry for your loss. If you ever need anything, I will be happy to help," she says with what I can obviously tell is fake sincerity. I look at her and the rest of the girls sitting at a table a few feet away.

"Thanks for your concern, Paige," I say, forcing down any hint of anger. "But I'm fine." I abruptly turn around and walk away before she can get a chance to reply.

Walking through the crowded hallway, I glance at the place where my best friend's locker used to be. The place where I would meet with her every day to complain about how awful our mornings were as we headed to our first class together. The place I will no longer be going to every morning. I trudge through the halls with memories surging my mind as I try hard not to break down right here and now. It's hard enough waking up this morning and driving past her house on my way here, but this . . . this just adds salt to the wound. The shrill ringing of the bell breaks me out of my trance, and I hurry to my locker before heading off to my first class of the day.

I can't seem to focus as Ms. Anderson promptly starts the lesson. I can't stop hearing her voice at the back of my head or picturing her next to me, not paying attention to the lesson at all as she makes snarky comments about how awful Ms. Anderson's outfit choice is that day.

"Alexa? Ms. Parker, are you with us?" The sound of Ms. Anderson's saccharine voice interrupts any further thoughts, and I try to clear my head.

"Yes. Sorry," I say quickly. She gives me a sympathetic look before continuing with the lesson, a lump forming in my throat. Time seems to be moving agonizingly slow as my next few classes go by; it doesn't help that every few minutes, I am approached by people saying how sorry they are for my loss and how she was such an amazing person. Half of them don't even know her. It infuriates me that these people didn't give her a second thought when she was alive, but now that she's dead, she suddenly matters to them.

When lunch finally comes around, I sit at a table towards the back. I'm relieved to get a break and a chance to sort my thoughts. My break is short-lived as I'm joined by company.

"Hi, Alexa. How are you?" Alison greets timidly as she and Madison sit down with their lunch trays. Alison and Madison are twins and probably the sweetest girls you will ever meet, but right now, I just wish they will get up and leave. I'm tired of people coming up to me with their pity and condolences, which only reminds me more of my loss.

"I'm fine," I reply half-heartedly, not having it in me to ask them to leave. "What brings you guys here?"

"Can't we have lunch with our captain?" Madison says with that bright smile that can light up any room.

"We just want to check on you, and the team wants to know if you'll be at cheer practice today." *Right. There's practice.*

"Yeah, totally." I flash them a smile. I can't let them see my weakness, and if moving on means that I have to resume the role of the girl I was before that day, then so be it. As lunch progresses and they make no move to leave, I struggle to stay focused. Everything reminds me of her.

The table near the center of the room used to be our table. The table we would sit at every day and talk about boys while also discussing our future. She would always talk about how we would attend the same college and become roommates and then rent an apartment together in a different city after graduation. It all just keeps leading me back to the question of 'why?'. I can feel my eyes start to blur with tears, and I stand up suddenly. The twins look up at me with concern-filled eyes.

"I-I'm going to go. I just remembered I have to go to the library and check out a book for my next class," I say while grabbing my things.

"Oh okay. I guess we'll see you at practice?" Alison asks.

"I'll be there," I promise her.

I emerge from the cafeteria and make my way to the bathroom with my eyes locked on the ground so no one can see the tears ready to fall.

"Sorry," I say after accidentally bumping into someone, not even bothering to look at them as I start to sprint to the bathroom in my frantic state. After making sure it's empty, I slide against the wall and do the one thing I promised myself I wouldn't do today— I cry. The tears pour out like a waterfall, the confusion and anger and pain with them. I cry until my vision is blurry and my eyes are red. I cry until I know that I can't be in here any longer because someone is bound to walk in, and I'm not sure I can handle confrontation in this state. It's been a month since she's been gone, and instead of things getting easier with time, everything seems to be getting harder. I wish that I can just go back in time and stop any of this from happening.

It's taking me some time to compose myself. I missed the remainder of my classes for the day, and I can't even bring myself to care. I end up leaving cheer practice early at the suggestion of the team. I can't focus on the routine, and I was messing everything up. Pushing through the double doors of the gym, I let out a frustrated sigh as I lean against the wall and pinch the bridge of my nose. I eventually head to the school's parking lot, which is mostly empty with the exception of a few cars.

"Alexa?" I hear my name being called and I go rigid. *Why can't I be left alone?*

"Hey, Matt." I turn to look at him and his friends surrounding his truck with sweat and dirt running down their faces. Matt Carpenter is the quarterback of our school's football team. I don't really recall having any real interactions with him other than at football games.

"It's been awhile since I've seen you," he says.

"I have a lot going on at the moment." I unlock my car door, not caring to continue this conversation after the crap day I've had.

"Wait," he says as I'm about to make my escape. I look at him expectantly, feeling annoyed that I'm being delayed from leaving.

"I'm sorry but I need to go." I shut my car door and leave, not allowing myself to feel bad for how harsh that probably sounded. When I finally enter my house, I'm greeted by the smell of my mother's cooking.

Before, I would be rushing into the kitchen, anxious to get a bite of whatever was on the stove. Now, I barely have an appetite.

"How was school?" she inquires with a smile as I throw my keys down on to the table.

"It was okay." Sighing, I watch as she dumps some pasta into the pot of boiling water.

"You know you can talk to me, Alexa. What happened isn't something you can easily recover from," she starts with a soft gaze in her eyes as she looks at me. "I know you both were close but—" I clench my hands into fists at her words.

We weren't *just* close; she was all I had. She's the only person that understood me, and now, she's gone. No explanation, no warning, and no apology.

"Mom, I know you're trying to help me and I appreciate it; I really do, but I just need time and space. She's my best friend and I don't want to think about the fact that she's gone." She looks taken aback by my words but she nods anyway.

"Okay. Well, I'm here if you need anything. I just want you to know that you're not alone," she replies with a sad smile, and I give her a quick hug before heading upstairs to my room. I lock the door and collapse on to my bed as I stare up at the ceiling. I grab my journal from the nightstand and open it up to a clean page but I freeze as a picture falls out.

It's of her and I at a party. We were holding red solo cups—which were filled with ginger ale—and smiling like there was no tomorrow.

"I can't believe you did that!" I exclaim as we both stumble into my room, hunched over in fits of laughter. *"The look on her face was priceless!"*

"It was definitely an accident," Cam says with a smirk.

"I think Paige knows you spilling that drink on her wasn't an accident."

I shut the journal and hold it tightly to my chest. It isn't fair. It isn't fair that Cam is gone, and I'm expected to just move on. How can I when most of my happiest memories are with her? How can I when all I can think about is her day in and day out? The tears fall down my cheeks for what feels like the thousandth time today. I curl into a ball with the picture clenched against my chest. I don't know how long I stayed like that, but before I know it, I'm asleep.

If you enjoyed this sample, look for
Say You Won't Let Go
on Amazon.

ACKNOWLEDGEMENTS

I'd like to acknowledge and thank my parents for supporting me and believing me when I didn't believe in myself. Thank you for making me who I am today. I don't think I'd be where I am at without your love and support.

A big thank you to my twin and brother. You guys have been with me from the very beginning and never gave up on me. I can't see myself without you both.

Another thank you to the website I grew on, Wattpad. I have this opportunity because I chose to write there. I met amazing people there and grew as an author. I am who I am today because I decided to start writing there at the age of 15.

AUTHOR'S NOTE

Thank you so much for reading *Loving Tragedy*! I can't express how grateful I am for reading something that was once just a thought inside my head.

Please feel free to send me an email. Just know that my publisher filters these emails. Good news is always welcome.
raneem_hasan@awesomeauthors.org

I'd love to hear your thoughts on the book. Please leave a review on Amazon or Goodreads because I just love reading your comments and getting to know you!

Can't wait to hear from you!

Raneem Hasan

ABOUT THE AUTHOR

Raneem Hasan is a Palestinian girl who was raised between California and Jordan. She started writing at the age 15 with her first book and since then loves to write. Her dream is to one day become a well-known published author, bring smiles on others faces as they read her work and to inspire people to achieve their goals like what she did.

Printed in Great Britain
by Amazon